HOW LOVE BEGINS

"I like you, Hank Richards," she said, lifting her face for the kiss she knew would come. Too soon to say love, but that was all right. There was no need for haste. Good things were worth waiting for.

She closed her eyes as he bent to capture her lips. Another miracle, Pat thought, letting Hank's warmth seep into her bones, letting the strength of his hands soothe away all her troubles, letting the hard bulk of his body shelter her. There were no skyrockets, no brilliant flashes of light—just a deep, thrilling heat of passion. This was the way it was supposed to be—a man and a woman, two souls blending into one, two hearts beating next to each other.

"Whew!" Hank said, when he finally released her. "That was . . ." Words failed him. He smiled and held her tightly in his arms. "So much for anticipation."

Pat smiled, her arms tightening around him, her eyes damp with happiness. "And it's only just beginning," she whispered, then offered her lips for another thrilling kiss.

SEALED WITH A KISS

STACEY DENNIS

ZEBRA BOOKS
KENSINGTON PUBLISHING CORP.

ZEBRA BOOKS are published by

Kensington Publishing Corp.
475 Park Avenue South
New York, NY 10016

First Printing: September, 1993

Printed in the United States of America

For my family,
My wonderful husband, John;
My two beautiful daughters,
Stacey and Cindi;
My charming son-in-law, Harry;
and my handsome grandson, David.
Love you all.

Prologue

Patricia Melbourne sighed, and pushed a strand of ash-blond hair away from her eyes. Actually the blond hair was liberally streaked with silver these days, and no wonder. She'd buried her husband barely four months earlier. Sorting through Clifford's clothes was a chore she'd been putting off for months, but now she simply couldn't postpone it any longer. Gail Ryan, one of the ladies she played tennis with at the country club, had called for the fourth or fifth time to urge Patricia to donate Clifford's things to a charity bazaar the Ladies Guild was holding in three weeks.

So, telling herself that procrastination was a mortal sin, Pat dug in. Now, as she lifted the last two suits from Clifford's walk-in closet—one a navy pinstripe, the other a gray flannel—she closed her eyes for a brief movent and let herself remember how handsome her husband had looked in both suits. An elegant man, that's what Clifford had been, from the day she met him, while he was still studying for his bar exams, until the day he died of a massive heart attack.

Oddly enough the familiar sting of pain and loss seemed weaker than it had been. Was she finally coming out of that awful, raw grief? Pat wondered. Was the excruciating agony of loss beginning to wane?

"It's about time, old girl," she told herself, squaring her shoulders and sticking her hand into the pocket of the navy pinstripe. Empty. Okay. Another one for the pile, she thought, tossing it on the bed. Then she picked up the gray flannel.

This time when she stuck her hand in the jacket pocket, she felt something crinkly, like a wadded-up piece of paper. She drew it out. Frowning, Pat's fingers stilled. Something was wrong.

She opened the paper, smoothing the creases with her perfectly manicured nails. Then all color drained from her face, and her blood turned to ice water as the meaning of the scribbled words hit home. The note was from Carolyn Evans, a colleague of Clifford's, and it left no doubt in Pat's mind that Clifford and Carolyn had been having an affair of long standing.

Pat sank down on the king-size bed and covered her eyes with her hands. Clifford having an affair? With Carolyn? My God, how many times had she invited that woman to dinner, feeling sorry for her because she was single and lived alone, and always looked like she was starving? Well, the bitch hadn't been starving for love, that's for sure! According to the note, she'd been getting a double dose from Pat's ever-loving husband!

"Bastard!" Pat cried, ripping the incriminating note to shreds. "Lying, cheating bastard!" Then she fell in a heap on the bed and sobbed herself into a migraine headache.

One

"I told you, Evelyn, I've made up my mind," Pat said firmly. "I want to sell the house. It's simply too big and grand for one person."

"But you've always lived there, Mrs. Melbourne. You're not used to being confined in an apartment. You'll miss the spaciousness. Are you sure you don't want to reconsider?"

"I don't need space. That was my husband's hang-up. All that empty space gives me the willies. I'm looking forward to moving into a smaller place, although I'm not sure I want an apartment. I was thinking more along the lines of a small house, something outside the city, with a yard and maybe even space for a vegetable garden."

"Vegetable garden?" Evelyn Lewis looked like the words were part of some secret code. Pat laughed.

"Yes. You know, tomatoes and carrots. Lettuce and fresh peas."

"Oh my . . . oh, you're teasing me, aren't you, Mrs. Melbourne?"

The young realtor smiled in relief, certain she'd finally figured out why Mrs. Clifford Melbourne, Sr. was acting so foolish.

"I've never been more serious, Evelyn," Pat said, shaking her head. "I want a place where I can have a garden. I may even get a little dog. Clifford never liked dogs, you know, but I've always loved them. Cats, too. In fact, I love all animals, but Clifford thought they were messy."

"Well, I'm sure he was right, Mrs. Melbourne. That gorgeous home of yours . . . I can't even imagine a dog running around shedding all over those lovely Persian carpets, having little doggie accidents on that imported marble tile. Oh dear, I cringe just thinking of it!"

"Mmm, well, be that as it may, I'd like you to list the property and start looking for a suitable house for me. Three bedrooms and two baths would be fine. I can use one bedroom as a hobby room, and keep the third as a guest room in case one of the children wants to visit. As I said, I'd like a yard, and if it's fenced, so much the better. I really think I will get a dog."

Evelyn Lewis rolled her blue eyes toward the tiled ceiling and shrugged. "Whatever you say, Mrs. Melbourne, but if you change your mind . . ."

"I won't," Pat said flatly. "I want out of the

house as soon as humanly possible."

She walked out of the realtor's office, certain that the young woman was staring after her in shock and dismay. Such a shame, Evelyn was probably thinking. All that money, and poor Mrs. Melbourne is going dotty!

Pat allowed herself to laugh once she closed the plate-glass door behind her. Everyone thought she was crazy. All her friends, Clifford's banker, even her own sister, Celia.

"Why in the world do you want to leave that beautiful house of yours, Pat?" Celia had asked, the night before last when she and Pat had dinner together. "It's not as though you can't afford to keep it. You're not broke, are you? Clifford always . . ."

"Clifford's accounts are all in good order, Celia. Money isn't the problem. You know how meticulous he was about financial security."

"Well, then I really don't understand this sudden desire to lower your standard of living, Pat. What's gotten into you?"

Celia Browning was as different from her sister, Pat, as two women could be. Celia was as round as a dumpling, and she always seemed to be smiling. Pat would never have dared gain weight when Clifford was alive. He thought overweight women were disgusting. Through the years Pat had also learned to be reserved with her emotional responses. Clifford hadn't liked robust laughter or open displays of affection.

No, you dog, Pat thought bitterly. You didn't like to be hugged or kissed in public by your wife or your children, but you didn't mind rutting between the sheets with your mistress, did you? Her barely suppressed fury brought a surge of color to her cheeks.

Celia looked at her younger sister in alarm. "Oh dear, are you having a hot flash, Pat?"

"No. I'm fine," Pat said, smiling in spite of herself. Celia had that way about her. You looked at her, a chubby woman with fat, carrot-colored curls marching across her head, and you had to smile. Celia dressed in polyester and knew every actor and actress on the soaps. She would give you her last dime, or the voluminous shirt off her chunky back. Pat loved her to pieces.

"Look, Celia, I know you don't understand, but don't probe, okay? Not right now. Just believe me when I say this is the best thing for me to do at this time of my life. It's what I truly want to do, and for the first time in twenty-eight years I am free to do exactly as I please."

"Oh." Celia looked surprised, then thoughtful, as she lifted a forkful of filet of beef tenderloin to her mouth. Then, the aroma of the food must have overcome her almost insatiable curiosity. She shoveled the food into her mouth and began to chew, a look of ecstasy on her round face.

When Pat got home from the realtor's that

afternoon, she called the housekeeper, Mrs. Hatter, into the living room.

"Sit down, Jane," she said kindly. "I have something to tell you."

A look of alarm crossed the older woman's face and Pat hastened to ease her mind.

"You know, don't you?"

"Well, I heard you crying that day when you were going through Mister Clifford's things, and since then you've been different. I need my job, so I've been wondering."

"You needn't worry, Mrs. Hatter. I've found a place for you to go when I sell this house. You can stay on until then, of course, and when you do leave I'll see that you get a month's severance. You know my friend, Mrs. Evans?"

Jane nodded. "She lives in that lovely place over on Walsh Avenue, doesn't she?"

"Yes. And she's not at all satisfied with her present housekeeper. So, if you're willing, she's agreed to give you a try once this house is sold. I think you could got along with her. She's not a demanding person."

"What a relief!" Jane said, her face relaxing into a grateful smile. "I was afraid . . ."

Pat smiled. "You've been a valued employee over the years, Jane. My goodness, you came to us when the children were just toddlers. Do you realize how long ago that was?"

"I surely do," Jane said, grinning. "I feel like I'm a fixture here."

"Well, I hope you understand that I wouldn't even consider letting you go if I didn't feel I needed to sell this house. It's simply much too big for one person, and I think I'll be more content outside the city."

After Jane went back to the kitchen to finish preparing dinner, Pat leaned back against the brocade sofa and closed her eyes.

She could see the room in her mind's eye. Expensive, elegant furnishings, wallpaper that reflected Clifford's impeccable taste. The Persian carpets Evelyn was so concerned about, not to mention the original oil paintings by some of the world's most famous artists. All the trappings of success. And she had been a part of it for twenty-eight years. She'd been the perfect "barbie doll" wife. She'd dieted and exercised to the point of exhaustion to stay slim and elegant for Clifford. She'd bought her clothes in only the best shops. Her hair was cut and styled by the most expensive stylist in Philadelphia. Every week her nails had been manicured, and her legs hot waxed. Pat stifled a nearly hysterical giggle. When she thought about it, she sounded like a commodity, a car being taken in for a wash and wax, instead of a living, breathing, flesh-and-blood woman.

In a sudden fit of rebellion, she stood up, unbuttoned her cream silk blouse and slipped it off. Then, with more pure pleasure than she'd known in months, she took off her bra and twirled it in the air. Her breasts bounced and she giggled. Free! She was free at last! Clifford, her lying, cheating husband was gone, and she was free to be herself, whoever the hell that was!

"Mother, have you lost your mind?" Ashley Ann Melbourne's strident voice blasted over the telephone wires and singed Pat's ear. "Daddy would roll over in his grave if he knew you were thinking of selling his house! How can you? Why are you doing this?"

Pat squared her shoulders. "How can I? Well, it was actually very easy. I just turned the house over to a realtor. You remember that pretty young thing, Evelyn Lewis? And as for the why, it's what I want to do, so why on earth shouldn't I? The house did not belong exclusively to your father, Ashley."

"Well . . . but . . ."

It was rare when Ashley sputtered, so Pat knew her news had hit her daughter pretty hard, but the children had to know sometime, and the sooner the better. Evelyn was bringing some people out to see the house in a few days, and maybe they'd want to buy it. If so, she might have to move quickly.

"You've got your own place now, Ashley," Pat said reasonably, "and you don't get home much to visit, so why do you even care?"

"Well, of course I care," Ashley said indignantly. "I come home as often as I can, Mother, but you know how busy I am. Is that the problem? Are you lonely?"

Pat laughed. "Not really. Gail and the other ladies in the neighborhood have taken it into their heads to keep me happily occupied at all times. It's getting so I have to hide myself away to get any peace and quiet. No, dear. I'm not lonely. I just feel it's the right time for me to make a change. I've lived in this house for a long time, and it's been wonderful, but now I want to try something different."

"Oh. Well, I suppose that makes sense. But you're not going to buy some tacky little tract house, are you? I couldn't handle that!"

Pat laughed. "There aren't many tract houses in this area, dear, and I'm not moving that far away, you know. I just want to get outside the city limits where it's quiet."

"Oh," Ashley said again. Then her voice perked up. "Oh. I understand now, Mother. You're getting older and you need peace and quiet, don't you? Why didn't I realize?"

Pat started to protest, then shrugged and smiled at the telephone. Let Ashley believe what she wanted to believe, if it made her feel better. What was the harm?

"I'm glad you understand, honey," Pat said. "You know I wouldn't want to upset you, or your brother."

"Oh him!" Ashley spat disdainfully. "He won't

care one way or the other. Why should he? He never cared about the finer things in life anyway. All he worries about is . . ."

"Please don't, Ashley," Pat said, her head starting to throb. "Clifford is my son, and your brother. Your only brother. Must you be so hateful?"

"Hateful? Mother, what in the world is wrong with you? Clifford is the one who . . ."

"I do not want to discuss this with you, Ashley, not now or any time in the near future. Do you understand?"

"Have it your way," Ashley said. "But one of these days you'll regret sticking your head in the sand, Mother, and don't say I didn't warn you!"

Pat hung up the phone and began to dial her son's number in California. Halfway through, she slammed down the phone. She couldn't talk to Cliff now, with Ashley's hateful words ringing in her ears. She'd call him tomorrow.

Pat had a hard time getting to sleep. She kept seeing her children as babies, especially Cliff. He'd been such a sweet, adorable little boy. But then Clifford took over, forcing the child to learn to play football, insisting that he go hunting and fishing with "the men," even though the thought of killing a helpless animal made the little boy throw up.

When Cliff got in high school it progressively

worsened. Clifford wanted his son to be a jock. He hated it when Cliff spent his time attending art shows and painting out in the garage studio. "What are you, some kind of fairy?" Clifford taunted repeatedly. Pat felt her eyes fill with tears as she remembered the way Cliff had looked when his father talked to him that way. First hurt, then as he got older, the anger began to come through. She'd tried to make Clifford stop, but he refused to listen to her. And finally, in his sophomore year of college, young Cliff threw up his hands and said, no more. He left school, refused to take any money from Pat and hitched a ride out to California. He was there now. Painting during the day and waiting tables at night. It broke Pat's heart. Not that he was painting. She truly believed that he was right to follow his dreams, but she hated being estranged from her son. And then there were the rumors that Ashley swore were gospel: That Cliff, her beloved only son, was gay. That the guy he lived with was his lover and not just a roommate. She prayed it wasn't true, but feared it was. Not that Cliff's sexual preference would change the way she felt about him. She was his mother, and she would always love him. But she was afraid for him. Desperately, achingly afraid.

"What's the matter, Tweetie?" Pat asked her African Lovebird the next morning. The poor little thing definitely looked like he was under the weather. His feathers were rumpled and he hadn't even touched the seeds she'd put in his cage the night before. A lack of appetite was definitely not normal for Tweetie!

"All right, I guess we'll have to pay Doctor Brookfield a little visit," Pat said. "Thank goodness it's spring, and the weather is mild. I wouldn't want you to get a cold on top of whatever else is wrong with you."

"I'm taking Tweetie to the vet, Jane," Pat said a half hour later. "I don't know how long I'll be gone. The answering machine is on, so don't worry about the telephone."

After settling Tweetie in the back seat of her Lincoln town car, Pat carefully backed out the driveway onto the street. And that was another thing, she thought. She was going to trade the Lincoln in for a minivan, something with enough room so she could take her new dog for rides. Yes, she was definitely going to get a dog, and she hoped Clifford *did* turn over in his grave! It would serve him right!

The animal clinic was having a busy day. The waiting room was filled with prospective patients, some of them barking, some of them meowing piteously from inside their cages. Rather than tempt fate, or the fat tomcat an elderly lady had on a leash, Pat handed the bird cage to the veterinary assistant and he put it up on a ledge out of harm's way.

"It may be a while, Mrs. Melbourne. Doctor Brookfield is swamped today, and you didn't have an appointment, so . . ."

"No problem," Pat said pleasantly. "I have plenty of time."

"That must be nice," a man with a thick shock of iron-gray hair said. He had the almost rust-colored skin of someone who had spent the better part of his life outdoors in the sun and wind. And his eyes were the color of a summer storm. Definitely not the suave, sophisticated type of man she was used to, but attractive in a rugged, no-nonsense way.

Pat smiled, then her eyes widened as she caught sight of the cardboard box at the man's feet. "Puppies!" she said, with an almost childish glee.

"Yep. Best of the breed, or at least that's what I'm hoping. A pretty sight, aren't they?" He reached down and scratched one of the fluffy white pups behind the ears. The little creature wriggled with delight.

Pat's smile widened and she inched closer. She looked up at the man inquiringly. "May I?"

"Sure. Just make sure you support the hind quarters. These little fellows are pure bred Samoyeds, from champion stock. I have high hopes for them."

"They're adorable," Pat said. She carefully picked up one of the puppies and held it against her cheek. The fur was thick and fluffy and as white as snow. Two incredibly dark eyes stared up at her, then a tiny pink tongue flicked out and licked her cheek.

"Oh-ho, I see Sam there has good taste. He knows a pretty woman when he sees one," the pups' owner said, grinning.

"Sam? Do they all have names?"

"Sure do. As soon as they're born I name them. Of course their new owners will rename them, but that's all right. The thing is, these little guys will stay with me for at least seven weeks, maybe longer, and I can't go around saying 'hey you,' now can I?"

"No, I suppose not," Pat said, reluctantly putting the puppy back in the box with its littermates. "Well, they certainly are adorable. Do they grow very big?"

The man grinned. "You don't know much about dogs, do you?"

Pat took a seat beside him and shook her head. "Not much. My husband didn't care for dogs, so the only pet I've had in the last twenty-eight years is Tweetie over there. He's an African Lovebird."

"Oh. Well now, I guess we're even. I sure don't know much about birds."

"I'm not an expert either, but a bird seemed to be about the cleanest, neatest pet I could think of."

The man put his hand out. "My name is Hank Richards. How about you?"

Pat gave him her hand, surprised at the strength of his grip. "Pat Melbourne. Do you do this for a living? Raise puppies, I mean?"

Hank laughed and shook his head. "Wish I could, but the way I do my dogs they don't bring in a lot of money. Still, I'd rather know they go to good homes than make a killing. No, dog breeding is just a hobby with me, or maybe I should say a passion. My wife always said . . ." Hank's voice trailed off and his gray eyes clouded. "Well, I guess Nancy was like your husband, Mrs. Melbourne. She wasn't much of a dog fancier."

"I'll bet she likes these pups though," Pat said. "I don't see how anyone could resist them."

"Nancy hasn't seen this bunch," Hank explained, putting his hand in the box to break up a mild argument between two of the fuzzy babies. "We've been separated for the last few years."

"Oh, I'm sorry."

"Me, too," Hank said. "Look, I guess it's your turn. The assistant is getting your bird down."

"But you were here before I was," Pat said, getting to her feet. "You should go first."

Hank shook his head. "This isn't my regular veterinarian, and these guys have to have shots and a good going over. It'll take a while. Go on, take care of your beaked buddy." He smiled. "It was nice talking to you."

"Yes. Thanks," Pat said, slightly confused by

her reluctance to end the conversation. What was it about this man that intrigued her so? Or was it his puppies?

Dr. Brookfield checked Tweetie over and pronounced him fit, except for the fact that he was molting. "Don't you remember when he did this last year, Pat?" he asked, chuckling. "You called me in a panic and I told you it was a normal function?"

"Oh, golly! Yes. Now I remember." Pat laughed. "You must think I'm a total idiot."

"Not at all," Dr. Brookfield said "I wish all pet owners were as concerned as you, but there's not much you can do except wait this thing out. Just be patient, and soon this little fellow will be back to normal, blabbing up a storm. He still talks, doesn't he?"

"He hasn't said much these past few weeks, now that I think of it," Pat said. "Does this molting affect his speech?"

Dr. Brookfield plucked a loose tail feather from Tweetie and dropped it in the trash can. He laughed. "In a manner of speaking I've always thought that molting for a bird was equivalent to a woman having PMS."

Pat grinned. "Get out of here, you chauvinist. Uh, by the way, that man out in the waiting room with those white puppies . . . do you know anything about him?"

"Hank Richards? Well, he's not one of my regulars. He lives outside the city. The vet he usually goes to is out of town. Why? Are you interested in buying a puppy from him?"

"I don't know. I might be. But I'd want to be sure he was a reliable breeder."

"Well, Hank breeds those Samoyeds of his as a hobby, but there's not many people who take as good care of their animals as he does."

Pat smiled. Somehow Dr. Brookfield's words didn't surprise her.

She couldn't resist sneaking one last peek at the pups on her way out, and against her better judgment she found herself asking Hank if they would be ready to be sold soon.

"About four more weeks," he said, getting ready to move the box into the other room. He grinned. "Why? You want one?"

"Maybe," Pat said, "but you still haven't told me how big they get."

"About like this," Hank said, measuring with his hands. "A Samoyed is a good-size dog."

"Well, I'll have to think about it," Pat said "I was thinking about a small dog, one I could keep as a house pet."

"You can keep a Samoyed in the house. They're real sociable animals. But I don't think you'd want to share your bed with one of them. A full-grown Sammy can take up a lot of room."

"Doctor is ready for you, Hank," a young assistant called. "Why don't you bring those beauties on in?"

"Gotta go," Hank said. "Take care of that bird."

As she drove home, Pat found herself unable to stop thinking of the man and his pups. He was definitely different from the men she'd become accustomed to. Clifford had believed in keeping with his "own kind" as he put it. Well, if the other men were cheaters like Clifford had been, Pat wanted no part of any of them. Actually, after what she'd learned about her late husband, she was down on men in general. But Hank had seemed like the genuine article, the kind of man a woman could depend on. "You are definitely losing it, Pat Melbourne," she chided herself. "You spoke all of twenty-odd words to the man, so what makes you think he's dependable?"

It must have been those adorable puppies that got to her, and the sad look on Hank's face when he mentioned his wife. She'd always been a sucker for a sob story.

When she got home Pat settled Tweetie back in his regular cage and put the carrier back in the storage room. Then she checked her answering machine for messages. There was one from Ashley, and one from . . . Pat's heart jumped . . . the second message was from her son.

She sat down at the telephone table and picked up the receiver. Cliff didn't call often, and she couldn't help wondering if something was wrong.

A man answered, and when Pat asked for Cliff there was a moment's hesitation. "Just a minute. I'll see if he's awake."

Awake? It was eleven o'clock in the morning by California time. Why would Cliff be sleeping?

He sounded sleepy when he came on the line, and Pat's forehead was crinkled in a frown. "Cliff? Honey? Are you okay?"

"Hi, Mom. I'm all right. Just getting over a nasty virus. I just wanted to say hello and check in with you. How are you? Are you making out okay?"

"I'm fine," Pat said. "I was just getting ready to call you. I wanted to tell you that I've decided to sell the house and move into something smaller. Ashley doesn't seem to think it's a very good idea, but it's what I want to do. I want to move outside the city and have a little garden, and I may even get a dog."

"Hey, Mon, that's great! Don't pay any attention to Ashley. Are you going to have a guest room so I can come and visit?"

"Of course. Can I look forward to that visit soon?"

Did Cliff hesitate, or was it only her imagination?

"I'm not sure how soon, Mom," Cliff replied after a moment, "but I'm definitely planning a trip home to see you."

"All right I'll look forward to it. Honey, are you sure everything is okay? Are you making out all right financially?"

"Money is not a problem, Mom," Cliff answered, "but thanks for asking."

Pat replaced the receiver and sat very still. Something was wrong. Her mother's instinct told her so. She briefly debated the wisdom of flying out to California to see for herself, but decided against it. She had to remember that Cliff was an adult, a grown man now. Their relationship was fragile at best, and interfering in his life would certainly not endear her to him.

He can take care of himself, she told herself. All I have to do is believe it.

The first prospective buyers came to see the house a few days later. A middle-aged man and his plump, gray-haired wife walked through the house at least three times, examining every inch of the property with a magnifying glass. Or at least that's how it seemed to Pat. She did as the realtor had advised and made herself scarce. Evelyn had told her that having the present owner hovering around made buyers nervous.

Armed with a book and a glass of iced tea, Pat sat in the meticulously landscaped backyard and stared into space. She couldn't stop thinking of the man she'd met at the vet's and his adorable puppies. The more she thought about it the more she wanted a dog. Something to look after, something to be glad when she got home. And maybe, if she was strictly honest, maybe she wanted a dog to spite Clifford. You can't spite a dead man, she reminded herself. Clifford doesn't know or care what you do from here on in. Come to think of it, maybe he didn't care when he was alive. Certainly he hadn't cared enough to be faithful. Bitterness so strong it made her shiver, swept over Pat. Every time she thought of Clifford with that awful Carolyn woman she wanted to scream. Maybe she should scream. Maybe it would release some of the tension inside her. But not now, not while the prospective home buyers were wandering around in her house.

"I think we've got a deal, Mrs. Melbourne," Evelyn said a few days after the visit. "Mr. and Mrs. Elkins really liked the house. Mrs. Elkins wasn't crazy about the wallpaper in the master bedroom, but her husband assured her it wouldn't be a problem to change it."

"I never liked that paper either," Pat said, surprising herself. It was true. She hadn't liked the wallpaper, but she'd never had the nerve to tell Clifford. He'd done most of the decorating in the house, and she had stood by like a dutiful, obedient wife, nodding approval even when it was false. "I don't like those gaudy gold faucets in the master bath either," she said, feeling the tension inside her start to dissolve. "Or that horrible dark brown carpet in the den. Come to think of it, there really isn't a whole lot about this house that I like at all!"

"Oh dear, what a thing to say!" Evelyn cried. "Why, your home is lovely, Mrs. Melbourne. A lot of women would be thrilled to have such a beautiful, big home."

"Maybe. Anyway, are the Elkins ready to sign an agreement of sale?"

"Just about," Evelyn said, "And I think Mister Elkins wants to see if he can make a deal with you for some of your paintings. Are you interested in selling?"

"Why not?" Pat said, shrugging. "I won't be taking them to my new house."

"None of them?"

"No. I'm going to decorate my new place very casually. It's going to be a complete change of pace."

"Oh. Well, I'll tell Mister Elkins, and maybe the two of you can get together and work out a price."

Two weeks later, the final papers were signed and the house was sold. Mr. Elkins ended up buying all but one painting, and Pat decided to give that to Cliff. She knew he'd appreciate it. She called Ashley and told her she was welcome to any of the furniture she liked, and then she started house hunting in earnest.

Finally, after trooping through more than thirty houses, she found the one that was perfect for her.

"This is exactly what I want," Pat told Evelyn.

The young realtor looked around doubtfully. "It's nothing like your old house, Mrs. Melbourne. The rooms are actually quite small. Won't you feel cramped?"

"No. I'll feel cozy," Pat said happily. For the first time since discovering Clifford's infidelity, Pat felt good. The little house was adorable. It had clapboard siding and a brick front. There was no formal dining room, but the kitchen was large and bright and airy. The master bedroom was just the right size. The spacious backyard was bordered with a natural wood fence. There was plenty of room to grow flowers and still have a small vegetable garden. It was even big enough for a small dog to romp.

"I'm going to take it," Pat told the puzzled realtor. "It's just what I want. I'm going to have so much fun furnishing this place. I can hardly wait!"

Evelyn nodded dubiously. "All right, if you're sure, Mrs. Melbourne. Shall I draw up the papers?"

"As soon as possible," Pat said eagerly. "I'm ready to get on with my life."

"You're giving away all your beautiful dresses and gowns?" Gail Ryan asked incredulously. Pat was having lunch with her friend, and she had just finished describing her new home. Now she laughed and put down her fork. "I'm changing my life-style, Gail. I won't have much use for silk dresses and evening gowns. I'll be leaning more toward jeans and cotton skirts."

Gail sipped her white wine and grinned. "You amaze me, Pat. I always thought you were perfectly happy living in that gorgeous home of yours, attending all those glamorous parties."

Pat grew thoughtful. "That's what I thought, too, but I'm just now beginning to realize that it was all a sham. That elegant creature wasn't really me. It was what Clifford wanted me to be. Remember the movie about the Stepford Wives? Well, that's what I was. I was a robot, a perfectly programmed model wife and mother." Pat eyed the delectable tray of goodies the waiter brought around. With a defiant grin she reached out and snatched a chocolate eclair. To hell with calories and fat content, she thought crazily. So what if she gained a few pounds? She didn't have to please anyone but herself from now on!

"Right over there, please," Pat said, a few days later. She pointed to the place where she wanted the moving men to deposit her new overstuffed, floral-printed sofa. She was doing the living room in soft corals and greens. She was convinced that when she was done it was going to be absolutely perfect. She'd spent weeks trooping from one furniture store to another until she found just the right pieces. She'd finally found her bed at a flea market, of all places! It had a lovely old brass headboard and footboard, and she'd cleaned and polished it until it shone like new. There was a peach and cream patchwork quilt for the bed, and an old-fashioned green glass lamp for the pine night-stand.

She'd brought Tweetie to the house first thing this morning, and now the lovebird was hopping from one end of his perch to the other, shouting his favorite phrase. "The British are coming, hurrah, hurrah!" he cackled, his beady eyes watching every move the men made as they carried in the furniture. "London Bridge is falling down!" Tweetie squealed. "Look out! Look out!"

"Does he do that all day?" one of the moving men asked, stopping to wipe sweat from his brow. "Doesn't he ever shut up?"

"When he's molting," Pat said. "I guess we should be grateful he's not in the mood to swear. Apparently the man who owned him before I did taught him a few choice words."

The men laughed. "No kidding? A bird that swears? What's he say?"

Pat grimaced. "Trust me," she said. "You don't want to know."

By eight o' clock that night the major pieces of furniture were all in place. The little round table and chairs were nestled in a corner of the kitchen, the living room furniture was placed exactly where Pat wanted it, and she'd even put sheets on her bed.

"We're home, Tweetie," she said. "How do you like it?"

"Hot damn!" Tweetie squealed. "Hot damn!"

Two

Pat stood up and dusted the dirt off her hands. She supposed she really should be wearing gloves, but she liked the feel of dirt on her skin. Maybe it was crazy, but for the first time in her life she felt like a real person, instead of a plastic doll. With Jane safely installed in another household, Pat now did her own cooking and cleaning, and she was thoroughly enjoying it. After a few false starts she'd learned how to use the washer and dryer, and while she was a long way from becoming a gourmet cook, her food was plentiful and tasty. In three weeks she'd gained five pounds. She'd have to stop eating chocolate bars every afternoon when she watched her favorite soap opera.

Pat laughed, imagining what Clifford would have said if he'd ever caught her watching a soap opera. At least she now knew how Cliff had felt when he finally broke away and went off on his own. What she was doing now was a form of rebellion, and it felt good. She'd settle into a routine one of these days, but there was no real hurry. Her life was her own now. She was determined to enjoy every moment.

She bent down to gather up her gardening tools and suddenly a familiar voice called out to her.

"Hey! Pat Melbourne. Is it really you?"

Pat looked up, and there he was, Hank Richards, the puppy man.

"Hank? What are you doing here?"

"I live across the road," Hank said. "One of our neighbors told me a pretty lady had moved in, but I've been working overtime lately, and I haven't been home much. Isn't this a coincidence?"

Pat laughed. "I'll say, but where are all your dogs? I haven't seen them out."

"My runs are out in back of the house," Hank said. "I try to keep my place as neat as possible for the neighbors' sake. Hey, did you get a dog yet?"

"Not yet. I thought I'd better get settled first."

Hank nodded, and reached out to lift the basket of gardening tools. "Here, let me. What are you planting?"

"Mostly flowers right now," Pat explained, "but I'd like to have a little vegetable garden, too."

"Well, that ground needs to be dug up good

for vegetables," Hank said, his dark eyes narrowed. "I could do it for you on my first free weekend."

"Thanks, but that won't be necessary," Pat said quickly "I can hire someone to do it."

"Now why would you want to do that? Why pay good money when you don't have to? Everybody's real neighborly around here. You'll find that out when you get to know us. We help each other out. In these tough financial times we've got to be thrifty."

"But . . ."

"Don't worry. There're no strings attached, if that's what's worrying you, Pat. Of course a home-cooked meal would be nice," Hank added. "Since Nancy left I mostly eat frozen dinners. Some of them aren't too bad."

"I'd be glad to cook you dinner, but I'm not much of a cook. All I can make are plain things, like meat loaf and spaghetti or fried chicken."

Hank's grin widened. "Any one of them would be ambrosia to me."

"Okay. You've got a deal. You dig my garden and I'll cook you a big plate of fried chicken." Pat matched Hank's happy grin. "I may even throw in a home-baked apple pie. I've never made one, but it can't be too difficult."

"You've never made a pie?" Hank asked. "What did you feed your family all these years?"

Pat opened her mouth to say that Jane had done all the cooking for the family, but something stopped her. She had the feeling that Hank wouldn't understand cooks and housekeepers, or houses with seven bedrooms and six baths. Her smiled widened, and when Hank extended his hand she gave him hers. Hank was a plain man, a man totally unlike her late husband. She didn't know much about him, but she did know she liked him, a lot.

"This is my champion bitch," Hank explained a few days later, "and that is Tundra's Silver Frost, my best stud dog. Isn't he a beauty?"

"I'll say," Pat said. She was awed by Hank's animals. And the pups she'd first seen in Dr. Brookfield's office were now almost as big as the adult dogs. The ones who were left, that is.

"You sold most of the litter?" she asked.

"All but these two," Hank said, pointing to the adolescent dogs romping in the fenced enclosure. "I kept one male and one female for breeding purposes."

"You're going to breed brother and sister?"

Hank shook his head. "It's been done, and sometimes you get good pups, but I want to introduce some new stock. I've got two new dogs coming from Wisconsin. They have a lot of Samoyeds out there. Lots of champions."

"You really love these animals, don't you?"

Hank grinned. "You can tell, huh?"

"Just a little." She stood back and surveyed the dogs as they played. "I'd be sorely tempted if they were just a little smaller," she said, "but I've just about decided to adopt a pup from the animal shelter. What do you think?"

"That's a good idea," Hank said. "Let me know when you decide to go to the shelter. I'll be glad to ride along and give you my professional opinion."

"Thanks," Pat said. "I'll remember."

Pat sat across from Clifford's attorney. The news he'd just given her should have shocked her, but after what she'd already learned about her late husband, she was pretty shock proof.

"So what you're saying is that there's actually more money than I thought? Are you telling me I'm rich?"

"That's about it, Pat. Of course there were some . . . rather large expenditures during the last months of Clifford's life. The condo in Florida, that little sports car . . ."

"What sports car?" Pat asked, "And what's this about a condo? We don't own any property in Florida."

Bruce Howard looked distressed. "I'm sorry, Pat. This kind of thing is never easy. I'm afraid that both the sports car and the condo are owned by a Carolyn Evans. Do you know the woman?"

Pat shook her head. "I thought I did," she said

flatly, "But I guess I was wrong."

"Well, disregarding that, there is still a very sizable estate, and we should be able to get things settled before the end of the year. I know that will be a relief to you."

As she drove home, Pat alternated between fury and disbelief. Maybe there was some mistake. Maybe Bruce had been reading some other man's file. Yes, and maybe the sky would fall in and she could forget she'd ever heard any of this drivel!

Well, what it all amounted to was the fact that Clifford was even more of a bastard than she'd originally thought. A condo and a sports car for his mistress! While the good little wife sat home alone and arranged flowers!

"Come on," Hank said, "let's see what they have back here."

They were both dressed in jeans and flannel shirts, and they'd decided that the time had come for Pat to pick out a puppy.

"Maybe I shouldn't do this," she said nervously, suddenly worrying about how Tweetie would react to a canine companion. "What if I get a puppy who doesn't like birds?"

Hank laughed and put his arm around her shoulders. "If you get a real young dog he'll get used to anything. Maybe you should worry about whether or not the bird will like the dog. From what I've seen and heard of that lovebird, his former owner must have been a sailor!"

"Tweetie's not so bad," Pat said loyally. "He just gets a little overexcited every now and then."

There were twenty-seven puppies waiting to be adopted. Pat's tender heart ached when she looked into the cages and saw the eager, expectant looks in the pups' eyes.

"I wish I could take them all," she said, looking up at Hank helplessly. "How can I choose just one?"

Hank shrugged. "It's hard," he said, "but you better remember that dogs can be expensive. There's food and shots and collars. You'll need a license, and when the pup matures you'll have to get it fixed."

"Must I?"

Hank nodded. "The shelter requires it. It's their way of making sure there aren't so many unwanted pups."

One of the attendants came up to them. "Every day we're forced to put healthy animals to death." The young man shook his head sadly. "Sometimes I go home feeling sick to my stomach, but there's no other way. We don't get enough people in here wanting to adopt, and we can only keep the animals for a limited time."

Pat felt like crying. All of the puppies were adorable, cute and cuddly, and all they wanted was a home and somebody to love them. "I'll take that one," she said, pointing to a small, spotted pup, "and that one over there." She looked up at Hank anxiously. "They'll get along, won't they?"

"Well, sure, but . . . are you sure you can handle two puppies, Pat?"

"I can handle it," she said firmly, holding out her arms for the spotted pup. The other one she'd chosen looked like a mix of poodle and cocker spaniel. It was small and jet black, with long, silky ears, and it had the most beautiful brown eyes Pat had ever seen.

"Can you use help here?" she asked the attendant. "I mean as a volunteer? I don't know much about animals, but I'm willing to learn. I could feed them or help exercise them, or maybe I can just love them."

"Lady, if you're serious, you've got a deal. We can use all the help we can get."

"Then I'll come by in a couple of weeks, after I get these little fellows settled."

"We'll look forward to it," the attendant said. "And thanks, lady. We need more people like you around here."

"Ditto," Hank said, his voice slightly husky. "You're quite a lady, Pat Melbourne." He was holding the little black pup, and Pat had the spotted dog. She was gazing at it with something very close to awe.

"Isn't he adorable? Oh, both of them are just precious! What shall I name them? Will you help me, Hank?"

Hank stared at Pat's pink cheeks and shining eyes. She reminded him of his daughter when she was little. Becky had had the same bright-eyed joy, and the same tender concern for animals.

"Uh, sure. We'll work on it," he said, embarrassed by the path his thoughts were taking. He thought of his wife, Nancy, just up and walking out one day as if the years they'd shared had meant nothing. But he'd never been able to satisfy Nancy, not even in the beginning when they were first married. He never made enough money, and he didn't go to work in a suit and a tie. Instead he fixed automobile engines. He got grease on his hands and under his nails, and toward the end Nancy hadn't even wanted him to touch her. She complained that he smelled of dogs. Hank frowned. He had no right to be spending time with Pat, no right to be drowning in her smile. He had a wife, even though he had no idea where she was.

"We better get these little guys home," he said gruffly, "before they pee all over us!"

Pat spent most of her time with the two little pups the next few days. She'd never had so much fun in her life. She'd named them Ink and Spot.

"Very original," Hank said teasingly, watching as Pat scooped up the spotted pup just as he was about to dampen her freshly mopped tile floor.

"This is great," Pat said. "I think I've already

lost that five pounds I put on since moving here."

"I can't see where you need to lose any weight," Hank said. "I like a woman with a little meat on her."

"Why, Hank Richards, are you complimenting me?"

Pat really liked Hank. He was a good neighbor and he was becoming a good friend as well. She liked knowing she could ask his advice on puppy rearing, and although she wasn't afraid of living alone, it was nice to know Hank was nearby just in case.

"Did I tell you my son is coming to visit me?" she asked, putting the pup back down on the floor. "He lives in California and I don't get to see him too often, so this will be a real treat."

Hank stood up and headed for the door. He didn't see his children much anymore. For some crazy reason they blamed him for Nancy's desertion. Right after it happened, his daughters had accused him of not trying to make the marriage work. He hadn't had the heart to tell them that there was no marriage left.

There was nothing he could have done. How can you make a woman care? How can you make her be satisfied with less than what she thinks she needs? Could he have given her more? Should he have tried harder to be what she wanted?

"Gotta go," Hank said abruptly, as the familiar uneasiness swept over him. He shouldn't be spending so much time with Pat. He wasn't a free man. "I'm glad your boy is coming. That will be nice for you."

"Bunch of bull!" Tweetie chirped. "That's a bunch of bull!"

"Smart bird!" Hank muttered as he crossed the road to his place.

Pat had to drive into the city to pick Cliff up at the airport the next day. She stopped to say good-bye to Hank.

"Hank, could you feed Ink and Spot while I'm gone?" she asked, after strolling over to his front yard. "I should be back by four or five."

"No problem." He didn't look up, just kept whittling on a piece of wood.

Pat fidgeted. "Look, if it's too much trouble . . ."

"I said I'd do it, didn't I?" Hank said, his voice a harsh growl. "What do you want, an engraved plaque or something?"

"What did I do, Hank? Why are you mad at me? I thought we were friends."

"We were . . . I mean we are, and I'm not mad. Oh hell, Pat, leave it, okay? I'm just in a foul mood."

"But maybe I can help. Is it . . . it is your wife?"

"Nancy?" Hank looked up, and his eyes were bleak. His face was pale and ravaged. "Yeah, it's Nancy. But there's nothing you or anyone can do."

"I'm sorry," Pat said softly. She wanted to put

her arms around Hank and just hold him. He wasn't the handsomest man she'd ever seen, and she supposed that some women wouldn't give a man like Hank a second look, but something in his eyes cried out to her. "It must be terribly difficult," she said, trying to prod Hank into talking about what was bothering him.

"Yeah, believe it or not, it still hurts," Hank said flatly. "I don't know where she is, or even if she's alive."

"I'm sorry," Pat said again, knowing how lame it sounded. But what could she or anyone really do for Hank? What could anyone say to comfort him? For all intents and purposes he was single, and yet he wasn't. She couldn't help wondering why Hank hadn't gotten a divorce.

She guessed he'd never felt the urge to remarry, so a divorce probably hadn't seemed necessary. Still, it must be like living in limbo. Married, but without a wife. Single, but not free.

Hank looked up, "I know you're sorry, Pat. Everyone is sorry, but it doesn't change anything. Go on, get to the airport and pick up your son. Don't worry about me. I get like this every now and again, but I'll get over it. I don't have any choice."

Pat nodded. Just like she would eventually be able to put the hurt of Clifford's betrayal behind her. Right now the wound was still raw and bleeding. There were still moments when she wanted to confront Carolyn Evans and push in her smug, lying face, but she didn't, and she wouldn't. Two wrongs didn't make a right, and Clifford was dead. It was over. It was better for everyone if she just left it alone. But just because she knew it was best to put the past behind her and move on didn't mean it was easy. There were still times when she wanted to tear up every picture she'd ever taken of Clifford, especially the ones of the two of them together, the ones where he smiled into the camera like a loving, devoted husband.

But even worse than the anger were the doubts, the fear that maybe it had all been her fault. Had she failed him in some way? Not given him everything he needed?

The sound of Hank's voice pulled Pat back to the present.

"Shouldn't you get going?"

"Oh, yes. Cliff's plane is due at two-thirty. Thanks for looking after the pups, Hank. I'll see you later."

As she drove toward the city, Pat thought about Cliff. He was coming home and that in itself was wonderful. Of course Clifford wasn't here now to hassle him, and that probably had something to do with this unexpected visit. When he was small, Pat had enjoyed a wonderful relationship with her son. It was only after Clifford started pressuring the boy that things went sour. Although he'd never said so, Pat believed that Cliff blamed her for not running interference between him and his father. And in a way he was right. She should have been stronger, should have stood up to Clifford and protected her young son. Instead she had stood helplessly by while Clifford emotionally battered the boy.

Tears stung Pat's eyes as she remembered. Then she shook her head. She couldn't do anything about the past, but from now on she was determined to be the best mother a son could ask for. She would be loving and supportive no matter what.

Pat arrived at the airport just in time to see the plane touch down. Her stomach was knotted with apprehension, but her mother's heart was singing. Cliff was her first born, her only son. Perhaps this would be her chance to breach the gap between them.

He strode into the waiting area, an overnighter in one hand, a topcoat slung over his shoulder. His expression was tense and wary.

"Cliff! Over here, son. How are you?"

She longed to take him in her arms, but something held her back. The look in Cliff's eyes, so anxious, the set of his shoulders . . .

"You . . . how was your flight?" Pat asked, daring to reach out and touch her son's hand. "Are you tired?"

Cliff shook his head, and visibly relaxed. "I'm fine, Mom, and you look wonderful. What have you been doing with yourself?"

Pat laughed and led the way to the baggage claim area. "Change of life-style, honey. I'm living in the country with lots of nice, fresh air. I've adopted two puppies, and I'm going to grow a vegetable garden. What do you think of that?" They collected Cliff's luggage, one suitcase and a garment bag, and headed for the parking lot and Pat's minivan.

Cliff smiled, then his expression sobered. "I doubt that Dad would approve."

Pat stood back while Cliff loaded his baggage into the back of the van. "I know he wouldn't approve, but I really don't care. I'm starting a new life, and I don't have to answer to anyone."

"Good for you," Cliff said, and suddenly, as he smiled, he was Pat's little boy again, and not her estranged son. He looked young and sweet and terribly vulnerable. And it seemed perfectly right for Pat to hug him close to her heart.

"I've missed you, son. I'm glad you're here."

"Me, too," Cliff said. "Me, too."

"So, what's with this big life-style change?" Cliff asked, as Pat drove out of the city limits. "I never knew you were a country gal at heart."

Pat took her eyes off the road briefly to smile at Cliff. "Neither did I, but I'm having a wonderful time. Wait until you see Ink and Spot, and I have a really nice neighbor who raises and shows purebred Samoyeds. My house is small, but there is a guest room. I insisted on that. I guess I was hoping for a visit just like this."

"Thanks, Mom," Cliff said "It's nice to feel wanted. After that letter Ashley wrote me, I . . . well, I wasn't sure if you'd want me to come."

"What are you talking about?" Pat felt the color drain out of her face. "When did Ashley write to you? What did she say?"

Cliff colored, and for a moment he refused to meet Pat's eyes. Then he seemed to draw strength from some unseen source. He squared his shoulders and looked Pat straight in the eye.

"She accused me of being gay. She said I was a disgrace to the family, a blot on our name, and that as far as she was concerned I am no longer her brother."

Pat pulled over to the side of the road. She had to. Her hands were shaking so badly she couldn't keep them on the steering wheel. She turned pleading, agonized eyes to her son. "Are you?" she asked, her voice harsh and hurting.

"Yes," Cliff said softly.

Three

Pat was more frightened than she'd ever been in her whole life. Not for herself, but for Cliff. The baby she'd held in her arms when the pain of teething kept him awake at night. The little boy she'd proudly escorted to kindergarten, the gawky, awkward twelve-year-old who came to her in agony because his father wouldn't let him paint and insisted on taking him hunting with the "men."

"Oh, Cliff."

She dared to look at him then and saw the pain and dejection in his gray eyes. She saw deep down into his soul to the misery inside as Cliff geared himself up for what he believed would be the final, total rejection.

Pat smiled and opened her arms, and after a tense moment of hesitation, Cliff came to her. And as she held him and let the warring, ambivalent emotions sweep over her, Pat knew that it didn't matter, nothing mattered where her mother's heart was concerned. This was her son, her first born. Nothing could alter that.

"Come on, let's go home," Pat said a few minutes later, when they both dried their eyes. "I've got two rambunctious pups there, and I can't wait for you to meet Hank. I know you'll like him."

They carefully kept the conversation neutral for the rest of the drive.

"How is your painting coming?" Pat asked. "You never say much."

She shot a quick glance at Cliff and saw his expression change. Gone was the wariness and fear, and in its place a glowing pride blossomed.

"I didn't write because I wanted to tell you in person, Mom. Some important people like my work, and if all goes well I'll be having a small show in a few months. It could be the break I've been waiting and hoping for."

"Oh, darling, that's wonderful! I'm so pleased and so proud of you! You must be thrilled!"

Cliff nodded eagerly. "I am and so is . . . Doug . . . my friend. He's a writer. He's loaded with talent, but so far he hasn't had many breaks. I'm hoping his turn will come next."

Pat nodded. Doug. Her son's . . . companion. Instead of a wife and children Cliff would have a male companion. She couldn't say the word "lover." She couldn't even think it, and maybe she would never be able to. One step at a time, she told herself. Just take tiny little steps and breathe deeply.

"Well," she said, as she turned onto Robin Road. "We're almost home. I hope you like my little house."

Hank was in her yard with Ink and Spot when she pulled into the driveway. He looked up and smiled, his earlier bad humor apparently gone.

"Is that your new friend?" Cliff asked curiously.

"Yes. That's Hank. Wait until you see the beautiful purebred dogs he raises. They're gorgeous."

She introduced Cliff and Hank, feeling a sudden knot of nervousness as Hank's intelligent eyes assessed her son. Then Hank held out his hand and both men smiled.

"And what's all this?" Cliff asked, dropping down on his knees to pet Ink and Spot.

Suddenly, as she saw the gentle, almost reverent way her son touched the pup's soft fur, Pat remembered when Cliff was eight years old, when the only thing he wanted for his birthday was a puppy. She had wanted to get one for him, but Cliff, Sr. adamantly refused. He said Cliff was too young to handle the responsibility for a pet's care, that the work would fall on Pat and the housekeeper. That doggie accidents would destroy the polished hardwood floors, and the house would smell like a kennel.

Pain slashed through Pat as she remembered. At the time it just hadn't seemed worth arguing about, but now she knew it had been. It was just one more way she had failed her son.

"Well," she said, clearing her throat, "how about a sandwich and something cold to drink." She turned to her son, her eyes pleading. "I wasn't sure what you'd like so I stocked up on beer and soft drinks, or I can make coffee if you like."

"A beer would be great," Cliff said. He touched Pat's arm lightly, reassuringly, as if to say that he understood.

Hank noted the exchange and frowned. Something was wrong here, and it was more than just a disagreement between parent and child. If ever there was love between two individuals, he was seeing it now. It was in Pat's eyes when she looked at her boy. Hank's frown eased as he followed Pat and Cliff inside. Boy, hell, Cliff was a grown man, and unless Hank missed his guess he loved his mother every bit as much as she loved him, but something was holding them apart, and for the life of him he couldn't begin to figure what it was. He knew tension between a parent and a child when he saw it and felt it. Lord knew there was enough of it between him and his daughters, especially Becky.

"Hank? Come on, join us. I've got your favorite rye bread."

When the three of them were settled around Pat's small round kitchen table, Cliff studied Hank and his mother carefully. There was something different about his mom, and it wasn't just the extra pounds she'd gained. No, there was something in her eyes, in the way she moved. A small smile tugged at Cliff's lips. Unless he was totally off base, he'd be willing to bet that his mom, the once painfully thin, elegantly dressed and coiffed Patricia Melbourne, was falling head over heels in love with the man next door!

"How long will you be staying, Cliff?" Hank asked, draining the last of his beer with satisfaction.

Cliff shrugged. "That depends. I'd like to hang around for a couple of weeks, if I'm not in the way."

"In the way? I wish you would stay forever! I wish . . ." Pat stopped in confusion. What was she doing? Nothing she could say or do would change anything. Cliff was who and what he said he was, and unless she wanted a complete and final estrangement, she would have to work on accepting that. It was time for acceptance. Time for unconditional love.

"Well, what I meant was you're welcome to stay as long as you like, and come back as often as possible. I've missed you."

"I think I'll be on my way," Hank said, pushing back his chair with a noisy scrape. "Got dogs to feed and water, and pups to cuddle. Come on over and meet my kids when you get settled in, Cliff," he said, once again extending his hand to Pat's son.

"Thanks. I'd like that. Mom says your dogs are something else."

Then Pat was alone with her son, and something twisted painfully inside her chest. She wanted so badly to love her son. She did love him, but there was no sense denying the fact that his way of life was very hard to understand and accept.

"Cliff, have you . . . ever thought of seeing a doctor?" she asked almost timidly.

Cliff sighed. Then he pushed back his chair and stood up and held out his hand to Pat. "Let's go in the other room and get comfortable, Mom," he said. "This may take awhile."

Afternoon shadows blended into evening darkness as Pat and her son talked, baring their souls and their hearts.

"I feel as though it's my fault, that if I'd stood up to your father more, everything would be different," Pat said brokenly.

"Mom, don't," Cliff said quietly. "I guess I felt that way at first, too. I did blame you for letting Dad ride roughshod over me, but I've met a lot of really nice, intelligent people in California, and yes, I did see a therapist. I thought he could cure me and I wouldn't be gay anymore. But it didn't work that way. I am what I am, Mom. I came home because I wanted to see if I could make you understand that and accept me as I am. Maybe my life would be easier if I was straight, but who really knows? All I know is that right now, at this moment in time I'm content. I have Doug, and we understand and care about one another, and my career dreams are finally starting to come true. But ever since I left home there's been a big hole inside me. I don't want to be separated from you any longer, Mom."

"Oh Cliff, I don't want that either!"

"But can you accept me as I am?" Cliff persisted "I can't pretend anymore, Mom, not even for you."

Pat drew a long, shaky breath. She wanted to tell Cliff that everything was fine, that she didn't care what he did or how he lived, but she couldn't. It wasn't true, not yet, and she wouldn't start off this new, fragile relationship with a lie.

"Son, I love you," she said softly. "No matter what, that will never change, but right now I can't make any promises. Can you give me a little time to absorb everything? Can we just enjoy each other's company and put the heavy stuff on hold for a while?"

Cliff swallowed his disappointment. What had he expected? That his mother would jump for joy when she learned that her only son was gay? "Sure, Mom," he said. "We'll take it one step at a time. Now, how about if we get some sleep? I've got jet lag, and tomorrow is another day."

"Yes," Pat said gently, letting Cliff take her hand and raise her to her feet. "It is, isn't it?"

She hugged him tight before showing him to the guest room. Pat touched her son's cheek tenderly. "Sleep well, son," she said. "I'll see you in the morning."

She lay awake for a long time, remembering. Cliff as a chubby, pink-cheeked baby, as a smiling, cherubic toddler, and then, as he grew into a boy, the all too frequent frowns that replaced the smiles. Cliff, Sr. had tried to force him into a mold. To make Cliff the perfect son, a husky high school jock, a son he could brag about to all his colleagues.

Was that when it began? Or had the seeds been there from the beginning? Pat admitted that she was woefully ignorant on the whole subject of homosexuality, but then she had never expected it to touch her. She had never thought the ugly threat of sickness and prejudice would come home to roost. Dear God, she thought, Ashley was right all along! Cliff *is* gay!

It was so hard, so painful to accept, and Pat wasn't sure she could do it.

Cliff was downstairs when Pat finally woke up the next morning. After falling into a restless sleep at dawn, she had a hard time dragging herself out of bed.

"You made coffee?" she asked her son. "Thank God! I feel like I could drink a gallon."

"Rough night?" Cliff asked sympathetically. "I hope I didn't dump too much on you all at once, Mom."

"I'll handle it." Good grief, were they going to spend Cliff's entire visit discussing his sexual preferences? If so, she'd just as soon he left today. As soon as the thought flew from her mind, she regretted it. Of course she didn't want Cliff to leave. This was a tough situation, but they'd get through it.

"What would you like to do today?" she asked, stirring cream into her coffee. Cliff had made it just the way she liked it, hot and strong.

"Well, I'd really like to go into the city and see my old art teacher, Mister Franks. Would you mind if I took off for a little while?"

Pat shook her head vigorously. "Heavens no. Just go on and do whatever you want. You can use my van. I've got plenty to do around here. How would you like a nice roast chicken dinner?"

Cliff laughed. "Why do mothers always want to feed their children? Yeah, I remember, Mom. Chicken will be great."

Pat straightened the kitchen while Cliff went to shower and dress. When he came downstairs later he was wearing chinos and a plaid cotton shirt.

"Cliff, you're not . . . well, you won't tell Mister Frank, will you?"

Instantly Pat knew she'd said the wrong thing. Cliff's smile disappeared and his jaw tightened. "Don't worry, Mother," he said sarcastically. "I'm not planning to take out an ad in the local paper, or rent a banner plane to fly across the city, but maybe there's something you should get straight right here and now. I'm not ashamed of being gay. I was in the beginning, and it took me a long time to get where I am today. I won't allow anyone to take that away from me, not even you."

An hour later, Hank came over. Pat was blotting the last of her tears and trying to straighten her hair.

"Pat! What's wrong? Why are you crying?"

Pat sniffed and tried to laugh. "What are you doing here, Hank? Shouldn't you be working?"

Hank shook his head. "No work today. The supplies didn't come in, so I thought maybe I'd hang out here and torment you. Where did Cliff go? I saw him drive off a while ago."

"He went to the city to see an old teacher. We had words and . . . oh, why can't I ever do anything right? I let him down when he was a boy and now I'm doing it again!"

Hank nodded. "Want to tell me about it? My shoulders are pretty broad."

"Not now," Pat mumbled. She wasn't ready to talk about this, to dump her confusion and fears on someone else, especially not Hank. They were forging a deep and trust-filled friendship. She didn't want to do anything to disturb that. She watched Hank from beneath lowered lids as she poured them each a glass of low-fat milk and set out whole wheat muffins. Hank was a man's man. How could he understand something like this?

"Come on," Hank said when he finished his muffin. "How about fixing a picnic lunch and taking it down the road to that little spot you like so much? There may not be too many more warm days like this."

Pat shook her head. Normally she enjoyed Hank's company. There was something steady and reassuring about him, and he had a wonderful sense of humor, but today she knew it would take more than his crazy antics to lift her spirits. "Not today," she forced a smile, hoping Hank wouldn't notice how her hands were shaking. "I'm making a roast chicken and all the fixings, and that takes time. Another day, okay?"

Hank shrugged. "Sure." He didn't know what was bothering Pat, and obviously she wasn't willing to share it. He turned away and grinned. From what he knew of Pat she wasn't all that talented in the kitchen, and if she planned on a roast chicken with all the fixings, it would definitely take some time! "Okay. I'll get out of your hair, but if you need anything just yell."

Pat stared after Hank as he walked back across the road. He was a nice man, a real man, and not a shiny-slick imitation like her late husband. Hank ate potatoes and meat and held a sick puppy with as much tenderness and care as any woman. He was tough and strong and yet he had a deep down gentleness that tugged at her heartstrings. It was a quality she had never seen in her husband. But how would

Hank feel about her son's homosexuality? Would he be able to accept it? Hank's had no sons of his own, only daughters, so how could he possibly understand?

"Fix the chicken, Pat," she urged herself. "Keep busy, and push the pain away."

By two that afternoon the chicken Pat had prepared so hopefully was a blackened mess. The whole kitchen smelled. The stuffing she'd mixed tasted like wallpaper paste, and the vegetables she had started to prepare sat in lonely splendor on the stove, the only thing she hadn't managed to ruin.

"Hey, what's going on over here?" Hank asked, tapping on the kitchen door and sniffing suspiciously.

Pat let him in and collapsed in a chair at the table. "I spoiled everything," she said, moaning. "But it looked so easy when . . ." She stopped in confusion. Hank still didn't know that for all of her married life she'd had a cook and a housekeeper, and for some crazy reason she wasn't ready to tell him.

"Anyway, it's been a long time," she lied. "I guess I forgot how to time it."

Hank nodded. "I'll say. Look, I've got a great idea. I made a big pan of lasagna last night, and I always think it's better the second time around. How about you and Cliff having dinner with me tonight? I'll fix a salad and pick up a loaf of Italian bread. What do you say?"

"Oh, I don't . . ."

Then Cliff walked in. "What . . ."

"I ruined the chicken," Pat said quickly before he could speak. "And Hank was kind enough to invite us to eat with him. Lasagna."

"Hey, all right!" Cliff said, grinning. "I've developed a real appreciation for Italian food since I've been in California."

"Great," Hank said. "Then I'll get to it. See you both around six?"

When Hank was gone, Cliff sobered. "I forgot you didn't know how to cook, Mom. How have you been managing since you've been on your own?"

Pat poured them each a glass of wine. She managed a shaky laugh. "I haven't tackled anything fancy yet but . . ."

Cliff's grin widened mischievously. "Until the chicken."

Pat snorted. "Chicken isn't fancy. Any idiot should be able to cook a chicken without burning it to a crisp. I can't believe I'm so stupid!"

"Hey, take it easy, Mom. Don't be so hard on yourself. I remember all those charity things you handled while Ashley and I were growing up. You helped a lot of people, and it's not your fault Dad wanted you out doing that instead of puttering in the kitchen."

"I just feel so helpless sometimes," Pat confided. "I'm finally learning things that I should have known years ago." She blushed. "Uh, Hank doesn't know how we lived before, you know. He doesn't realize that I never had to cook and clean."

Cliff's brows rose. "Oh. It's like that, is it?"

"Like what?" Pat asked.

"You like Hank, don't you, Mom? I mean really like him."

"Oh, don't be silly!" Pat cried. "Why, I hardly know the man, and he's my neighbor. I like him, but . . ."

"Hey, don't get so uptight, Mom. For what it's worth, I approve. Hank seems like a great guy, and you deserve whatever happiness you can find."

Tears welled up in Pat's eyes and suddenly she found herself in her son's arms. She let Cliff hold her for a long moment, then she sniffed and stepped back.

"Come on, tell me about Mister Frank. Did he remember you? Is his hair still as unruly as it always was?"

Cliff insisted on running out to buy a bottle of wine before they went across the street to Hank's for dinner. After all, what kind of Italian dinner would it be without wine?

Pat showered and changed her clothes while Cliff was gone, and she paid special attention to her makeup, hoping to disguise the ravages of her tears. The next time she went shopping she was going to buy a good, basic cookbook. After all, if she could read, she could learn to cook, right? And now that she was alone she had to take care of herself. If she didn't, who would?

"Pat, Cliff, come on in," Hank said, opening the door wide to them. "Wow, don't you look nice." He grinned at Pat. Then he caught sight of the wine bottle Cliff was carrying. "That's one of my favorites. Thanks."

Suddenly two perfectly groomed Samoyeds sauntered into the room, heads held high in the regal posture so characteristic of the breed. They eyed the visitors curiously, and approached them without fear.

"Hi, Frosty," Pat said, bending to pat the head of the big male. Then she turned her attention to the female. "Aren't you pretty today, Princess?"

Cliff was speechless. "These are the dogs you breed? They're sled dogs, aren't they?"

"That's what they were originally bred for, yes," Hank answered, as he poured them each a glass of wine, "but I doubt these pampered pooches will ever see a sled."

"Well, Mom was right. They're beauties, all right," Cliff said, accepting a glass of wine from Hank.

"I love your apron," Pat said, winking at Hank. "Is there anything I can do to help?"

Hank grinned. "I think the best thing you can do is stay out of the kitchen, Pat. Why don't you and Cliff just relax and enjoy your wine while I finish things up?"

Cliff put his wine down on the table and sat cross-legged on the floor with the two dogs. They seemed to take to him right away, and Pat couldn't help smiling.

"Wait until you see the puppies," she said. "They're absolutely adorable. Hank has two litters now."

"I'll show them to you after we eat," Hank called from the kitchen. "Say, could one of you give me a hand here for a minute? I'm afraid I need a little help after all."

Pat started to get up, but Cliff beat her to it. "I'll do it, Mom," he said. "I do most of the cooking at home, so I know my way around a kitchen. Doug's talents don't go past the written page."

"Oh. I . . . see. How did you learn to cook?" Pat asked weakly. She envisioned Cliff in the kitchen wearing an apron while his male lover sat at a table waiting to be served.

"Not from Doug, that's for sure. I took a

culinary course at night school. I enjoyed it, and now we eat pretty good."

He disappeared into the kitchen then and Pat tried to get herself together. She couldn't keep doing this, getting all wound up every time Cliff said something that reminded her of his life with Doug. She was being paranoid anyway. Lots of men enjoyed cooking. Hank was in the kitchen this very minute, for heaven's sake, and it would be hard to find a more masculine man than him. She had to stop watching every move Cliff made and listening to every inflection of his voice. If she didn't she would drive him away again, and this time it might be for good.

Then suddenly dinner was on the table, without Pat having to lift a finger. "Everything looks wonderful," she said, glancing around Hank's warm, comfortable dining room. The furniture was old and well used, but it had been lovingly polished to a soft patina, and the lace tablecloth looked like an heirloom.

"Is this handmade?" she asked, fingering the delicate cream-colored lace.

Hank put a tray of sliced bread in front of her and nodded. "My grandmother. She was a true craftswoman. She made quilts and all the clothing for her family, and in later years she crocheted these tablecloths. I have several more."

"It's lovely," Pat said. "It must be nice to have things that have been handed down from generation to generation."

"Don't you?" Hank deftly slid a man-size portion of lasagna onto Pat's plate and passed her a glass jar containing freshly grated cheese. "Eat," he commanded. "You've been looking a little pale these last few days. You need some meat on your bones."

Cliff grinned and accepted his own gigantic portion of lasagna. "My sentiments exactly, Hank. When I go back to California I know I'll be leaving Mom in good hands."

"You'll be leaving Mom in her own hands, young man," Pat said indignantly, a forkful of salad halfway to her lips. "I don't need a keeper."

"Okay, sorry, Mom. I just meant . . ."

"Your mother knows what you meant, Cliff," Hank said, laughing. "Now why don't you shut up and eat before you really put your foot in your mouth?"

Four

The rest of the meal passed with light-hearted banter. Cliff asked Hank a dozen questions about dog breeding, and Hank, warming to his favorite subject, hardly noticed Pat's nervousness.

Finally, when they all declared they couldn't eat another morsel, Hank stood up and began to clear the plates. "We'll have coffee and cake a little later, all right? You can't go home without trying my Italian Cream Cake."

Cliff groaned. "Many more nights like this and I'll lose my boyish figure and Doug will . . ." A dark flush covered Cliff's handsome face and his words trailed off helplessly. "What I mean is . . ."

Hank's gaze swung from Cliff's agonized expression to Pat's obvious discomfort, and suddenly it all made sense. The wary distance between Pat and her son, the pain he'd seen in Pat's lovely green eyes. A heavy silence hung over them until Hank cleared his throat. "Help me clear up, Cliff? Let's let your mother relax tonight, shall we?"

Cliff gratefully began scooping up dishes and silverware, and Pat went into the living room. Hank knew. She'd seen the recognition in his eyes. What would happen now? Would it be the end of their friendship?

She sat alone for almost half an hour and she couldn't imagine what Cliff and Hank were doing in the kitchen. What were they talking about? Had Cliff confided in Hank?

Then, just when she thought she'd go crazy wondering, Cliff came into the room carrying a tray with coffee, followed by Hank with a sinfully rich cream cake.

She opened her mouth and nothing came out, and she knew she must look like a total idiot. "Is . . ."

"Everything is okay, Mom," Cliff said quietly. "Hank and I had a good talk."

Hank put the cake on the coffee table and sat down beside Pat. He took her hand in his and smiled tenderly. "Relax. Everything is going to be all right. You don't have to pretend anymore."

The tears came then, drenching Hank's shirt

as he drew her sobbing, shivering form into his arms, but they were warm, healing tears, and when they finally dried, Pat looked over at Cliff and smiled. Then she held out her hand.

That night Pat and her son sat with Ink and Spot cuddled between them on the sofa and talked again. Pat was as honest as she knew how to be.

"I wish things were different. I'm afraid I can't pretend otherwise, but I'm trying hard to understand and accept. Please be patient with me."

Cliff smiled sadly. "I wish things were different, too, Mom." He reached out and brought Pat's hand to his cheek. "I never wanted to hurt you this way. I don't want you to be ashamed of me, but I can't pretend to be something I'm not, and I can't wish Doug out of my life. He's important to me, to my happiness. And he's a good person. I think you would like him."

"Cliff, I can't . . . I'm not ready . . ."

"Don't worry, Mom. I won't ask you to do anything that makes you uncomfortable. I just hope you'll try to keep an open mind."

"I'll try," Pat said.

Ashley's strident voice woke Pat the next

morning, when she answered the shrilling phone. Panic swept over her for a minute. "Ashley? Where are you? You're not . . ."

"For heaven's sake, Mother, I'm in New York. Where else would I be when I'm in the middle of a shoot? Don't you ever pay attention to anything I tell you?"

"I'm sorry. I guess I've had other things on my mind. How are you, dear? How's the shoot going?"

"The shoot is going beautifully as always," Ashley said, "and I'm fine, or at least I would be if I wasn't worried sick about you. Have you come to your senses yet, Mother? You're not really going to stay on in that tumbledown little cottage, are you?"

"Who on earth told you it was a tumbledown cottage?" Pat demanded, her hackles rising. Ashley sounded more like Clifford, every day. It was eerie.

"Well, really, Mother, the way you described it left very little to the imagination. Don't you miss the house?"

"Not at all," Pat replied, "and by the way, Ashley, Cliff is here for a visit. We're having a lovely time. He's doing well with his painting. Isn't that wonderful?"

"Cliff is there with you? And you didn't tell me?"

"I'm telling you now, Ashley." Pat felt dangerously close to the breaking point, or maybe it was more accurate to say she was ready to explode. Lately she and Ashley had come perilously close to an out and out argument on several occasions. Ashley seemed to think she had to take over where her father had left off, giving orders, issuing commands . . .

"There's no need for you to get upset, dear," Pat said, willing her voice to stay calm and quiet. "I just thought you would want to know that your brother is in town."

"I don't know why I should even care," Ashley said, sounding like a whiny child. "Cliff doesn't like me any more than I like him."

"Thank you for calling, Ashley. I'm glad your shoot is going well. I'll tell Cliff you said hello."

"Are you hanging up on me, Mother?"

The tiniest hint of a smile tugged at Pat's lips. "Yes, Ashley," she said. "I certainly am!"

Once again Cliff had coffee made when Pat went into the kitchen. "This is a real treat," she said.

Cliff slid a mug across the counter to her and smiled. "And good morning to you, too. Who was on the phone so early? Was it Hank?"

"No. It was your sister," Pat said, shaking her head. "She's doing a shoot in New York, and she just called to find out when I'm going to give up this 'tumbledown shack' I'm living in."

"What?" Cliff's brows rose in disbelief. "Has she seen this place?"

"Not yet," Pat answered, stirring cream and sugar into her coffee. "And I'm not sure I want her to. You know how Ashley is. She's her father's daughter. She'll probably take one look at this place and try to have it condemned and me committed."

Cliff refilled his mug and sat down across from Pat. "She sure is Dad all over again. She's the most rigid person I've ever known. Everything is either black or white. There are no shades of gray in between."

Pat nodded. Then she stood up and went to the freezer. After a brief search she triumphantly pulled a package of brown-and-serve frozen cinnamon rolls out and waved it in front of Cliff. "Your favorite, remember?"

Cliff grinned, and in Pat's eyes he was a little boy again, standing in the kitchen dancing from one foot to the other while the scent of cinnamon filled the kitchen.

"Can I make the confectioners' sugar icing?" he asked.

An hour later, bleary-eyed and satiated with the sweet, sugary rolls, Pat and Cliff eyed the lone survivor. "Want it?" Pat asked.

"No way," Cliff said, rubbing his belly. Then he grinned at his mother. "You never did this when Ashley and I were growing up. How come?"

Pat's face grew still and sober as she remembered. Not only had she avoided cinnamon rolls, she'd practically starved herself to stay slim and trim for Clifford. How many times had she picked at a salad while he and the children ate home-baked bread, potatoes stuffed with cheese, and the finest cuts of beef? How many times had she filled up on plain, unsalted popcorn before going out to eat so she could be satisfied with smaller portions? How many times had she denied herself the simple pleasure of a dish of ice cream just so Clifford would continue to look at her with approval? And then what good had it done? He went looking for someone else anyway.

"I was a fool," she said, turning to look at her son.

There was a knock on the door then and Pat's heart started doing funny things inside her chest when she saw Hank.

"Come on in," she called, getting up to find him a mug.

"Morning all," Hank said cheerfully. He accepted a steaming mug from Pat with a grin. "I'm off work again today, so I thought I'd try and finish that new kennel I'm building.

What do you know about nailing plywood, Cliff?"

"I can handle a hammer with the best of them," Cliff said. "I did a little of everything when I first went out to California. Why? Do you need some help?"

Hank nodded. "I could sure use another pair of hands. My dogs are getting pretty crowded."

"You got it," Cliff said. "How about you, Mom? Want to volunteer?"

"Not me. I have to run into town and pick up a few things. I'm making dinner for you two gentlemen tonight, and I promise not to burn it."

Hank scratched his head and pretended to debate. "Well, now I don't know . . ."

"Go on, get out of here, both of you," Pat said. "Go build your kennel."

When the men had gone, Pat quickly straightened up the kitchen, then went upstairs to dress. She was going to buy a good, basic cookbook and she was going to work her way through it from first page to last. After all, she was a reasonably intelligent lady, and if she could read, she could follow a recipe.

When Pat returned from the store she let Ink and Spot out into the fenced backyard to romp. Then she propped the new cookbook up on the counter and unloaded her groceries.

A half hour later she had all the ingredients assembled on the counter and she was ready to take the plunge.

Somehow, Ashley's telephone call had fired her determination. Her daughter's haughty assumptions that Pat was behaving irrationally had made her blood boil.

She was forty-nine years old, for heaven's sake, not ninety! She still had all her faculties and was perfectly capable of making her own decisions!

Try telling that to your daughter, Pat, she mumbled silently, as she dredged boneless chicken breasts in flour as though she'd been doing it all her life. She continued to fume as she browned the chicken in butter and chopped mushrooms and onions. She certainly didn't want to argue with Ashley, but it might just come to that if the girl continued to treat her like a brainless twit. "I changed your diapers, young lady," she grumbled. "It wasn't the other way around!" Plop! The butter sizzled as Pat added chopped vegetables to the pan. "I'm free now," she muttered, flipping the page of the cookbook. "I can do as I please!"

Hank worked steadily, nailing boards in

place, listening and nodding as Cliff talked.

"My father was a prick," Cliff said bluntly. "I don't know what happened, but I think my mom finally realized it, too. She used to . . . well, let's just say that she pretty much did whatever he told her to do. And my sister Ashley is just like him. She even looks like him, coloring and all, which I guess is good for her because she's doing great as a model up in New York."

"Your sister is a model? I don't remember Pat telling me that."

Cliff nodded, pounding a nail with more than average force. "Mom is a private person. My father didn't like displays of emotion."

Bastard, Hank thought, banging his hammer harder than necessary. He'd taken a liking to Pat the very first time he saw her in the vet's waiting room. She was soft and gentle. It was in her eyes and her voice, in the way she smiled as she petted one of her pups. She was just the type of woman a domineering man would like to get his hands on.

"So you and your dad didn't get along," Hank prompted, leaning back on his heels and laying down his hammer.

Cliff shook his head. "That is the understatement of the year. I was a big disappointment to him. I was never very good at sports and I didn't like to do the 'man things' he and his friends did."

Hank nodded. "Some parents have a hard time realizing that their children have their own individual personalities." It was more than that. Hank could tell just by what Cliff wasn't saying that the young man's father had verbally abused him for most of his life. He wasn't much on psychology, but he'd read enough to know that being constantly put down could have a devastating effect on a child. And he didn't understand this homosexual business either. He'd always thought that the old-fashioned man-woman thing worked just fine, but Cliff was a nice young man, and he seemed to care about his mother, and in Hank's book that made him okay. The rest of it, he figured, just wasn't any of his business.

By four-thirty Pat was finished. The Chicken Breasts Supreme were simmering gently in a rich, creamy sauce. The brown-and-serve rolls were neatly lined up on the cookie sheet just waiting to be popped into a warm oven. A salad was crisping in the refrigerator and there was a half gallon of Cliff's favorite ice cream in the freezer. Pat smiled and placed her hands on her hips as she looked around. She had managed to prepare an entire meal, and the kitchen was still intact. Nothing was burning, and she still had all her fingers.

"Whoa, Mom, what smells so good?" Cliff entered the dining room covered with dust and grime and looking happier than Pat could remember seeing him in a very long time.

Pat finished folding the last napkin, placed it beside the plate and turned, smiling. "Me?" she teased.

Cliff sniffed again. "Mmm, that, too, but I was talking about food. Are you going to tell me you actually cooked something?"

"A gourmet delight," Pat replied proudly. "You and Hank are going to be very impressed."

"I think Hank already is impressed, Mom, but not by your cooking."

"You are a fresh kid," Pat said, but she couldn't help smiling. Of course Hank liked her. She liked him, too. They were neighbors and friends, but that's all. That's all it could be. Hank was still married, and Pat wasn't interested in any heavy relationship, not with everything she was beginning to discover about herself.

"Did you tell Hank dinner would be ready at seven?" she asked.

"I did, and he said to tell you he'll be here with bells. The man is brave, Mom."

"Don't you start, Clifford Allen Melbourne. I'm not a complete imbecile, you know. I can read and I can follow a recipe as you will soon discover for yourself."

Cliff's face sobered. "I always knew you were a smart lady, Mom. I'm just sorry it took so long for you to realize it."

"Me, too," Pat said, smiling ruefully. "But better late than never, right?"

Cliff went upstairs to shower while she put the finishing touches on dinner. It was crazy, Pat decided, but she was wildly excited about this simple dinner. She desperately wanted Cliff and Hank's approval. She actually felt as if she needed it, and she didn't have the faintest idea why. Was it because she had spent most of her married life running in circles to please her husband, and never quite being sure she measured up? And now, since discovering Clifford's infidelity, she knew she hadn't been good enough.

"Now wait just a minute," she muttered under her breath. "I *am* good enough! I've always been good enough! If Cliff wasn't smart enough to see that, then he's the one who had a problem, not me!"

She didn't realize her son had heard her until she heard Cliff's low, pleased chuckle.

"Way to go, Mom," he said.

By eight-thirty, after an absolutely delightful meal where the three of them talked, laughed, and ate themselves into a near stupor, Pat was ready to clear the table. But when she stood up and reached for a plate, Hank laid his hand over hers. For a moment her breath caught in her throat. Such a simple, innocent gesture, yet it sent very un-innocent shivers racing up and down her spine. Hank's hands were so different from Clifford's. His nails were short and blunt and there were callouses on his palms, mute testimony that he worked hard for a living. No trips to a manicurist for this man, but somehow his touch did things to her that Clifford's had never done.

"Uh-uh," Hank said, shaking his head vehemently, "After a meal like that there's no way we're going to let you do the clean-up, too. Come on, Cliff. Let's get to it!"

So Pat sat and watched her two favorite men clear the table and load the dishwasher. She sipped a second cup of coffee and basked in their extravagant praise of the meal.

"You do amaze me, Mom," Cliff said, deftly wiping the countertops. "Everything was perfect. I can't believe you made that salad dressing from scratch."

Hank looked a little puzzled. "I always

thought women were born knowing how to cook."

Pat laughed. "Now that is definitely a chauvinistic statement if ever I heard one. Were you born knowing how to change a tire?"

"Touché," Hank said, as he loaded the last dish into the dishwasher and closed the door. "How about going into the other room and changing the subject?"

They sat on the floor in front of the coffee table and played gin rummy. They laughed, sipped wine, and cheated outrageously, and Pat couldn't remember when she'd last had so much fun. She felt completely relaxed, totally at ease, and thrillingly alive. A couple of times, when she glanced up and found Hank smiling at her, she felt herself flush, but it was a pleasant warmth, not an uncomfortable feeling at all. Hank was a comfortable man to be around.

"This was great," Cliff said, when they finally called it a night. Then he turned to Pat. "I'm glad I came back, Mom, really glad."

Pat felt her mother's heart swell with love. "Me, too, son," she said softly. "Me, too."

As he walked back across the street to his own house, Hank felt suddenly bereft. He would like to have stayed with Pat and Cliff. Especially Pat. He was starting to like her in a way he hadn't expected. As a woman, and the relationship he was beginning to long for, was not simply friendship. He wanted a man-woman thing . . . a committed, caring relationship. He frowned in the darkness. What he wanted was to love and be loved.

"Hank is a really neat guy," Cliff said, when he and Pat were alone. "And he sure seems to like you, Mom."

Pat blushed. She was starting to realize that her feelings for Hank went beyond simple friendship, but this was her son she was talking to, not one of her woman friends.

Not that he would censure her. She knew he wouldn't, but their relationship was so fragile at the moment, so new and tenuous, she just wasn't ready to confide in him.

So she shook her head and smiled. "And I like him. We're neighbors and friends, and that's all, dear. Please don't start making up fantasies about me."

Cliff stretched his long legs out in front of him and grinned. "Whatever you say, Mom," he replied. "I just wanted you to know that I approve." Cliff hesitated, then spoke again.

"Hank and I had a long talk today. He knows about me, Mom, and he's not judgmental. That makes me feel good because I really like the guy. He's decent, you know?"

"Yes," Pat said softly, impulsively leaning over to kiss Cliff's cheek. "I know."

* * *

"So Ashley's coming home," Cliff said dully. "Do you want me to clear out? I don't want to cause any trouble."

"Clear out?" Pat said. "Absolutely not. You have as much right here as Ashley does. Probably more, actually, because I'm sure she is going to hate this place."

"Then that's her problem, isn't it?" Cliff asked. They were having breakfast in Pat's bright, sunny kitchen, but the day that had started out so happily had taken on a definite pall. "I'm not afraid of her disapproval, Mom. It's just that I don't want to make things unpleasant for you." Cliff's eyes were serious. "I don't know what happened after Dad died, and you don't have to tell me if you don't want to, but I know something went on, because you're different now, and"—he added, almost shyly—"I like you better this way."

Pat sipped her coffee. "I like myself better, Cliff. And you're right. I'm not going to tell you what happened. Let's just say that I woke up and smelled the roses. Your father was an imperfect mortal, just like the rest of us. Let's leave it at that, all right?"

Cliff nodded. "Sure, but what about Ashley? Why did she suddenly decide to visit . . . now? Do we just sit and wait for the bomb to drop?"

"That's one way of putting it," Pat said thoughtfully. "I don't know why she's coming or what's going to happen when she gets here. I wish I could promise you that she would be sweet and loving, as a sister should be. But one thing I do know: Ashley cannot be allowed to control either my life or yours. We are all consenting, capable adults, and we each have a right to live our own lives the way we see fit. If Ashley can't understand that . . ."

Pat left the rest of her sentence unsaid. Knowing her daughter as she did, she was pretty sure that the impending meeting was going to be unpleasant.

Ashley arrived late that afternoon in her small blue Chrysler convertible. She was dressed in a chic walking suit and wore sunglasses that hid her lovely dark eyes.

"Here comes trouble," Cliff quipped, trying to smile.

Pat could see that he was geared for a fight. With all her heart she wished that Ashley and Cliff could have a warm, affectionate relationship. After all, when she was gone, what other close family would they have?

"Maybe it won't . . ." Pat began, but her words were cut off by the slam of the door and Ashley's strident, decidedly displeased voice.

"Mother? Cliff? Where are you? Good heavens, I thought I'd never find this godforsaken hole in the woods! Mother?"

"Right here, dear," Pat said, moving toward the door to embrace her daughter. As always she was struck by the young woman's classic beauty. It was no wonder Ashley's modeling career was such a smashing success.

But if her arms longed to wrap themselves around the woman who had once been her adored baby girl, Pat's heart knew that it simply wasn't meant to be. Much as she might wish that things would be different, deep down she was afraid that she and her daughter would never be close. Ashley had started pulling away from Pat even before the difficult teen years when daughters notoriously rebel against their mothers. She had leaned toward her father from the time she was a toddler, and with every passing year she had become more like him, in looks and mannerisms, and in her rigid, unforgiving attitudes.

"I'm glad to see you, dear," Pat said. It was strange, but in her daughter's presence Pat suddenly felt less competent. Somehow, with just the slightest lift of a brow, Ashley could make her feel awkward and unsure of herself. It was almost like having Clifford back.

"Well, I must say this is certainly a far cry from the lovely, elegant home Father provided you with. Are you really going to tell me you like this?" Ashley stood with her hands on her slender hips. She whipped off her sunglasses and let her eyes sweep the modest, but lovingly decorated living room. She disregarded the peach silk floral arrangement Pat had labored over, shook her head at the peach and green floral-patterned sectional sofa and matching easy chair, then she spotted Ink and Spot frolicking on the mint-colored carpet.

"Good heaven's, Mother! Have you lost your mind? Are those animals yours? They don't live in the house, do they?" Ashley touched her forehead dramatically, and behind Pat, Cliff snorted. "Oh tell me I'm having a nightmare," Ashley cried. "This can't be real!"

"Afraid so, sis," Cliff said, coming to stand beside Pat and brace her for the oncoming storm. "Those little fellows are Mom's new companions. Cute, aren't they?"

Ashley's cool gaze swept over her brother and neatly discarded him. "You really must have a thorough checkup, Mother," she said haughtily. "Perhaps a neurological workup is in order as well."

Pat took a deep breath. "Let me assure you that my health, both physical and mental, is just fine, Ashley," she said, "and while you are in my home I would appreciate it very much if you would treat your brother in a decent, cordial manner."

Ashley's jaw dropped. Pat had never spoken to her so harshly. "You can't mean that you approve of his . . . life-style, Mother! Really!"

Pat's stomach lurched. This might turn out to be even worse than she had imagined. Beside her Cliff stood, stiff and determined, but she felt his anguish. "Ashley," Pat said quietly, "unless you can control yourself I'll have to ask you to leave."

She felt horrible, like she was being forced to choose between her children, but what could she do? She simply could not stand by and watch Ashley rip her brother's pride to shreds.

"What? You're taking his side against me?" Ashley screamed. "Mother, I can't believe this! What's wrong with you? What has changed you?"

Pat sighed. She reached out and clasped Cliff's hand and squeezed. He returned the pressure.

"Nothing is wrong with me, Ashley, and as

for what has changed me, let's just say it was life."

Ashley stared, speechless.

"Ash? I'd like us to be friends," Cliff said tentatively, stepping forward and extending his hand. "Can't we talk?"

"About what?" Ashley sneered. "Your lover? Your . . . life-style? I don't know what happened to you, Cliff, but as far as I'm concerned I no longer have a brother!"

"Ashley! How could you?" The sickness was rising up in Pat's throat now, threatening to choke her. How could this be happening? It was like a bad, bad dream, only this time there was no waking up. "Please . . ." She clutched Cliff with one hand and extended the other hand to her daughter. "Please, Ashley . . ."

Ashley backed away, her lips twisted with revulsion. "Don't touch me!" she cried. "As long as you side with him, you and I have nothing to say to one another. Oh, how can you behave this way, Mother? Daddy would turn over in his grave!"

Yes, Pat thought, as her daughter whirled and ran out of the house, sobbing. Clifford probably would turn over, and he would have been just as rigid and unforgiving as Ashley was. Well, be that as it may, there was no way she was going to cut herself off from her only son.

"Mom?" Cliff stood behind her, his face pale and set.

Pat turned and saw the pain in his eyes.

"I never wanted anything like this to happen. I never wanted to come between you and Ashley."

Pat sighed heavily. "You didn't. I'm sorry she was so hateful, but if it hadn't been you it would have been something else. I'm sure you could tell that your sister wasn't too impressed with my new living quarters."

Cliff managed a short laugh. Then he pulled Pat close for a brief hug. "She's a snob, just like Dad was. All she cares about is impressing people. I feel kind of sorry for her."

Pat nodded. She felt the same. Ashley's whole life revolved around maintaining the perfect image. Well, that was modeling, but Ashley had taken the concept into her personal life as well. But Pat was determined not to spend what was left of her life brooding about things she couldn't change.

That evening Hank came by offering to treat them all to "dinner" at a local fast-food restaurant.

"We'll go all out," he said heartily. "Milkshakes, fries, the works. We'll grease up our arteries and boost our cholesterol. How about it? Doesn't that sound great?"

Pat smiled wanly. Ordinarily she would have loved Hank's invitation, but she just didn't have the heart for it. Cliff was in the guest room, and had been since shortly after Ashley left. Pat knew he was deeply affected by his sister's harsh attitude.

"Not tonight, Hank. Neither Cliff nor I would make very good company. We had a run-in with my daughter, Ashley, this morning."

Hank's smile faded. "Your daughter was here?"

Pat inched closer to Hank on the sofa. Somehow his solid bulk represented security and safety. "Briefly," she said, grimacing. "She didn't like the house, or the fact that her brother was in it. She doesn't approve of Cliff, and she made no bones about it."

Pat longed to throw herself into Hank's arms and sob out all the anguish and pain that had built up inside her. It seemed that was all she did lately, ever since she'd found the incriminating note in Clifford's suit pocket. And she'd never been allowed to cry. But now she felt like crying again, just to release some of the tension. Hank would think she was crazy. After all, they were just friends, weren't they? Neighbors. How dare she even think of dampening his shirt with her tears?

Then, as if he'd read her unspoken thoughts, Hank was gently nudging her into the circle of his arms. Warm, strong arms that promised shelter and safety. "Let it go, hon," he coaxed softly. "Just let it all out. You're entitled."

And she did. The tears came then, tears for her marriage that had never been what she thought it was, tears for her beautiful, cold-hearted daughter, tears for her son, who she feared would have a long, hard road ahead of him, and finally, tears for herself, who could do nothing but stand by and watch it all happen.

She felt like she was drowning in tears, like the flood would never, ever end, but finally it did.

Pat raised her head to look to Hank, knowing she must look a fright. Her nose was running and she knew her eyes were swollen and red-rimmed. Her face got all blotchy when she cried. It always had. She wouldn't be surprised if Hank took one look and bolted for the door, never to return.

"I'm . . . sorry," she said. "I just . . ."

Hank raised her chin with his fist and smiled gently. "I'm glad. You needed this, and I've been wanting to hold you in my arms for a long time."

Pat laughed shakily. "Like this? With me looking like something out of a horror magazine?"

They were nestled in the corner of the sofa, and now Hank smoothed a few stray strands of hair away from Pat's eyes. "You always look beautiful to me, even when you're down on your knees grubbing in the dirt."

Their eyes met and something melted inside Pat. Something hard and cold, something that had been frozen for a long time. Suddenly she was as young as spring, as fresh and dewy as a rosebud opening in the early morning hours. Her body tingled, and her flesh yearned for Hank's sweet, tender touch.

"Pat, I . . ."

"Hey, you two, what's going on? Are we ever going to have some dinner?"

Cliff stood in the doorway, a wide, pleased smile on his handsome face. He made a circle with his thumb and forefinger. "Way to go, Mom," he teased.

"Clifford Allen, you're a brat. How dare you sneak up on us this way?"

"Wasn't sneaking. If you two weren't so wrapped up in each other . . ."

"Enough!" Pat cried. "Hank has invited us to gorge on fast food. Shall we?"

"Hey, all right!" Cliff said. "I haven't done that in ages. Let's go!"

So they sat on what Pat had always considered midget-size chairs and stuffed their faces with burgers, fries, and thick chocolate milkshakes. And if that wasn't enough they each had a soft-serve cone afterward. When they finally got up to go home they were all groaning.

"Ten pounds," Pat said, moaning, "And every ounce of it on my hips!"

"You could handle that with no problem," Hank said. "You're too thin."

"Too thin?" Pat's eyes widened and sparkled with pleasure. No one had ever said that to her before. She didn't really believe it, of course, but it was nice to hear. A sudden echo from the past cast shadows over her green eyes. She could still see the disdain in her husband's eyes as he surveyed her swollen form after the birth of each of the children. "You've got to get that blubber off," he'd said over and over when her weight failed to drop fast enough for him. "There's nothing I hate more than a fat, sloppy woman!"

"Pat, what's wrong?" Hank said, touching her arm and jerking her back to the present. "You look like you saw a ghost."

"I did," she murmured, "or at least I heard one, but it doesn't matter, not anymore."

And it didn't. Clifford, was dead, and with him, the old Pat had also died. She was different now, new and brave, and she was living in a different time and place, with different people. She looked up at Hank and smiled.

She was just about done crying.

Five

"I really do have to go home, Mom," Cliff said, a week later. "There are a couple of paintings I need to finish before my show, and . . . well, to tell the truth, I miss Doug."

Pat still hadn't gotten used to hearing Cliff speak of his companion. There was no way to miss the softening of his voice when he mentioned Doug's name, no way he could hide the warm, eager light in his eyes. She was still struggling to accept what she'd learned about her son, and she was still confused. But the one thing she did know was that she loved Cliff, and nothing could change that.

"Then I guess it's time for you to go," she said. "You have to do what you have to do."

"Yes, I do," Cliff said quietly. "I see the way you turn pale whenever I mention Doug's name, Mom, and believe me I'm not doing it to provoke you. It's just that I can't pretend he doesn't exist. Doug is an important part of my life. I'd like you to meet him someday."

"Maybe someday," Pat said, hating herself for being so evasive. She was willing to grant Cliff the right to live his life as he saw fit, but that didn't mean she could embrace it, or feel comfortable with his companion.

Cliff smiled, reading her thoughts. "It's okay, Mom. We'll give it some time."

They hugged and Pat hated to let go. "Let me know about your show, will you?"

Cliff grinned and stepped back to look at his mother. "Why? Are you planning to come out to California to see it? Doug and I could put you up. Our apartment has two bedrooms."

Pat swallowed and managed an answering smile. "I'm not planning to do any traveling right now, but maybe someday."

"Sure," Cliff said, nodding. "Someday."

She drove him to the airport, hugged him close for one last goodbye, then stood there while he boarded the plane.

As she drove home, Pat listened to the car

radio. Some of the songs she heard were sad and made her want to weep, but she'd promised herself there would be no more tears. Life was too short, at best. Who wanted to spend it wallowing in buckets of useless tears?

Before going home Pat stopped at the animal shelter. She spoke to the young man who had helped her adopt Ink and Spot.

"Hey, Mrs. Melbourne. How's it going? How are those pups doing?"

"Oh, they're fine. I'm spoiling them rotten, and they love it."

"Great. That's great," the young man said. "I wish it could be that way for all the animals we get in here. Look over there. See that litter of kittens? We found them on the front step in a big, plastic bag. It's a miracle they didn't suffocate. Then again, I guess it wouldn't make much difference. If we don't find homes for them soon they'll have to be put to sleep."

Against her better judgment, Pat edged close to the cage holding the kittens. There were four of them. They looked like powder puffs. One was a cream color with dark gray tipping his ears and nose, and one was jet black. "They're all adorable," she said. "But there's something about this one . . ." She carefully lifted the cream-colored kitten from the box. Immediately the tiny animal began to purr. In fact he purred so hard his whole body vibrated.

"I'm taking this one home," she said, making a sudden, rash decision. "Will it be hard to train him to a litter box?"

"I've already done that," the young man said, "and since it looks like you're going to be a regular around here, I should tell you my name. It's Dale Kennedy." He grinned mischievously. "Sure you don't want to take two, like you did with the pups?"

Pat shook her head regretfully. "I wish I could take them all, but I'm already building quite a menagerie as it is. I have to hang on to some common sense."

While she waited for Dale to ready the kitten for the trip home, Pat wandered around the shelter. It wasn't a very big building, and there was evidence that it sorely needed renovation and expansion. An idea began to form in her mind, but she decided to give it some serious thought before she said anything to anyone. She grinned. If Clifford knew what she was thinking he really *would* turn over in his grave!

Hank's truck wasn't in sight when Pat pulled into her driveway, and she felt a sharp surge of disappointment. She told herself it was because she wanted his help in introducing the kitten to her dogs. After all, he was the dog expert. But as she lifted the carrier out of the back seat, Pat felt her lips curve. Hank did know a lot about dogs. There was no doubt about that, and she loved the way he related to the animals, but that wasn't the only reason she was disappointed to see that he wasn't home. "I just genuinely like the man," she admitted out loud. "And what's wrong with that?" The kitten purred, dragging Pat's thoughts back to the matter at hand. "Okay, little guy," she said "It's time to introduce you to the rest of the family."

That evening Celia called, her warm, affectionate voice a soothing balm to Pat's ambivalent feelings.

"Celia! What a treat! How did you know I needed to talk to you?"

"You do? Heavens, I thought you were so busy these days you didn't have time for your old sister anymore. What's wrong, dear? You sound a little down. Are you sorry you gave up your house?"

"No, not that, Celia. I love my little place in the country. In fact, I want you and Jake to come out and spend a weekend with me soon. Will you?"

"Well, of course. We'd love to, but if you're happy in your new home, what's bothering you?"

Pat sighed. She and Celia had always been close. They had shared secrets as teenagers, and even after Pat's marriage to Clifford, when her life changed drastically, the two women had managed to maintain their closeness. But sister or no, did she really want to confide in Celia about Cliff, and about Ashley's hateful attitude? Who was it who once said that if you failed with your children, nothing else mattered? Well, Pat knew she had certainly failed with Ashley . . .

"Come on, little sis, let's have it. What's making you blue?" Celia demanded. "Keeping things bottled up inside never helps. You should know that by now."

"I do," Pat said, nodding into the phone as though Celia could see her. "Oh, sis, it's the kids. I had a terrible run-in with Ashley and . . ."

Celia snorted. "Ashley! I'm not surprised that you two are at each other's throats. What has she done now?"

"Lots of things, all of them nasty. And Celia, this time I'm not sure we can patch things up. I don't even know if I want to.

Ashley is a beautiful, talented young woman, but frankly I don't like her very much."

"And it hurts like hell to admit that, doesn't it? Do you know it took me a long, long time to accept the fact that I didn't have to love everyone who was related to me? Take Brian, for instance. He's my first born, right? I should smother the boy with love, right? Wrong. We have absolutely nothing in common. We have different moral values, a different code of honor. We simply don't speak the same language, yet he's my son and I'm supposed to adore him, but I don't."

Pat was stunned She'd never realized Celia felt that way about her eldest child. Personally, she had never cared much for Brian either, even when he was little. He was just not an endearing person, but Celia . . .

"I'm sorry," she said. "I didn't realize."

Celia's sigh flowed through the lines. "No one does, except me and Brian. We finally had a long, honest talk a few months ago. I guess we both decided it was time to stop pretending. Brian cares about me, as I care about him, and we will always have some ties, but the loving affection and adoration we're supposed to feel for one another just isn't there. We agreed that it's no one's fault, and that neither of us should feel guilty. And you know what? Things are better now. They really are. Isn't that amazing?"

"It certainly is, but I doubt that Ashley and I could stay in the same room long enough to have a heart-to-heart talk, and after the things she said to Cliff . . ."

"Ah, Cliff, how is that sweet boy? You know I often wished he was my son instead of Brian. I think I could have related to Cliff."

"I'm not so sure about that, sis. Cliff is . . . well, he finally admitted to me that he's gay. His roommate, Doug, is actually his lover." There. She'd said the words. The truth was out. Now what would Celia say?

After a long, painful silence, she heard Celia clear her throat.

"Patty," she said, using Pat's childhood nickname for the first time in years. "I know it must have been hard for you to hear that, just as it must have been for Cliff to tell you. How did you handle it?"

Pat toyed with an empty yogurt container. "I told him I loved him, and that nothing would ever change that. I'm trying to accept his right to live his own life, but it's hard,

Celia. It's so damned hard!"

"I'm sure it is," Celia said slowly, "but you did the right thing, honey. I know how much you've always loved that boy. If you lost him . . . well, the way I see it there isn't much you can do about Ashley. Unless she undergoes some sort of miraculous metamorphose, you two may never get together, but Cliff is different. Just keep on loving him, little sis, and the other will take care of itself. It's really amazing how tolerant we get as we age, isn't it? Some of us, anyway."

Pat could hear Celia's amused chuckle and she suddenly felt a lot better. "I've missed you," she said. "Let's do that weekend soon, shall we?"

"Absolutely," Celia replied, "and give Cliff my love, will you?"

Pat felt slightly dazed. She'd expected Celia to be supportive; she hadn't, however, expected her to accept the news about Cliff quite so calmly. But Celia was amazingly modern and well read. She kept up with things, and she had none of the hard-nosed rigidity that had been bred into Ashley. Celia believed in the "live and let live" philosophy.

Pat's kitten, as yet unnamed, twined itself around her ankles, purring madly. Spot, peacefully snoozing in a corner, instantly came alert and bounded over to see what was going on. He was quickly followed by Ink, who wagged her stubby tail in ecstasy.

Pat laughed. With a group like this, what was there to feel morose about?

The next morning the kitten was still without a name, Hank's truck was nowhere to be seen, and Pat had a beastly headache. She started a pot of coffee, swallowed two aspirins, and fed the animals. Tweetie, ensconced in the adjacent dining area, was loudly protesting the entry of the newest family member.

"Bunch of bull!" he raged, hopping back and forth on his perch. "That's a bunch of bull!"

Pat smiled around the headache. "Maybe so, Tweetie, but he's here to stay so you may as well get used to him. Life is change, you know."

Tweetie cocked his brilliantly plumed head and stared at Pat with beady eyes, as though he was trying to decipher what she had said. Then he hopped down into the bottom of his cage and attacked his sunflower seeds with a vengeance.

She spent most of the morning getting the kitten accustomed to his new home. Fortunately the two dogs accepted him wholeheartedly, so she didn't have to act as referee. But although she had plenty to keep her occupied, she felt all out of sorts. Maybe it was the emptiness of the house now that Cliff had gone home, or the unresolved agony she felt over the split with Ashley. No matter how Celia rationalized it, Ashley was still Pat's daughter, flesh of her flesh. Pat had carried Ashley under her heart, she labored to bring her into the world. How could she calmly dismiss all that as though it had no importance? The thing was, she couldn't. She simply couldn't be as cavalier as Celia had sounded, speaking of her Brian. There should be a way that she and Ashley could at least remain on speaking terms, shouldn't there? Maybe not. Ashley had delivered an ugly ultimatum. She had as much as told Pat to choose between her and Cliff, and in Ashley's eyes Pat had already done that.

"Who do they think I am, Solomon?" Pat cried, knowing that only her animals could hear her, but needing to vent some of her frustration. How was it possible for a mother and a daughter to drift so far apart that they could not even carry on a civil conversation?

Yet, Pat knew that it happened all the time. There were instances of family feuds on television talk shows just about every day. So, why did she feel as though she was the only mother anything like this had ever happened to?

The telephone rang, breaking into her thoughts, and Pat answered it absently. "Hello?"

"Mrs. Melbourne? This is Dale Kennedy over at the animal shelter. How are you today?"

"Fine," Pat answered automatically, although she was anything but. "What can I do for you, Dale?"

"A lot, I hope," the young man answered. "Look, I know you just took that kitten last night and you're probably still getting him settled, but . . . well, we're in a real bind here, and I could use a pair of caring hands."

"What's wrong?" Pat asked, her heartbeat accelerating. "You sound upset."

"I am," Dale answered. "Look, this isn't a pleasant situation here and if you want to beg off, I'll understand. It's just that I'm desperate. Pete picked up a bunch of abused and injured animals this morning and all hell has broke loose here. We've got calls out to several local veterinarians, but it's more than Pete and I can handle alone. Some of the animals are pretty bad off."

"I'll be right there," Pat said. "Just hang on. I'm on my way."

Her headache forgotten, Pat hastily arranged the kitten's litter box in the garage and filled the dog's dishes with fresh water. She felt it best to keep the animals separated until she was sure they were going to get along. Glancing down at her jeans, Pat decided her outfit would have to do. She hadn't taken the time to put on makeup, but she doubted the animals would care. All that mattered was that she get over there as soon as possible and do what she could.

As she drove, Pat fumed at the human cruelty. How could people treat animals so badly? Her heart ached just thinking of what she was about to encounter, but nothing could have prepared her for the horrifying reality.

There were six adult dogs, four of them nursing bitches, two adult males, and thirty-one puppies, all filthy and covered with fleas and in a state of near starvation.

"We rescued these poor creatures from a so-called 'puppy mill,' " Pete explained. He shook his head and a lock of dark brown hair fell over one eye. He wore jeans and a T-shirt and he looked about Cliff's age, but his eyes were saddened by all that he'd seen. "Those people . . . they get dogs and just keep on indiscriminatingly breeding them until the females are too old or die from neglect. Look, see that one over there? She's got a broken leg. It was never set and now it's healed wrong. She has to hop on three legs, and you can count her ribs through her skin!"

Pat felt sick. She knelt beside a makeshift box where a sad-eyed female and her four, scrawny pups lay. The pups weren't even trying to nurse. They were too weak. Pat doubted that it would have done them any good anyway because the female probably had no milk. How could she? Her bones stretched her skin and her eyes were dull and empty. Briefly she looked up as Pat touched her head, then lay back down as though she'd given up.

"What can we do? Can we save them?" Pat asked. "We can do something, can't we?"

Dale came skidding into the room then, a tall, silver-haired man in tow. "Here's Doctor Johnson," he said excitedly. "He'll help us assess the situation."

Pat backed up to allow the veterinarian room to work, and also to try and compose herself. Funny, but in all the years she'd been married to Clifford, even though she had always liked animals, she'd never given much thought to what went on in animal shelters. Maybe she hadn't wanted to know, but now she was face-to-face with the grim realities of abuse and neglect and human greed. She had read about puppy mills, about unscrupulous breeders who churned out puppies one litter after another, never giving the bitches a chance to regain their strength between one litter and the next. And she knew that often the puppies were inferior and sickly, and that they were carelessly shipped to equally unscrupulous pet store owners.

Pete stepped close to her side for a moment. "Are you okay, Mrs. Melbourne? You look a little pale."

Pat nodded. "I'll be all right. I'm just stunned. I'm having a hard time believing that human beings could be this cruel."

"Incredible, isn't it? And all for a few dollars." His dark eyes shifted away from her. "Some of them will probably have to be put down," he said. "I doubt we can save them all, and even if we did, who knows how many we can find suitable homes for?"

Pat digested Pete's words, knowing that everything he said was true, knowing that what she was seeing today would change her forever.

It seemed to take weeks for Dr. Johnson to finish examining all the animals. Unable to stand by doing nothing, Pat wandered back to one of the offices and made a fresh pot of coffee. No matter what the veterinarian's verdict, she knew it was going to be a long, difficult day for all of them. A hot, strong cup of coffee might help fortify them.

"Mrs. Melbourne?"

It was Dale, and although it wasn't even noontime, he looked tired and haggard.

"Call me Pat. If we're going to work together, let's not stand on ceremony."

Dale managed a ghostly smile. "Great. Welcome aboard, Pat. I'm just sorry we have to indoctrinate you in such a rotten way."

"I'll survive," Pat said. "Now what can I do? What did the veterinarian say?"

"Two of the bitches will have to be put down. It's the only humane thing to do. They're just too far gone. Doctor Johnson thinks we can save most of the puppies, but we're going to have to bottle-feed some of them. It's going to be a real hassle for the next couple of weeks, and then, if we do save them . . ."

Pat stopped Dale before he could go any further. "One step at a time, Dale," she said. "Let's just concentrate on saving them for now, okay? We'll worry about finding homes for them later."

"Right. I guess that's all we really can do. Doc suggested putting the weakest ones to sleep, but . . ."

Pat shook her head vigorously. "Let's give it our best shot. Those puppies deserve a chance."

Dale grinned, and some of the sadness in his eyes faded away. "You're on, Mrs. Mel . . . I mean, Pat. Let's get to work!"

Dr. Johnson showed them how to mix formula for the puppies and provided them with doll-size bottles. Pat blinked back tears as he and Pete carried the two weakest bitches into the other room, then she determinedly squared her shoulders and got to work.

Holding the tiny, emaciated puppies in her hands gave Pat a strange, almost powerful feeling. For the moment at least, she was responsible for these little lives. What she did now might very well make the difference between life and death.

As she coaxed the puppies to nurse from the tiny bottles, she spoke softly, as she once had to her own babies. "It's a lovely day outside, you know," she whispered. "You must eat and get strong so you can romp and play on the soft, green grass. It really is a beautiful world, despite what you've known so far."

Next to her, Dale shook his head as the puppy he held refused to nurse. "Sometimes I really wonder," he said, his voice thick with bitterness. "What's wrong with people who do things like this? How can they sleep at night?"

"I don't know," Pat said, keeping her voice low and soft so as not to startle the puppy she was holding. The life was so fragile. She was almost holding her breath.

Later, Pete and Dr. Johnson joined them and helped feed the puppies. By late that afternoon the four of them had managed to get some nourishment into most of the pups, but Dr. Johnson regretfully announced that at least three of the pups would have to be put down. "It's kinder than letting them hang on for several more days and slowly starve to death. They're just too weak to nurse."

Again tears stung Pat's eyes and she turned away as the tiny animals were carried away. Such a waste! So much death and destruction and all because of man's greed and neglect. Her stomach churned and bile rose in her throat. She had to hurry to the rest room.

"What will happen now?" she asked when she returned to the main building. They all drank the coffee Pat had made gratefully. For the moment at least, they had done all that could be done, but Pat knew that in a couple of hours the feeding process would have to begin all over again.

Dr. Johnson spoke first. "I'm taking some of these youngsters with me," he said. "I've got a soft-hearted wife and three adult children who will be more than glad to pitch in and lend a hand feeding these little scraps for the next couple of weeks. With any luck we'll be able to start weaning them then."

"Pete and I are going to bunk right here for a while," Dale said. He grinned. "Heck, my folks will be glad to have me out of their hair for a few days."

Pat's heart lifted. How could she doubt the basic decency of the human race when there were people like this around? Sure, there were rotten apples in the barrel, but there were plenty more decent, caring people, and those were the ones who really counted.

"Then you can manage without me tonight? I'll be back in the morning."

The three men grinned.

"Pat, you're a dream come true. How can we thank you for what you did today?"

Pat flushed. She wasn't all that used to compliments from men. Most of her adult life had been spent trying to keep ahead of the criticisms Clifford doled out. Pat smiled, her imagination running wild as she imagined what Clifford would have said if he'd seen her in soiled jeans, her hair every which way, with nary a smudge of makeup on her face. He'd have been appalled.

"I'm just glad I could help," she said, "and if I didn't already have two pups and a kitten at home . . ."

"Hey, if you're going to work here, you have to realize that you can't take all the strays home with you. Heck, we all feel the same way, but there's only so much one person can do."

"Well, I'll just bet that there are a lot of nice people out there who would be willing to open their homes to a sweet little puppy. We've simply got to get the word out."

"Yeah, but how do we do that?" Dale

asked, raising his dark eyebrows.

Pat's smile widened. Maybe her years of organizing charity bazaars and volunteering hadn't been wasted after all. Maybe it was time to use all the tricks she'd learned. Maybe it was time to call in some favors.

"Let me think about this for a couple of days, guys," she said. "I just may be able to come up with something."

"Go to it, Pat," the three men chorused. "We're willing to try anything."

Pat drove home feeling totally drained and exhausted. Her heart ached for the dogs that had been put to sleep, but she felt a strong sense of pride when she thought of the ones that would be saved. Her head was spinning with ideas, ways to find good homes for the puppies once they were strong and healthy, but she was really too tired and hungry to think coherently.

"Think about it tomorrow," she told herself. "What you need right now is a warm meal, a hot shower, and eight hours of sleep."

Ah, it sounded like heaven, but the problem was that if she really wanted a warm meal she would have to prepare it. And she was so tired.

Her heart leaped when she saw Hank's car

in his driveway. Lights were on in his house. As she pulled into her own drive, Pat debated going over and knocking on his door. She wanted to tell him about her day, about all the feelings churning inside her. And maybe, with any luck, he would hold her in his arms and soothe away some of the pain she was feeling. Maybe . . .

No. Hank had packed up and left without a word. Apparently, he hadn't thought it necessary to tell her he was going away, so what made her think he would appreciate her knocking on his door at seven o'clock at night? What if he had company? What if he was entertaining a woman?

Slamming her car door harder than necessary, Pat grabbed her handbag off the seat beside her and hurried to her own front door. Get a grip, she told herself. Hank is a friend, and a neighbor. But he has a private life you know nothing about. Good grief, he still has a wife!

Pat greeted her pets affectionately, joy washing over her as she surveyed the healthy, happy animals. This was the way it should be, she thought.

"Okay, kids," she said, laughing, when Ink and Spot started racing around her legs in circles. "Settle down. Anybody hungry around here?"

"Hot damn!" Tweetie sang loudly "Hot damn!"

The doorbell rang just as Pat finished mixing the food for Ink and Spot. Against her better judgment her heart skipped a beat before settling down into a nice, even rhythm.

She tried to smooth her hair before opening the door, but it was hopeless. She looked disheveled, and probably smelled to high heaven after hours of cuddling soiled puppies. Well, there was nothing she could do about it now, and Hank would just have to accept her as she was.

And he did. She opened the door to a broad, happy grin, and then Hank opened his arms. Pat walked into them without hesitation, forgetting the rank canine perfume that clung to her.

"Hank," she murmured thankfully, suddenly realizing what a loss it would be if she couldn't open the door to him.

"Pat," he whispered huskily. "Do you have any idea how much I've missed you these past couple of days?"

She wanted to know where he'd gone, what he'd done . . . why he hadn't said goodbye, but she swallowed the recriminations and just hung on to him. "Oh, Hank, I'm such a mess!"

He held her shoulders and put her away from him. "Mmm, now that you mention it . . ." He sniffed and made a silly face. "What have you been doing, woman, wallowing in a mud hole?"

Pat stepped back and shook her head. Now she needed space between them before she said or did something silly. "Worse."

Hank watched her eyes darken with pain and his gut tightened. There was something about this woman that got to him, something in Pat's eyes that hit him where he lived. He had the damndest urge to protect her . . . to wipe away the lingering sadness he sometimes saw in those beautiful eyes. But he was getting in too deep and he knew it. He wasn't free, and Pat wasn't the kind of woman a man trifled with.

"What's happened?" he asked, stepping inside when she stood back to let him enter. "You're okay, aren't you?" He couldn't resist grinning at her. "Aside from being on the ripe side, that is."

Pat managed a weak smile. "I know. I need a hot shower in the worst way." The smiled faded. "I've been at the animal shelter all day. Dale and Pete took in a bunch of abused and neglected dogs and puppies. It was more than they could handle on their own so they called me."

Hank sat on one of the stools at Pat's kitchen counter. "And?" he prompted.

Pat sat down across from him and shivered. "It was terrible, much worse than anything I could have imagined." She told him then, and Hank listened intently.

She could see the anger build inside him as she spoke. As a breeder himself, Hank knew the proper procedures to insure healthy animals.

As Pat finally wound down, she realized she felt better for the telling. It didn't change anything, but at least she had vented some of her anger and frustration.

Hank was quiet and thoughtful, then a puzzled look came over his face as "Cat" raced into the room with Ink and Spot in hot pursuit.

"What in the world?"

"The newest member of my family," Pat explained. "I stopped at the shelter on my way home from the airport the other day and Dale said they had just found some kittens on the front step, stuffed into a garbage bag. I couldn't resist."

"Well, he's a cute one, that's for sure,"

Hank said, the smile returning to his face. "What's his name? Or is it a she?"

"Dale said it's a boy, and he doesn't have a name yet. I was waiting to get your advice."

Hank considered for a moment, then a new thought brightened his eyes. "Hey! You haven't had any dinner, have you?"

"Not yet," Pat said. "I just got in."

"Then go hop into the shower while I whip us up a gourmet's delight." He winked. "How does scrambled eggs and toast sound, with fresh tomatoes and a bottle of Chardonnay?"

"Heavenly," Pat said. "I won't be long."

Six

She sang in the shower, something she had done only once in all the years she was married to Clifford. He'd caught her at it, and had ridiculed her so strongly that she never attempted it again. Now, Pat let her voice swell to the heights. Hank wouldn't hear her out in the kitchen, and even if he did, she was willing to bet the most he'd do was join in. A wave of heat flooded her body as she felt the warm water pelt her breasts. She was having some very erotic thoughts about Hank, and that would never do. They were just friends.

An hour later, seated across from Hank, with a plate of fluffy scrambled eggs in front of her, Pat sighed. "What did I do to deserve this? I was trying to figure out what I could eat on the way home and the thought of bungling around in the kitchen made me crazy."

"Well, now you don't have to," Hank said, digging into his own eggs with gusto. "I'm far from a gourmet, but I have learned to survive since Nancy left."

Pat was silent for a moment, then she took the plunge. "Why did you and your wife separate, Hank? You can tell me to mind my own business if you want, but every time you mention Nancy you look so sad."

"Yeah, well it still smarts. I'm not in love with her anymore," he added hastily, "but the reason she left . . . and my daughters' reactions . . ."

He lowered his head and stared at the food. He'd lost his appetite, but it wasn't Pat's fault. He was the one who had mentioned Nancy's name, and he couldn't blame Pat for being curious.

"Nancy left me because I couldn't give her the life she hungered for," he said slowly, as though he were measuring the words. And maybe he was, because each one carried a pound of hurt, a ton of rejection, and the scars were still raw and aching.

"I'm sorry," Pat said softly. "I know that doesn't help, but I don't know what else to say."

"Actually it does help. When Nancy walked out it was as if I closed off a part of myself. I refused to discuss it with anyone, even my daughters. Oh, I know Nancy told them her side of it, and Becky, my youngest, apparently believed what her mother told her. I've only seen the girls twice since Nancy left."

"Oh Hank!" Pat knew the suffering. She'd been through it herself. The pain of estrangement . . . the fear of never being able to regain what was lost.

"At first I blamed everything on Nancy, but I never even tried to explain how I felt to Becky and Laurie, and I know now that was wrong."

A million questions swirled through Pat's mind, but there was one she had to ask. "What was it your wife wanted that you couldn't give her?"

Hank sighed, pushed away his still full plate and sipped his wine. "I should never have married Nancy," he said. "We were from two different worlds. Her father was a bank president, her mother an artist. Nancy was an only child. She grew up having her every wish fulfilled. For some crazy reason she decided she wanted me."

Pat tried to lighten the mood. "Why not?"

Hank laughed bitterly. "I was young and full of myself, and flattered that a girl like Nancy would have anything to do with me. I couldn't see two feet in front of my nose. So we got married and Nancy's parents bought us a big, fancy house. My father-in-law tried to get me to go back to school and take business courses so I could go into banking, or some other suitable profession, but all I ever wanted to do was work with my hands. I'm not cut out for business. When I refused to fit the mold things started to go sour, but by that time we had two kids. We finally sold the big house and moved into this one. Nancy hated it from day one. She felt it was beneath her, that we were going downhill fast."

"So, it was material things she wanted?"

Hank nodded. "Along with prestige and social standing. Let's not forget those. She wanted to send the girls to private schools and I couldn't afford it on what I make. And I couldn't allow Nancy to keep taking handouts from her father."

"And one day she just walked out?"

"Just about," Hank said. "Oh, she left me a note saying she felt we had irreconcilable differences, and that since I wasn't willing to compromise . . . ha! Compromise! Do you know what she meant by that? She wanted me to give up the dogs and the work I love and wear a suit and a silk tie to work every day and carry an imported leather briefcase. I couldn't do it, Pat. It just wouldn't be me."

Pat nodded, her heart aching for Hank's pain, and for the sudden realization that although he didn't know it yet, she was from that same different world. What would Hank say if he knew the size of the estate Clifford had left her? If he knew that she had been married to the man in the suit and silk tie, and that she had once bought Clifford an imported leather briefcase? She had a strong feeling that he would run in the opposite direction just as fast as he could. And what else could she expect?

She smiled, forcing the painful truth away. "So, where were you the last couple of days anyway? I missed knowing you were right across the road." She tried to smile, but it was tight and forced, and if Hank hadn't been so distracted she knew he would have seen through it.

But Hank was drained dry by his revelations. He looked pale and tired and sad.

"I went to see a private detective," he said slowly. "I want to locate Nancy. It's time to end our charade of a marriage and get a divorce."

Pat's heart lifted briefly, then slowly sank back down. What good would it do her if Hank did get a divorce? Now that she knew the reason for his wife's desertion, she also knew that she and Hank could never be anything but friends, and maybe not even that when he found out what she really was. But what if she'd told him in the very beginning? Would he even have allowed her this close? She thought not, and both of them would have missed the wonderful companionship they had shared so far.

She studied Hank's weary features for a moment and decided that her confession had to wait.

"Well, now that I sobbed in the soup, what's next?" Hank asked, forcing a smile. "It sounds like we've both had quite a day."

"Mmm, that we have," Pat said, standing up and gathering the dirty dishes. "I'm going back to the shelter tomorrow and help feed those orphaned puppies again. And then I'm going to see if I can come up with some ideas to find good homes for them. I'm determined that those little mites are going to make it, Hank."

The smile Hank gave her then was not quite so forced. As Pat looked at him she could almost see some of his tension drain away. "Good for you," he said.

He gave her a light kiss on the cheek when he left, and promised to check in with her the next evening to see how things were going. After Pat closed the door and secured the lock she touched her fingertips to her cheek. Hank. He was everything Clifford hadn't been, everything she'd always hungered for and hadn't even known existed until she met him.

Flipping light switches on her way to her bedroom, Pat tried to make sense of her jumbled thoughts. But she was so very tired, both physically and mentally. In a daze she stripped off her clothes and pulled a cotton nightshirt over her head. Then she crawled into bed with a grateful sigh. Tomorrow, she promised herself. Tomorrow.

The telephone pealed insistently the next morning, as Pat swung her legs over the side of the bed, and rubbed her eyes. Groaning, she reached for the receiver. "Hello?"

"Pat? This is Dale. I just wanted to let you know that we made it through the night without any more casualties. In fact, Pete and I both think our pups are slightly improved. Uh, can we count on your help today? As you can imagine, Pete and I didn't get a whole lot of sleep."

"I'll be there as soon as I dress and grab some breakfast. How about if I bring you guys something to eat. How about bacon, egg and cheese muffins, juice and coffee?"

"Pat, you're a priceless gem," Dale said. "We'll be waiting with hearty appetites and grateful hearts."

She was grinning as she hung up. She'd been right. The puppies were going to make it. Now all she had to do was find good homes for all of them.

Ink, Spot, and "Cat" didn't seem too pleased to see her go, but Pat knew they'd be fine until she returned that evening.

She backed out of the drive, carefully averting her eyes away from Hank's home. It wasn't a mansion, certainly, but Hank had made it into a pleasant, comfortable home, yet it hadn't been enough to satisfy his wife.

Grimacing, Pat found herself thinking that Hank's wife probably would have been the perfect mate for Clifford. It was strange how tangled people's lives could get. She could stand back now and see that she and Clifford had been all wrong for each other, and Hank could probably do the same, yet at the time, when she was young and innocent and hopeful, Clifford had seemed the perfect beau. Handsome and intelligent. Ambitious.

Pat laughed softly. That said it all. Why hadn't she looked for warmth and caring? For compassion and gentleness? Any one of those qualities could have outweighed the material gifts Clifford had heaped on her. When Cliff, Jr. was born he'd given her diamond earrings. For Ashley, there had been a gorgeous, sinfully expensive emerald necklace. For each anniversary there was an expensive, sometimes almost gaudy bauble, and she had rarely worn any of them. Most of the items were still in her small jewelry safe, and she supposed that one of these days she should sell them, but she didn't need the money, so maybe they should be passed on to Ashley. Her daughter would doubtlessly appreciate the jewelry, and she would wear it with style.

She stopped at a fast-food restaurant to buy breakfast for Pete and Dale, and she added a glass of orange juice for herself. Too much coffee made her jittery these days, and she wanted all her wits about her as she worked with the animals. They deserved her full attention.

"Ah, our own private guardian angel," Dale cried, as Pat entered the shelter carrying two large bags of food. "What have we here?"

"Enough for breakfast and lunch," Pat said. "I noticed a microwave in the back room yesterday, so I thought this would save us from having to run out at noon."

"Fantastic!" Pete cried, falling on the bags like a starving animal. "Pat, I love you. Will you marry me?"

Dale laughed loudly. "Oh-ho, and what about that cute little blonde I saw you with the other night?"

Pete grinned as he unwrapped a still warm breakfast sandwich. "She can't cook, and she doesn't much care for animals," he explained. "I probably won't see her again."

"Good for you," Pat said, sipping her juice. "Compatibility is very important in a relationship."

She knew she sounded like a mother hen, but so what? Pete and Dale were both young. Their whole lives were ahead of them. After only one day of working with them, she felt a fond maternalism for both of them, and she would hate to see either of them make a mistake that could haunt them for the rest of their lives.

"You sound as though you speak from experience, Pat," Pete said, closing his eyes in ecstasy as he sipped hot, strong coffee.

"I do. I know what it's like to live with someone you have nothing in common with."

"We'll remember that the next time we see a cute chick, won't we, Pete?"

Pete nodded affirmatively, but Pat had her doubts. When hormones raged, common sense flew right out the window. And she should know!

The puppies did seem a little stronger to Pat. She picked one little fellow up and held him next to her cheek. To her amazement a tiny pink tongue flicked out and lapped her ear. She laughed joyfully and continued mixing the formula for the tiny bottles. Yes, this one was definitely going to make it, and if she had anything to do with it, the rest of the animals would recover as well.

It was after five when she got home that

night, and Pat's eyes automatically flickered toward Hank's driveway. Yes, there was his truck and the house was ablaze with lights. She thought about knocking on his door and telling him about her day, but quickly decided against it. She'd been too busy all day to even think about the things Hank had revealed to her last night, and until she did it was probably best to keep her distance.

Once again, Pat was joyously greeted by her animal family. Even Tweetie joined in the greeting by announcing loudly that "The British are coming! Hurrah! Hurrah! The British are coming!"

"Past history, you bag of feathers, you," Pat said, laughing. "I think I'll have to teach you some new phrases."

"Hot damn!" Tweetie cackled. "Hot damn!"

"You're definitely in a rut," Pat declared, petting Ink and Spot and letting "Cat" out of the garage.

She ladled out cat food and dog food, all the while listening for the now familiar, and welcome, knock on the door. But it failed to come, and finally, when she saw that it was nearly seven o'clock, Pat reasoned Hank had probably decided to keep his distance for a while.

It was really for the best, she told herself as she fixed a tuna sandwich and heated a bowl of chicken noodle soup. Hank had enough complications in his life without adding a woman who was not what he thought she was. And she didn't need any more problems either. There was still the feud with Ashley to deal with, and her feelings toward Cliff, and with every passing day she was becoming more and more committed to helping the animal shelter in a much grander way than she had originally imagined. No, she didn't need anything to clutter her already confused mind. What she needed was time and space to work through the most important aspects of her life—her relationships with her children. That deserved and required top priority.

"So stay home, Hank," she muttered as she sliced her sandwich in two. "It's for the best."

Pat worked at the shelter the rest of the week, and by Friday afternoon, when Dr. Johnson stopped by to evaluate the dogs' conditions, she was more than ready for a break. She had thoroughly enjoyed her time at the shelter. It gave her a wonderful feeling of satisfaction to see the pups grow stronger every day, but there were other areas of her life that needed attention, and she was greatly relieved to hear Dale and Pete say that they could manage without her over the weekend.

"Be sure to get the Sunday paper," Pat told them before she left for the day. "Check out the family living section. I think you'll be pleased."

"What have you done now, Pat?" Pete asked, smiling.

"You'll see," Pat said mysteriously. "All I can say is, be ready for a flood of phone calls."

With those parting words, she left, feeling quite pleased with herself and all she had accomplished that week. Now, if she could just establish some neutral ground with Ashley, everything would be perfect. Well, maybe not perfect, Pat amended, but being on speaking terms with Ashley would at least be a step in the right direction.

She stopped for groceries on the way home, knowing that her supply of dog food was getting low. She laughed softly, remembering Hank's warnings about the price of feeding and caring for a pet. If he only knew! Ah yes, if he knew he'd probably never set foot on her doorstep again, and she couldn't honestly blame him. Why should he take a chance on letting himself in for the same kind of grief he'd already gone through with Nancy? And how could she ever convince him that she was different? That she honestly didn't care about fat bank accounts and material possessions. No, she was quite convinced that at this time of her life she would be perfectly content to sit by a fire and read or watch television or listen to music, and if Hank was at her side, so much the better. But Hank probably wouldn't believe that, and she was certain he would find her inherited wealth intimidating.

"Oh pooh!" Pat said under her breath, as she loaded bags into the back of her automobile. Every time she started to think, her thoughts got all muddled and confused. One problem blended into another and it ended up giving her a headache. "I'm going to relax this weekend and forget everything," Pat promised herself as she slid behind the wheel for the drive home.

But the phone was ringing off the hook as Pat hastily inserted her key and opened the front door. Leaving the grocery bags on the step, she hurried to pick up the phone.

"Mother? Where on earth have you been? This is the third time I've tried to call today, although why I should have to be the one to make the first move, I'll never understand. I'm up to my ears in work and . . ."

"Hello, Ashley," Pat interrupted. "It's good to hear from you, dear. Other than busy, how are you?"

"Do you really care, Mother? Or maybe you do now that your precious baby boy has gone back to his lover. Honestly, Mother, how can you defend Cliff?"

Pat sighed, and quickly counted to ten. "Please don't say something we'll both be sorry for, Ashley. Cliff is my son and your brother. I never said I was happy about his life-style, but I certainly don't intend to make him miserable about it. I love him, Ashley, and nothing will ever change that."

There was a long, pregnant silence, then Ashley spoke again, but this time her voice was somewhat subdued. "Mother, I can't help . . . worrying about him."

"You are not responsible for your brother,

Ashley. You don't have to approve of Cliff, you just have to accept him as he is. He is a kind, honest young man, loving and caring, and he seems to have a brilliant future ahead as an artist. And he wants to establish a relationship with you, Ashley. He truly does. We talked about it at length during his visit."

Now Ashley sounded as if she were crying, but Pat knew that couldn't be. Ashley never cried. At an early age her father had taught her that tears were a sign of weakness, and that the meek definitely would not inherit the earth.

"Mother, I just . . . I don't know if I can do that. Father would have . . ."

"Why don't we leave your father out of this, Ashley? Despite what you might like to think, your father was not the perfect, immortal being you imagined him to be. He had faults as we all do, and he's gone now. You are a mature, adult woman. It's time for you to make your own decisions, based on how you feel inside. If you have any feelings at all for your brother, I beg you not to cut him out of your life."

"But I . . . Mother, sometimes that's what I feel you've done with me. I know we haven't always seen eye to eye. I know we have different values, but I do . . . love you. You're my mother."

Now Pat was crying and she'd thought she was done with tears. Only these tears were healing, not hurtful tears, and now she could dare to hope that she would not lose her daughter after all.

"And I love you, sweetheart," Pat replied. "You're my daughter, my adored baby girl. I will always love you, no matter what, and despite our differences we can build on that, can't we?"

A moment's tense hesitation, then a warm, resounding "Yes! Oh, yes, Mother, we can! I'll come see you as soon as this shoot is finished. We need to talk."

"Of course," Pat said happily. "The sooner, the better."

By the time she hung up the telephone, Pat's tears had dried to be replaced by a feeling of wild, sweet hope. Underneath Ashley's sophisticated veneer, there was still a little girl, hungry for love and approval. Ashley had spent her life striving to make her father proud of her, struggling to attain financial and social success. Pat smiled ruefully. If she only knew! All she'd ever had to do to win her mother's approval was be a decent, caring person. Seeing Ashley's face on the cover of a magazine wouldn't mean nearly as much as seeing her open her arms to embrace her brother. Well, maybe it wasn't too late. Progress had been made today. Maybe, when they finally met face-to-face, some of the old mother-daughter feelings would resurface. It was a goal Pat was prepared to work toward. Maybe, in her quest to shield Cliff from his father's badgering, Pat had neglected Ashley. Maybe Ashley had felt left out, and maybe that, even more than Cliff's way of life, was the basis for the animosity between brother and sister.

Debating between a grilled cheese sandwich and a diet dinner, Pat stood in front of the refrigerator mulling over her choices. She really wasn't very hungry, not for food anyway. What she really longed for was someone to talk to, besides her salty-versed lovebird. She missed Celia like crazy.

When the doorbell rang, Pat was certain it was Hank, finally coming to check on her, but when she looked through the peephole Cliff had installed, her heart swelled with joy.

"Celia! Jake! Why didn't you let me know you were coming? Oh my goodness! This is wonderful! Just what I needed."

Celia grinned, her carrot-colored sausage curls bouncing as she returned Pat's exuberant hug. "Mental telepathy, sis," she said. "I got up this morning and told Jake it was high time we checked this new place of yours out."

"We had nothing better to do," Jake teased, giving his sister-in-law a hug.

"You devil," Pat said. "Oh, come in, please. Where are my manners. Just don't trip over the cat, Celia. He likes to wind himself around your ankles."

"Cat? You have a cat, too? I thought you said you'd adopted two puppies from the animal shelter?"

"I did, and it's a long story. Come on in and get settled and then we'll talk. We've got all weekend."

"Get the groceries, Jake," Celia said. "My baby sister needs some fattening up."

"Oh, Celia! You never change, do you? And thank goodness!"

Instead of a sandwich, the three of them feasted on Chinese take-out that Celia and Jake had picked up on the way. Pat ate until she thought she would bust.

"Lord, I haven't eaten like that since Cliff went back to California. Oh, Celia, guess what? Ashley called me earlier. She started off as her usual, stuffy self, but then the most amazing thing happened. She began to talk like a reasonable, rational human being. She's coming for a visit as soon as her current shoot is finished and we're going to try and iron things out. She even hinted that she would try to accept Cliff as he is."

Pat shot a worried look in Jake's direction. "Did Celia tell you about Cliff?"

Jake nodded. "I know," he said simply, "and it won't change the way I feel about that boy, if that's what's worrying you, Pat. I always felt that Cliff got a raw deal from his father."

"Thank you," Pat said, tears stinging her eyelids. She really did have to put a lid on these tears. They came entirely too frequently these days. "You don't know what it means to me to hear you say that, Jake."

"Does anyone want dessert?" Celia asked eyeing a cream cheese frosted carrot cake she'd brought.

"Maybe later," Pat said, groaning. "Right now I'm so full I could pop. How about some coffee?"

When the coffee was ready they took their cups into the living room to get comfortable.

"I like this place, sis," Celia said, settling her bulk into a puffy print armchair. "It's warm and homey. It's you."

"I like it, too," Pat said, "And it's easy for me to take care of. Everything is convenient and compact, and I love the fresh air and space here."

"And your sweet furry little friends," Celia said, petting Ink, while Spot took a seat on Jake's lap. "Cat" perched on the back of the sofa behind Pat, surveying the situation. From the dining room they could hear Tweetie bouncing from perch to perch whistling a tuneless melody.

"Quite a menagerie, isn't it?" Pat asked. She laughed. "Can you imagine what Clifford would think?"

"Lord, yes," Celia said, laughing. "He'd have a blooming fit!"

Jake filled his pipe and nodded. "Poor Clifford," he said. "I feel kind of sorry for him. He missed out on a lot in his lifetime."

Something twisted inside Pat. That was probably true, but then again there were some things Clifford hadn't missed out on, like extramarital affairs. The bitterness would probably never completely go away, but it was fading slowly.

"Yes," she agreed quietly. "He did miss out on a lot, but it was his choice, and now I have no choice but to live my life the best way I can. I've decided to start by pleasing myself."

"Hurrah, hurrah!" Celia cried, clapping her hands together. "I always did think you gave in to that man too much, but . . ."

"No soapbox, Celia," Jake warned, grinning. "We're here to visit with Pat and relax, remember?"

"Aye-aye, Captain," Celia said, giggling like a schoolgirl. "I need this man, sis," she said, turning to Pat. "He helps me keep my head on straight, not to mention the fact that he makes the best seafood chowder in the world. He's going to do that for us tomorrow. We brought all the ingredients with us."

"Oh, wonderful!" Pat cried. "I haven't had your chowder in ages, Jake. Are you sure you won't give me the recipe?"

Celia chuckled mischievously. "What good would it do you, Pat? You don't have a cook to give it to!"

Pat laughed along with her sister for a moment, then she sobered. "Believe it or not I have learned to cook a few basic dishes, and . . . well, my neighbors don't know about the way I used to live, so . . ."

Celia nodded wisely, her carrot curls dancing around her chubby face. "So you want me to button my lip, right? Okay, I'll try, but you know me, sis. I make no promises."

Pat groaned inwardly. She loved her sister with every fiber of her being, but Celia could be a terrible blabbermouth, and sometimes things just slid out without her even realizing it. If she got through this weekend without Hank finding out it would be a miracle.

Around midnight, Jake gave up and went to bed, telling the women that he needed a good night's sleep to be able to work his magic on his seafood chowder. Pat made hot herbal tea and she and Celia settled in for girl talk.

"So, now tell me everything you've been doing since you moved out here, Patty. You look absolutely wonderful. You've got a glow about you . . . why, if I didn't know better I'd think you were pregnant!"

"Heaven forbid!" Pat said, with a groan. "I'm thankful that those days are over."

Sipping her tea and glancing longingly at the untouched carrot cake on the table, Celia shrugged. "I don't know. Sometimes I think about those days and wish they were back. It was such an exciting, busy time. Now, well sometimes I wonder what I'm going to do with the rest of my life."

Pat temporarily forgot her own problems as she studied her sister's perplexed expression. "I never realized you felt that way, Celia. I thought . . . well, you're always so cheerful."

Celia nodded. "It's what everyone expects from me. You know the scenario. Fat, jolly old woman. Always ready for a laugh."

"Are you unhappy about your weight?" Pat dared to ask. She'd always thought that Celia was indifferent to her size. Now it seemed she was wrong. Perhaps she didn't know her sister as well as she'd thought.

Celia looked down at her teacup. "I hate looking the way I do," she whispered, her voice heavy with sadness. "But it's a vicious circle, Patty. I try to diet, then I get so hungry I binge, then I hate myself and I'm so miserable I just keep on stuffing my face. It just goes on and on."

Pat was stunned. She'd never even imagined her beloved sister felt this way. "Have you seen a doctor? Maybe there's some sort of medical problem, or maybe a doctor could give you something to curb your appetite."

Celia hung her head. "I'm ashamed to go to the doctor. I'm afraid of what they'll think of me."

"Oh, Celia!" Pat felt as if her heart was breaking, and she was determined that somehow, someway, she would help her sister break out of her prison of fat.

Finally, when they started to go hoarse from talking so much they hugged each other and reluctantly agreed it was time to go to bed.

Pat lay awake for a very long time. How could she have not seen Celia's pain all these years? Why had she simply assumed that her sister was happy being the jolly fat lady? Had she ever even taken the time to try to really get to know the woman she claimed to love so much?

Well, it wasn't too late, and thank God she had the means to help Celia solve her problem. She'd make inquiries over the next few weeks and find the very best weight-loss program available. And then she'd make damn sure Celia enrolled in it and stuck to it. After all, it wasn't just a matter of Celia looking and feeling better about herself. There were health risks involved in being overweight, too. And she wanted Celia to live a long and happy life.

With that thought firmly implanted, Pat fell into a deep, sound sleep.

"How do you feel about flea markets?" Pat asked the next morning after breakfast. There's a great one just a few miles away. We could take a ride over, if you like."

"Not me," Jake said, shaking his head. "I have to get started on my world-famous chowder. You women go ahead, but don't spend too much money," he admonished Celia good-naturedly.

"Ha! I've only got one twenty in my wallet. Kind of hard to splurge on that, old man."

Jake grinned and wagged his finger. "Watch how you talk to the cook, woman!"

Pat watched her sister and brother-in-law fondly. The genuine love and respect between

Celia and Jake was so strong you could feel it whenever you were around them. They'd been married thirty-three years and had raised three children, and Pat was willing to lay odds that Jake had never even looked at another woman.

Well, some men were that way, she reminded herself. And others were never satisfied. A pain ripped through her, but it was gone in a flash, and Pat suddenly realized she must be starting to heal. It didn't hurt as much these days when she thought about Clifford's betrayal.

"Okay, let's go," she said a few minutes later, after she'd changed into comfortable walking shoes. She still hadn't mentioned Hank to Celia, and she suddenly realized she'd better do it before they walked out the door.

"Uh, Celia? There's something I've been wanting to tell you. About my neighbor, Hank."

Celia's eyes lit up like twin Christmas lights. "Oh? There's a man in your life?"

"Oh no, not like that . . . I mean, well, Hank and I are just friends and neighbors. He raises purebred Samoyeds and he was very nice to Cliff. He . . ."

"Sounds like the exact opposite to Clifford,

which is probably just what you need. Is he cute?"

"Celia, that's not what . . . oh, look, there he is! Whatever you do, don't mention Clifford or the way I used to live, okay?"

She felt like a fool and the worst kind of cheat as she warned Celia not to spill the beans. Of course she would have to tell Hank the truth someday, but when she did it she wanted them to be alone, so she could explain in detail.

"Well, hello, ladies," Hank said pleasantly, coming up to Pat and her sister as they stood beside Pat's little van.

"Good morning, Hank. I'd like you to meet my sister, Celia. Celia, this is Hank Richards. Celia and her husband, Jake, are visiting me for the weekend."

"That's nice," Hank said. "It's good to meet you, Celia."

"We're heading for the flea market," Pat said, "And poor Jake is inside slaving over a hot stove. He's preparing his famous seafood chowder for dinner tonight. Can I twist your arm and entice you to join us?"

Hank grinned. "Seafood chowder? Twist away, ladies. I'll be here with bells on. What time?"

Celia laughed as she and Pat drove away. "Well, that was an easy conquest. So, that's Hank."

"Yes. What do you think of him? He's nice, isn't he? I mean . . ."

"I think I know what you mean, sis. You're smitten, aren't you?"

"Smitten? No, of course not. I told you Hank is just my neighbor, but he is very nice and I enjoy talking to him."

"Is that all you do?" Celia asked devilishly. "Goodness, Pat, you must be older than I thought you were!"

"Come on, stop it. I hardly know the man. We met at the veterinarian's once, just before I moved in here, and then I was amazed to find out he was my neighbor. I told you he raises dogs, didn't I?"

Celia grinned and nodded, noting the way Pat's hands had tightened on the steering wheel. "But is he single?" she insisted.

The grin slid off Celia's face when Pat answered.

"No," Pat said. "He has a wife, somewhere."

Seven

Pat and Celia spent the better part of the day wandering through the stalls at the flea market, laughing and catching up on family news, and just enjoying being together. Finally, when her feet began to protest, Pat suggested it might be time to go home.

Her sister sighed with relief. "I thought you'd never ask. I'm ready to drop!"

"For heaven's sake, why didn't you say something? I didn't want to be a party-pooper and admit that I was winding down. After all, you are older." This she said with a sly, teasing look, but to her horror, Celia burst into tears.

"I know!" she wailed. "I'm getting older every day, and if that isn't bad enough, I look like a fat cow. Oh, what am I going to do?"

Pat held the car door while Celia struggled to wedge her bulk into the passenger's seat. Then she slid behind the wheel and waited for Celia to calm down.

Finally her sister's tears dried, and Pat smiled compassionately. "We're going to do something about your weight," she said firmly, "and soon you'll be feeling good about yourself again. And in the meantime, I love you, and Jake loves you, and we accept you just the way you are. If you never lost an ounce we would still adore you."

"Oh, Patty! You're so smart. You always were the smart one. Do you really think I can get some of this blubber off?"

"Do you want to?" Pat asked softly. "Do you really want to be slim and trim and energetic again?"

"Yes! Oh, yes! I want that more than anything!"

"Then you can do it, and I'll help you all I can. We'll find a weight-loss program that's right for you, and this time you'll stick with it."

"I will," Celia said eagerly. "This time I really think I will!"

"Good, then dry those tears and put a smile on your face. We're going home."

They found Hank comfortably ensconced in the kitchen with Jake. Somehow Pat was not surprised. Both men had tall, frosty mugs of beer in front of them and looked like they were thoroughly enjoying themselves.

"Well, what is this? A masculine version of a hen party?" Pat asked.

She stood in the doorway, her hands on her hips. She was smiling and the sunlight from the wide kitchen window caught sparkles in her hair. Hank thought she was just about the best-looking woman he'd ever seen. But maybe he was a wee bit prejudiced. He liked Pat and the liking was turning into something more. It scared him. He'd struck out once. What gave him the right to think it would be different this time? Because you're older and wiser, he told himself. He had learned that people often weren't what they appeared to be, and that love and fidelity wasn't always enough to satisfy a woman. And he'd learned the raw, hateful pain of being rejected. But his every instinct cried out that Pat was different. That she wasn't the type of woman to be bought with fancy frills and big bank accounts. But what if he was wrong? Could he take another rejection at this stage of his life?

"Uh, I was trying to wheedle Jake's recipe away from him, but no luck," he said, when he noticed the way Pat was staring at him. Lord! He sure hoped she couldn't read minds!

"Still holding out, eh, Jake?" Pat teased. She smiled as Celia went to her husband and kissed his cheek. Jake beamed. "Hello, sweetie," he said, giving Celia a quick hug. "Did you have fun?"

Celia whispered something in his ear and Jake actually blushed.

"Cut that out, Celia," Pat admonished. "You behave yourself."

Jake laughed. "Save your breath, Pat. She doesn't know how!"

Dinner was a delight. Jake and Hank seemed to have established a comfortable rapport and together they ganged up on the two women to tease and torment throughout the meal. But it was more fun than Pat had enjoyed in a very long while. No one was angry, the food was delicious, there were no dark secrets lurking overhead. Pat suddenly stopped chewing, knowing the last statement wasn't strictly true. There was one secret. One that could very well affect her whole future, a future she was beginning to hope she could share with Hank.

"Penny for your thoughts, Pat," Hank said softly, leaning over the back of her chair, his breath warm on her neck. From the corner of her eye Pat saw Celia watching. She'd explained the circumstances of Hank's missing wife to Celia, but Pat knew her sister was not satisfied. To her married was married, whether the wife was in the house or not.

"I'm too full of Jake's delicious chowder to have any thoughts," she said evasively. "Why don't we all take our coffee into the living room?"

They settled down in the living room, and Pat was both gratified and embarrassed when Hank purposely maneuvered himself next to her on the sofa.

"Has Hank told you about his dogs, Jake?" she asked. "He really has some very beautiful animals."

Hank laughed. "I talked his ear off all afternoon while you ladies were shopping. He's probably sick of hearing about dogs."

Jake grinned and shook his head. "On the contrary. I think it's great that you're able to do something you so obviously enjoy."

"It must be wonderful," Celia said, sounding a little wistful.

"Unfortunately, I got a chance to see the other side of pet breeding," Pat said. "I've spent the last few days at the animal shelter helping hand-feed some orphaned puppies."

"Really?" Celia looked very interested and she leaned forward eagerly. "How did you get involved in something like that, Pat? Did someone invite you to join?"

Pat shook her head. "It's nothing like that. Hank and I went there so I could adopt Ink and Spot, and then, on the way home from the airport I stopped by and they had a litter of kittens that had been dumped on the doorstep, so I ended up taking 'Cat' home. I don't know, when I saw all those homeless, unwanted animals it did something to me, and I asked if they needed volunteers."

"Oh, goodness, I would never have thought of doing something like that! But what a wonderful idea!"

Pat grimaced. "Not so wonderful when the animals we can't find homes for have to be put down, or when an animal comes in that is so sick and weak it can't be saved."

"Oh dear, that's dreadful! Are there really that many animals needing homes?"

"There are more animals than homes, and more come in every day." She stopped and looked at her sister. "You don't have a pet, do you, Celia?"

"Hey, wait a minute," Jake said, laughing. "I'm not sure I want to go through all that peeing puppy stuff again. Celia and I went that route quite a few times when the kids were growing up."

"Oh, Jake, wouldn't it be nice to have a little dog again? We could get a nice small dog, and one that won't shed too much and . . ."

"See what you've done, sis?" Jake demanded, trying to glare fiercely at Pat, and failing miserably. "All right, I guess we can handle one small dog, if you really want to do this, Celia. But just one, understand? I'm not interested in anything like this menagerie Pat's got going here."

Pat smiled. "It keeps life interesting, Jake."

Just then Tweetie decided it was time for him to put in his two cents. "That's a bunch of bull!"

he squawked. "That's a bunch of bull!"

On Sunday, knowing that Dale and Pete would be at the shelter caring for the orphaned pups, Pat took Celia to pick out a pet, but first she stopped at the corner store to pick up the Sunday paper. "Turn to the family living section, will you, Celia?"

Celia did as she was told, and then she let out a whoop of delight. "Holy cow! Did you arrange for this, Pat? It's a full-page article about the shelter and all the animals that so desperately need homes. If this doesn't empty some of those cages, nothing will!"

"Good. It's in there. Now all we can do is wait and see what happens. I guess I better be prepared to go to work tomorrow, just to answer the telephones."

Celia eyed her sister thoughtfully. "You are content, aren't you, Pat? I wasn't sure, but after seeing you this weekend, well, I think you look happier than you ever did when Clifford was alive. Back then you had a sort of pinched, worried look all the time, as if you were never sure you were doing or saying the right thing."

Pat laughed. "I wasn't. I tried so hard to please Clifford, and then . . ." Her words trailed off and she shrugged. "That part of my life is over. This is a new road I'm traveling."

"I think that's what I need," Celia said wistfully. "Something new and interesting in my life." She blushed when Pat eyed her skeptically. "Oh, not a new man, silly! Jake and I are a matched pair. Why, neither one of us would know what to do without the other, but I've just been at loose ends since Vicki moved out. The house is so quiet and empty."

Pat nodded, remembering how noisy and filled with laughter Pat's home had always been when her nieces and nephews were young. There was always a varied assortment of small friends as well as Celia's own brood, and there were pets everywhere. Hamsters, gerbils, parakeets, dogs, and kittens. She smiled as an idea occurred to her.

"What would you think of opening a day-care center in your home, Celia? Doesn't that sound like fun? You and Jake always enjoyed the hustle and bustle of lots of kids underfoot. I think it might be perfect for you. You've got that great big backyard, and that wonderful old tire swing. Is the sandbox Jake made still there?"

"A day-care center? In my home?" Celia looked stunned. Obviously it was a new and intriguing idea. "Do you really think I could? Wouldn't it be hard to get permits and things . . . to qualify with the state and whoever handles those sort of things?"

Pat nodded. "I'm not sure of all the details, but I know there would be some hassles getting started, but don't you think it would be worth it? Maybe this could be the new and interesting thing you've been looking for, Celia."

Celia was beaming, her eyes shining. "Oh, if I could . . . and I think Jake would love the idea, too. I think he's been kind of lonely, too. Now that he's retired he sometimes get tired of puttering in the garden."

"There, you see? It might be just the thing for both of you."

Pat pulled up in front of the shelter and parked, and turned to her sister. "We ain't done yet, sis," she teased. "We've still got a lot of living left to do!"

An hour later, after meeting Dale and Pete and scrutinizing every animal available for adoption, Celia settled on an adorable mixed breed with a thick, fluffy tan coat.

"I thought you were looking for a dog that wouldn't shed, Celia." Pat joked, running her fingers through the little dog's long hair. "This little guy is going to need plenty of grooming."

Grinning sheepishly, Celia nodded. "I know, but I just can't resist those shoe-button eyes. Isn't he precious, sis?"

Dale and Pete exchanged amused looks. "Do we have another volunteer in the making?" Dale asked.

"Oh no," Celia said quickly. "I live some distance from here, and besides I'm opening a daycare center in my home soon. I'm afraid I won't have time to volunteer."

Pat smiled. What a weekend it had been!

Just as she'd suspected, Pat spent most of the day answering the phone on Monday. Hundreds of people wanted to know more about adopting a pet from the shelter, and most of the callers made appointments to come by and look at the animals.

"If this keeps up we'll have no problem finding homes for all the puppies," Dale said that afternoon, when Pat took a welcome break. Pete was manning the phones now, and every now and then he made a victory sign with his fingers.

"Isn't it wonderful?" Pat sipped her coffee and relaxed.

"It was a great idea to put that article in the paper," Dale said. "How did you manage it, Pat?"

"Oh, I've got some friends here and there," Pat said. She didn't tell Dale that she and the newspaper editor had once worked together on a charity telethon, or that because of the work Pat had done for various civic organizations, Margaret Farmer owed Pat a favor. Well, the score was even now. If today was an indication, and if Margaret kept her promise to periodically remind people of the work the shelter was trying to do, there would be less animals being put down.

"Look at this little guy," Dale said, pointing to the puppy curled on his lap. "Three days ago I wouldn't have given him a chance, and now I know he's going to make it. I almost wish I could keep him myself."

Pat finished her coffee and stood up. "I know what you mean. Look, if you guys can manage without me now I've got some errands to run. Think you can muddle along on your own for a while?"

Pete laid the phone down and grinned. "Look at you," he teased. "A few days on the job and you already think you're indispensable. Well let me tell you . . ."

"Yeah, let's tell her, Pete," Dale broke in. "Let's tell Pat how well we would have managed without her these last few days. Let's tell her how we could have managed feeding and caring for all these animals with our hands tied behind our backs, huh?"

Both young men were grinning, and Pat felt a hot flush warm her cheeks. It was a heady feeling to know that she had accomplished something worthwhile, and it was incredible to know that her efforts were appreciated.

"Let me out of here before my head balloons all out of proportion. But thanks, guys. I needed to hear that."

Pat checked her watch as she slid behind the

wheel of her white minivan. It was still early, and there was plenty of time for her to drive into the city and pay Clifford's attorney a visit. She'd made the appointment that morning, and Bruce Howard had assured her he would be more than happy to see her. But maybe he wouldn't be when he found out what she intended to do. Somehow she couldn't imagine the silver-haired, debonair Mr. Howard feeling a lot of sympathy for homeless animals. Still, she didn't know a thing about the man's personal life, and she knew she could be misjudging him. Anyway, it didn't matter if he approved or disapproved. The money was hers to do with as she pleased, or at least it would be in another two or three months. Bruce's latest phone call had informed her that Clifford's estate would be settled on or before the end of the year.

As she drove, Pat went over plans for renovating and enlarging the shelter in her head. The whole building was hopelessly outdated and Dale and Pete deserved a decent, comfortable lounging area. The work they did was hard and often unrewarding. The very least they deserved was a decent environment to work in. With more runs and better sanitation facilities, everyone would benefit, humans and animals alike. And once the paperwork with Bruce was taken care of, Pat knew her next step was to check with all the local veterinarians and set up a rotating volunteer schedule, so the animals could be assured proper medical care. And the last and final thing she planned to do was engineer a major campaign to make pet owners more aware of how devastating unwanted litters of puppies and kittens could be. She wasn't quite sure how she was going to accomplish all this, but it could be done. It had to be done.

Bruce Howard looked a little startled when his secretary ushered Pat into his office. Too late Pat realized he'd never seen her in casual, knock-around clothes. Always before when she'd had occasion to consult him, she had been perfectly groomed and expensively dressed. Now, as she took the seat he offered, she realized how disheveled she must look. She started to smile, then burst out laughing, causing the poor man to look very alarmed.

"Pat? Are you all right? May I get you something? Water? A drink?"

"No, I'm fine," Pat said, wiping her eyes. "I'm sorry, Bruce. Please don't mind me. I've just come from the animal shelter where I've been helping out and I suddenly realized what a mess I am, and then the expression on your face . . ." Against her will, she dissolved in giggles, and when she finally got control of herself, Bruce was smiling.

"Well, Pat, I must say that you seem to be doing just fine. I don't know when I've ever seen you happier. And you're keeping busy?"

"Oh, indeed I am! As I said, I've been helping out at my local animal shelter. Actually, that's why I'm here. I want to discuss some plans with you, plans that will require a substantial amount of capital."

"Oh?" Bruce's eyebrows rose and he leaned forward expectantly. "What exactly are you planning to do, Pat?"

She outlined her plans then. They were still pretty sketchy, but she needed to know that there would be no problem with the funds before she went any further.

"So, it won't be a problem, will it?" she asked anxiously. "I mean I know that legally the money is mine, but I wasn't sure if Clifford had laid down any specifics."

Bruce shook his head. "There's none that I know of, Pat. As I told you before the will names you as the sole heir, and of course in the event of your death, the estate would pass to young Cliff and Ashley. When will you need these funds?"

Pat shook her head. "I'm not sure. I'll have to get estimates, talk to contractors, see about permits, all that sort of thing. Is it all right if I get back to you?"

"Of course." Bruce hesitated a moment, then

his expression softened. "You're a decent woman, Pat, and I admire what you're doing. You're moving on with your life, aren't you?"

Pat smiled. "Yes, I am," she answered. "I really am."

The next few weeks were busy ones for Pat. She had little time to worry about Hank, or Ashley, or anything but her plans for expanding and renovating the shelter. When Dale and Pete learned of her plans they were ecstatic. "More space!" Dale sang. "I'm beginning to believe in miracles!"

"Yes, well, in between all of this," Pat said, spreading her hands, "I've got to find time for some holiday preparations. Do either of your realize that Thanksgiving is almost here, and after that Christmas is right around the corner?"

Dale grinned and poked Pete in the arm. "Yeah, we know all right. Old Pete here has been saving his pennies to buy his new girl a nice present. What do you think, Pat? Should it be perfume or candy? Or maybe some sexy underwear?"

Pat eyed both young men sternly. "Does the lady in question still live at home with her parents?"

"Yeah, she does," Pete said, not sounding too happy about the situation.

"Well, then sexy underwear is definitely not an option, not if you want to score points with her pop."

"I guess you're right, but perfume is so ordinary."

Pat left Pete and Dale to their gift lists and went out back to the runs to check a couple of older dogs who had been brought in a few days earlier. Both animals were healthy and she had no idea why the owners had brought them in. Maybe they were moving, maybe they were just tired of the responsibility, but in any case they now had two healthy adult dogs that she knew would be hard to place. Everyone gravitated toward cute, cuddly babies, but with mature animals it was another story. Many people were afraid of taking on an older pet, afraid of getting attached and then having the animal die or get sick, or they expressed doubts about ingrained bad habits. Or they just plain didn't find older dogs as appealing as a puppy.

"Well, all of those things have validity," Pat admitted to Pete and Dale later, "but what about the freedom from housebreaking? Not having to go through the terrible teething, chewing stages of a puppy? What about the pleasure of giving an animal who sorely needs it, a good, safe home?" She made a mental note to give Margaret Farmer a call and stress the need to push for adoption of older animals, not just the youngsters.

"Yes, you've got a lot of love to give, haven't you, girl?" she asked a sad-eyed retriever.

The dog wagged its tail and nuzzled its nose against the fence seeking contact with Pat's hand.

Blinking back tears, Pat patted the animal's head and turned away. Like a nurse or a doctor, she was beginning to realize that the only way she could do a good job here at the shelter was to remain objective, and that meant not getting too attached to any of the animals. But it was hard. Harder than anything she'd ever done before.

Three weeks before Thanksgiving, Ashley drove up. She'd given no advance warning. Pat bit her lip as the beautiful, poised young woman got out of her car and stood looking around her. Maybe it was best this way. If she'd had time to prepare, she would also have had time to worry and fret. This way she would just have to wing it and hope for the best.

Ashley finally turned back to her car and opened the trunk. She pulled a small overnight bag out and straightened.

"Hello, Ashley," Pat said, opening the door wide and smiling. "I'm glad to see you." She wanted to hug her daughter, but something held her back. Years of being pushed aside in favor of Clifford, Sr., memories of all the harsh words she and Ashley had exchanged. It was all there between them, haunting them, taunting Pat, forcing her to wonder what she had done wrong.

But instead of the haughty sneer that had become almost a permanent feature on Ashley's lovely face, Pat was treated to a soft smile. "I'm glad to be here, Mother," Ashley said. "I've missed you."

The years fell away then, all the old hurts dissolved into nothingness. "Oh honey, I've missed you, too!"

She held her in her arms then, her little girl. Memories flashed before Pat. Ashley as a fretful, colicky infant, as a sweet, slightly precocious toddler, then Ashley as she blossomed into a woman's femininity. And that, Pat remembered, was when the distance between them really began.

"Come in, honey. Let's not stand out on the steps and weep all over each other. Would you like some hot chocolate? You always loved hot chocolate when you were little."

"I'd love some hot chocolate, Mother, but please try to relax, okay? I know this visit may be difficult for both of us, but at least it's a step in the right direction, don't you think?"

"Oh yes, it is!" Pat cried. "Sit down, honey, and I'll get the hot chocolate. I won't be long."

As she headed for the kitchen, Pat saw Spot and Ink cautiously approach Ashley. She winced. Like her father, Ashley had never been particularly fond of animals, and she hadn't even seen the cat yet.

But she needn't have worried. There was a wistful softness on Ashley's face as she eyed the two puppies. Pat had never seen that look before.

"Well, I suppose we'd better get acquainted, hadn't we?" Ashley asked, hesitantly extending her hand. "It doesn't take much brains to figure out that the two of you have got it made here with my mom. I'll bet she spoils you both terribly."

But there was no malice in Ashley's tone, and Pat dared to hope that the rift that had existed between herself and her daughter could someday be completely healed. It was almost enough to make her believe in miracles.

When she returned with the hot chocolate and a plate of homemade cookies, Ashley eyed the sweets longingly. "No cookies for me, Mother," she said, shaking her head regretfully. "I have to keep a close check on my weight."

Pat nodded. "Sorry, honey. I wasn't thinking. It's just that I've gotten to enjoy baking. You know I never did much in the kitchen when your father was alive."

Ashley sipped her hot chocolate and briefly closed her eyes. "It tastes just the way I remembered it. Do you know this is the first time I've had hot chocolate in years?"

Pat nodded, waiting. There was much she wanted to say, many things she needed to tell Ashley, but she sensed that her daughter also had things she needed to get out in the open.

Ashley put her cup down and leaned back. She looked around the small, but lovingly decorated room and nodded. "This is actually kind of nice. A lot different from what you were used to, but nice." She looked at Pat and smiled. "You didn't like the way we lived when Father was alive, did you?"

Pat hesitated, then quickly decided that honesty was the best policy. "I don't think I did, honey, but I was so used to doing what was expected of me, I didn't take the time to think about it. I was playing a role, acting a part, and then . . ."

She stopped in confusion. One thing she didn't intend to do was tarnish Ashley's memory of her father. That would accomplish nothing. Ashley apparently had enough to work through without learning that her father had had feet of clay.

"I'm glad you're happy now, Mother," Ashley said. "I really mean that. I know I said terrible things about this little house, and I am sorry. I acted like a spoiled brat. If this is what you want . . . if having these pets makes you happy, then this is what you should do."

"That's how I feel, too, honey," Pat said, swirling the marshmallow in her hot chocolate. "I was married to your father for a long time, and I tried to be the best wife I knew how, but now that part of my life is over, and hopefully I still have a few good years left. I plan to enjoy them."

"Good. You should enjoy yourself, Mother. You deserve to be happy. I've done a lot of thinking since we talked on the phone a few weeks ago. I'm beginning to see that I've been wrong about a lot of things." Ashley stopped, swallowed nervously, then swung her eyes away from her mother. "I always thought Daddy was perfect, the handsomest, smartest, most successful man in the world. I never stopped to think that some of the things he said and did with you and Cliff weren't always kind."

"He wanted Cliff to be a certain kind of son, and your brother just couldn't force himself into the mold," Pat said quietly.

"I know. I can see that now. But back then it seemed as though there were two sides, me and Daddy on one, and you and Cliff on the other. I felt like . . . you didn't love me as much as you loved Cliff."

"It wasn't a matter of love, Ashley. It was need. I felt Cliff needed me, to act as buffer between him and his father, to ease the pressure Clifford put on him. You were always so self-assured, so poised. Even as a tiny girl you appeared to be sure of yourself."

Ashley fidgeted, and Cat chose that moment to pounce on her and settle in her lap. Ashley looked startled, then she grinned. "A cat, too? I guess I should have known. You really have gone over to the other side, haven't you, Mother?" She stared down at the animal on her lap. "Strange-looking creature, isn't he?"

But Pat saw the way she stroked Cat's silky fur, the way she visibly relaxed as Cat began to purr contentedly.

"Anyway," Ashley continued, "I guess I wasn't as sure of myself as everyone thought, and as I watched you coming to Cliff's aid time and time again, I guess I drew away from you and concentrated on getting Daddy's attention. But I never completely succeeded with that, either. He was always so busy . . . so preoccupied with his clients . . . with one important case or another. God, I sound like a real nut case, don't I? I'm sorry, Mom. Maybe I shouldn't be dumping all this on you. You've got your own dragons to slay, haven't you?"

Pat nodded. "I suppose I do, but I'm glad we can finally talk this way. I never realized you felt like this. You didn't seem to need me, so I concentrated on Cliff, although not enough, or he wouldn't have been compelled to run away the way he did."

"What are we going to do about him, Mother?" Ashley asked, her voice changing. Hardening back into its former stiff posture.

Pat sighed. Today, for the first time, she and her daughter had made a start at understanding each other, and maybe with time and patience they could put the past to rest and build a fresh, new relationship as two loving, caring adults. But Cliff's situation was apparently still a thorn in Ashley's side, and it was going to take a long time, if ever, for her to realize that there was only one option where her brother was concerned.

"Honey, Cliff is who he is, and all we can do is accept him and love him as a son and a brother."

Now Ashley's lovely eyes filled with tears and she shook her head vehemently. "But Cliff is in danger . . . what if he gets sick? What if he contracts . . ." But she couldn't say it, and Pat held her own tears in check and forced the ugly image out of her mind.

Pat stood up and began to pace around the room nervously. "We . . . Cliff and I didn't discuss . . . that, but I'm sure he is being careful. Just as I'm sure you do. I guess that's all we can hope for."

Ashley shook her head, unconvinced, and Pat's heart silently agreed with her. The fear walked with her, day and night, and all she could do was try to keep pushing it back. Ashley would have to learn to do the same. There was nothing else they could do.

Eight

They had a quiet dinner together that first evening. Ashley said she could only stay for a few days. "I'm due to start a new shoot in a week, and there are things I need to do back in New York."

Hank hadn't called, although Pat had seen his truck in his driveway. He'd probably seen Ashley's little convertible and guessed who it belonged to. She smiled. Hank was lying low, giving her much needed time alone with her daughter. Bless him.

The next morning Pat called the shelter, assured herself that Dale and Pete could manage without her, then set about making a big country breakfast for herself and Ashley.

But when Ashley entered the kitchen, it was as if the previous day had been only a dream. The cold mask was back in place and she eyed the plates of food disdainfully.

"I can't eat that, Mother!" she said contemptuously. "I would have thought you'd realize. All that fat . . . do you really cook your eggs in bacon grease?"

Pat flipped the egg to its other side and bit her lip. Had she imagined the new, soft Ashley she'd glimpsed the other day? She glanced up, stared hard at her daughter and was rewarded when Ashley dropped her eyes contritely.

"Sorry," Ashley mumbled. "I'm doing it again, aren't I? That damned queen of the manor act. It's getting old, isn't it?"

Pat let her breath out in a whoosh. Rome wasn't built in a day, she thought. "Yes, it is, but I'll hang in there if you will. What would you like for breakfast, honey?"

"Do you have any grapefruit? That's usually all I eat for breakfast. Half a grapefruit and a slice of toasted whole wheat bread."

Pat nodded. "Very sensible. I should have thought. I suppose I just wanted to show off my new culinary talents. I only recently learned how to flip eggs without breaking the yolk, you know."

"Well, it's very impressive," Ashley said, sitting down and sipping the juice Pat had poured.

She looked like she hadn't slept well, Pat thought, and no wonder. She had also lain awake most of the night thinking about what they had revealed to one another. Getting right into the heart of a matter wasn't always easy, she decided. She smiled as she watched her daughter bend down to scratch behind Ink's ears.

After breakfast, when Pat had scraped most of the uneaten fried eggs into the dog's bowls as a special treat, she tidied the kitchen and took off her apron.

"Now," she said, smiling brightly at Ashley. "What would you like to do today, honey? It's pretty cool out, but if we bundle up we could take a nice long walk. There is some lovely country scenery around here."

"A walk would be great, Mom. There aren't many nice places to walk in the city."

Pat grimaced. "I remember. I suppose it's old age creeping up, but I truly enjoy the quiet, slower pace out here in the country. It suits me."

Ashley nodded. "It must. You look wonderful, Mother. Almost as if you've been rejuvenated. You didn't get a face lift when I wasn't looking, did you?"

"Not a chance," Pat said, laughing. "You know what a chicken I am about doctors. What you see is what you get, is my motto."

Ashley laughed softly. "Good for you, Mom.

Good for you."

They took the two dogs with them on their walk, and Ink and Spot had a great time frolicking in the occasional piles of leaves by the side of the road.

"So, do you really enjoy this volunteer work you're doing at the animal shelter, Mom?" Ashley asked. "I mean it was hard to picture it at first, but now that I see your new little family it's beginning to make sense. I never knew you liked animals that much."

"I always loved animals, but your father . . . well, he thought they made too much mess, and I suppose I just never wanted to argue with him. Anyway, none of that matters anymore. I'm doing what I want to do now, and that's what is important. I suppose I may as well tell you now that I am planning to use some of my money to enlarge and renovate the shelter. It's something I really want to do."

Ashley shrugged. "I'm sure there's plenty of money for you to do just about anything you want, Mom."

"There is," Pat agreed, "but don't worry, I'm not planning to squander all of your father's estate. I'm sure there will still be a sizable inheritance for you and your brother when the time comes."

"Daddy probably would have cut Cliff out

of his will if he'd known," Ashley said softly, absently kicking a pile of bright autumn leaves.

Pat nodded, but made no reply. What Clifford would have done no longer mattered.

They walked for a long time, until Ashley began to complain that she was starving. Then they headed back home, and after settling the dogs, they drove off to a quaint little tearoom for lunch.

"Mother, this is lovely," Ashley said, looking around in delight. "Don't you just love this Victorian decor?"

Pat nodded and sipped her lemon tea. They were served tiny, delicious finger sandwiches, a tray of artfully arranged fresh fruits and cheeses, and the most delicious tea in the world. She was gratified to see Ashley enjoying her food.

Long ago, Pat had dreamed of times like this, of enjoying pleasant, quiet moments with her daughter, but as the years passed she began to believe it would never happen. She had started to think that she and Ashley would never meet on common ground.

"You know, sitting here like this I'm beginning to think we can really do this, Mom," Ashley said, bringing Pat back to earth. I think we're going to be friends." She hesitated, then smiled. "You're not the woman I thought you were."

Pat grinned. "Ditto," she said. "Ditto."

That afternoon, while Pat was preparing dinner, a simple pot of homemade soup, she heard the familiar tap on the back door. Her heart leaped in her chest. Hank! She'd been so busy enjoying Ashley's company she hadn't given him much thought, but now she realized he'd always been at the back of her mind.

"Hi," she said eagerly. "Come on in."

Hank entered the kitchen, bringing a sense of warmth with him, despite the chilly air that swept into the room. It was always that way. He carried warmth and peace with him wherever he went, Pat thought. She was suddenly aware of how much she would miss him if he went away.

"My daughter Ashley is here visiting," she announced. "She's upstairs shampooing her hair. I'm glad you came by. I want her to meet you."

"I saw the car yesterday and thought I should make myself scarce," Hank explained, "But today . . . well, I just had to come by and make sure you were okay."

Pat smiled, her eyes meeting and holding with Hank's. "I'm glad," she said again. "I missed you."

She fixed him a cup of coffee and sat down across from him at the kitchen counter. "Stay for dinner?" she asked. "You like homemade vegetable soup, don't you?"

"Homemade soup on a cold winter night? How could any man resist that?"

"Mother?" Ashley stood in the doorway looking shy and uncertain and at least ten years younger than she actually was. Her face was scrubbed clean of makeup, and her freshly shampooed hair hung around her shoulders, curling in damp tendrils. Pat thought she had never looked more beautiful.

"Ashley, there you are. I was hoping you'd hurry down. I want you to meet my neighbor and good friend, Hank Richards. Hank, this is my daughter, Ashley."

"Pleased to meet you, Ashley," Hank said pleasantly. "Are you enjoying your visit?"

As Pat watched the play of emotions on her daughter's face, she knew the struggle that raged inside Ashley's slender form. Here was a man sitting in her mother's kitchen. Ashley had never seen Pat with any man but Clifford, and she had always been fiercely possessive of her belongings. It had to be hard for her to see a man who might possibly take her father's place sitting across from her mother.

"I . . . how do you do?" Ashley said formally. "It's nice to meet you, too."

Pat briefly closed her eyes. Thank you, Lord, she murmured silently.

"Well, the soup is almost done and I've asked Hank to stay for supper," Pat told Ashley. "Whenever I make soup there's enough for an army."

Ashley nodded. "May I have some coffee?"

Pat poured the coffee, mentally cursing the awkward silence. How to break it? What to say? Then Hank saved the day by asking Ashley about her modeling.

"I'm afraid I don't know much about high fashion," he said, "but your mother showed me one of your covers. I'm impressed."

Ashley actually blushed.

Surprised, Pat realized there were many facets to her daughter's personality she would have to learn.

"Thank you," Ashley said. "But as you can see, a lot of photography and lighting tricks go into making those covers look good. I'm just an ordinary girl."

"Oh, I doubt that," Hank said, smiling. "Do you like living in New York?"

Ashley started talking then, and suddenly Pat was the outsider looking in. Hank and Ashley chatted on and on, about city life versus country living, about the logistics of having a pet in a high-rise apartment, about crime and politics . . .

Pat hummed softly under her breath and stirred the soup. This was nice. This was the way it should be.

Then it was time for Ashley to leave and go back to her own life. It was too soon, and yet Pat felt oddly relieved. She and Ashley had made a good start at building a new relationship, but there were still bridges to cross, and fences to mend. Something in Ashley's eyes told Pat it would not be all smooth sailing.

Pat realized, as she had when she drove Cliff to the airport, that no matter what had gone before, or would come in the future, her life was separate from her children's lives now. Each of them had their own dreams and desires, their own priorities, and that, of course, was as it should be.

She spent the morning straightening up the guest room, smiling as the lingering scent of Ashley's perfume swirled around her. Pat eyed the small room critically. She had no idea what had ever possessed her to decorate the room in such dark colors. The room was completely at odds with the rest of the house and she decided she would have to do something about it soon. If Ashley was going to spend occasional weekends, the room definitely needed a lighter, airier look.

But first things first, Pat decided, dumping Ashley's sheets in the hamper and loading towels into the washing machine. Her top priority at the moment was the renovation of the animal shelter. She could hardly wait for the construction to begin. They would be able to shelter more animals when it was completed, and if her plan to recruit donations worked, they would be able to keep the animals for a longer period of time before being forced to put them down. And with Margaret Farmer's help, hopefully they would eventually get to a place where none of the animals would have to be put to sleep.

That was the goal she was working toward. Maybe it was an impossible dream, but she had to try. The animals were helpless. They had no defenses.

Pat smiled as she dusted and vacuumed. It was wonderful to have things that had to be done, to have a real reason to get up in the morning, and to live the way she pleased.

She thought of Clifford. She remembered his betrayal and her heart twisted. That hurt would always linger, but lately, especially since she had begun to realize what she could accomplish with the money Clifford had left her, the pain had softened somewhat. At least Clifford had thought enough of her, and the years they had shared to make her the beneficiary of his estate. The money couldn't reduce the betrayal she felt, but at least it gave her the freedom to thoroughly enjoy the rest of her life. Pat knew that not many widows had that kind of ease.

"Oh, Clifford, what went wrong with us? How did we get so far apart?" There were no answers, no echoes from the past to enlighten Pat, but then she hadn't expected any. Clifford had carried his own secrets to his grave. She would never know now what he had thought and felt all the years of their marriage, and she could only take comfort in knowing that she had given their union all that she had to give at the time. There was no more she could have done.

By the time Pat had finished cleaning house, she felt as though her soul had undergone a cleaning as well. For a long time after learning of her husband's infidelity, she had carried a core of bitterness around inside her. She had felt diminished as a woman, but now she was finally starting to realize that there were good memories as well as bad, and that was what she should focus on. Bitterness begot more bitterness, and pain and hate. It ate at you until there was no room for love or joy.

"I forgive you, Clifford," she said, looking out the window at the bare trees and dormant lawn. And as she stared, the first pure, pristine snowflakes of the season began to drift down from the sky. It was a benediction, a blessing, Pat thought. An end to one season, the bright and glorious beginning of another.

"Your daughter is lovely, Pat," Hank said later that evening when they sat in front of a roaring fire in Hank's living room.

The snowfall had accelerated into a full-scale storm, and when Hank had suggested relaxing in front of a fire with hot mulled wine, Pat had enthusiastically agreed.

"This is lovely," she answered, leaning her head on Hank's shoulder. "Yes, Ashley is beautiful. She was beautiful the day she was born. I suppose I should have foreseen her future even then."

"And the two of you managed to get things sorted out?" Hank asked, sounding a little wistful.

"Not everything, but I think we made a start. What about you, Hank? Don't you think you should try to talk to your daughters?

Surely Becky has had time to think by now, and she must realize that your breakup with your wife wasn't all your fault."

Hank shook his head. He was growing a beard and the fuzz of graying hair tickled Pat's chin. She shivered, and Hank's arm tightened around her shoulders.

"I'm not real good with words the way you are, Pat. I don't know where to start, how to explain it all to Becky and Laurie. And I don't want to badmouth their mother. I'd just like them to understand that I had no choice. I just couldn't be what Nancy wanted me to be."

"That's exactly the way you should explain it to them, Hank," Pat said, sitting up eagerly. "Just the way you told me. Fancy words aren't necessary."

"Maybe not, but Becky is a stubborn girl. Even as an infant she was determined to have things her way. Laurie would probably be more reasonable."

"But they're both adult women now, Hank, and I'd be willing to bet they miss you as much as you obviously miss them. Don't forget, I saw the way you looked at Ashley, and I knew you were thinking of your own daughters. Don't wait, Hank," she pleaded. "Life is too short. Go to them and tell them how you feel, that you love them and miss them. Heal the wounds and start over. If I can do it, so can you."

Hank was silent for a long time, and Pat began to fear she'd gone too far. They were friends, but maybe she'd overstepped the bounds of friendship. Hank talked very little about his personal situation.

"Hank? Did I offend you? I didn't mean to interfere. It's just that . . ."

"Please don't apologize, Pat. I love the fact that you care. I guess I'm just a coward."

His hand was on her hair now. He smoothed his palm lightly over her head. What was it about this woman that made him feel shy and tongue-tied? Why did the mere sight of her make his heart dance in his chest as if he were twenty years old again? Why was he, after years of being alone, daring to dream of sharing his life again?

"Pat, I . . ."

Panic overtook Pat then. She sensed what Hank was about to say. She felt it in the deepest recesses of her heart, and she simply wasn't ready. And he wasn't, either, not really. It was just the mood of the evening, the magical, snow-crusted landscape outside, the warm, fire-lit shadows inside. If Hank spoke now he would regret it later.

"Please, Hank," she said gently, reaching up

to lightly caress his cheek. "Not now. Not yet. We're friends. That's enough for the moment."

Was it? He wasn't sure. Sitting here in front of a crackling fire, with Pat so close he could smell her sweet, feminine musk, he wasn't sure at all. Deep in his gut, feelings he had thought were gone forever raged anew, but Pat wasn't ready, and the last thing he wanted to do was ruin the wonderful, warm closeness building between them.

"Whatever you say, pretty lady," he said. But then he couldn't resist dropping a chaste kiss on the top of her head. "It'll keep."

"Yes," Pat said strongly. "It'll keep."

"This place is a zoo!" Dale complained good-naturedly, as he contemplated piles of sawdust, workers hurrying back and forth and the piles of lumber and other supplies outside the building a couple of days later.

Pat laughed. She had a clipboard in her hand and she was dressed in what had rapidly become a uniform of sorts. Soft, faded jeans and a thick flannel shirt. Her hair, recently cropped in a short, easy-to-care-for style, was slightly mussed, but she really didn't care. There were many more important things to worry about. Like the plumber who hadn't yet shown up, the electrician who was demanding overtime for working through his lunch hour, and the problem of keeping the animals from going crazy every time a different worker arrived.

"Not quite," Pat said, "but you're close. Don't worry, pal," she said, patting Dale's arm consolingly. "It'll all be worth it in the end."

Dale nodded. "I know. That's what I keep telling myself. Uh, when do you think all this will be finished?"

"By Christmas for sure," Pat promised. "At least that's what I've been told over and over again."

"Well, all this extra space is going to be a blessing, no doubt of that," Pete said. "Are you still going to get that friend of yours to run a special article about Christmas adoptions?"

"Definitely," Pat answered. "Do you know how many people give pets for Christmas presents? If we can just get people to realize that these animals here are just as loving and healthy as purebreds, half the battle will be won."

But there was another problem nagging at Pat's conscience. She had yet to tell Hank of the shelter expansion and renovation, and she knew she would have to do it soon. The problem was, she didn't know what to say, or how to say it. Oh, by the way, Hank, I'm not a poor, lonely widow the way you thought. Actually, I'm independently wealthy. Kind of funny, isn't it? You worried about my being able to afford food for my pets, and I could buy out your kennels if I wanted to. Anyway, I just thought I'd cut loose some of my excess cash and jazz this place up a little. How do you like it? It didn't cost that much, really. Just more than you probably make in a couple of years. But what the heck, it's only money, right?

Oh yes. That's perfect, Pat, she told herself. Just throw it right in his face. Make a mockery of all the time you've spent together so far, the friendship that's been built on lies and half-truths and evasions. Let him have it right between the eyes, and watch his respect and concern for you die by degrees as the truth sinks in.

"Pat? Hey, Pat, there's somebody here to see you!"

Dale was beaming, and so was Hank as he stood in the doorway surveying the workmen with amazement. Yes, both men looked happy, and Pat felt as if her world had just dropped out from under her.

"Wha . . . what are you doing here? You're not working?"

Hank grinned. "Slow day. I thought I'd stop by and see how things were going around here, but I had no idea about any of this. Why didn't you tell me what was going on? This is great!"

He turned to Dale. "Where did you guys scrounge up the dough for all of this?" He waved his hands to indicate the workmen.

"Hey, I can't take credit for this. It's all thanks to Pat. She's our benefactor. She engineered this whole thing."

Pat could see Hank struggling to understand. "You mean you found a way to raise the funds for this?"

"I . . ."

"Hell, man, this fantastic little lady just dug deep into her own private bank account," Pete said loudly, coming into the room behind Hank. "Ain't this something? Can you believe it? These animals are going to be sheltered in style from now on, not to mention the luxurious new digs Pete and I are going to have. And we owe it all to Pat. Ain't she something?"

Hank's face was pale, his eyes bleak as the meaning of Dale's effusive compliments slowly sunk in. "Oh yes," he said, sounding choked. "She sure is something!"

"Hank, let me explain!" Pat had dropped

her clipboard and run outside after Hank as he hurried from the building, but he seemed determined to escape from her as quickly as possible.

"No explanations necessary, Pat," he called over his shoulder flatly. "There's no reason you should have to tell me any of your private business." He turned then and glared bitterly. "But tell me one thing, what were you afraid of? Did you think I'd want you for your money? God, I can't believe how I spilled my guts to you . . . telling you all about Nancy, and her preoccupation with things . . . how you must have laughed, thinking of your own bulging bank account." Hank laughed, a hard, grating sound that made Pat wince. "And I was worried about you paying someone to dig up your garden. What a laugh!"

"No, Hank . . . it wasn't like that! If you'd just let me explain . . ."

"No thanks. I'm not interested in any more lies."

"I never lied to you," Pat said brokenly, blinking back tears.

"No, that's right, you didn't," Hank said harshly. "You just refrained from telling me the truth, and that makes it all right in your book, doesn't it? Well, it won't wash with me, Pat. You knew how I would feel when I learned of this . . . you must have realized . . ."

"I did . . . I do! That's why I didn't say anything. I was afraid you would misunderstand!"

"Oh, there's no misunderstanding, Pat. None at all. Everything is suddenly crystal clear."

He jumped in his truck then and slammed the vehicle into gear. Pat stood, staring after him, feeling as if her heart had been ripped out of her chest.

"Hey, Pat, is something wrong? Boy, Hank took off out of here like a . . ."

Pat hurried away from Dale's puzzled, concerned expression. "Everything is fine," she said bitterly. "Just perfect!"

The afternoon dragged on and on. Dale and Pete wisely gave Pat a wide berth. She was desperate to get home, crazy to see Hank and try once again to explain, but she couldn't leave while the workmen were all milling around.

What good was it going to do anyway? she wondered, sitting in Dale's cramped little office, sipping warmed-over coffee. Hank had been bitten once, he wasn't about to put his hand out again. He would equate her with Nancy now, and maybe that was what she deserved. In all honesty, how much different was it from what Clifford had done to her? Coming home like a dutiful husband, pretending they had the perfect marriage, even making love to her at regular intervals, and all the time he was bedding his colleague, a woman Pat frequently entertained in her home. Had Clifford lied? No. He had just neglected to mention that he had a hot babe on the side. So how different was what she had done in not telling Hank her true status? Even if she'd hinted at the fact that she was "comfortable" it might have helped, but she hadn't even done that. Instead she'd gone merrily along, accepting Hank's help, letting him think she was a struggling widow. Well, she would have plenty of struggles from now on. She'd struggle with her conscience, with her regrets, with her "I wish I hads."

"The plumber is leaving, Pat," Pete called hesitantly. "Is there anything you need to tell him?"

"I'm coming," she said, getting to her feet like a tired old woman.

When Pat finally got home that night, Hank's truck was not in his driveway and the house was dark. He'd probably been home, cared for the dogs, and then taken off, so he wouldn't have to see her.

Shoulders slumping Pat let herself into the house and was immediately surrounded by her pets. She smiled despite her pain. At least she still had her animals.

For the next two weeks Pat never saw Hank. He apparently left early in the morning and returned late at night. In desperation she called Celia one night to tell her what had happened.

"I know you don't want to hear this, but maybe it's for the best," Celia said. "After all, he is a married man."

"Oh, Celia! In name only! I told you Hank and his wife haven't lived together in years, and he doesn't even know where she is."

"Still, he's not free, and I could tell you were starting to care about him. I don't want you to get hurt again, Patty."

"It's too late, sis," Pat said. "I already am hurt. I have to find a way to make Hank understand that my money doesn't have to come between us."

"I got the impression he was a strong, bull-headed man," Celia replied. "That may not be easy."

"Nothing worthwhile ever is. Look, I've been so busy weeping on your shoulder I haven't even asked about you. How's the diet coming along?"

"It's not a diet," Celia said quickly. "The people at the center said I should look on this as a new way of eating, and not just a diet. Oh, Pat, I'm so glad you helped me do this!

So far I've lost nine pounds, and my counselor said that's very good. My clothes are starting to feel loose. Isn't that wonderful!"

"It's fantastic," Pat agreed. "Is Jake being supportive?"

Celia's voice softened. "You know Jake. He's the best man that ever lived. I know I couldn't do this without him by my side."

"Great. That's just what I wanted to hear," Pat said, then she made some lame excuse to hang up before she started to cry.

That was what she had hoped for with Hank. She had dared to dream about having a good man by her side for the rest of her life, but maybe it simply wasn't meant to be. Maybe all she would ever have was her work at the shelter and her pets, and of course, her children. Maybe it was simply too late for love.

Nine

Pat woke up one crisp morning and realized it was less than a week until Thanksgiving. She already knew that Ashley wouldn't be able to make it home. She was doing a shoot in California.

She had debated inviting Celia and Jake for the holiday weekend, but decided against it. Celia was working hard to lose her excess weight, and it wouldn't be fair to tempt her with holiday goodies. So what does that leave? Pat wondered dejectedly. Just her and the animals. She barely glimpsed Hank these days, and although she took full responsibility for not telling him the truth, she was beginning to think he was carrying his anger too far. Even the worst criminals sometimes got a second chance. Was he perfect? Who did he think he was anyway?

But in the light of day, as she dressed to drive

to the shelter, she knew that in Hank's mind he felt fully justified in maintaining this cold war. Well, so be it, she decided as she pulled a heavy corduroy jacket on over her sweater. She could manage on her own if she had to, and she could have a lovely Thanksgiving dinner all by herself, too. She'd always loved the holidays, and she sure wasn't going to sit in a corner and suck her thumb just because she didn't have a house full of company. Instead of a turkey, she'd buy a chicken. She could still have all the trimmings, stuffing, cranberries, creamed cauliflower. Apple and pumpkin pies. Pat smiled and patted her tummy. She could almost taste the rich gravy and fluffy biscuits she would make, with the aid of her cookbook, of course. She'd have a feast all by herself, and to hell with everything!

"What are you doing for Thanksgiving, Pat?" Dale asked that afternoon, when they took a well-deserved coffee break.

"Oh, I'm just having a quiet little dinner," she said. "My daughter and son are both in California, and neither of them can get home."

"Hey, how about coming to our house?" Pete asked. "My mom makes enough food for an army, and there's always room for one more."

"Thanks," Pat said, "but I'll be fine. I'm actually looking forward to cooking my own dinner this year."

"Well, let us know if you change your mind,"

Dale said. "No one should be alone on a holiday."

The work on the shelter was progressing nicely. Pat looked around with a feeling of pride. It made her feel good to know that she had helped, but there was much more that needed to be done. Margaret Farmer had contacted her a few days earlier and suggested that Pat go on a local television show before Christmas. "You could make an appeal for people to give an unwanted animal a home for Christmas. It might work, Pat. Christmas is such a sentimental holiday anyway. People are feeling generous. It's worth a shot, isn't it? How many animals do you have over there now anyway?"

Pat sighed. "Too many. Your articles have sent a lot of people in, but it's still not enough. I won't be satisfied until every one of these creatures has a good, loving home."

Margaret laughed. "Such fervor. I'm glad to see that in you, Pat. We were all so sorry about Clifford."

"Yes. Well, life goes on, doesn't it? That's what I'm trying to do, get on with it."

"All right, I'll see what I can find out in regard to the television station. Bob Penders is a friend of mine."

"Thanks, Margaret. Say, do *you* have a pet?"

"Oh, no you don't, Pat! I have all I can handle with my job and my little family. Maybe in a few years when my nest empties."

Pat smiled as she replaced the receiver. She hadn't known Margaret well before, but lately they were getting to be quite friendly.

"Problems, Pat," Dale said, coming into the room with a dejected expression on his face later that afternoon. "Someone just left a basket of newborn kittens on the front step. They can't be more than four or five hours old. No sign of the mama cat."

Pat sighed. She was getting used to this sort of thing, but she would never understand it. How could a thinking, caring human being just casually abandon helpless animals?

"We'll have to bottle-feed them," she said. "I'll call Doctor Johnson and ask him how to mix the formula. We still have those doll bottles somewhere, don't we?"

"Sure, but . . . well, Pete and I both have heavy dates tonight, and kittens this young need to be fed every couple of hours."

Pat nodded. She couldn't be angry with Pete and Dale. They were two of the most caring, dedicated young men she'd ever known, but a heavy date was a big thing at their age. She shrugged. "I'll take them home with me for the night," she said, "but remember, you and Pete both. You owe me!"

By five-thirty Pat was heading home, the box of kittens behind her seat, and a carton of supplies next to it. Thank goodness there were only four tiny, striped kittens. As it was she would have her hands full. Any more and it would have been an impossible task.

Pete and Dale had helped her feed the kittens just before she left, so for the moment her brood was quiet. Pat felt her mind begin to wander as she drove.

When Ashley had called to say she was doing the shoot in California, Pat's first thought had been that perhaps she would pay her brother a visit. But Ashley had quickly squelched that hope.

"I won't be seeing Cliff, Mother. I thought about it, but I'm just not ready. I don't know if I'll ever be ready."

"You do what makes you feel comfortable, honey," she told Ashley. "That's really all any of us can do."

"Well, I'll send you some gorgeous postcards and I'll be in touch when I get back. Maybe, well I was wondering if you wanted me to come for Christmas?"

"Want you? Oh, sweetheart, it will make the day! You know how I've always loved the holidays, and part of it was the fun of having lots of people around . . . good food and lots of laughter."

"That's the way I remember our holidays in the big house. I think that's one of the reasons I was against your selling it. It felt like you were sweeping all our memories under the rug."

"Never," Pat said fervently. "Some of our memories are very happy ones." She felt herself soften, as she remembered the Christmas eve that Clifford had stayed up until four-thirty in the morning putting a dollhouse together for Ashley. And then there was the year he built the magnificent platform for Cliff's train set. Yes, there were many good memories, and they deserved to be cherished.

"We'll have a wonderful Christmas, honey," she had promised. "You'll see."

Well, now she would have to make good that promise, Pat reminded herself as she pulled into the driveway. A minute later, as she lifted the box of kittens out from behind her seat she shuddered, thinking of what would have happened if the baby animals had been left outside. It was bitterly cold now, and the temperature was expected to drop even more before morning. It looked like another snowstorm was imminent.

"Come on, little ones," Pat crooned, nudging her front door open with her hip. "It's time for me to introduce you to the rest of the family."

The two dogs took the newcomers in stride, but Cat was more suspicious. "It's all right, Cat," Pat assured her feline boarder. "They're not moving in permanently. You're still top cat around here."

Either her words or the tone of her voice reassured Cat because he sauntered off as though the whole situation bored him. Pat quickly fed the dogs and made sure they had fresh water, then grabbed a quick sandwich and glass of milk for herself. Before she knew it it would be time to feed the kittens again. She sighed. It was going to be a long night.

By morning Pat was exhausted. She'd been up and down all night like a yo-yo. Feed the kittens, try to catch a couple of hours sleep, feed the kittens, sleep . . . it went on and on until finally, when dawn streaked the sky, she gave up and stumbled out to the kitchen to make coffee.

She shook her finger at the now sleeping kittens as the coffee perked. "It's a good thing you're all so cute, and I'm so tenderhearted."

The kittens slept on, their little bellies full, their bodies warm from the hot water bottle under their blanket. For the moment at least, all their needs had been fulfilled.

Pat sighed as she poured a cup of hot, strong coffee into a mug. Would that it were as easy for humans, she thought. If a full belly and a warm bed were all anyone needed, how simple life would be.

She slumped wearily in her chair, hoping the coffee would give her enough energy to get dressed and drive over to the shelter and deposit the kittens in Dale's lap. Then she was going to drive straight home and sleep for the rest of the day. Well, maybe not all day, but at least until she had recharged some of her batteries. She felt like an old, wound-down clock.

How on earth had she ever survived her colicky babies and the two o'clock feedings? Just thinking of it made her shudder.

Pat laughed as the coffee began to work its magic. You were a lot younger then, old gal, she reminded herself.

Pat was waiting when Dale and Pete drove up to the shelter.

Both young men laughed when they saw the dark circles under her eyes. "Rough night, Pat?" they teased. "You look like you didn't get much sleep."

"Less than that," Pat grumbled. "Here. They're all yours. They're all eating well, and they seem to be doing fine. I'm going home and back to bed."

"Right on!" Pete cheered. "Go to it, Pat, and thanks. Dale and I had a great time last night."

"Good. I'm thrilled," Pat mumbled, shoving the box of sleeping kittens into Pete's outstretched arms. "Have a nice day, guys."

The little minivan headed for home at a faster than normal clip, and as soon as she got in the house Pat kicked off her shoes and headed for her bedroom.

She woke about two in the afternoon. She sat

up, pleased to note that she felt almost human again. And she was hungry.

Deciding that she deserved a little indulgence, Pat made herself a three decker ham, cheese, and tomato sandwich, poured a glass of diet cola and carried her combination lunch and dinner into the living room. She turned on the television, plopped down in her favorite chair and sighed with pure pleasure.

Such luxury, such decadence, and no one to know or care. It was one of the benefits of living alone.

From her living-room window she had a clear view of Hank's front yard. She saw him drive up at precisely five fifteen, saw him slide out from behind the wheel of his pickup, stretch and then let himself into the house. She leaned forward in her chair, trying to see his face, but the days of twenty-twenty eyesight were gone. All she could make out was a blur, and the blur never even glanced in her direction.

It got dark, and Pat switched channels on the television. She glanced across the road and saw a light go on in Hank's living room. What was he doing? How was he feeling? She wondered if he would hang up if she phoned?

Finally, when she could stand it no longer, Pat dressed in jeans and a sweater, slid her feet into fur-lined boots and ran a comb through her hair. She didn't bother with makeup. She wasn't interested in impressing Hank, only in helping him to understand why she'd been less than honest with him.

She picked her way carefully across the street. It had rained earlier and there was a thin layer of ice forming on the blacktop. Then she was standing on the front step, her hand poised to knock. She hesitated, then gathered her courage and pounded hard on the door.

She heard a noise, then a muffled curse, and then the door swung open and Hank's face peered out at her.

"Pat? What are you doing here?"

She smiled tentatively. "It's nice to see you, too, Hank. May I come in for a minute? It's awfully cold out here." Even when he was angry it was impossible for Hank to completely hide the warmth that was so much a part of him.

"Come in? Uh, sure, come on." He stood back to let her enter, and tried desperately to curb the flood of longing that swept over him. How could he feel this way about a woman who had lied to him . . . well, maybe she hadn't exactly lied, but she hadn't told the truth either. And after he'd bared his soul to her! Hank would have died before admitting how much he'd missed seeing Pat, talking to her, basking in her smile. But he'd loved and trusted one woman, and what had it gotten him? Pain, grief, and estrangement from his children. No way would he let himself in for that kind of loss again.

He led the way into the living room and Pat saw a cheerful fire glowing in the fireplace. "Mmm, that looks wonderful," she said. "Winter arrived with a vengeance, didn't it?"

"Always does," Hank muttered noncommittally.

So, Pat thought, he's not going to make this easy for me. Well, she hadn't thought he would. She would just have to go with the flow and hope for the best. If nothing else maybe she and Hank could find a way back to the lovely friendship they had shared. She wanted more from him. She knew that now, but friendship was better than nothing.

"Hank, I want to . . . I need to explain some things to you," she began. "I know you were hurt by what you feel was a deliberate deception, but I really didn't mean it to be that way, and I was trying to figure out how to tell you about . . . about the money. I wanted to figure out how to convince you that it doesn't make a difference."

"Really? That's interesting. And did you figure out how to do that?"

Hank stood, feet slightly apart, arms folded across his chest, his jaw firm and tight. By most woman's standards, Pat supposed he wouldn't be considered handsome, but there was something warm and solid about him, something that made her heart pound and her skin prickle. He was a real man, strong, yet tender. He was blunt and he was honest, and that was probably why he was finding it so hard to understand how she could have omitted the tiny little fact that she was wealthy.

"It just isn't that important to me, Hank," she said. "Why won't you believe that?"

"Because life has taught me the opposite. Money is damned important, Pat, especially when you don't have any!"

"I know. I didn't mean that. What I was trying to say is that I'm not Nancy. When my husband died we were living in a house more than three times the size of the one I have now. It was filled with all the trappings of wealth and success. I sold the house, Hank, and the paintings and all the antique furnishings. I gave most of my old clothes, many of them designer originals, to the thrift shop, and believe it or not, until I moved here I'd never worn a flannel shirt in my life. All of those things didn't make me happy, Hank."

She paused and waved her arm toward the little house across the road. "That's what makes me happy. My little house, my animals, your friendship, and yes, my work at the shelter. I never realized there was so much that needed to be done, so many young, healthy animals being put down every single day. I want to help, and if using some of my money can make things happen, why not? Is that so terrible?"

Hank's jaw was a little less tense, his eyes a smidgen softer, but his voice was still harsh with pain when he spoke.

"Pat, I believe everything you're telling me. You're a terrific lady. I know you genuinely care about those animals at the shelter, and I think it's wonderful that you're in a financial position to help them. I admire you for what you're doing, but it doesn't change things between you and me. We're from two different worlds, Pat. There's no way you and I can be a couple."

"I'm in your world now, Hank," Pat said softly. "This is where I want to be. This is the way I want to live the rest of my life."

Hank shook his head sadly. "No. I don't think so. I don't know the circumstances of your marriage, Pat, but I think you're just slumming right now. One of these days you'll wake up and start missing the theater, the diamond earrings . . . your mink, and you'll go back where you belong and forget all about me."

"No. I won't. I know I won't."

"It doesn't matter," Hank said. "I'm not willing to take that risk."

He was gentleman enough to walk her to her door even though she protested. On her front step he reached out and tipped up her chin.

"I'm sorry, Pat. I wish things could have been different."

Pat nodded. "Me, too," she whispered after him. "Me, too."

Three days later, as Pat shopped for supplies for her solitary Thanksgiving dinner, she reminded herself to focus on the things she had to be grateful for. First and foremost, she was healthy, and that was priceless. She was forging a good relationship with Cliff and Ashley, and that was something that could never be measured in dollars and cents. Then there was her work, which gave her immense satisfaction, and last but definitely not least, her cozy little home and her beloved pets. In just a few months she had become firmly attached to her animals and now she couldn't imagine her life without them. They gave her complete, unconditional love. And they asked for nothing but affection in return. When she tallied everything up, Pat realized she actually had quite a lot to be thankful for.

"Mmm, sweet potatoes," she murmured. Always one of her favorites. She walked along leisurely, dropping items in her basket. She had always enjoyed food, but until recently she had never been able to indulge. She decided that this Thanksgiving would be a feast to remember.

"Shopping for one?" a voice asked from behind her.

Pat turned, saw a dignified-looking man of her own age smiling at her.

"Yes," she admitted. "It's the first time. It's kind of hard to judge quantities, isn't it?"

The man shrugged. "Never tried. I just scout out one of the local restaurants and let someone else worry about it." He smiled sheepishly. "I guess you think I've got a lot of nerve, but I couldn't help noting the size of the can of cranberries in your basket. It was a dead giveaway."

Pat returned the smile. "My family is too far away to come home," she explained, "but I plan to enjoy myself anyway."

"Good for you. Do you . . . live around here?"

Pat hesitated. She had no idea who this man was, and she wasn't about to start giving out her address to perfect strangers. And anyway, even though he had a nice smile, she simply wasn't interested. Despite her lingering bitterness over Clifford's betrayal, she had opened her heart to Hank, and what had it gotten her? More pain. No, she could manage quite nicely without a man in her life, thank you.

"It was nice talking to you," she murmured, turning away. "Have a nice holiday."

Thanksgiving Day dawned bright, clear, and bitterly cold. The smell of snow was in the air, and as Pat stuffed her little chicken and basted it, she kept an eye on the window, eagerly awaiting the first fluffy snowflakes.

The house was starting to smell like a holiday, she thought, proud of how far she'd come with her cooking skills. She was actually becoming quite competent, and she knew that this chicken would not end up in the garbage like the one she'd attempted to cook for Cliff and Hank. She'd decided on only one pie since there was no one around to help her eat leftovers, and now it reposed in perfectly browned splendor on the countertop.

Pat tied a frilly apron on over her skirt and fiddled with the knob on her portable radio. Music was what she needed. Something peppy and cheerful.

She zeroed in on a country-western station and heard the last strains of Billy Ray Cyrus's "Achy-Breaky Heart." She grimaced. Very appropriate indeed!

Ten

In between checking on her chicken and stirring the sauce for the creamed cauliflower, Pat watched Macy's Thanksgiving Day Parade on television. Funny how easy it was to become a creature of habit, she thought, but somehow, without the parade it wouldn't have been Thanksgiving.

But just as she was ready to sit down and enjoy the fruits of all her labor, there was a knock on her door. Before she could reach the door, the knock came again, louder this time, more insistent.

"Okay, okay, don't knock it down," she said, somewhat irritated. Who on earth was pounding on her door on Thanksgiving Day, just as she was about to enjoy her solitary dinner?

She looked out the peephole, saw Hank and quickly opened the door.

"Hank! What on earth!"

Stamping fresh snow from his boots, Hank looked just a bit sheepish. "Look, I know this is a terrible imposition, but I've got an emergency on my hands and I need help."

"What's wrong?"

"Princess has gone into labor, and it looks like there may be complications. I can't get in touch with my vet and . . ."

"Just let me change and I'll be right over," Pat said, her festive dinner forgotten. "Or if you want to wait . . . ?"

"I'll wait," Hank said. "The road is slippery. Of all times for a snowstorm!"

Pat disappeared, and Hank paced, waiting for her. He couldn't miss the delectable smell of roast poultry and his eyes involuntarily rested on the perfectly browned, fragrant apple pie sitting on the counter. And then his eyes settled on the beautifully set table with one single place setting. His heart twisted. Pat had gone to all this trouble just for herself, and was prepared to eat alone, on Thanksgiving. He shook his head. It seemed the lady had even more grit and guts than he'd given her credit for.

Yeah, and here you are practically begging for a helping hand, when you just about slammed the door in her face a couple of nights ago. Some big man, you are, Hank Richards!

Angry at himself, and angry at Pat for making him angry at himself, Hank paced the small room. No fool like an old fool, he chided himself, and he had sure been acting the part! What did he want from Pat anyway? Did he expect her to get down on her knees and beg his forgiveness? Well, she'd just about done that and he'd refused to budge an inch. Did he expect her to keep coming back and asking for more? Hell no! She'd be a fool to do that, and despite everything, Pat Melbourne was nobody's fool! She was a lady, a real lady, and why couldn't he just accept her apology at face value and get on with it? Because he was a stubborn, mule-headed caboose, that's why! He'd always been stubborn. That was probably the main reason he'd been estranged from Becky for so long, and why his relationship with Laurie wasn't warmer.

Well, it was never too late, was it? He'd start with Pat, by telling her just what a fool he was. He'd tell her today, just as soon as Princess was safely delivered.

"I'm ready," Pat said, hurrying back into the room.

She'd changed from her bright jersey dress to jeans and a flannel shirt. She wore thick socks and low-heeled boots.

"Just let me put this chicken on hold warm," she said. "Everything else can be reheated in the microwave later."

Hank couldn't hold back a grin. "You almost sound like you know what you're doing in the kitchen."

Pat smiled proudly. "I'm learning more every day. It's amazing what a cookbook can do."

No, Hank thought, it's amazing what a woman like you can do. Not only had Pat forged a new and different life for herself, she was rapidly changing the way he looked at life as well. Before he'd been insulated, safe inside his own little shell, with his small house, his dogs, and his job. He'd stayed clear of women, even his own daughters. Then Pat came along and changed all that. Suddenly his self-imposed cage was confining. He began to long for light and fresh air, for more than what he had.

"Ready?" Pat asked brightly.

"Ready," Hank said, but he wasn't sure he was. He guessed this was a little like jumping in the lake when you weren't a hundred percent sure you could stay afloat. It was sink or swim now. Time to take the plunge and get on with it.

Hank's kennels were heated in the winter

and air-conditioned in the summer, but of course it was cooler in the kennels than it would have been in the house. Pat slipped off her jacket so her arms were free, and she was immediately glad she'd put insulated underwear on under her shirt.

"Ah, here's our girl," she crooned, gently petting and soothing the agitated animal. Princess lay in her whelping box, but her big dark eyes were anxious. "What's wrong with her, Hank? Why are you worried about complications?"

"It's just taking too long. I'm afraid there may be a dead fetus slowing things down."

"So what can we do?"

"Nothing but wait right now. Look, Pat, maybe I shouldn't have bothered you, but I know how much you love animals, and you can see how nervous Princess is. I thought maybe you'd be able to calm her down a little." He lowered his eyes shyly. "You're a woman. You know what she's going through."

"I'll do my best," Pat promised, her hand gently stroking the dog's swollen belly. "She's one of your favorites, isn't she?" Pat looked up at Hank, and her heart felt like it did a flip in her chest when she saw the look in his eyes. But it wasn't for Princess, it was for her.

Hank met her gaze for a moment, then

turned away. "Yeah," he mumbled. "She's my favorite."

The afternoon wore on as Princess labored with no visible results. "Can't you try another vet?" Pat asked worriedly. The bitch was tired, and that was a bad sign. There had to be something they could do to help her.

"I'll go make some calls," Hank said. "Will you be okay here until I get back?"

"Sure, but bring some warm milk, will you? I think Mama needs a little nourishment."

Once Hank had gone Pat began to croon softly to the laboring bitch. From time to time Princess would strain as though trying to force her unwilling babies from her body, but nothing seemed to be happening, and Pat's concern escalated. Hank took such good care of all his dogs. What could have gone wrong?

Her back started to ache from bending over and she briefly straightened up to ease the kink. At that moment, Princess stood up, hunched over and strained mightily. Pat's adrenaline started to pump. Was this it?

As she watched in wonder, a tiny pup enclosed in a mucus-like sac slid from Princess's body. She waited, as Hank had instructed her to do, to give the bitch a chance to do what nature intended. But Princess was weary, and she lay back down without even glancing at the pup. Pat hesitantly reached for the pup. It was still in the sac and she knew she had to break the sac and help it breathe. It was a good thing she'd paid attention when Hank had explained the whelping process to her.

In a second she'd torn the sac, but the tiny pup didn't move, and a terrible feeling of foreboding swept over Pat. Was this the dead fetus that had given Princess so much trouble?

Just then Hank rushed in. He saw the tiny gray-looking pup and shook his head sadly. "It's no use, Pat. That one didn't make it, but look, Princess is straining again!"

And strain she did, this time to bring forth a pup that she promptly took care of in the way nature had intended. She chewed at the sac until it tore, then proceeded to lick the tiny pup all over until it wriggled and squealed in protest.

"This one is alive!" Pat cheered. "Oh, Hank, it's okay!"

Hank saw the high color in Pat's face, the joy in her eyes, the triumph in her softly curved lips. His own heart rejoiced. This was no high-society, well-heeled widow. This was Pat. His Pat, unless he was stupid enough to scare her off again. He reached out and touched her cheek, momentarily stunned by the velvety softness.

"It's a miracle!" Pat whispered, watching in

amazement as princess almost effortlessly delivered four more perfect puppies. And all of them, except the first little mite, seemed strong and healthy.

It wasn't until the last pup was delivered and Hank bent to care for Princess, that Pat realized he'd actually touched her. She put her hand up to the spot on her cheek, and the warmth was still there. Something inside her tingled as she crouched beside Hank, watching as he gently cleansed the bitch, then offered her warm milk.

"Good job, Princess," he said tenderly. "You're a real good mama. You've got five pretty little babies."

Princess accepted Hank's praise and shifted so the pups, all clean and dry now, could begin to nurse.

Hank stood up and helped Pat to her feet. "That was a close call. I was afraid I was going to lose Princess."

Pat delighted in the feel of Hank's arm as it rested on her shoulders. "Birth is a miracle, isn't it?" she asked softly. "But does this sort of thing happen often? The stillbirth, I mean?"

Hank nodded. "Now and then, and we never really know why. Anyway, all's well that ends well. How can I thank you for your help, Pat?"

Pat cocked her head and pretended to consider. "Maybe you could start by coming back to my house and helping me eat the Thanksgiving dinner I prepared. After all, now you do have something to be thankful for, don't you?"

Hank grinned and gave Pat a little squeeze. "More than you know, Pat. More than you know."

A half-hour later, as Pat hastily set another plate at the table and put the finishing touches on her dinner, she looked over at Hank. He was uncorking the wine he'd insisted on bringing, and the harsh lines in his face had softened.

"It was almost like being in the stable . . . almost a religious experience, wasn't it? With the snow falling outside and the laboring mother."

Hank smiled. "Every time one of my dogs gives birth it's like that for me, Pat. I never get over the miracle of it." He grinned and sniffed appreciatively. "And speaking of miracles, you've come a long way in the kitchen, haven't you?"

Pat nodded. "Like I said, cookbooks can work wonders. Now, come on. Let's sit down and eat. I'm starved!"

The meal was every bit as delicious as Pat had hoped. The chicken was moist and tender. The creamed cauliflower was perfect, and her gravy was smooth and tasty.

"On a score of one to ten, this meal rates an eleven," Hank said, pushing his plate away with a groan. "Five stars, Pat. Definitely!"

"Thank you. I'm glad you agreed to share it with me. I really wasn't looking forward to eating all alone."

She busied herself clearing the table then, almost afraid to look at Hank. The meal was over. Would he leave now? Was this the end?

"Pat? Can you stop all that busy work for a minute and listen to me?" Hank asked, coming up behind her and circling her waist with his strong arms. "I've been a stubborn old fool. Can you forgive me? Do you think maybe we could start over? Take things slow and easy, one step at a time, and really get to know each other this time."

Pat shivered. This was what she'd wanted, what she'd prayed for. That Hank would at least give them a fair chance. "I'd like that," she said, slowly turning in his arms until they were face-to-face. They were closer than they'd ever been. There had always been so much between them, her half-truths, his wife, but now suddenly all the barriers were down. Nancy had walked out on Hank. She didn't deserve to be counted as his wife, and now that Hank knew who Pat really was, now that he could accept her as she was, there was nothing left to separate them.

"I like you, Hank Richards," she said softly, lifting her face for the kiss she knew would come. "I *really* like you."

Too soon to say love, but that was all right. Good things were worth waiting for.

"I *really* like you, Pat Melbourne," Hank murmured, his voice warm and husky. "And I'd *really* like to kiss you. I've been waiting for the right moment, and I think this is it."

"Then shut up and do it," Pat suggested, closing her eyes.

Another miracle, Pat thought, letting Hank's warmth seep into her bones, letting the strength of his hands soothe away all her troubles, letting the hard bulk of his body shelter her. There were no skyrockets, no brilliant flashes of light, but this was so much better than that youthful frenzy. It was so much stronger. She leaned into Hank, letting her body mold itself against him, letting him feel the contours of her femininity, as she delighted in his hard masculinity. This was the way it was supposed to be. Two souls blending into one, two hearts beating next to each other. Two minds making the best of both.

"Whew!" Hank said, when he finally released her. "That was even better than I thought it would be. So much for anticipation!"

Pat smiled, her fingers splayed against his chest, her eyes damp with happiness. "And it's only just begun," she said.

"I haven't done a bit of Christmas shopping," Pat complained a few days later. "I don't know where the time has gone."

Pete grinned. "See how time flies when you're having fun?"

Pat made a mock swipe at his head. "Some fun," she said, looking around at the piles of sawdust and bits of lumber scattered everywhere. "Do you think this will ever get done?"

"They promised December first," he said. "I think it looks worse than it really is. What is it you're always saying about it being worth all the aggravation in the end?"

"I know, I know. It's just that some days I feel like the workmen are going backward, you know?"

"They're doing okay," Dale said, coming into the room with three containers of fresh coffee. "Here. Sip and be rejuvenated."

"Thank you, thank you," Pat said. She'd been grooming dogs all morning. Three of their adult dogs were going to new homes this afternoon, and she wanted them to look their best.

"Rough morning, Pat?" Pete teased.

She nodded. "Rougher on me than them, I think. Look at me. I'm wetter than the dogs!"

"That's what I like, a woman who gets into her work," Dale joked. "Seriously, Pat, the pups look great. Their new owners won't be able to resist them."

"That's the plan," Pat said. "Our campaign to get folks to adopt older pets seems to be working, doesn't it?"

"Thanks to your efforts," Dale said. "Say, how did your sister make out with her little dog?"

"Celia? Oh, she's as happy as a June bug. She gave the pup some outlandish name I can't even pronounce and she's spoiling him rotten. That is definitely a story with a happy ending."

"Well, we can use as many of those as we can get," Dale said. "Lord knows we've seen enough of the other kind."

And that was what they couldn't afford to forget, Pat thought. Things were going good now, but they had to keep up the momentum, and they had to educate people on the importance of spaying and neutering their animals. It was the only way to keep the pet population manageable.

She and Hank ate chili for dinner that night, seated at the kitchen counter with pencils and pads beside them.

"So, it's settled. We head for the city to shop bright and early Saturday morning, right? We really can't wait much longer, Hank. The stores will be sold out."

Hank had a vaguely troubled look in his dark eyes, and suddenly Pat had a flash of insight.

"Let's not buy each other gifts. Hank, How about we donate what we would have spent to our favorite charities?"

Hank's relief was almost palpable. "You really want to do that?"

"I love the idea," Pat said honestly. "There's nothing I need right now. I have all the important things."

"I'll second that," Hank said, reaching up to touch her cheek. "I'll definitely second that."

"So, I won't be arriving until the twenty-third, Mother. Is that all right?" Ashley asked.

"That's perfect," Pat said. She'd been worrying about getting everything ready for Christmas, and she'd been almost hoping that Ashley wouldn't arrive until the last minute.

"Wait until you see what I bought you, Mother," Ashley said, sounding very young and eager. "I know you're going to love it. I got it in California and . . ."

"Whoa! Don't tell me any more. You never could keep a secret, even when you were little."

"All right, I'll hush," Ashley said. "But I'm excited. This is going to be a good Christmas, I think." Then Ashley's voice changed, became thick with unshed tears. "But I'll miss Daddy."

"I know, hon," Pat said softly. "I know." But it was going to be a wonderful Christmas, Pat thought, carefully replacing the telephone in its cradle. The only thing missing would be Cliff. He couldn't come home. His first show was only weeks away and he was, as he put it, "painting like a maniac." And maybe that was for the best, Pat thought. Under the circumstances maybe it was best that she and Ashley have this time alone to work through the remaining barriers in their relationship. Of course they wouldn't be completely alone all of the time. Celia and Jake would be on hand from Christmas eve until the 26th, when they would have to go back home and remodel their house. Plans for a small day-care center were in the works and Celia was twenty pounds lighter than when she last visited. And of course Hank would be on hand to help them celebrate.

Pat bit her lip as she mixed dry and canned dog food for Ink and Spot, and set out a dish of kitten kibble for Cat. She had no idea how Ashley would respond to Hank, but she was done with lies and evasions, and besides, Ashley was an adult woman, not a fragile child. She was old enough, and should be mature enough to realize that her mother was entitled to a life of her own.

When the animals were all fed and content, Pat sat down with her Christmas list. Shirts, socks, and underwear for Cliff, as well as a check so that he could buy whatever he needed on his own. For Ashley she planned to buy a pretty piece of jewelry, something to symbolize their new, closer relationship. And of course, pretty clothes. No young woman ever had enough pretty clothes, Pat thought fondly, not even famous models. And perfume. There was a new scent on the market that sounded as though it would be perfect for Ashley. It was advertised to be light, yet sophisticated and provocative.

Celia would be a delight to shop for this

year. With her newly svelte figure, Pat had all kinds of ideas for gifts. And Jake; dear, sweet Jake. Every year, for as long as he had been married to her sister, Pat had bought Jake a box of cigars along with his other gifts. She chuckled, wondering what would happen if she broke tradition and did something different.

Pat smiled as she absently chewed on her eraser. Dale and Pete were no problem. With all their "heavy dates" she had decided to buy them each fragrance gift sets. And for Pete there was also a book on animal training. Dale rated a miniature Corvette, the car he someday hoped to own.

And that, Pat thought, brought her to Hank. Even though they were donating to their favorite charities in lieu of gifts for each other, she wanted to buy him some small token of her affection, but what?

Leaning her head back against the sofa, Pat briefly closed her eyes. What could she buy Hank that would not be intimidating, and yet show him how deeply she cared? When nothing came to mind after a few minutes, Pat gave up. All she could do for now was wait for inspiration to strike.

But wasn't this part of the fun of Christmas, wondering and worrying over just the right gift? Hurrying and scurrying to get everything done in time.

Pat sobered. It was, as Ashley had pointed out, their first Christmas without Clifford. Under ordinary circumstances, if she had been a sincere, grieving widow, there was no way she would have invited another man to share this time with her and her family. But she wasn't grieving, at least not the way Ashley was. Clifford's infidelity had seen to that. She was sorry Clifford had died. He should have had more time, but even if he had lived, they probably would have parted once Pat found out about his mistress. She couldn't have stayed quiet and lived with that.

Shaking her head, and chasing the gloomy thoughts away, Pat stood up and put her list in a safe place. She would add to it as inspiration struck, and it would, no matter what, be a very good Christmas.

"All right, all right, let's get this show on the road," Hank said, taking Pat by the elbow and firmly propelling her to the door on Saturday. They had arranged with another neighbor to look in on the animals while they were gone, but Pat still felt a pang when she saw Ink and Spot's big sad eyes.

"I hate to go out and leave them," she admitted sheepishly. "Isn't that silly?"

Hank chuckled. "It's your maternal instincts. And the fact that animals, like human kids, know just how to lay a guilt trip on you. They'll be fine, Pat. Paul will let them out and make sure they have food and fresh water."

Laughing, Pat hurried to keep up with Hank's long strides. "I know, and this is really the last chance we'll have to shop. Did you make out a list like I told you?"

Hank's face clouded as he helped Pat into her minivan and went around to the driver's co-side. "Nobody to make a list for," he mumbled, fumbling with the key. "Every time I send Becky or Laurie a present, they send it back."

"Maybe you should take them gifts instead of sending them," Pat suggested. "Haven't you ever thought about that?"

Hank's features twisted, and for a moment his face was a mask of agony, then anger lit his eyes and he turned to Pat.

"For Christ's sake, let it go, Pat! What are you trying to do, ruin the entire day? You're the one with the family to shop for, so let's just concentrate on that, okay? Just leave me out of it!"

For a moment Pat was tempted to tell Hank to turn the van around and take her home. What was bugging him anyway? She'd never heard him shout like that.

But then, as she dared to peek at his stiff, stern profile, she caught a glimpse of the pain underneath. His estrangement from his daughters hurt him deeply, and probably more now, at this time of year, than any other. And it was something he had to work out on his own, without any help from her or anyone else.

In a few minutes, as the car radio played Christmas music, Pat watched Hank visibly relax. She let her breath out in relief. Good, now they could start over and have a nice day.

She began telling him about Celia's plans for a day-care center, and how excited Jake was at the prospect of working again.

"I suppose some people just can't retire gracefully," she said lightly, "But Jake was a wonderful father. I know he'll enjoy working with children again."

"It's good to keep busy," Hank said quietly. "I wouldn't know what to do without my work and my dogs."

But you still need your children, Pat thought. There's a big hole that needs to be filled. She fell silent, thinking.

Keep snapping at her like that, old boy, Hank chided himself, sneaking a look at Pat's solemn profile, and you'll be all alone again, just the way you were before she came into your life. You'll get up in the morning and go to work, you'll tend to your dogs, you'll go to sleep and do it all over again the next day, with no one to share with. No one to care if you live or die.

Hank wriggled uncomfortably. He was being morbid and he knew it, and he rarely ever thought this way. Usually he accepted life as it happened, and he didn't complain. But now, since he'd known Pat, everything was different. He was wanting things he'd stopped wanting a long time ago, needing things he'd never thought to need again. It was wonderful and terrible at the same time. And he still needed to find Nancy. He had a private detective trying to find her, but it was expensive and he didn't know how long he could continue. And until he found Nancy and ended that chapter of his life, what could he offer Pat?

Oh hell, what could he offer her anyway? If he did divorce Nancy, he'd probably have to give her half the house. That meant he'd have to sell and divide the proceeds. What would he do with his dogs then? Starting over, that's what it would be. Hank shook his head. He wasn't sure he could.

"Look, I'm sorry I yelled," he said, gauging Pat's reaction from the corner of his eye. "Got out of bed on the wrong side, I guess. Let's start over, okay? Good morning, Pat. My name is Hank. Lovely day for Christmas shopping, isn't it?"

Pat laughed. "Apology accepted. Incident forgotten, and yes, it's a wonderful day for Christmas shopping!"

The drive into the city took less than ninety minutes, and after Hank parked the van in a parking lot, they were off and running.

And run they did. Hank had never seen a woman with so much energy when it came to selecting and buying gifts. Once or twice he felt a pang when he noted the price tags on some of the items Pat purchased for her daughter, but he swallowed his misgivings and tried to be a good sport.

"Really, Hank," Pat said, when he was finally able to persuade her to stop for lunch. "Don't you exchange gifts with any of your coworkers?"

Hank sipped his coffee, then shook his head. "Never have," he admitted. "And I don't see the sense in starting now."

Pat cocked her head and smiled. "Very sensible, I suppose," she said, "But not much fun. I love to shop for Christmas gifts."

Hank laughed. "I can see that. You're wearing me out, lady!"

"But isn't it fun?" Pat persisted. "The crowds, the Christmas music, the noise and confusion."

"It takes all kinds," Hank said, as the waitress brought him a thick roast beef sandwich.

They ate hungrily. Even Pat had to admit that she had worked up an appetite.

But when they finished, they both looked at the bags and packages sitting on the floor between them and shook their heads. "How about if I take these things back to the van and meet you in a couple of hours?" Hank suggested. "I do have a couple of things I'd like to look at and I'll be better off on my own."

Pat was surprised, but she readily agreed. Anything not to have to tote the things she'd already purchased for the rest of the day.

"Okay, three o'clock at the fountain in the center of the mall," she said. "How's that?"

"Perfect," Hank said, scooping up the packages. "See you then."

As soon as Pat got in the van that afternoon she slipped off her shoes. Hank turned on the heat and the welcome warmth swirled around them.

"Brrr, it's getting cold," Pat said. "Just that short walk to the car was enough to freeze my toes, not to mention the fact that I probably have a dozen blisters. Oh, thank goodness this holiday only comes once a year!"

Hank laughed and reached out to clasp Pat's hand. "I thought you thrived on all the hustle-bustle, lady," he teased. "Having second thoughts?"

"No, I do love it. I guess I just don't have the stamina I used to have." She looked at Hank through lowered lashes. "Do you think maybe I'm getting old?"

Hank squeezed her hand and his eyes said it all. "Not in my book, lady," he said huskily. "Not in my book!"

Between wrapping gifts, decorating the house, and baking, Pat had all but forgotten the most important thing, the Christmas tree.

"Do you really want to go to all that trouble?" Hank asked the next evening, as they sat in front of his fire, sipping wine. "Trees are messy. They drop needles all over the carpet. They turn brown and dry out and . . ."

"Knock it off, Scrooge!" Pat cried. "There's no way you can deter me. How can you have Christmas without a tree?"

"They're expensive," Hank added stubbornly. "Seems a shame to spend all that money on something you throw out in a couple of weeks."

"I don't intend to throw my tree out. I want to buy a real tree with roots, so I can plant it after the holiday is over. Will you go with me and help me pick one out?"

Hank sighed. "Do I have a choice?"

Pat laughed. "There's always a choice, pal, but you know you're dying to help me pick out a tree. Come on, admit it!"

Hank couldn't help laughing, and that was the most wonderful thing about Pat. She never allowed him to take himself too seriously. She simply wouldn't let him wallow in dark thoughts or self-pity.

"Well, I don't know about that, but I like being with you, so I guess that ties it."

"It sure does," Pat said happily, putting up her hand so Hank could help her to her feet. "Tomorrow?"

Hank groaned. "Tomorrow."

They finally found the absolutely perfect tree and it only took them two hours of tromping back and forth in the freezing cold. Hank decided he should be grateful for small favors.

"It was worth every minute," Pat insisted as

she thawed out her hands over the stove burner and waited for the milk to heat. "And now we can really enjoy our hot chocolate."

"Somewhere there's logic in that," Hank said, shaking his head. "I just have to find it."

Early on the morning of the twenty-second, Pat went to the shelter to deliver her gifts to Dale and Pete, then she was off to the television station to make an emotional appeal for people to adopt pets for the holiday.

"Can we open these now?" her two coworkers asked boyishly.

Pat shook her head. "Not on your life. Christmas is three days away. You'll just have to wait."

Both young men grinned, then Pete brought his hand out from behind his back. "We got something for you, Pat. It's not much, but we hope you like it."

"I'll love it," Pat said. "Look, I'd like to stay and chat, but I'm on my way to the television station. How do I look? Do you think I can persuade some of the viewers to come over here and take home a pet?"

"If anybody can do it, it will be you, Pat," Dale said.

Before she left Pat took a quick tour of the shelter. Almost all of the renovation was done, except for a few small jobs that would be completed after the first of the year. It looked good, if she did say so herself. There were thirty new runs, a large new infirmary where animals with medical problems could be kept separated from the other animals. And the lounge she'd designed for Dale and Pete was wonderful. Bright and cheerful, it boasted a brand new coffeemaker, a state-of-the-art microwave, and a small refrigerator. There was a small round table and four chairs, a comfortable sofa, and a television. At least now when Dale or Pete had to spend the night to care for sick or injured animals they could be comfortable.

Bob Penders, the manager of the local television station, turned out to be a confirmed animal lover just like Pat.

"I think this is a great idea," he said enthusiastically, as he and Pat discussed what she should say when they went in front of the cameras.

Pat's years of being on charity committees stood her in good stead when she sat in front of the cameras with Bob later that day. She'd expected to be tongue-tied, but instead the words flowed out of her as she talked of all the homeless, needy animals still at the shelter waiting for new owners.

"So," she concluded, "if you have room in your home and your heart for a loving, lovable pet, please visit the animal shelter today and give a homeless animal a Merry Christmas. You'll be glad you did."

"Perfect wrap-up, Pat," Bob Penders said, shaking her hand after they'd gone off camera. "If that doesn't send people flocking to your shelter, nothing will. Say, would you like to go for a drink? I'll be through here in an hour or so."

Pat smiled. Bob seemed like a nice man, but her heart was already spoken for. "Thanks, but I've got someone waiting for me at home. Merry Christmas."

Eleven

And then it was the morning of the twenty-third. Pat woke, feeling excited and eager. Everything was just about ready, and this afternoon Ashley would arrive. She had decided to wait to decorate the tree, remembering how Ashley always loved rooting through all the lovely ornaments Pat had collected through the years.

The tree stood in unadorned splendor in a corner of the living room, strings of lights and boxes of ornaments piled beneath it. And on the other side of the room were the brightly wrapped presents. The turkey was thawing in the refrigerator, and tomorrow, on Christmas Eve, Pat would make the stuffing and bake the pies.

Sliding her feet into furry scuffs and belting her thick velour robe, Pat hurried to the kitchen to start her coffee. Coffee, toast, and a glass of juice and she'd be ready to tackle the world, she told herself. Well, her small world at least. It was going to be a wonderful holiday.

As the coffee perked, Pat toasted two slices of whole wheat bread and spread them with sugar-free jam. And she remembered the Christmas holidays from the past.

Clifford had always considered all the fuss and preparations a lot of nonsense. He viewed the time spent away from his practice as a waste. When the children were small he did loosen up just a little, but then, as they grew up, he reverted back to his stiff rigidity. If he took part in the festivities at all, it was grudgingly, and Pat often felt as though she and the children annoyed him.

"But that was then, and this was now," she said aloud, once again shaking her head. Clifford was gone and she was alive. It was time to lay old traditions to rest and make new ones.

She huddled in her robe as she sipped hot coffee, waiting for the house to warm up. She really would have to think about a new heating system. Now that the weather was getting really cold, it seemed barely adequate. Pat looked around, wondering if she had room for a small fireplace. She enjoyed sitting in front of Hank's, watching the flames leap and dance, hearing the crackle and snap as the logs burned, feeling the warmth and glow on her face.

Yes, there was definitely something magical about a fire on a cold winter night. She smiled. And it didn't hurt to have a nice man by your side either.

Pat worked like a beaver all morning, polishing here, dusting there, wrapping one last gift she'd almost forgotten. When she finally broke for a quick lunch, she was tired but happy. She took her sandwich into the living room and sat by the window, looking across the road to Hank's place. He was working half a day, and he had promised to stop in as soon as he got home.

Dear Hank, she thought. A kind and loving man, a man she trusted and admired. She would make him a part of her family this holiday, but she couldn't help thinking that he needed his own two daughters at his side. She knew he grieved for the lost relationship, yet he seemed reluctant to even try and patch things up. She ached to help him, but he'd made it abundantly plain that he didn't appreciate her interference.

Finishing her sandwich, Pat mentally checked off the chores still waiting to be done.

Make up the bed in the guest room, now painted a soft shade of blue, with white woodwork and a delicate blue and white patchwork quilt on the bed. Blue was Ashley's all-time favorite color. Pat could hardly wait to see her reaction. She'd even unpacked one of the antique dolls Ashley collected and had set it in a small wicker rocking chair. Ashley's room. That's what it had become. Even though he hadn't actually said the words, Pat knew that Cliff's visits would be few and far between, especially if she was unable and unwilling to accept and welcome Doug in her home.

She turned on the radio, swirling the dial until she found a station playing Christmas carols. When the familiar old songs filled the room, banishing the last of the slight chill, she began to hum, and she pushed all the sad thoughts away.

"Open up! It's freezing out here!"

Hank was covered with snowflakes and Pat couldn't help laughing as she opened the door and stood back to let him in.

"You look like the abominable snowman," she teased. "Isn't the snow wonderful? Just in time. Maybe we'll have that white Christmas I've been hoping for."

"Hmm, are you planning to shovel the driveway, too?"

"Shovel?" Pat cocked her head to one side,

pretending to ponder the meaning of the strange word. "Shovel?" she repeated dumbly.

"I might have known," Hank grumbled, shrugging out of his coat and hanging it on the coat stand in the hall. "Where's that hot chocolate you promised me the other day? I'm frozen all the way from my nose to my toes."

"Come on, stop complaining. The hot chocolate will be ready in a jiffy. Did you finish everything up at the shop?"

"Yep. I'm clear until January second." He laughed. "All my coworkers think I'm nuts, taking my vacation this time of year, but I'm really looking forward to just bumming around and relaxing."

Pat nodded. "It will do you good, and your dogs will love having your company. I can't believe how big Princess's pups are getting. They're adorable."

Hank perched on a stool at the kitchen counter and nodded. "Another month and they'll be ready to go to their new homes. I've got some people coming by to see them after the first of the year."

Pat filled two mugs with hot chocolate and slid one of them across the counter to Hank. "How can you tell your pups are going to good homes?"

"I think I'm a pretty good judge of character," Hank said. "I try to feel out my people, see how much they really know about dogs, why they want a Samoyed for a pet. If I think they're just buying a pup on a whim, I do my best to discourage them. I tell them all the bad habits Samoyeds have, how much they like to chew, especially the first year. I lay it on extra thick about how much it costs to feed a big dog, and how expensive veterinarian care can be. In general, I paint a bleak picture. Usually they reconsider and make a fast getaway!"

"And if they don't?"

"Then if I really feel they wouldn't take good care of my pup, I'll just be honest and tell them I don't think a Samoyed is the right dog for them. And they're not right for everybody, you know. Some folks are better off with little dogs, or maybe a cat."

Pat grinned. "What about birds? Do you ever recommend birds as pets?"

Hank swung his gaze to the living room, where Tweetie was wildly hopping from perch to perch. "Only if the bird is not schizophrenic," he said dryly.

"Poor Tweetie," Pat said, sipping her hot chocolate. "No one understands him but me. He's just looking for attention, you know."

Hank smiled and reached out to cover Pat's hand with his own. "Lady, you are really something. Do you know that? Every time I think I'm getting to know you, I see a different side of you."

"Why? Because I think Tweetie has feelings and needs just like other animals?"

"No, because you care so damned much about every living creature you come in contact with. Is there anything you don't like?"

Pat nodded vigorously, enjoying the feel of Hank's fingers pressing hers. Hand-holding might not be very exciting, but it was wonderful just the same. "I do not like snakes," she said, "and I *hate* spiders. Does that shatter your image, sir?"

Hank laughed, stood up and pulled Pat off her stool and into his arms. "So, you're not perfect after all," he murmured huskily. "That must mean you're human."

Pat lifted her face, determined to show Hank just how human she really was. They were both feeling the tug and pull of strong physical attraction, but she sensed Hank holding back. What she didn't know was why. She knew he wanted to take things slow and get to really know one another, and that was what she wanted, too, but sometimes, especially during the last few weeks, she'd lain awake at night filled with vague and some not-so-vague yearnings. One of these days they were going to have to do something about it.

"You're standing under the mistletoe, Hank Richards. What are you going to do about it?"

Hank lowered his head until their lips were almost touching. "I guess," he whispered huskily, "I'm just going to have to do my duty and kiss you."

The first hesitant pressure of Hank's lips against hers sent shock waves of longing rocketing through Pat's body. Wow! she thought. Oh, wow!

It had been building for a long time, this ache of wanting, and Pat was slightly surprised at the strength of her desires. During the last years of her marriage, the physical side of her relationship with Clifford had dwindled. Of course, now she knew why, but at the time she had accepted it as normal for a couple married more than twenty years. Now, with Hank, it was almost as if she were young again, almost as though her hormones had received a drink from the fountain of youth. She felt them clamoring, felt the warmth spread slowly through every inch of her body. And then, as Hank pressed her ever closer, she knew that he felt it, too.

But before the heat consumed them, Hank was putting her away.

"Isn't Ashley due almost any minute?" he asked huskily.

Pat nodded dreamily. "Mmm, yes."

Hank grinned ruefully. He stepped back, putting a safe distance between them. "Then I think we'd better put a lid on it, as the kids say. I don't think you want your daughter to catch us in a compromising situation, do you?"

Pat's breathing quieted. Right now she wished Ashley's arrival was several hours away, but then she reminded herself that she and Hank had plenty of time, and that when they finally did come together as lovers it would be all the better for the anticipation.

She looked up at him, letting him read the promise in her eyes, and she was rewarded by Hank's quick intake of breath.

"Our time is coming, Pat," he promised softly.

When Hank went home to take care of the dogs, Pat checked the rich seafood chowder she was preparing for dinner. Jake had finally relented and given her his prized recipe.

Ashley adored seafood, and Hank was partial to it as well. With it Pat planned to serve a mixed green salad and crusty French bread. And for dessert, a light citrus sherbet.

Pat, old girl, you do amaze me, she congratulated herself, as the chowder's rich aroma wafted around her. You're smarter than the average bear!

Laughing softly to herself, Pat headed for the shower. She wanted to be dressed and pretty when Ashley arrived and Hank returned.

So far everything was working out well. She prayed that it would continue.

Ashley arrived just in time for dinner, and when she smelled the chowder her face broke out in a smile. "Mother, how did you manage all this," she asked, making a sweeping gesture with her arm. "All the wonderful decorations, and good food as well. And you look fantastic. I'll bet we could almost pass for sisters."

"Don't sound so surprised. I'm not a complete imbecile, you know."

"Of course you aren't," Ashley said quickly. "I never thought that. It's just that everything was so different when Father was alive. I thought . . . I guess I'm surprised at how well you're coping."

"We do what we have to do, honey," Pat said, as she finished setting the table. "Life goes on, even when we lose a member of our family."

"Speaking of," Ashley said, her voice taking on a tightness that made Pat feel incredibly sad, "what do you hear from Cliff?"

"His show is definitely on," Pat said, "and as you can imagine he's very excited about it. He wants me to come out for it."

"Oh. I see. Will you?"

"I don't know. I know I'll feel bad if I don't go. Cliff wants someone from the family to be there at this important time of his life, and I let him down so much in the past . . . I know I'll be eaten up with guilt if I don't go."

Ashley nodded. "I guess I can understand that, even though I'm not a mother yet, but can you handle it, Mom?"

"I don't know that either," Pat admitted. "Cliff wants me to meet his companion. I know he'll expect me to stay with them and I'm not sure if I can do that."

"Does he know you feel this way?"

"Yes. I told him, but I know he's hoping that in time I'll feel differently. I'm hoping so too."

"Cliff and I never really clicked, did we?" Ashley asked thoughtfully. "I mean, right from the start, when you brought him home from the hospital, there was a distance. I guess some of it was normal sibling rivalry, and the fact that he was a boy, the son all men are supposed to want so badly. I think I felt like his birth put me in second place, and not even a close second."

Pat filled the water glasses and shook her head. "That wasn't true, dear. Your father always doted on you. Cliff's birth didn't change that. You were always Daddy's little princess. If anyone was left out, it was your brother, because he could never measure up to his father's expectations."

"Daddy was pretty hard on Cliff, wasn't he?

The Publishers of Zebra Books
Make This Special Offer
to Zebra Romance Readers...

At the time I think I relished seeing the tension between the two of them, but now . . . well, that was pretty mean, wasn't it? And when I began to suspect that Cliff was gay, I was almost happy about it, because I felt like it made me the best again. Boy, I'm a pretty nasty piece of work, aren't I?"

"You're human, honey. But I'm the one who should have stepped in and called a halt when Cliff was growing up. I didn't, and your brother resented me for that for a long time. I think he's finally forgiven me, and that's why I don't want to let him down now."

Ashley was quiet for a moment, then she impulsively put her arms around her mother. "You'll do the right thing, Mom," she said. "I'm sure of it."

By the time Hank arrived for dinner, the snowstorm had intensified. Pat grinned as she brushed snowflakes from Hank's hair. It was definitely going to be a white Christmas.

"I'm glad you got here before the snow really started accumulating," Hank told Ashley, as the three of them sat down at the table. "I think this storm is going to be a doozy."

"Well, I don't have to be back in New York until the twenty-seventh, so I'm planning to settle in and just enjoy myself."

"Your Aunt Celia and Uncle Jake will be here tomorrow," Pat said. "I can hardly wait to see Celia's svelte new figure. And I told you she and Jake are starting a day-care center in their home, didn't I?"

"You did, and I guess that was your idea, too," Ashley said, eyeing her heaping bowl of chowder hungrily.

"Well, she just seemed to be at loose ends. I always thought she was the most cheerful, outgoing person I've ever known. To see her unhappy . . . well, it worried me."

"And now she's on top of the world, or at least that's how it sounds. It will be great to see her and Uncle Jake again." Suddenly, Ashley's face clouded. "Father never cared much for Jake, did he?"

Pat frowned. Ashley had apparently been doing a lot of soul-searching in the past few weeks. Perhaps it was just as well she realized that her father had been an imperfect mortal, but on the other hand, Pat hated to see all her daughter's illusions shattered.

"They were just very different, honey. You know how Jake is. He says what he thinks and let the chips fall where they may. As an attorney, your father learned early on to think before he spoke, to measure his words. I don't think he quite knew what to make of Jake."

"And that," Hank said, interjecting his point of view, "is what makes this old world of ours so fascinating. Every one of us is different and unique. We really wouldn't want it any other way, would we?"

"I suppose not," Ashley said, but there were question marks in her eyes, and Pat had a strong feeling that Ashley was just beginning to question a lot of things she had always taken for granted.

The meal was a huge success. Both Ashley and Hank heaped praise on Pat, until she finally called a halt.

"Enough," she cried. "I'm glad you enjoyed the chowder, but how about helping me clean up the kitchen so we can get down to some serious tree trimming?"

"I'm glad you waited for me, Mom," Ashley said, sounding almost shy. "Trimming the tree has always been one of the nicest parts of Christmas for me."

"I know," Pat said, putting her arm around Ashley's slender waist and hugging her. "I remembered."

With carols playing softly in the background, and the crisp scent of pine filling the air, Pat's small living room was transformed into a holiday miracle. Ashley and Hank laughed and chatted easily, as if they'd known each other in another life. Pat watched her daughter, her lips curved in a tender smile. Just a few short weeks earlier, she could never have envisioned this perfect scene, never have imagined Ashley relaxing and letting down her beautiful, dark hair. She was like a different person now. She was the daughter Pat had always hoped to have. But there were still problems to work through, and maybe it was all a part of living, a part of human growth. Maybe she and Ashley would still be struggling to understand one another a dozen years from now.

"I hope this tree will take root and live," Pat said, sniffing the clean pine scent appreciatively. "I never had a live tree before."

"Remember how hard Father tried to persuade you to buy an artificial tree?" Ashley asked. "He thought real trees were such a mess!"

"They are," Hank said, winking at Pat, "but your mother seems to think it's worth it."

"Of course it's worth it," Pat said indignantly, lovingly placing a somewhat tarnished silver angel on the tip of a branch. "And since Christmas only comes around once a year, why shouldn't we fuss a little?"

"Fuss away, Mom," Ashley said, exchanging an amused look with Hank. "This is your party."

And a party it turned out to be. When the tree was trimmed to everyone's satisfaction, Hank lit the lights and they sat on the floor in a semicircle to admire their handiwork. Pat had set up a small buffet table with a punch bowl filled with hot mulled wine and cinnamon sticks and a plate of cheese and crackers and slices of fruitcake. The smell of cinnamon mingled with the pungent pine, and when the radio blared "Joy to the World," Pat felt like joining in.

It was only when Ashley began to yawn that they realized just how late it was.

"Wow! That long drive did me in, I guess," Ashley said. "I think I better call it a night."

Hank got to his feet quickly. "Me, too, and I need to check on the dogs before I turn in." He smiled at Ashley, then turned to Pat. "Thanks for a wonderful evening. I'll remember this for a long time."

He made no move to kiss her, but then she hadn't expected him to, not with Ashley watching avidly.

"Good night, Hank. We'll see you tomorrow."

"Yes," Hank replied, "you certainly will."

"The room looks lovely, Mother," Ashley said, when Pat stopped at the guest room to say good night. "But you didn't have to go to all this trouble for me."

Pat smiled. "Why not? Blue is your favorite color, isn't it? And you are my only daughter, aren't you?"

"All right, I give up. I'm too sleepy to debate with you. In any case, thank you. I'm going to enjoy sleeping here."

Pat went to her own room, brushed her teeth, and slipped into her nightgown, all the while bathed in a contented glow. Everything was working out perfectly.

The next morning, as Pat and Ashley lingered over their coffee, they discussed sleeping arrangements. "I can take the sofa, Mother, and let Aunt Celia and Uncle Jake have the guest room. It won't be a problem."

"No, that's what I'm going to do, honey. The sofa is really very comfortable, and Celia needs a firm mattress. She's had trouble with her back for years."

"Well, I'll help you change the sheets in your room then," Ashley said. "And then . . . do we have time to bake some cookies?"

"I was just waiting for my cookie-making helper to arrive," Pat said, warm, sweet memories sweeping over her. Ashley at three, with an apron tied around her, standing on a chair so she could help roll out cookie dough.

Ashley sighed and finished her coffee. "Making cookies was always one of my favorite things. Especially the sugar cookies with the red and green sprinkles."

"The red and green sprinkles are in the cabinet and the sugar cookie dough is chilling in the refrigerator. I made it yesterday."

Ashley's happy smile turned into a grin. "Mom, you really are something else. This is going to be a great holiday."

But a moment later Ashley's happy expression melted into pain. "Except that . . ."

Pat nodded, not wanting to hear the words, but knowing Ashley needed to say them. "I know, dear," she said. "You miss your father."

Nodding, Ashley deliberately avoided meeting Pat's eyes. "It's funny, too, because he never really joined in our holiday preparations, did he?"

"Holidays just weren't his thing, hon. Not everyone enjoys all this fuss and fervor, you know."

Ashley nodded. "I'm glad you do, Mom."

By the time Celia and Jake arrived at three that afternoon, Pat was exhausted and exhilarated. She and Ashley had baked dozens of sugar cookies. The pies were cooling, one apple, one pumpkin. The stuffing was mixed and in the refrigerator, and Pat was absolutely amazed at her daughter's expertise in the kitchen.

"Exactly when did you learn about the culinary arts?" Pat demanded. "When you lived at home you didn't know a spatula from a fork!"

Ashley laughed. "I wasn't quite that bad, Mom, but you're right. I didn't know my way around a kitchen very well. Actually, it was one of the first things I did after I got my own apartment. I took a course in cooking, then I went on to baking and last fall I graduated from a gourmet cooking class."

"I am impressed," Pat said, "and here I am, so proud that I managed to read and decipher the instructions in a cookbook."

Ashley impulsively hugged her mother. "You're doing great, and don't forget, you had a late start. I'll bet you could catch up with me if you wanted to."

"Maybe, but I probably won't. I've got other fish to fry these days. My work at the shelter takes up a lot of my time."

Ashley finished peeling the last potato and nodded. "I know, and I think it's great that you're doing something you enjoy so much."

"As you are." Then, catching sight of the quick flash of pain that crossed Ashley's face, she sobered. "Aren't you enjoying your work anymore?"

"Oh sure," Ashley said. "It's just . . . well, it's all tinsel and glitter, you know? All the friends I've made . . . I'm never really sure if they're my friends or if they're just hanging around because I'm successful right now. What would happen if I fell from grace? Would all those so-called friends rally around me, or would they just quietly fade away? And then there's the pressure to stay thin and young looking."

Pat couldn't help laughing. "Ashley! You're twenty-eight years old. Surely you're not worrying about aging yet!"

"I have to worry about it, Mother, because after a certain point, I'm finished. My career will be over."

Pat sat down on a stool and rested her elbows on the counter. "You know I never really thought about that . . . about what it must be like for you to wake up every morning and realize you're a day older."

"Well, it's something I've had to accept," Ashley said calmly, "and I have to plan for the day when I'll be too old or too fat to model anymore."

"And what will you do when that time comes?" Pat asked.

"Well, hopefully I'll be married and have children. I'll have a family and who knows, maybe I'll open a gourmet bake shop or a catering service. How does that sound, Mom?"

"If that's what you want to do, it sounds marvelous, honey, but I still think that's a long way into the future."

"Maybe," Ashley said, "but I'll need to be prepared."

When the door chimes sounded Pat knew the time for mother-daughter confidences was past. From now on there would be laughter and merriment, eating and drinking, and all the festive trappings of a holiday. But there would be no privacy. She smiled. It had been a marvelous day. She and Ashley had been closer than she could ever remember. Her daughter was softer now, more understanding. A different girl. It was wonderful.

Twelve

"Celia, you look gorgeous! Doesn't she look wonderful, Ashley?"

Pat was amazed and gratified by the visible change in her sister. Celia's eyes were shining with happiness, her body was slimmer and trimmer than it had been in years, and even the trademark carrot-colored sausage curls were gone.

"My goodness, who did your hair? I love it!"

"Really?" Celia touched the soft, ginger-toned waves self-consciously. "I wore my hair the same way for so long . . . it was like losing an old friend. But Jake likes it, so I suppose that's all that matters."

"You bet I do," Jake said heartily. Then he reached out, clasped Ashley in his arms and swung her around in a circle. "And who is this big-city beauty? It can't be our little Ashley, can it?"

"Uncle Jake, you never change," Ashley said, beaming as she planted a kiss on his bald spot. "Aunt Celia, it's true. You look beautiful. It's so good to see you both."

Celia followed Pat into the kitchen while Ashley and Jake went into the living room to chat.

"Good heavens, what did you do to her, Pat? She's a different girl. Not that she wasn't always a beauty, but . . ."

"I know what you mean," Pat said. "She was a snotty little bitch, wasn't she?"

"Well, I wouldn't . . ."

"But I would, because it's true," Pat said. "I always loved her because she was my daughter, but I didn't like her very much. Since the last time we talked . . . well, she's undergone a metamorphose."

"I'll say! And I like her a lot better this way!"

"So do I," Pat said happily, giving her sister a quick hug.

"Is Hank coming over?" Jake asked, as they sat by the tree sipping hot spiced cider.

"He'll be here for dinner," Pat explained, "but he said he had something important to do this afternoon."

"Nice guy," Jake said. "I like him."

"Me, too," Ashley said, surprising everyone.

Pat smiled. "Then I guess it's unanimous, isn't it?"

Hank arrived just in time for dinner. He brought doggie biscuits for Ink and Spot, and a catnip mouse for Cat.

"Well, we know who rates with this man," Celia said, smiling. "Merry Christmas, Hank. It's nice to see you again."

"Same here. You're looking pretty spiffy these days, Celia. Old Jake must be treating you pretty good."

"Old Jake didn't have a thing to do with it," Celia said. "It was this lady right here. She's the one who pulled me out of my rut and got me back on track."

Hank's eyes lingered on Pat until she flushed. "Come on, all of you, lay off," she said. "It's time to eat. Is anyone hungry?"

With Ashley's help, Pat had prepared a delicious Beef Burgundy. With it there were tender baby carrots and browned potatoes. Ashley had prepared a spinach salad with hot bacon dressing, and baking-powder biscuits.

"A feast fit for a king," Jake said appreciatively. "I've been eating diet dinners lately right along with Celia. This is a rare treat."

"And when we go home we'll go right back to our regular routine, old fellow," Celia said, trying to look stern. "I'm not about to gain all that weight back."

Pat couldn't help noticing the tiny portions Ashley put on her plate. Of course. Ashley had to watch her weight even more carefully than the average person. Her career depended on it.

She wasn't sure she would have had the will-power to make the kinds of sacrifices Ashley was making. Basically, her career was her life. Her schedule revolved around the shoots she did. She had to be ready to pack up and leave town at a moment's notice. And sure it was exciting and glamorous, but like Ashley had admitted, there was also a lot of tarnished tinsel. Ashley's life wasn't any more perfect than anyone else's.

"How's your pup, Celia?" Hank asked, as Pat poured coffee and cleared the dinner plates.

"Mortimer? He's doing beautifully. He's already learned to sit up and roll over and . . ."

"Mortimer? I thought you named him . . . oh, I still can't pronounce it!" Pat cried.

"Neither could anyone else, so we changed his name," Celia said brightly. "Mortimer has a nice ring, don't you think?"

"Mortimer," Pat mumbled as she stacked the dishes in the dishwasher. "Mortimer." She shook her head.

Later, when they were all comfortably settled in the living room, Ashley asked Celia about her cousins. "Couldn't any of them get home for the holidays?"

Celia shook her head. "You know how Darlene is. She likes to be in her own home with the children, and I understand that. Some years Jake and I go there, but this year Jake didn't feel like such a long drive."

"Seems like you spend the whole weekend on the road," Jake grumbled.

"Anyway, Betty Lou was invited to go skiing with a good friend, so I told her to take advantage of the opportunity. She can visit us after the New Year."

"And Bruce?" Ashley prodded. "What about Bruce?"

"Bruce is . . . well, he's terrible busy this time of year, getting ready for tax time and all that. He just couldn't spare the time."

Pat saw the sadness in her sister's eyes and she ached to hug Celia. But then Hank jumped in and saved the day, and soon they were all laughing.

Later, when they all began to wind down, Hank spoke.

"I have a special gift I'd like to give Ashley," he said. "I'll go get it now, if I may."

"A gift for me?" Ashley looked surprised, and Pat was surprised. They hadn't discussed exchanging gifts, except to decide on what charities they wanted to donate to.

"Shouldn't we wait until morning?" Pat

asked. "That's when we usually open our gifts."

"I'm afraid this gift won't wait," Hank insisted.

"Then go get it before we all die of suspense," Celia prodded. "And hurry!"

While Hank was gone they all speculated, but no one could even begin to guess what the gift might be. Then the front door opened and Hank stepped inside, leading a fluffy white puppy behind him. Pat saw that it was one of the pups from Princess's last litter.

"What in the world?" Pat's hand flew to her mouth. Was Hank giving Ashley one of his pups? Would she want it? Her daughter had never shown much interest in animals, and even now she merely tolerated Ink and Spot.

"For me?" Ashley squeaked. She was out of her chair and kneeling on the floor before anyone could utter a sound. Gone was the beautiful, sophisticated model, and in her place was an eager, excited little girl.

The pup came right to her as if he was guided by radar.

"Oh my gosh! He's beautiful! Oh Hank! This is wonderful!"

The young woman who had always been so prim and fastidious, scooped the pup up in her arms and laughed with delight when it lapped her cheek with a tiny pink tongue. White dog hair covered Ashley's black dress in an instant, but she didn't seem to care. She was mesmerized by her present. She cuddled the pup the way she had once cuddled a rag doll, and she crooned to it the way a mother would croon to her child.

The four adults were also mesmerized. Only Hank was smiling, a hint of smug complacency in his eyes. The others were slack-jawed with amazement. It was a sight none of them had ever thought to see.

Celia leaned close and whispered in Pat's ear. "Are you sure that's really Ashley? I hear some of those modeling agencies do strange things. Do you think they sent us a clone?"

Pat burst out laughing, then she sobered as a new thought struck her.

"Ashley, how can you take care of a dog when you're always running off to shoots. I'd hate to see one of Hank's dogs in a boarding kennel."

Ashley smiled, and the radiance lit the whole room. "It's okay, Mom. I'll work it out. There's a woman in my building. She loves animals and she house-sits for some of the other tenants when they have to go away. I'm sure she'd sit for me and look after . . . hey, what am I going to name this fellow?"

"He is a she, Ashley," Hank said, "And I want you to be strictly honest with me. I'd like you to have this dog, but if it will make problems for you, I'll take her back with no hard feelings."

"Take her back? What are you, an Indian giver? No way, Hank! This is my dog now. You gave her to me, and I have a whole room full of witnesses." She laughed then, and suddenly Pat saw Ashley at seven.

Dark-haired, with deep, intelligent eyes, with the promise of mature beauty even then. She had dropped her favorite doll, and it cracked in a dozen places. Sadly, Pat had confirmed that it was beyond repair.

"But now I won't have anyone to love," Ashley had whispered, tears streaking her round cheeks.

Pat blinked. Ashley had something to love now, thanks to Hank. How had he known?

But she still felt she had to warn Ashley. "Honey, are you sure you have the time and patience to train a dog? Hank will be the first one to tell you that Samoyeds love to chew, especially until they get past the puppy stage, and are you sure they'll allow a pet in your apartment?"

"I'll manage, Mother," Ashley said, and now her tone was sharp and biting. "I'm an adult, you know. I'm not a little girl anymore."

Uh-oh, the wall was up again, Pat thought. Now she'd done it.

But a moment later the tenseness faded from

Ashley's face as she was properly christened by her new pet.

"Oh no! Oh, bad girl!" Ashley couldn't help laughing, and she looked up at Hank helplessly. "Now what do I do?"

Hank grinned. "Before or after you change your clothes?"

Hank took the pup for a walk while Ashley changed.

"I'd never have believed Ashley would get so excited over a dog," Celia said, "but she certainly seemed smitten."

"Yes, and then I had to ruin everything by sounding like a mother."

"Oh, Pat, don't be so hard on yourself. Why, anyone can see that you and Ashley have made great strides, but you can't expect everything to be perfect all the time."

"I guess you're right, but when she takes that haughty tone with me, I want to take her over my knee and spank her," Pat said.

"Don't forget," Celia said. "Clifford was her father. It's only natural there be a little of him in her."

"All set," Hank said, returning with the chastised pup. "Pat, if you'll give me some paper towels I'll wipe up the stain."

"It's already taken care of," Pat said.

"Well, it won't take long to train this pup. Samoyeds are very smart."

Ashley came skipping down the steps then, like she was closer to thirteen than thirty. "I decided what I'll name her," she told Hank. "How about Fancy Lady? I'll call her Fancy."

"Fancy Lady?" Jake cocked his head. "Sounds kind of honky-tonk to me."

"Oh, Uncle Jake! I like it. It suits her. She's going to be a very elegant lady when she grows up, aren't you, Fancy?"

The pup struggled out of Hank's grip and made a beeline for Ashley, and that clinched it. Fancy Lady it was. Hank's pup had a new owner, and a new name.

Reluctantly, Ashley allowed Hank to take Fancy back to the kennels until morning.

"I'll give you a crash course in dog training tomorrow," Hank promised. "And Samoyeds are smart. You'll be surprised how fast Fancy learns."

Pat walked him to the door. Hank stood there, with the puppy in his arms, looking perfectly bland and innocent.

"Hank Richards, why didn't you tell me what you had up your sleeve? I almost fell over when you walked in with this dog."

Hank grinned, looking so much like a mischievous little boy that Pat had to smile in return. "Isn't this what Christmas is all about? Surprises? Besides, I figured you'd try to talk me out of it, telling me Ashley was too busy to take care of a dog."

Pat nodded. "You're right. I would have. I still can't get over the way she reacted. I never even thought she liked animals."

"Probably didn't know she did herself," Hank said. "How could she, when she never had a pet?"

"Touché," Pat murmured, wondering what other surprises might be in store for her. "We'll be up bright and early tomorrow," she said. "I can never sleep in on Christmas morning. So get yourself over here in time for breakfast. Celia is doing the honors and she's promised it will be something special."

"I'll be here," Hank promised, then he bent down and kissed Pat.

A small pink tongue flicked out and lapped Pat's cheek, and she and Hank broke apart, laughing. "So much for private, intimate moments," Pat said.

By the time Pat returned to the living room, she saw that the tree lights were out. Everyone had gone off to bed. She smiled. Ashley had laid out bedding on the sofa for her, and her nightgown and robe was there as well. This holiday was yielding one surprise after another.

Pat woke before any of her guests the next morning. Wrapping herself in her warm robe, she slid her feet into furry scuffs and padded out to the kitchen to start coffee. While the coffee perked Pat turned on the tree lights and removed her bedding from the sofa. Unless she was mistaken, Ashley would be up any time now, and Celia and Jake would not be far behind.

Enjoying the early morning solitude, Pat sat down and briefly closed her eyes. Later, after everyone had opened their gifts, she would find a moment to call Cliff. She couldn't let the day go by without wishing her son a Merry Christmas.

Pat shivered, wishing she could absolve herself of the ambivalent feelings toward her son. A part of her wished he were here beside her right this moment, but another dark part of her was glad he was far away. Glad she didn't have to deal with the push-pull of the emotions Cliff evoked in her. No matter what she told herself, no matter how many books she read, there was still a core of grief and disappointment deep inside her mother's heart. And the fear. Dear God, the fear simply would not go away! And it was worse when Cliff was where she could see and hear him.

"Mother? Merry Christmas."

Ashley stood in the doorway in a pale blue nightgown and robe, her face washed clean of makeup, her beautiful dark hair hanging long and loose.

She held out her arms. "Merry Christmas,

baby," she said thickly. "Merry Christmas."

Then Celia and Jake came stumbling into the room, and there were hugs and greetings all around. Pat brought coffee and mugs into the living room, and they decided they would open gifts before breakfast.

"Mother, I don't know what to do about Hank," Ashley said, pulling Pat aside.

"How do you mean?"

"Well, he's giving me that beautiful puppy, and all I got him was a plaid flannel shirt. I mean, I really don't know him that well and . . . well, I didn't think an expensive gift would be appropriate."

Pat had to smile. There were times when Ashley reminded her strongly of Clifford, but where once that would have annoyed Pat, now she was able to smile. Perhaps her daughter had received the best qualities of both her parents.

"Hank will love a flannel shirt," Pat said. "And he doesn't give his dogs away casually. I think you should know that."

"I do," Ashley said, "and that makes Fancy all the more special."

"All right, let's get this show on the road," Jake called. "Where's Hank?"

As if on cue there was a knock on the door. Ashley beat Pat to the door.

"Oh, look at Fancy! She's all dressed up for

the holidays!"

Indeed she was. Hank had apparently brushed the pup until her white coat gleamed with sparks of silver, and around her neck was a huge red bow.

Leaving Ashley on her knees on the floor with Fancy, Hank moved to Pat and drew her into his arms in front of everyone. "Merry Christmas," he whispered huskily, his lips nuzzling her hair. "Are we under the mistletoe?"

Pat shook her head. "No," she said. "But don't let that stop you."

And it didn't. But in deference to their interested audience, it was a soft, gentle kiss, with just the barest hint of the hunger beneath.

"Okay, break it up," Jake insisted. "It is time to open presents. Grab a cup of coffee, Hank, and join in."

For the next hour and a half there was laughter and jokes and as much family warmth as anyone could reasonably expect. Pat stood back for a moment, assessing her group. Hank had quietly moved in as though he'd always been a part of their family, as if there had never been any question of his belonging. Celia and Jake were having a grand time, and Ashley reminded Pat of the little girl she'd once known, before that little girl had grown into a woman and lost some of the magic and wonder of life.

For a moment the ghosts of Christmases past

rose up to haunt Pat. There were good memories, and there were some not so good. The inevitable impatience Clifford had always shown after the first blush of holiday goodwill faded. The football gear he insisted on buying for Cliff the year the boy practically begged for an art set. The expensive jewelry Pat always received, which had almost always been chosen by Clifford's secretary.

There had always been warmth, because Pat had insisted on it, but there had been none of the ease, the spontaneity that graced this special day. Pat knew it was the very best Christmas she had enjoyed in many, many years.

"If you'll all excuse me I have something I have to take care of," she said quietly, hating to break the magical spell, but knowing it was time. "Celia, are you about ready to start that fabulous breakfast you've been bragging about?"

"I'll help you, Aunt Celia," Ashley volunteered, "if Hank will baby-sit Fancy." Ashley grinned disarmingly at Hank and the deal was sealed.

Pat quietly went into her bedroom and closed the door. It would have been nice for Ashley to wish her brother a Merry Christmas, but she'd been afraid to ask.

It took a few minutes to get through to Cliff, and then, once again his phone was answered by an unfamiliar male voice.

Pat swallowed. "May I speak to Cliff, please? This is his mother."

"His mother? Well, Merry Christmas, Mrs. Melbourne. I'm Doug."

"Doug? Merry Christmas to you, too. Is Cliff there?"

"Sure. Just a minute and I'll get him."

Pat heard muffled voices, then Cliff was on the line.

"Merry Christmas, Mom," he said. "It's great to hear from you. Are you having a nice holiday?"

"Wonderful," Pat said. "Your Aunt Celia and Uncle Jake are here. They send their best."

"You've got company. That's good. Uh, what about Ashley? Is she with you?"

"Yes, she is, and she seems to be having a wonderful time."

"Good. I don't suppose she sent her best, did she?"

"Cliff, I . . ."

"Hey, it's okay, Mom. I didn't really expect it. I'm just glad you called. Will you tell Celia and Jake I said hello?"

"Of course. And thank you for the lovely sweater, dear. The color is perfect."

"Glad you liked it, Mom. Doug helped me pick it out."

"Oh. Well, I'd better go. Celia is making

breakfast and she may need some help in the kitchen."

Cliff sounded disappointed. "Sure. Thanks for calling, Mom. It means a lot. I love you."

"And I love you, son," Pat said softly. "Goodbye."

Tears stung her eyelids as she carefully replaced the receiver.

It was hard. So hard. Sometimes she wasn't sure she really could deal with it.

Celia outdid herself with breakfast. There was a tray of the delicious miniature cinnamon buns she was famous for, a large platter of fluffy scrambled eggs, seasoned with cheese and herbs. There was crisp bacon, small, perfectly browned sausages, and a tray of fresh fruit.

They all ate like stevedores, and when the meal was over, Hank and Jake insisted on cleaning up the kitchen.

Taking mugs of coffee into the living room, the three women made a fast getaway before the men changed their minds.

"Well, you've certainly got a beautiful dog there," Celia told Ashley. "If you treat her right, she'll be your best friend."

"The only pets I ever had when I was growing up were goldfish," Ashley reminisced. "They were pretty, but not very affectionate."

"Dogs give unconditional love," Pat said. "I

should have insisted your father let me get Cliff a puppy that year he asked for one. I still can't believe I was so dense and unfeeling. Instead of the pet he wanted, Clifford bought his son a hunting rifle, when the very thought of killing an animal made Cliff sick."

Ashley was silent, and Pat knew she had her own memories. She hadn't meant to bring up past hurts, but the words had just slipped out.

"Father wanted things his way," Ashley said quietly, stroking the sleeping puppy on her lap. "I'm sure he didn't mean to be cruel. He just thought he knew what was best for all of us."

"I'm a little worried about Jake," Celia said, casting a look toward the kitchen. They could hear the muffled sounds of men's laughter, mingled with the sound of running water. "He tires so easily lately. Do you think his color is off?"

Pat forgot all about her late husband as she tallied the changes she had noted in her brother-in-law recently. "I did think he seemed a little quieter the past couple of days. Has he had a checkup recently?"

Celia shook her head worriedly. "You know how men are. They think they're immortal. Whenever I say anything he insists he's fine, and says I'm imagining things."

"How old is Uncle Jake?" Ashley asked.

"He'll be sixty-nine on his next birthday,

which is next February, but he's always been remarkably healthy. Why, I can't remember him ever taking time off from work during all those years at the postal department."

"Nag him into getting a checkup, Celia," Pat said. "He may just need some vitamins or something, but you don't want to take any chances."

"I hate to nag," Celia said, "but if I have to, I will."

The rest of the day passed pleasantly. It was everything Pat could have hoped for.

The traditional turkey dinner was wonderful. Everyone ate until they were stuffed, and then, while Celia and Pat cleaned the kitchen and Jake relaxed, Hank and Ashley took Fancy for a walk.

"Ashley certainly seems to like Hank," Celia said, rinsing plates and stacking them in the dishwasher. "I'm surprised. I thought she'd be all bent out of shape when she found out you had a . . . boyfriend."

"Hank is not really a boyfriend, Celia," Pat said quickly. "We're friends and maybe someday it will be more, but . . ."

"Has he found his wife yet?" Celia asked bluntly. "Seems to me that's the first thing he'd do if he was entertaining any thoughts about . . ."

"He has a detective working on it, but you

know how that kind of thing goes. And it's expensive. He's not sure how long he can afford to continue the search."

"And if he doesn't find her? Where does that leave you?" Celia asked bluntly. "I know you think I'm hopelessly old fashioned, Pat, but . . ."

Pat impulsively hugged her sister, wanting to chase the look of worry off Celia's face. "I wouldn't want you any other way, darling," she said, "but what Hank and I ultimately decide to do will be our business and no one else's. And I won't be seeking permission at this time of my life, Celia. Not from you or anyone."

"Oh. Oh, dear, you have changed, haven't you?"

Pat laughed. "A little. I'm pleasing myself these days, Celia. I think it's time."

Hank gave Ashley some tips on dog training, and showed her the best way to teach a young pup how to walk on a leash.

"Samoyeds are very smart, but they are also known for their stubbornness," he explained. "So what you have to do is show Fancy right from the start, that you are the boss. If you do that she'll respect you and be easier to control."

"I think there is a dog training school near my apartment," Ashley said. "Do you think that might be a good idea?"

"Sure. Can you fit it into your schedule? I meant what I said last night, Ashley. Please don't feel you have to accept Fancy if she's going to be a problem. I guess I just love dogs so much, I think everyone should have one."

Ashley smiled. Then she reached out and laid her hand on Hank's arm. "Fancy is the very best present I ever received," she said, "and you don't have to worry. I'm going to take good care of her. You'll see. She'll be the best loved, most pampered pooch in the country!"

"Well, don't worry about the pampering. Just love her. That's what pets want, you know. Lots of love."

"Speaking of," Ashley said, almost casually, "are you in love with my mother?"

Thirteen

Hank stopped walking. He tried to gather his thoughts, tried to decide what to say and how to say it. Ashley didn't seem to hold any malice toward him, but from the things Pat had told him he knew that the mother-daughter relationship had not always been what Pat wanted it to be. Right now things seemed to be smoothing out between the two women, but he was afraid that one careless word on his part would blow everything sky high.

He laughed nervously. "Now that is definitely a loaded question, young lady. Your mother and I haven't known each other all that long and . . ."

"It doesn't take years, or even months to fall in love, Hank, even for senior citizens like you and Mom." Ashley grinned mischievously, and Hank let his breath out slowly in relief.

Whatever Ashley was doing, it wasn't meant

to be an entrapment. Perhaps it was just genuine concern for her mother. Still, Hank knew he wasn't prepared to discuss his deepest feelings with this young woman, sweet though she was. What he and Pat felt for one another was private.

He smiled and patted Ashley's hand to take the sting out of his words. "I'm not willing to talk about that right now, Ashley. I hope you understand."

For a moment Ashley looked almost petulant, but then she smiled. "Put me in my proper place, didn't you? All right, Hank. I'll back off, but don't hurt my mother, understand? She's a good person."

Hank impulsively squeezed Ashley's hand. "I couldn't agree more."

By nine o'clock that evening they were all yawning.

"I think we should make it an early night," Pat suggested, "before we all fall asleep sitting here."

Jake sighed with relief. "I was trying to figure out how to make a graceful exit," he said. "I guess I'm just not as spry as I once was. I'm beat."

Pat glanced at her brother-in-law with some concern. Jake had always been the life of the party, the last one to give up. Now, Pat thought he had a rather odd color, and there were very pronounced circles under his eyes.

They all said their good nights. Pat's houseguests headed upstairs while she walked Hank to the door.

There was a sudden, awkward silence as they faced each other. Then Hank spoke, his voice a husky whisper.

"This was the nicest Christmas I've had in a long, long time, Pat, and all because of you. You're a very special lady."

Pat tried to laugh, but it came out sounding like a sob. "And you, Hank Richards, are one hell of a man," she murmured. Her arms were at her sides, and she waited, half eager, half fearful, for Hank to draw her into his arms.

But he didn't. Instead, he gently tipped up her chin with his fist and touched his mouth to hers for a fleeting second.

"Good night, Pat, and thank you," he said. "You'll never know how much this time meant to me."

Then he was gone, striding across the frozen lawn, stopping at the roadside to make sure the way was clear, then continuing the trek to his own home, his own bed.

Pat quietly closed the door and leaned against it, all the strength suddenly going out her legs as she imagined what her life would be like without Hank. It wasn't that she couldn't manage on her own. She'd proved she was perfectly capable of doing that, but she didn't want to manage alone. She wanted someone to share her feelings with, someone she could confide in. Someone who would stand by her, through good news and bad. She didn't, she realized, want to spend the rest of her life flying solo. But was Hank willing to be her copilot, or had his unhappy marriage made him afraid to fly?

Finally, knowing she'd collapse if she didn't get into bed soon, Pat doused the lights and checked the door lock. Then she spread her bedding on the sofa and laid down.

Hank cared about her. She didn't doubt that. But they had never discussed anything deeper than the fact that they were strongly attracted to one another. In her heart, Pat knew it was merely a matter of time until she and Hank became lovers. What would their lovemaking mean to Hank? Would it be just a pleasant interlude of physical satisfaction? Pat squirmed uncomfortably. Lord knew she was ready for some of that herself! But she also wanted more. She wanted a piece of Hank, part of his heart, maybe even a bit of his soul. Was he willing to give that up . . . to risk love again . . . at this time of his life?

Pat turned on her side and sighed. She remembered a quote she had once read. "Love's like the measles—all the worse when it comes late in life." It was Douglas Jerrold who wrote that.

Maybe you were right, Mr. Jerrold, she thought, as her eyelids slowly closed. Maybe being in love is more trouble than it's worth!

It seemed her eyes had barely closed when she became aware of light and movement, and a terrible wailing sound.

Pat jerked upright, rubbing sleep from her eyes so she could focus on Ashley's trembling form.

"Ashley? What's wrong? What is that terrible noise? Is it . . . oh Lord, that's Celia! What is it? Has something happened to Jake?"

Ashley's face crumpled. "Mama," she moaned, "he's gone . . . Uncle Jake is . . . dead!"

"What? No . . . you're mistaken . . . Celia's just frightened. I'll go to her and we'll wake him . . . he'll be all right. You'll see . . ."

Fumbling into her robe, Pat noticed that the sky was brightening. A new day. Surely Jake couldn't die . . . it had to be a mistake!

Then she was stumbling up the steps, calling her sister's name, entreating Celia not to cry.

"Celia? He . . . Jake . . ."

"Gone," Celia sobbed, unable to catch her breath. "He's gone, Pat. I woke up and he was . . . so cold, so still. Even before I looked,

I knew. He's gone, Pat. My Jake is gone!"

Pat gathered her sister's quivering body into her arms, and she tried not to look at her brother-in-law's still form. Jake gone. It was hard to imagine. It was nearly impossible to believe that she'd never again hear his hearty laugh, or see him smile at his beloved wife of nearly forty years.

"Oh, Celia," Pat whispered. "Not Jake . . . not our Jake!"

The two women held each other for a long time, then Celia seemed to gather her last reserves of strength. She straightened and blinked, gently pushing Pat's comforting arms away.

"Please," she said quietly. "I need to be alone with him for a few minutes before they . . . before they take him away." She looked at Pat pleadingly. "Please. I'll be all right."

Pat nodded and backed out of the room. Just before she closed the door she saw Celia bend to kiss her husband's forehead before she gently drew the sheet up over his face.

Hank was waiting downstairs, and she flew straight into his arms as though she were a homing pigeon.

"Easy now," Hank crooned, patting her back gently. "Easy."

"Hank called a doctor and an ambulance,

Mother," Ashley said, her face pale but determined. "They'll be here soon. Should I go up to Aunt Celia?"

Pat blinked. Clearly Ashley was taking over. She'd called Hank. And now she was prepared to try to comfort her bereaved aunt.

"No," Pat said, moving out of Hank's embrace. "Not yet. She wanted some time alone with him before . . ."

Pat's face crumpled and she held out her arms to Ashley. "I'm so glad you were here this Christmas . . . that you got to see him again. Jake always had a soft spot for you."

Ashley smiled wanly. "Uncle Jake was special," she said. "I'm going to miss him."

"I'll make some coffee," Hank said, heading for the kitchen. "It's going to be a long day."

And it was. It was the longest, hardest day Pat had ever gone through, with the exception of her own husband's death. Celia surprised them all by exhibiting an inner strength that was awesome. But when she thought no one was looking, she faded, drawing into herself and her pain. Pat took on the sad duty of notifying Celia and Jake's children. Their daughter Darlene promptly became hysterical, Betty Lou was skiing and could not be reached immediately, so Pat left a message. And then finally, there was Bruce.

He reacted much the way Pat would have

expected, with a calm, cool acceptance. "Is Mother all right?" he asked dutifully.

Pat gritted her teeth, wishing Bruce was standing right in front of her so she could shake him until his teeth rattled. "I'm looking after her," she informed him, "but she needs her children around her right now."

"I'll be home as soon as I can clear my desk," Bruce replied stiffly. "Tell Mother I'm . . . sorry."

Pat was trembling as she hung up the phone. How could a son be so cold and unfeeling? So cruel and callous? But what if he really wasn't? What if it was all a mask to hide his true feelings?

Pat sighed. Things were never what they seemed. That was a lesson that had been brought home to her with stunning clarity when Clifford passed away. So, she would try not to judge Bruce, and maybe this family crisis would have a bright side. Maybe it would be the beginning of a new closeness between Celia and Bruce.

Hank agreed to look after Pat's pets and Fancy as well, while Pat, Ashley, and Celia accompanied Jake's body back to the city.

"I wish I could be with you," he told Pat gently. "Even though I'm not really a member of the family, I feel as though Jake was my friend, but someone's got to look after these animals."

"Yes," Pat said. "Someone does. Knowing you'll be here when I return means a lot."

"Oh, I'll be here," Hank promised huskily. "I'll definitely be here."

The next few days were both sad and bitter-sweet. Ashley enjoyed seeing her cousins again, and only wished it could have been under happier circumstances. She took her youngest cousin, Betty Lou, under her wing, and tried to convince the young woman that she shouldn't feel guilty for not coming home for the holidays. There was no way she could have known what would happen.

"Still, I should have known that Dad wasn't getting any younger, that his days were numbered," Betty Lou said wistfully. "I feel cheated. I never got to say goodbye."

"But he had a pleasant holiday," Ashley explained, "and he spoke of all his children with pride. He was contented. That's what you should try to remember."

Pat had never been so proud of her daughter. Ashley had been through this same trauma herself, and she knew everything Betty Lou was feeling. Only weeks earlier, Pat would never have imagined that Ashley would be capable of such wisdom and compassion.

In the days before and just after the funeral, Pat saw some old friends. Everyone remarked on how well she looked. But her primary concern was for Celia. She and Jake had been so close, almost intertwined. Would Celia be able to cope? As soon as she had the thought, Pat chased it away angrily. Of course Celia would cope! She was a strong woman, a survivor, and she would go on with her life for herself, her children, and because Jake would have wanted it that way.

The day after the funeral, Ashley reluctantly took her leave. She kissed her aunt, then hugged her mother tightly. "I have to go, Mother," she said, "but I'll be home to visit you soon, and despite everything, I had a wonderful time."

"I love you, sweetheart," Pat whispered. "Godspeed."

Then, Pat knew she also had to leave. "Celia, would you like to bring Mortimer and come home with me for a while? You'll be more than welcome."

"Thank you, no," Celia said quietly, looking over at her son, Bruce, who sat, stiff and silent at her side. "Bruce and I have some things to talk over, and we need some quiet time alone."

Pat nodded. There had been so many people in and out of the house Celia had hardly had time to breathe, but now that Jake had been laid to rest, there was much for her to think about. There were decisions to make, and a new life to plan. She hugged her sister tightly. "Then I'll go and leave you in peace," she said. "But remember that I'm only a phone call away."

Celia nodded, her eyes swollen and red-rimmed from her grief. As Pat turned to leave she saw Celia reach out to her son. She was gratified to see that Bruce didn't pull away.

Back in her own little home, with Ink and Spot dancing around her ecstatically, Pat drew a long, deep breath. She'd attended two funerals in little more than a year, and she felt empty. Death was so final, so unforgiving. It came, and it took, and then it was over. Too late to say the things you wished you'd said. Too late to go back and change things. Too late.

She heard the knock on the door, and her tired, aching heart rejoiced. Hank. Dear, kind, caring Hank. She needed him now, desperately.

She opened the door wordlessly. Hank held out his arms and she walked into them, and the moment his strength closed around her Pat felt whole again. An instant and the holes inside her closed up, the wounds became less raw and painful. She was home, in Hank's arms where she belonged.

They talked for a long while, sipping a sweet, light rosé wine. "Celia will be all right," Pat said confidently. "She's a strong woman, and she was lucky to have Jake's love and devotion for nearly forty years. Not many women can claim that."

Hank nodded, his chin resting on top of her head. She was cradled against him gently, and for a time it had been enough, but now it wasn't.

Suddenly Pat was hungry, nearly faint with the need to be part of him, to feel him inside her. She wanted to feel alive, to know that her blood still pumped within her veins. She needed to feel the living warmth of Hank's flesh against her own. She needed him to hold her and touch her and make the awful, cold emptiness go away.

"Make love to me, Hank," she begged softly, touching his face, looking deep into his eyes. Cold steel that could warm to silver velvet in an instant. They were warm now, warm with compassion and concern, and something else Pat didn't dare try to decipher.

"Please, Hank," she entreated. "Please. I need you so."

It was as if the floodgates had been torn down by the force of a gigantic swell, a swell of passion and need and caring. Hank turned her until her breasts were crushed against his chest, until her lips were a mere fraction of an inch from his, until the warm, damp center of her was pressed hard against his urgent, throbbing need.

"Oh, Hank," Pat moaned. "You want me as much as I want you!"

His answer was a caress, a featherlight touch of fingertips to her quivering lips. Then his fingers moved, tracing a fiery line across her chin, down her neck and finally teasing the tender tips of her breasts until she arched against him, pleading for more.

They slid down against the sofa, shifting until their bodies were nearly fused together, but there was still the unwanted barrier of clothing . . . the nuisance of removing garments that kept them apart.

Pat sat up, shivering as Hank's hard, calloused hands unfastened the clasp of her bra. Her breasts, full and heavy, spilled into his hands.

Hank groaned, and then he was tearing at his belt buckle as Pat slid her slacks and underpants down over her ankles. Naked at last, they came back together, the creamy femininity of Pat's flesh a startling contrast against Hank's leathery, wind-roughened skin. But the contrast only excited them more, making them appreciate the difference that made them male and female.

Pat was floating on a soft, cottony cloud. She'd known sexual fulfillment in her life, but there had never been the breathless, hungry anticipation she felt now. She'd never known the almost insane need to please and receive pleasure that consumed her at this moment with Hank. Her hands roamed his firm, work-hardened body, her lips feathered down his neck, across his chest until he groaned and clasped her hands to still them, to quiet the raging forces that urged them on.

"Easy, my darling," he crooned gently, smoothing sweat-dampened hair off Pat's forehead. "We have all the time in the world."

Pat shook her head, memories washing over her, threatening to cool the heat of passion. "No," she murmured. "Time is our enemy. It's slipping away. All we have is now . . . this moment."

She began to move against him then, in a way he simply couldn't ignore. He entered her, swiftly and surely, then he, too, began to move. It was as though their love dance had been perfectly choreographed, as though each movement was accurately timed to provide pleasure and joy. When they exploded, they were together, clinging like children frightened by forces greater than themselves. And then, when the spasms quieted, when their heartbeats slowed, they continued to hold each other, awestruck by the power of their hearts and bodies.

Pat wasn't sure what to expect after she and Hank made love. Would it change their daily interaction with one another? Would Hank back away? Or would the passion they had shared draw them closer?

By far she preferred the latter possibility, but after kissing her tenderly, and telling her how much their union had meant to him, Hank had covered her with a light blanket and left her alone on her sofa.

And now, in the bright light of morning, as she sipped her coffee and laughed at Ink and Spot's antics, she wondered.

I practically raped the man, she thought, amused as she felt a warm flush on her cheeks, but it had been inevitable. Jake's death, and the feelings that had invoked only hastened what would have happened eventually. And she wasn't a bit sorry. She felt different this morning. Alive and hopeful, as though she'd been cleansed of everything dark and sad in her life. Of course she wasn't. Not even Hank's artful lovemaking, wonderful as it had been, could do that. But her body had been starved for a man's touch, her senses had been deprived too long. She was alive again, a fully functioning woman, and it felt wonderful.

When she heard Hank's knock, she called out for him to come in, because the mere thought of seeing him again made her knees so weak she was afraid to stand up.

"Good morning," Hank said, almost shyly. "I wasn't sure if you were up, but I couldn't wait another minute to see you."

"Oh, Hank!" Pat did stand up then, but only so Hank could draw her into his strong, warm embrace. "You could have stayed, you know," she said softly. "My bed is big enough for two."

Hank shook his head. "I was too bedazzled. I needed time to think. What happened between us last night . . . I knew it was going to happen eventually, Pat, but I wasn't prepared for the force. It blew me away."

Pat laughed, loving this new, childlike side to Hank. "Me, too, I'm still weak in the knees."

Hank smiled, then he sobered. "That's why I came over so early. I'm leaving town for a few days. Will you look after the dogs for me?"

"You . . . you're leaving?"

Hank nodded. "I have to, now more than

ever. I need to see my daughters, Pat. I need to mend my fences with them, and I have to find Nancy. In my heart I believe that the girls know where she is and just don't want to tell me."

"Why?" Pat asked quietly. "If she doesn't want to be with you, why should she care if you know where she is?"

"I don't know, but I'm going to do my best to find out. This thing between us, Pat . . . it can't be just a casual fling. I want more for both of us."

"Yes, so do I." There was no time for pretense, no time for shyness. "I love you, Hank Richards."

He stared at her for a long, poignant moment. Pat's eyes were soft with love, warm with promise, and he wanted . . . oh, God, how he wanted what she had to offer! He wanted all of her, and he wanted her as his wife. He wanted what Celia and Jake had had.

"I'll be back as soon as I can," he said.

But he hadn't said he loved her, Pat thought after he'd gone. For all that his body had said, he hadn't been able to mouth the words. But it was all right, she decided, because life had taught her that words were often not as important as actions. How often had Clifford voiced the familiar sentiment, only to leave and spend illicit hours with his mistress?

No, she could wait for Hank to say the words, and she knew he would, soon.

Looking after Hank's dogs as well as her own small menagerie kept Pat busy for the next few days. She called the shelter, found out that her television message had been wildly successful, and that Dale and Pete were coping very nicely without her.

"Not that we don't miss you, Pat, because we do," the two young men chorused into the telephone receiver, "but we figure with all that you've already done you deserve a little rest. We were sorry to hear about your brother-in-law," Pete added quietly.

"Oh? How did you know?"

"Hank called. He said you'd probably be out of commission for a while."

"Well, I'll be back. Don't worry about that. But right now Hank is out of town and I'm looking after his kennels."

"You do what you have to do, Pat, and don't worry about us. Me and Dale are basking in luxury here with our great new lounge. There's not much more we could ask for."

"Good, then I won't worry about you. See you in a few days."

But the days stretched into a week, and she was starting to get alarmed when Hank finally called.

"Pat, I'm sorry," he said. "I know I should have called before this. Is everything all right at home?"

"The dogs are all fine," Pat said, "but what about you? I was beginning to worry."

"I know, and again I'm sorry. It's just been so hectic since I got here, but I'll explain everything when I see you. I should be home late tomorrow afternoon."

"All right. I'll be waiting."

"Good," Hank said, sounding strong and confident. "That's just what I needed to hear."

Pat hung the phone up thoughtfully. She prayed that Hank had managed to resolve the problems he'd had with his daughters. She'd seen the paternal hunger in his eyes when he talked to Ashley, and she well knew the ache of estrangement. Wonderful as he was, he wouldn't be a whole man until he established a relationship with his girls. A shiver went through her as she wondered how Hank's children would react to their father having a new love in his life. If they hadn't been able to accept their mother's leaving, how could they cope with a new woman in Hank's life?

We'll cross that bridge when we get to it, she told herself. Don't go borrowing trouble. It can come and find you quick enough on its own!

The next day, as she waited for Hank's return, Pat alternately soared high above the clouds and plunged deep down in despair. What if Hank was unable to find his wife? It wouldn't change the way she felt about him, but she knew that it would color Hank's every waking moment. He was simply not the kind of man to revel in an extramarital affair. He would want everything open and aboveboard. He would want no walls between them.

But if Nancy couldn't or wouldn't be found, there would always be a wall, there would always be a piece of Hank that Pat couldn't reach. It wasn't a question of marriage, although lately she had begun to imagine what it would be like to live with Hank as his wife, to share every facet of her life with a man she had come, not only to love, but to respect and admire.

But marriage wasn't a requirement for loving Hank, not at this stage of Pat's life. She would love him no matter what, but would he feel the same? Would he be able to forget the fact that he was still legally married?

Just after four o'clock she heard the sound of his truck. A sweet warmth flooded her body and her lips curved in a welcoming smile as she hurried to the door. Then he was in her arms, their hearts beating in a perfectly matched rhythm. "Welcome home," Pat said softly. "Welcome home, my love."

She poured them each a glass of wine and sat next to him on the sofa, her feet curled under her. She was wearing a soft blue jumpsuit and small gold earrings glittered against her earlobes. Her face was soft with love and gladness, and Hank knew he'd never seen a lovelier sight.

"If you knew how anxious I've been to get back here but the girls . . . well, things went pretty well, and I didn't want to rock the boat."

"Tell me," Pat invited, snuggling close against his side. "I want to hear all about it."

"Becky was the hardest one to talk to," Hank said, shaking his head. "She's too much like me, I guess. Gets a notion in her head and just can't let go. Anyway, I think I finally managed to convince her that I did everything I could to make my marriage work, and that it was Nancy's choice to leave."

"What about your other daughter, Laurie?"

"Ah, Laurie," Hank said, smiling proudly. "She's grown up so much since I last saw her. I could kick myself for missing out on these last few years of the girls' lives."

"So, basically both girls were glad to see you," Pat prompted.

"After the initial angry words," Hank said, sobering. "There was a lot of hostility, and it had to come out. But I think the girls finally realize I'm not the bad guy."

"And Nancy? Did either of them know where she is?"

"They both swear they haven't heard a word from her since she left here." Hank shook his head. "It makes no sense, Pat. Even if Nancy was unhappy with me, why would she abandon her own children? The girls have nothing to do with what went wrong in our marriage."

Pat was silent for a long moment, then she voiced the thought that had been in the back of her mind for a long time.

"Do you think she could be dead, Hank?"

Hank's shook his head. "I hope not, but I'm beginning to think it's a definite possibility. It would certainly explain why she never tried to contact the girls. There's no other explanation that makes sense, Pat. Nancy wasn't much of a wife to me, but she loved our daughters. It's hard to believe that she would just write them off."

Pat nodded, unable to even imagine walking away from her children. She shivered. After what Hank had just told her, she didn't know whether she wanted Nancy to be found.

Fourteen

Pat went back to work at the shelter the day after Hank's return. She had missed the easy friendship she'd formed with Pete and Dale, and she missed the interaction with the animals, even though she was frequently saddened by the plight of some of them.

"Well, here she is!" Pete boomed. "Welcome back, Pat! We missed you."

"Same here," Pat said, giving each young man a brief hug. "How's everything going?"

"Good," Dale said. "Real good. We've got empty cages and that's always good news. All that advertising you did really helped."

"I'm glad," Pat said. She followed Dale and Pete to the new lounge area where she accepted a cup of coffee. She glanced around the large, brightly decorated room with pride. "This is nice, isn't it?"

"Nice?" Pete asked, his dark brows raised.

"You call this nice? Dale and I call it heaven, and I think the animals feel the same way."

Pat nodded. "Good. Mission accomplished." She sat down in one of the comfortable new chairs and sipped her coffee thoughtfully. "I've been kicking some new ideas around," she began, "and I want your input."

Pete laughed and Dale put his hands to his head. "Uh-oh, Pat's got another idea! What now? Are we in trouble or what?"

Pat laughed. "No more remodeling, so relax," she promised the two men. "But what do you think of our screening some of our adult dogs for use as companion animals? They're using dogs to help the hearing-impaired now, and also people who are confined to wheelchairs. I'll bet that some of the dogs we get in here could be used for that. We'd have to find out where to send them for the proper training and . . ."

"Wow! What an idea! If it worked, we could avoid putting a lot of adult animals to sleep," Dale said excitedly. He looked at Pete accusingly. "Why didn't we think of that?"

Pete grinned and shrugged. "This is what we have Pat for," he said cheerfully.

Pat spent the rest of the morning in the office making telephone calls. Before she left that afternoon, she had made several promising contacts. A woman named Janet Marlborough would be coming to talk to them at the end of the week. She would explain what they looked for in companion animals, what traits an adult dog had to possess to be properly trained.

"It's not a total solution," Pat explained to Dale and Pete as the three of them ate lunch, "but I think it could be a step in the right direction."

"I'm willing to give it a try," Pete said.

"Count me in," Dale agreed.

Pat stopped at the grocery store, picked up the fixings for a simple steak dinner, then drove the rest of the way home in relaxed contentment.

As soon as she got home, she put the dogs out in the yard for a few minutes and called Celia. She was determined to keep in close touch with her sister. She truly believed that Celia would do fine on her own, but she would need lots of loving support during the next few months, until her grief began to dim.

"Celia? How are you, dear? I was thinking of you today, and I just wanted to call and see how you were doing."

"I'm glad you called, Pat. I've been needing someone to talk to. Bruce went home yesterday, and last night was my first night alone in this house. I didn't sleep a wink."

"I know," Pat said gently. It had been the

same for her, in the first days and weeks after Clifford's death. "It will get easier," she added. "How did things go with Bruce?"

She heard Celia sigh.

"Nothing has changed," Celia said, her voice filled with regret. "I know Bruce will grieve for his father, but Jake's passing hasn't changed his feelings for me. Nor mine for him. It's an unfortunate situation, Pat, but I don't believe I'll ever be close to my son."

"I'm sorry," Pat said. "I was hoping . . ."

"Yes. I know. The girls thought the same thing, but I guess it just wasn't meant to be."

"How are you otherwise?" Pat asked. "You're eating and taking care of yourself, aren't you?"

"I'll be all right, Pat. Jake wouldn't want me to sit in a corner and pine away, so I'm going on with our plans for the day-care center. It will keep me busy, and it's what Jake would have wanted."

"Good for you," Pat said. "Be sure and let me know if you need any help. I don't know much about day-care centers, but I'm sure if we put our heads together we can find the answers we need."

Celia managed a soft laugh. "We're women of the nineties, right?"

"Right," Pat said, her throat threatening to close up. "We can do anything!"

Pat wasn't sure if she felt better or worse after she hung up. She was proud of her sister for carrying on, but it hurt to think of the pain Celia was feeling. And there was really very little she could do. She could be there for her sister. She could offer loving support and soothing words, but the hurt and the loss would never really go away. It would be with Celia until the end of her own life. She would have to learn to live with it, to deal with it on a daily basis, and as Pat had learned during the past months, there would be times when there was nothing she could do but crawl off by herself and lick her wounds.

It was hard to even imagine Celia with any man but Jake, but Pat hoped that someday, somewhere, her sister would find a compassionate, loving man when the time was right. And if that happened she was sure Jake would heartily approve.

After feeding and caring for her pets, Pat bundled her groceries and carried them across the street to Hank's house. It was bitterly cold now, and she was looking forward to enjoying the warmth of Hank's fireplace after they'd eaten.

Hank's door opened before she could even knock. He drew her into his arms, groceries and all, mumbling how much he'd missed her.

"We were together last night," Pat reminded

him, her lips smiling against his, as he dipped his head once again.

"Umm, I know, but it's been a long day," Hank said. Reluctantly he released her. He looked at the bag she was holding ruefully. "No eggs, I hope?"

Pat shook her head. "No eggs, but I do have a delectable sirloin steak that is just begging to be broiled. I also have potatoes to be baked, and the makings of a mixed green salad."

Hank grinned. "A woman after my own heart. Come on in, woman, and let's get cooking!"

Pat unpacked the supplies while Hank set the table and rattled around getting the proper pans and utensils. She was relieved to see that Hank had accepted her wish to buy dinner without apparent discomfort. She knew he still had doubts about the difference in their financial situations, and she knew those doubts would not be dispelled easily, not after the disastrous outcome of his marriage. But she was determined to show him that her modest wealth did not have to be a barrier between them. And maybe the best way was just to love him with every fiber of her being. To show him that she needed him in other, more important ways. To make him understand that he was the most important part of her future.

"I called Celia today," she said, as she washed and tore lettuce into a large salad bowl. "She sounds like she's coping pretty well, but it breaks my heart to hear the sadness in her voice. She and Jake had such a good marriage. They were ideally suited to one another. His death has left a big hole in her life."

Hank placed the steak on the broiler tray and seasoned it with garlic powder and onion salt. He turned to face Pat, his expression solemn. "Those two had something rare, that's for sure," he said. "Jake was a fortunate man."

"Yes, and I think Celia realizes she was a lucky woman. I hope that will see her through some of the rough times ahead."

"And what about you, Pat? What helped you get through the rough times?" Hank asked quietly. He slid the tray under the broiler, closed the oven door, and turned to face her.

Pat's hands stilled, and the onion she had been chopping slid from her fingers. It rolled off the counter and landed on the floor with a dull plop.

"Talk to me, Pat. Tell me about your marriage, about what your life was like before I met you. I told you about Nancy, but you never seem to want to talk about your past. It's like your life before this past year was a blank slate, and I know that's not true."

Pat bent to pick up the onion, but Hank beat her to it. Their fingers met and her eyes were drawn to meet Hank's.

"There . . . isn't all that much to tell," she fibbed. "I was a wife and a mother. There aren't any deep, dark secrets."

"Maybe not on your part," Hank said soberly, placing the onion back on the counter. "But what about your late husband? Were you happy? Was he good to you? Do you still miss him?"

"For heaven's sake, what does it matter?" Pat asked nervously. Whenever the subject of Clifford came up she felt anxious . . . almost scared, and she didn't understand why. She hadn't done anything wrong. It was Clifford who strayed. Clifford who betrayed their marital vows, Clifford who slept with his colleague after telling Pat he loved her.

"Don't let that steak burn," Pat warned, keeping her eyes on the salad bowl in front of her. "I'm getting awfully hungry."

"So am I, but not for food. I want to know about you, Pat, and I'm not going to drop the subject, so you may as well spill the beans."

A strange fear took control of Pat then, a totally irrational fear that Hank would no longer find her desirable if he knew that her late husband had been unfaithful. It was crazy, and in the deepest part of her intellect she knew it, but she could not control it. She began to shake uncontrollably, and the chopping knife slid out of her hand, landing on the counter with a clatter.

Hank was at her side instantly. "Honey, what is it? Tell me what's upsetting you, and together we'll make it go away."

Pat shook her head, sobs screaming in her throat, only they couldn't get out because her lips were frozen shut. She just kept shaking her head.

Hank released her for an instant, and Pat felt her legs buckle beneath her. But as soon as Hank had removed the partially cooked steak from the oven he was back. He pulled her into his arms, pushed her head down on his shoulder and held tight.

"Cry, baby," he urged. "Let it all out. I've felt you holding back so many times. I always knew there was something deep inside that was hurting you. Let it out. I'll take care of you."

I'll take care of you. Those simple words released all the pent-up anger and fear and bitterness that Pat had carried around for so long. The tears flowed and her chest heaved, and still Hank held her.

Finally Pat felt the tears drying on her cheeks. She felt her breathing slow and gradually return to normal, and she was conscious of a curious weightless feeling. It was almost as if she were floating, as if she were so light and free she could float off into the atmosphere.

She raised her head, and Hank surveyed her ravaged face lovingly.

"Feel better?" he asked gently, wiping a stray tear with his thumb.

"I think I do," Pat said, realizing with amazement that it was true. "I didn't know there were that many tears left in me."

"Let's go in the other room and sit down," Hank said. "We'll have a late dinner."

So they sat on the sofa. Pat watched the flickering flames in the fireplace and she told Hank about her marriage.

"The funny thing is," she finished much later, "I didn't even realize what had happened to me until after Clifford's death, when I accidentally discovered his infidelity. That's when I saw what I had become. A perfumed, hot-waxed robot. I did what I was programmed to do, never even daring to think that anything should be different." She sighed. "No wonder young Cliff was so bitter. I allowed his father to ride roughshod all over him, and never lifted a finger to help. And then, when I found out that it had all been a lie . . . that Clifford had been with a woman I had frequently entertained in our home . . . I guess I went a little crazy. That's when I put the house up for sale and donated most of my expensive designer clothing to the thrift shops."

"Well, that answers a lot of my questions," Hank said quietly. "I guess now I can understand why you turned your back on . . . all that."

Pat took the tissue Hank handed her and dabbed at her eyes. "None of it made me happy," she said, "not the way I'm happy right now."

She saw Hank smile, but the smile looked a little crooked, and something twisted inside Pat. "Hank?" she asked questioningly, "is anything wrong?"

Hank shook his head. "No, honey, everything is fine. Now, how about if we get ourselves some dinner? I don't know about you, but I'm as hungry as a bear."

They ate dinner off trays in the living room. For some reason Pat felt she didn't want to move too far from the fire.

"Now this is a steak," Hank said heartily, spearing a juicy piece of beef. "Cooked to perfection, if I do say so myself."

"It's wonderful," Pat agreed, and it was.

The meal was perfect, but something was wrong with Hank. He was trying too hard to act like nothing had happened, but something had. There was a distance between them that hadn't been there before. Since the night they had made love, Pat had felt a growing closeness with Hank, a connection that she had dared to hope would never be broken. Now it was as if a chasm had opened up between them. Hank smiled and said all the right things. He even hugged her as they carried their dishes out to the kitchen, and when she was ready to go home he kissed her tenderly, but the wall was there, and she was afraid that this time she would be unable to tear it down.

Hank walked Pat to her door. They were both shivering against the cold, night air. "We're definitely in the deep freeze," Hank said. "You'd better do something about that heating system soon."

"Yes, I was thinking the same thing. One of these days it will conk out and then where will I be?"

"Good night," Hank said softly, tipping Pat's face up for a light kiss. "Hurry inside before you get chilled."

Pat nodded wordlessly, not bothering to tell Hank that it was too late. She already was chilled, all the way into the depth of her heart and soul.

Hank lay awake a long time, berating himself for what he'd done. He'd wanted to know about Pat's past, about her marriage, and now that he did know he understood so many things . . . her determination to separate herself from all the trappings of wealth and social position. It was suddenly all so clear, and so frightening, because he'd begun to dream of a future with her. Spending Christmas with her and her family had given him a glimpse of what it could be like, and now he was scared stiff that it was all going to be snatched away.

What would happen when Pat finally worked through her feelings? Would she still be satisfied with a small, three-bedroom cottage, or would she begin to miss the spaciousness and luxury of her previous home? What if she grew tired of doing her own cooking and housework . . . if she decided she'd had enough of blue jeans and flannel shirts? What if she decided that her plainspoken, homespun boyfriend was dull and uninteresting? What if picnics on a country road paled beside the thought of a luxurious vacation in Europe?

I can't give her any of those things, Hank thought wearily. I couldn't give them to Nancy and I can't give them to Pat, and knowing she has enough money to do just about anything she wants will eat at me until there's nothing left of what we feel for one another.

Hank flopped on his side. He'd made a terrible mistake getting involved with Pat in the first place, and now he had to rectify it. The only thing was, he didn't know how, not without breaking her heart, and his own in the bargain.

Fifteen

Pat didn't see Hank for three days. Oh, he hadn't run away. He was still right across the road, but he might as well have been on another continent. She knew why. It was because she'd told him about her marriage, about her failures. He saw her differently now, and he'd probably decided he didn't want to be involved with a woman who'd made such a dismal mess of her life.

It was like applying for a job and not having good references, Pat thought. Her references as a wife and mother left a lot to be desired. For a while she had almost managed to convince herself that Clifford's infidelity was not her fault; that it was her late husband's own lack of morals that had allowed him to stray beyond the bonds of matrimony, but now she wasn't so sure. She'd failed Cliff, and maybe she'd failed Ashley as well, in a different way.

How could she be sure she hadn't also failed Clifford?

Pat listened to Tweetie's scolding as she absently filled his food cup. Her mind was a trillion miles away until she heard Tweetie's familiar lament.

"That's a bunch of bull!" he squawked. "That's a bunch of bull!"

Like the caricature of a light bulb flashing inside her skull, everything was suddenly bright and clear. That was a bunch of bull! Her own half-buried insecurities were rising to the surface to torment her, and she wasn't going to stand for it. Not anymore. Not now, at this time and place in her life. She'd paid her dues. She'd devoted years of her life to her family's happiness, and if it hadn't been enough . . . then so be it. She wasn't a failure, and she'd be damned if she'd act like one!

"Can you guys manage without me today?" she asked a few minutes later, when Dale answered the telephone at the shelter. "I've got some important personal business to take care of."

"Well, you know we'll miss you, Pat," Dale said, "but I think we can muddle through. It's pretty quiet here right now."

"Good. I'll see you tomorrow."

Pat hung up the phone as a wave of fresh new energy pulsed through her veins. She didn't know what it was that was nagging at Hank, but in her heart she was sure he didn't consider her a failure. No, it was something else, something he hadn't been able to verbalize. Well, tonight was the night. Once and for all they were going to get everything out in the open. They'd slay all the dragons from their pasts together, and lay all their doubts to rest.

Pat spent the better part of the morning picking out the outfit she would wear, giving herself a facial and shampooing her hair. Hank wasn't the kind of man who had to be impressed, but for her own sake she wanted to look her best. Either way things turned out, this was going to be an important night in her life. If she managed to get through to Hank it could be the beginning of a wonderful future for them, and if she didn't . . . she didn't want to think of that possibility, but if it happened she would deal with it. She was a strong, capable woman and no one could take that away from her.

By four o'clock that afternoon, everything was in readiness. A pot of French onion soup was simmering on the stove, a salad was crisping in the refrigerator, and an old-fashioned chicken pot pie was ready to go in the oven. A bottle of white wine was chilling, and Pat was ready. A nice dinner, a glass of wine, and then she and Hank would get down to it. No more unexplained silences, no more evasions. The whole truth would be spread out in front of them and then they would deal with it. One way or the other.

At five fifteen, Hank's pickup pulled into his driveway. Pat gave her hair one final pat, checked to make sure her lipstick wasn't smeared, grabbed her jacket, and marched across the street.

She met up with Hank just as he started to put his key in the lock.

"I want you to come to dinner tonight," she said without preamble. "We have to talk."

Hank's expression was wary. "Pat, I don't think . . ."

"That's your trouble. You think too much. Take care of the dogs and come over, Hank. This thing between us has got to be settled once and for all. I'm not a yo-yo that you can bounce up and down at will, you know."

"I don't . . ."

"Dinner will be on the table in forty-five minutes, Hank," Pat said firmly. "Be there."

Hank let himself into his house, shaking his head in bewilderment. This was a new side to Pat. He'd always considered her a soft, completely feminine woman, but now . . . he couldn't help chuckling. He wasn't sure he'd want to meet up with her in a dark alley!

But she was right. He'd been hiding out like

a scared little kid, and it had to stop. Even if he and Pat couldn't manage to get together as lovers, they were still neighbors, and he knew he'd hate to lose her friendship. So, Pat was right. They had to settle things once and for all. It was time to come out of hiding and face the music. Only, to Hank it felt more like a one-woman firing squad. How could he make Pat understand his fears, the doubts that kept him awake at night?

Hank sighed as he stepped into the shower. He didn't know how the evening would end, but he was sure of one thing. Pat Melbourne was one determined lady!

Forty-two minutes and some odd seconds after Pat had confronted him at his front door, Hank was walking into her house. He smiled hesitantly and couldn't help sniffing appreciatively as the good smells of home-cooked food encircled him.

"It smells like you spent the whole day in the kitchen," he said awkwardly. "You shouldn't have gone to all this trouble."

"I wanted to," Pat said crisply. "I've discovered that I think better when my hands are busy."

"Oh. Well, in that case you must have done a lot of thinking," Hank said, noting the beautifully set table, the wine chilling in a silver ice bucket.

"You must be hungry," Pat said. "We'll eat first, and then we'll talk."

Hank gradually felt his tense muscles begin to relax as he sampled the delicious onion soup and crisp French bread Pat served him. He remembered telling Pat once that good food always made him mellow. Apparently she hadn't forgotten.

"So, how is Princess's litter?" Pat asked. "Have any of the pups gone to their new homes?"

"All but one," Hank said, "and I'm thinking of keeping her for breeding purposes."

Pat laughed. "Pretty soon you'll be adding on to your kennels."

Hank laid down his spoon and shook his head. "No. I don't think so. Breeding Samoyeds is just a hobby. I don't want to turn it into a big-business venture."

They finished off the meal with casual chatter. Pat remarked that Ashley had called and reported on Fancy's health and well-being.

Hank beamed. "I guess giving her that pup wasn't a mistake after all. I have to admit I had my doubts."

"I would never have believed Ashley would be so besotted by a pet," Pat admitted. "But then, as a child she never really had much contact with animals, not at our house anyway."

A trace of bitterness had crept into Pat's

voice as she spoke. Her cheeks flushed as she began to clear the table.

"I have to lay all my bitterness to rest," she said. "It's hard, but I'm working on it."

"Pat, there's something I . . ."

"Wait," she said, holding up her hand. "Let me load the dishwasher and then we'll take our coffee into the living room and talk."

Hank nodded. "All right." He stood up and began to help Pat clean up.

Finally they were settled. They eyed one another uneasily, and Pat found it hard to believe that the solemn-faced man next to her was the same man who had held her and made such beautiful, tender love to her. This Hank had dark circles under his eyes and worry lines etched into his forehead. His gray eyes, eyes that could be warm and velvety, were troubled.

"Pat, I . . . I feel like a little kid who has been chastised by his teacher, but I know that what you said this afternoon was right. We do have to settle things between us."

"Yes." Pat nodded and tried to clear her throat. "We do. You know you insisted I tell you about my marriage the other night, and then, after I opened up to you, you changed. Why, Hank? I think I have a right to know. Did you lose respect for me once you found out that my late husband was unfaithful? Did that make me less of a woman in your eyes?

Are you afraid to get involved with a loser?"

"Loser? You? Oh, Pat, no! I could never think that!"

"Then why have you been avoiding me these past few days? Why do you hurry in and out of your house like you're afraid I'm going to tackle you?"

Why, indeed! All at once Hank saw how ridiculous the whole thing had become. Instead of coming right out and telling Pat how he felt, he'd hidden, like a frightened little kid. He'd left her wondering and hurting, and his own hurt had multiplied a thousandfold. "I acted like a jackass, didn't I?" he asked.

"Yep. You sure did. Now how about telling me why?"

"I just . . . when you told me about your husband, how he treated you . . . what he did, I thought I understood why you turned your back on all the trappings of wealth, and I thought . . . I still think that one of these days you may change your mind again. You'll miss the things you once had, and this . . . what you have here, won't be enough for you. I don't think I can handle another woman walking away from me, Pat."

"I see." Pat nodded, letting Hank's explanation sink in slowly. So that's what it was. It wasn't that Hank saw her as a failure, but that he was still unsure of her. In his mind she was still "one of the others." A wealthy woman playing at seeing how the "other half" lived. Well, it wasn't true. Looking back now she knew that she'd never quite fit the mold Clifford had tried so hard to force her into. She'd never been comfortable with the society matrons he'd insisted she hobnob with, and deep down she'd always thought the expensive antiques he furnished their home with were ugly. But Hank didn't know all that.

"I don't know what to say to you, Hank," Pat said slowly, her voice filled with despair. "If you can't or won't believe what I tell you, what's left? You know I'm not a quitter. I never have been, and I wouldn't walk away from you unless you told me to go. I care for you, Hank Richards. I care deeply, but I can't stay with you if you won't allow yourself to trust me. I can't give you an iron-clad guarantee, you know. No one could do that for you." She sighed heavily and moved away from him. It seemed wrong to sit next to him now, wrong to pretend a closeness that didn't exist. "It's your ball game, Hank. There's nothing else I can say."

Hank was silent for a long moment, a moment that seemed to stretch into eternity. He wanted so badly to believe Pat, and a part of him did believe her, but deep inside there was still a core of fear . . . a terrible, dark dread that refused to go away. He swallowed. He had two choices. He could remain silent and let Pat walk out of his life, or he could open up and be honest and hope she'd hang around while he did his best to work through his doubts.

"Pat, I want to believe you. A part of me does, but another part, the Hank that was nearly devastated when Nancy walked out, is having a hard time. I think . . . no, I know I can work through this, but it may take a little time. Will you stick by me? I know it's a lot to ask, but I don't want to lose you. I don't want to lose what we have together."

Pat shook her head. "I don't want to lose that either. I never had that before, you know. I never had a man who cared for me just as I am."

Hank's face crumpled into a grin. "Then do we have a deal?" he asked, stretching out his hand.

"We've got a deal," Pat said just before she leaned over and kissed him.

"My show is scheduled for March third, Mom," Cliff explained, his voice ringing excitedly over the telephone wires. "It would really mean a lot if you could come out. Like I said before, our apartment has two bedrooms. You can stay with me and Doug."

"I don't know, son," Pat said hesitantly. "I'm pretty involved with the shelter here now and . . ."

"Mom, you're talking about stray dogs and cats. This is me, Cliff . . . your son. What about me? Aren't you even a little excited about my success? I've waited a long time for this."

"Of course you have, and I'm as proud as punch," Pat said quickly. Then, before she could lose her courage, she made a decision. Hard as it would be, she had to do this for Cliff. She owed him her support and love at this critical time of his life.

"All right, Cliff, I'll come out, but I think it would be better if I book a room in a hotel. Is there a decent place near your apartment?"

"I'll check. Thanks, Mom. I had my fingers crossed that you'd come. This is an important time for me."

"All right. Let me see about making airline reservations, and I'll get back to you," Pat said.

All along she had known that she would go out to California. How could she not? How could she not support Cliff when he had worked so hard to reach his goal?

But she was sick at the thought of confronting Cliff's partner. What could she say? How should she act?

She waited impatiently that evening until she saw Hank's truck, then she grabbed her jacket and hurried to him.

Hank held her tight against his chest, but there was no hint of sexuality in the embrace. He seemed to sense that what she needed was comfort.

"Come on, let's get inside before those tears freeze on your face," he said, putting her away so he could open the door.

Then they were inside, and the warmth and coziness of Hank's home wrapped itself around Pat like a protective cocoon.

"Now, what's wrong? It's not Ashley, is it? Or Celia?"

Hank unwrapped a plaid muffler from his neck and unzipped his jacket as he waited for Pat to reply.

Huddling deeper into her down jacket, Pat shook her head. "No one is sick or hurt," she explained quickly. "It's Cliff. I told him I'd go out to California for his first show. Oh, Hank, I'll have to meet the young man he lives with and I'm not sure I can handle it!"

Hank nodded. "A tough situation." He looked thoughtful for a moment, then his expression lightened. "I've got it. I know just what you need, Pat."

"Oh? You're dealing in miracles these days?" Pat quipped.

"Not exactly, but it just seems to me that lately you've been spending just about all your time worrying yourself into a frenzy over other people's problems and troubles. How does a night out on the town sound to you?"

"A night out? Where? For heaven's sake, Hank, it's a Wednesday!"

"So? Is there any law that states a man can't take his girl out for dinner and a couple of drinks on a week night? There's a great new Italian restaurant not far from here. Come on, Pat. What do you say? Dig out some glad rags and let's do it!"

She had to laugh. Dear as he was, Hank was a long way from anyone's idea of a party animal, yet he actually looked enthused.

"You really want to do this?"

"You bet," Hank replied. "Maybe after dinner we can find a place to dance. I used to be pretty good on the dance floor."

Not knowing quite what to expect, Pat hurried back across the road to her own house, her worries over Cliff temporarily forgotten. She suddenly realized that she and Hank had never had a date. They'd gotten to know one another pretty well, and they had shared the deepest physical intimacy a man and woman could share, but they'd never gone on a date. She grinned. It was high time!

An hour later, in response to Ink and Spot's

alert, Pat hurried to open her front door. Then she stood there gaping like a tongue-tied, brainless adolescent, until she was finally able to voice one squeaky word. "Hank?"

His grin stretched from ear to ear. "In the flesh," he said, stepping inside and closing the door behind him. "You look just as beautiful as I thought you would, Pat."

"My God!" Pat said, her voice breathless. "I can't believe this! You look . . ."

Hank's gray eyes twinkled. "I know," he said, lowering his head in mock modesty. "Incredibly handsome, intoxicatingly masculine, supremely sensual . . . have I missed anything?"

The spell was broken by his silliness. "Oh you!" Pat said, laughing as she stepped close and adjusted his dark blue tie. "You," she said, lowering her voice to a husky, sensually promising whisper, "are a fine figure of a man, sir. I'm proud to be your date."

"The feeling is mutual, lady," Hank said. "Are we ready?"

On the short drive to the restaurant, Pat sat in a stunned silence, taking in this new side to Hank. She'd always found him attractive, but she'd become used to seeing him in jeans and plaid shirts, with his thick gray hair slightly rumpled. Somehow she had never pictured him in a dark suit and tie, looking every inch the determined lothario. A delighted giggle wangled its way past Pat's lips.

"What's so funny?" Hank asked, thick gray brows raised questioningly. "Do I look that strange?"

"You look marvelous," Pat assured him quickly, tracing her fingertip up his arm and lightly teasing his neck. "In fact I'm not sure I want to waste my time on dinner."

Hank smiled, then shuddered under Pat's increasingly sensual touch. "Later, lovely lady," he promised, his voice thick with his own desire. "We have a whole wonderful night ahead of us."

And a wonderful night it was. Pat couldn't remember when she'd last felt so relaxed, so pleased with herself and the world around her. And she was glad she'd chosen her favorite black dress. It had been sinfully expensive, and like most pricey clothing, it was deceptively simple. But it had a neckline low enough to display an enticing amount of cleavage, a fact that was not lost on Hank.

"We're going to have to do this more often," he said. "It's a crime to hide all that . . . luscious flesh under a flannel shirt."

"I thought you liked flannel," Pat teased. "I distinctly remember you saying it was comfortable."

"Umm, it is, and so are old slippers and my

well-worn lounge chair, but I wouldn't put any of those above the view I'm enjoying right now," he said, wiggling his thick brows.

Pat laughed, and felt her cheeks warm. She and Hank were actually flirting with one another, something they'd never done.

They ordered an antipasto platter and the house specialty, lasagna. Then the waiter disappeared to return with a carafe of robust red wine and a large bowl of salad, and the tastiest garlic breadsticks Pat had ever eaten.

They ate and laughed and touched, light, feathery caresses that promised much. And then, when the table had been cleared and they were sipping their coffee, a young accordionist appeared and began to play a romantic love song.

Pat knew her eyes were glowing. "Did you know about this?" she asked.

Hank shook his head. "I had no idea, but it works out perfectly. May I have this dance?"

Pat stood up and moved into Hank's arms. It seemed so right and natural, so perfect for the way she was feeling. She felt light and free, young and lively. All her worries had been left at home. This was her night with Hank, her time to concentrate on feelings and forget all the day-to-day cares. Her time. She laid her head on Hank's shoulder and let her eyelids drift downward.

"Are you ready to leave?" Hank asked a trillion years later. "I want to be alone with you, Pat."

"Umm, sounds wonderful," Pat murmured. She opened her eyes, blinked and discovered that she and Hank were the only ones left on the postage stamp-sized dance floor.

She sighed as they made their way back to their table. "I hate to see the evening end."

"Don't worry," Hank said huskily. "The best is yet to come."

And it was the best. Once again Hank and Pat reached the highest heights together. Their bodies had the hunger and greed of youth, the wisdom and patience of maturity, and the all important ingredient that enhances the physical act, a true and genuine affection for one another.

Pat cried out as she scaled the highest mountain, held tight and warm against Hank's firm, masculine body. She had worried about pleasing Hank before their first time together, but now she was secure in her womanliness, safe in her femininity. Hank accepted the crow's-feet and tiny wrinkles, the faded stretch marks that crisscrossed her abdomen, and he loved her all the more.

"Ah, Pat," he said, when they drifted back to earth together. "Don't you see that the signs of age are badges of bravery . . . of all that you have been and done? How could I not love each and every tiny line on your lovely face?"

Pat smiled and sighed happily. "You're a smart man, Hank."

Sixteen

Pat slept well that night. For the first time, Hank spent the night. After a quick trip across the street to check on the dogs, and make sure his home was secure for the night, he returned, and they drifted off to sleep in each other's arms, curled against each other spoon fashion.

But morning brought crisp winter sunlight, and all Pat's problems came home to roost.

As she brewed coffee and made toast, she filled Hank in on her conversation with Cliff. "He wants me to be there for his show, and I simply couldn't say no," she said.

"And the crazy thing is that part of me desperately wants to be there. This will be the culmination of all his dreams, his validation as an artist. I want to share in his joy and triumph."

Hank sipped his coffee and nodded. "But you're having a problem with meeting Cliff's roommate, right?"

"I guess I'm really not very broad-minded, Hank."

Smiling sympathetically, Hank laid his hand over Pat's. "I can understand how you feel, but I think what you have to remember is that Cliff's sexual preference is only one small part of his life. He's a fine young man, and he wants and needs your approval."

Pat warmed her hands around her coffee mug. The house was uncomfortably chilly, due to the way she'd been dragging her feet about getting a new heating system. But something inside was also making her cold. She wanted so much to be a good mother to Cliff, and she was afraid she wouldn't measure up.

She sighed, and her eyes sought Hank's. "I guess I don't have a choice. I have to go out there and do the best I can," she said.

Hank nodded approvingly. "You'll do the right thing, Pat. You love your boy, and he'll know it. And isn't that all that really matters?"

After Hank left for work, Pat hurriedly dressed in jeans and a plaid flannel shirt. How different her life was from the way it had been a year earlier. After being with Hank she realized how love-starved she'd been for years. The hasty, routine couplings she'd had with Clifford had merely been a means for physical release, but this, what she had with Hank, was so special; she felt warm and very well loved.

Before leaving for the kennels, Pat called the number Hank had given her to arrange for an estimate on a new heating system. And while she was at it, she intended to see about having a fireplace put in.

Ashley called that evening. "How's Fancy?" Pat asked.

Ashley laughed, and she sounded very young and carefree. "She's adorable. You wouldn't believe how smart she is, Mother. I swear Hank must have given me the pick of the litter. Mrs. Bentley, the woman in my apartment building who looks after Fancy while I'm at work? Well, she's just insane about her. She said she never saw a dog with such a sweet, loving disposition."

"Well, I'm glad. I was hoping you wouldn't have any problems with her. Pets are worth their weight in gold as far as I'm concerned, but they also represent a huge responsibility."

"Well, Fancy and I are doing just fine. In fact, I can't imagine what I did before she came into my life. When you see Hank tell him I said thanks again, will you? Fancy is just about the best present I ever got."

Pat hung up feeling warm all over. At least one of her children was content. Then she gave herself a shake. Cliff was content, too, or at least that's what he maintained, and who was she to say different?

She gave Ink and Spot a biscuit and put on her jacket. "You kids be good now," she called as she left the house.

Dale and Pete were glad to see her, and after a quick cup of coffee, Pat did a tour of the animal runs. She was saddened to see a newly arrived litter of six young puppies, of an undetermined breed. They were adorable, but Pat knew that unless they were adopted within the next few days, their lives would be cut short.

"I see we have a new crop," she said as Pete walked up behind her. "When did they come in?"

"Just yesterday," Pete explained. "Some guy brought them in a cardboard box. He said somebody left them in his yard."

"Right," Pat said disgustedly, turning away from the puppies' excited yapping.

"Has Janet Marlborough called?" she asked Pete as they walked back to the office.

"Yeah, she did. She called yesterday. She said to tell you she'd be here sometime this afternoon to explain the companion dog program to us."

"Good. That will be one step in the right direction," Pat said. "I'd like to see you and Dale get started on that before I leave for California."

Pete nodded. "Going to visit your son?"

"Yes," Pat answered, her heart filling with pride. "Cliff is an artist and he's having his first show. He wants me to be there."

"Wow! I guess so!" Pete said admiringly. "I admire anyone with artistic talent. I can't draw a straight line."

Pat laughed. "Maybe not, but you're awfully good at feeding orphaned puppies and kittens. What you and Dale are doing here is very worthwhile, you know."

"Yeah, I think so, too. The way I look at it, I may never be filthy rich, but I can sleep at night. Not everyone can say that."

"When did you get so smart and philosophical?" Pat asked, impulsively hugging her co-worker.

Pete grinned. "I'm young," he said. "I haven't realized my full potential yet."

Pat sat down in the office to catch up on some paperwork. Dale and Pete were wonderful with the animals, but they hated the paperwork that went along with their work with a passion, so Pat had taken over most of it. Oddly enough, she found the routine comforting. She enjoyed bringing order to chaos, liked knowing that the hours she spent at the shelter were making a difference.

She was just finishing up some filing when Janet Marlborough arrived. A plump, cheerful woman in her mid-forties, Janet wore no makeup and was casually dressed in a sweat-suit.

"Hello everyone," she called briskly. She zeroed in on Pat. "I'm so glad you called and asked me to outline our program. May I call you Pat?"

"Please do," Pat said, nodding. Janet was like a small, round tornado. She moved around the small office with all the force of a mini-hurricane.

"Well, Pete and Dale. You two look capable. That's a help. You'd be amazed at the people I sometimes have to work with. I hope you have some adult dogs for me to look at today."

"We have a few," Dale explained, "but Pat here has been campaigning to get our older animals adopted."

"That's good," Janet said, "but you'll never have a hundred percent success rate, you know, and that's where I come in. I can take an animal with reasonable intelligence and a sound disposition and make sure he'll have a good, safe home."

"I'm for that," Pete said.

"Ditto," Dale echoed.

"That makes three of us," Pat said. "If there's any way to prevent a healthy animal from being destroyed, I'm for it."

Janet nodded. "Good. That's what I wanted

to hear. Let's get to work."

They spent nearly an hour with each of the three adult dogs currently in residence. Janet pronounced the first dog, a collie-shepherd mix, a perfect candidate for the program. After briefly getting acquainted with the dog, she deliberately tugged its tail, patted its back a little more roughly than necessary, and carefully gauged the dog's reactions.

"See?" she asked, her eyes sweeping from Pat to Dale and then on to Pete. "See the way he carefully pulled away? I didn't really hurt him, but I'm sure my touch was uncomfortable, yet he didn't snap or nip." As if to reassure the dog that her roughness was accidental, Janet crooned and fussed, and the dog responded with forgiving kisses and an energetic wag of its tail.

"I think I'm getting the idea," Pat said. "I know that some of your animals are trained to work with paralyzed people and the hearing-impaired, but some of them are also taken for regular visits to children's hospitals and nursing homes, right?"

Janet nodded enthusiastically. "And if you could see the faces of some of the nursing-home patients, you'd understand why this program excites me so much. But the point is that old people sometimes tremble, their hands don't always do what they want them to do.

And it's the same with the kids in the hospitals. You know how kids are. They can grab a dog's tail and yank before you can blink an eye. If we are dealing with a timid or nervous animal, we could have a big problem. Most dogs bite out of fear, you know. And if a dog feels cornered or threatened they can react in a dangerous way."

"So basically, you look for dogs who are mellowed out," Dale said, bending down to pet the collie he and Pete had named Shep.

"That's about it," Janet said. "Let's check the other dogs out, shall we?"

Of the other two dogs, Janet pronounced the small buff-colored cocker spaniel unsuitable because he was too hyper. "But he would make a delightful pet for an active, energetic child. Not a toddler, mind you, but perhaps a child of nine or ten."

The third dog, a lab mix, seemed to have the calm, docile nature Janet was looking for. "I'll take these two right now, if it's all right," she said. "I have a couple of trainers who just recently graduated their dogs. They're at loose ends and would love a new project."

"Hey, all right!" Dale said happily. "Now all we have to worry about is the buff cocker, and I think I know just the ten-year-old for him."

"Really?" Pat asked. "You think you can find him a home?"

"Yeah. I don't know why I didn't think of Jimmy before, but when Janet said he'd be good for a child of nine or ten, something clicked. See, Jimmy's mother is my neighbor. She and her husband just got divorced. Jimmy's having a real hard time. He's missing his dad like crazy. A pet would be just the thing to help him over the hump."

"Mmm, sounds like a match made in heaven, but what about Jimmy's mother? Will she agree?"

"I think so. Maggie is really worried about Jimmy, and she doesn't know how to help him." Blushing, Dale continued. "I've been trying to spend a little time with the kid, you know? Like a big brother thing, but I'll bet having his own dog will be the best possible medicine."

Pat helped Pete get the two dogs ready, and she reminded Janet that the collie would have to be spayed.

"Don't worry," Janet assured her. "I'm familiar with the shelter's rules and regulations, and believe me, I couldn't agree more."

As she waved goodbye to Janet and the two dogs, Pat felt a wonderful feeling of satisfaction. Two of their dogs were on their way to a new, productive life, and if Dale was successful with his young neighbor, the buff cocker would have a home, too. Dear, sweet Dale, blushing as he admitted that he had tried to help a young boy who was hurting. She had known that both Pete and Dale were caring people, but to know that Dale donated even his free time to helping others . . . it made her feel warm all over. No matter how many bad things happened in the world, as long as there were loving, caring young people coming along, you couldn't help but believe that good would triumph over evil.

When she turned into her driveway, Pat immediately noticed the strange car in Hank's driveway. Hank apparently wasn't home yet, and she didn't see anyone sitting in the small red sedan. Did that mean the person was inside Hank's house, or perhaps wandering around the kennels?

That was probably it. Someone had stopped by to see the dogs. Briefly, she debated about walking across the road and telling the person that Hank would be home shortly, but just then she saw the familiar pickup rattling down the road. She smiled, her lips curving with pleasure and her body warming as she pictured Hank's sturdy frame unwinding itself from the truck after a hard day's work.

Getting out of her minivan, Pat decided to leave Hank to tend to his prospective customer while she freshened up and made herself pretty for him. She'd made homemade vegetable soup the night before and Hank would be over for supper shortly. Pat hummed contentedly as she let herself in the house.

Hank stretched and yawned. It had been a long, busy day, and he was looking forward to a nice hot shower and some of Pat's delicious vegetable soup. Not to mention the fact that sitting across from Pat and seeing her smiling face would definitely perk him up.

Frowning, Hank noted the small red car with out-of-state license tags for the first time. He hadn't made any appointments for anyone to see the pups and he wasn't expecting company, so who in the world could it be, and where was the occupant of the car anyway? He peered inside the small sedan and saw that it was indeed empty. His frown intensifying, Hank walked around behind the house to check the kennels. When they caught sight of him, the dogs set up a ruckus.

Hank laughed. "Okay, guys and gals. I'll take care of you in just a few minutes. Meanwhile, has anyone been snooping around here?"

He watched the dogs, almost as if he expected them to answer him, then he shrugged and turned back to the house. Maybe someone had pulled into his driveway and had car trouble.

Hank inserted his key in the lock and had the door open before a new thought occurred to him. Then he laughed again. His imagination was working overtime. If someone had intended to break into his home they sure wouldn't park their vehicle right out front in plain sight.

Still, he stepped inside cautiously, a funny, prickly sensation making his skin tingle. He felt like someone was staring at him, watching and waiting . . .

"Hello, Hank," a low, throaty voice said. "I'm back."

He blinked, stared at the slender woman standing in front of him and closed his eyes. Dear Lord, he was more tired than he'd thought! He was hallucinating!

But when he opened his eyes the woman was still there. She had a sad, regretful smile on her face and she looked just the way he'd remembered her. "Nancy? Where the hell have you been? Where did you come from? Is that your car out front? Good Lord! Do you realize the girls and I were beginning to think you were dead?"

It was a dream . . . no, it was a nightmare. If this had happened even a year earlier . . .

but it was too late now. Much too late.

Nancy smiled gently. "I'm sorry about all that, but I can explain, or at least I can try, but you look done in, Hank. Why don't you go take a nice, warm shower. I'll put some coffee on and we'll talk. We do have to talk, you know. I'm still your legal wife."

"Yes. I know. I . . ." Hank started to say he'd been trying to rectify that little issue, but his tongue felt like it was tied in knots, and he did need a shower badly. "All right. Give me a halfhour. And make the coffee good and strong."

Nancy moved around the kitchen comfortably, amazed at how little things had changed. Hank was understandably shocked, but he had always been a reasonable man, and she was sure that once she explained everything to him he would understand, just as the girls had. Nancy smiled, thinking of Becky and Laurie. How wonderful it had been to see them, and how hard it had been for her to stay away all this time, but it was something she'd had to do. If the girls had known where she was, they'd have pressured her to come back, and she'd felt as though she were suffocating here in this house, with Hank and the dogs, with the boring, everyday sameness of things . . .

with nothing exciting or interesting to look forward to. Oh, some of that had been her fault, she knew that now, but it had taken her several years to realize where she'd gone wrong, where both she and Hank had fallen short of the promises they had once made to one another. She'd fallen into a middle-aged rut, and she'd blamed all her unhappiness on her husband. And then, finally, she'd escaped. She'd run away, because she knew if she didn't she would drown in self-pity.

But poor Hank! Until yesterday she hadn't known that he thought she'd left because he couldn't give her the material things she craved. Well, that had been a part of it. She did hunger for beautiful things, but she wasn't a total dummy and she knew there was a lot more to life than fat bank accounts and designer clothes, and she'd come to realize that Hank was the kind of man a woman could depend on in a crisis. And after all, she was almost fifty-four years old. She couldn't go traipsing all over the country by herself indefinitely, could she? But would Hank believe her? The girls said he was pretty bitter, that he'd even hinted that he'd met someone else.

There was a tap on the back door. Startled, Nancy nearly dropped the coffee mug she was holding. Then she saw a woman's face peering in at her. She hurriedly opened the door.

"Yes?"

Pat's smile froze. "I . . . is Hank here?"

Nancy smiled. "Yes, but he's in the shower right now. Maybe I can help you. I'm Nancy, Hank's wife."

"Hank's wife?"

"Oh, where are my manners?" Nancy said. "Come in, please. It's too cold to stand outside. Hank should be down any minute. Would you like a cup of coffee?" Maybe this was the woman, Nancy thought. There was something in her face that made Nancy uneasy.

Pat shook her head numbly. Hank's wife? But how could that be? He'd said he had no idea where she was, or even if she was still alive, and the woman standing in front of Pat was definitely alive! Suddenly, Pat felt like a world-class frump. She'd showered after coming home from the shelter, but knowing that she and Hank were planning to stay in, she'd worn clean jeans and a soft peach-colored sweatshirt. But this woman who said she was Hank's wife was dressed to the nines—a well-tailored suit, hose, and slim-heeled pumps, her hair in the latest style, flawless makeup.

She shook her head dumbly when Nancy pointed at the coffeemaker. "No. No, thank you. I just . . ."

The crisp scent of after-shave preceded him into the room. Then Hank was standing there, looking from one woman to the other with a strange, almost panicked expression on his face.

"Pat, this is . . ."

"I know," she said quickly, wanting only to escape before she made a colossal fool of herself. "I better go. I just wanted . . . I didn't know . . ."

"I'll call you," Hank yelled, as Pat turned and fled. "I'll call you, Pat!"

"Well, goodness, what was all that about, Hanky-panky?" Nancy asked, pouring two steaming mugs of coffee.

Hank grimaced. Once he'd thought Nancy's pet name for him was cute, now, hearing it roll off her tongue so glibly irritated him beyond belief.

"More to the point, what the hell is all this about?" Hank asked sharply, glaring at Nancy furiously. "You just turn up in my kitchen after more than three years. Surely you don't think you can just walk back in here and take up where you left off."

"Hank, it's . . . the reasons why I left in the first place are complicated. Even I didn't understand them until recently. If you'll just sit down and listen, I'll try to explain. And please, will you stop glaring at me like that? You used to look at the girls that way when they did something wrong."

"The girls!" Hank held his head in his hands and groaned. "They don't understand any of this, especially how their mother could just disappear off the face of the earth, and not even try to contact them."

Nancy perched on a stool at the kitchen counter and shook her head. "I went to see the girls before I came here. I explained everything to them. They were very understanding and forgiving."

"Great! I'm happy for you. Did they tell you that I was estranged from them because of you?"

"Yes, and I'm terribly sorry about that. I never thought the girls would blame you for my leaving."

"You're terribly sorry," Hank repeated dully, shaking his head in amazement. "Is that supposed to make everything all right, Nancy? Do you think that makes up for all the pain and grief the girls and I suffered?"

Nancy crossed one slim leg over the other. This wasn't going at all the way she'd planned it. She'd expected Hank to be almost pathetically glad to see her, and she'd truly believed that he would accept her back into his life and his arms with no questions asked. Oh, not that Hank was a pantywaist. He'd never been that, but once they had been very much in love, and she was the mother of his children. That had to count for something.

"I know just saying I'm sorry is inadequate, Hank, and anyway, I'm more than just sorry. I regret what I did and the way I did it with all my heart, but it's done and I can't change it. All I can do now is try to make up for it in every way I can, and look to the future. And that is why I'm here."

Hank shook his head. "What are you saying, Nancy?"

"I want to come back to you, Hank. We're still legally married. It will be hard at first, but in time we can put the past behind us and it will be like it never happened. I want to be a mother to my girls, and I want to be your wife again, Hank."

Seventeen

Hank and Nancy talked in circles for hours. Finally, when hunger pangs threatened to overcome Hank, he made scrambled eggs and toast, thinking wistfully of Pat's homemade soup and baking-powder biscuits.

When Hank glanced at his wristwatch and saw that it was after midnight, he called a halt. "Look, Nancy, it's late. I'm tired and I have to get up and go to work tomorrow."

"All right," Nancy said agreeably. "I know this is a serious matter and not something we can just jump into. We'll take things slow and easy, one step at a time, but you'll see, Hank. In a few days it will be like I never left."

Hank's jaw dropped. "You mean . . . you actually think you can just move back in here and . . ."

Nancy's lower lip formed a pretty little pout. "Now, Hanky, you're not going to turn me out into the cold at this hour of the night, are you? I didn't think I would have to make hotel reservations, so I already took my bags upstairs."

"You what? Good Lord, Nancy! Where do you get your nerve?"

"All right," Nancy said. She hoped she didn't look as uneasy as she felt. She'd never known Hank to be this stubborn, this cold and hard. "I guess you're just not quite ready to take up where we left off, but that's no problem. I'll sleep in Becky's old room for the time being."

"My God, I can't believe this!" Hank cried. He felt like tearing his hair out by the roots. Had Nancy always been this self-centered, this insensitive to other people's feelings?

"Do whatever you like for tonight," he growled, "but tomorrow we'll talk again, and get this mess straightened out once and for all."

Nancy smiled. "I knew you'd be reasonable, Hank," she said. Then she stood on tiptoe and kissed his cheek. "I'd really like to do more," she whispered huskily, "but I can see you're not ready. But it was good between us once, Hank, and it can be even better now."

Hank's blood was on overheat. He felt like an auto radiator that was ready to overflow.

Any minute he expected steam to start pouring out of his ears, and flames to burst out of his skull. And Pat! Poor Pat! What on earth was she thinking?

He waited until Nancy had gone upstairs, swishing her slender hips seductively, then he peered out his front window. A surge of disappointment gripped him. All the lights were out at her house. It wouldn't be right to call her now, and besides what could he say to her? Until he got things straight with Nancy it was better if he just stayed on his own side of the street. But he wished he could run out of the house and straight to Pat. He wished he could hold her and love her and make this whole crazy mess go away.

He stretched and yawned. Now he really was tired. Actually he felt completely drained, as if all the energy and strength had been sucked out of his body. Despite the way his head was spinning, he was sure he'd be able to fall asleep.

Pat tossed and turned restlessly. Hank's wife was lovely, a woman any man could be proud of. Did Hank still love her? He had said he didn't, but that was before, when he thought she might be dead. How did he feel now? Pat scrunched her eyes closed, trying not to imagine Hank kissing and caressing Nancy the way he'd so recently caressed her. But Nancy was his wife, and from what she knew of Hank's daughters, they would be overjoyed to have their mother back in the nest. Pat's head ached, and she remembered Hank calling out that he'd call her. But he hadn't, and the last time she peered out the window, she'd seen that all the lights were out in his house. She shivered. Was he in bed with Nancy this very minute, making passionate love to her?

Celia warned you, she reminded herself. She told you you were playing with fire to get involved with a married man, even though there was no wife in evidence. But Hank had seemed so sure when she said his marriage was over, yet now his wife was back, in his home, maybe even in his arms.

Pat sighed and determinedly closed her eyes, willing the unwanted images away. Go to sleep, she told herself firmly. Tomorrow is another day. And whatever was going to happen would happen. She remembered the alcoholic's saying and said a quick prayer that she would be able to accept what she could not change.

Nancy was bustling around the kitchen

making breakfast when Hank entered the kitchen. He stopped, did a double take, then reassured himself that his eyesight wasn't failing, that Nancy was indeed wearing a frilly apron and flipping eggs in a skillet.

"You don't have to do this," he mumbled. "I don't normally eat a big breakfast."

"But you should," Nancy insisted, smiling as she poured him a glass of orange juice. "Sit down, dear."

Sighing, Hank pulled out a chair and sat down. He glanced out the window wistfully. Where was Pat? What was she thinking?

"Nancy, this isn't going to work," he began slowly. "Despite what you seem to think, we can't just resume 'business as usual.' You walked out of here what . . . ? Three years ago? You said you were tired of living like the lower classes. You said I was dull and boring . . . that you were sick to death of a washing machine that clanged during the rinse cycle and a husband who smelled like dogs. You said . . ."

"Oh, Hank! You didn't really believe all those silly, horrid things I said, did you? I was just letting off steam. I was having a crisis. I'd just celebrated my fiftieth birthday and it seemed like everything good and worthwhile was behind me. I couldn't image that there was anything at all to look forward to. And then, when Doctor Ellis said I needed a change . . . well . . ."

"Who the hell is Doctor Ellis?"

Nancy had the grace to flush. "He's . . . well, he's the therapist I was seeing before I left. He was . . . is very young and progressive, and he believes . . ."

"Wait a minute!" Hank snarled. "You were seeing a therapist and you didn't even tell me?"

"Well, I knew you wouldn't approve. As I said, Doctor Ellis is very modern and I didn't think you would understand."

"He's the one who told you to leave me? He's the reason you took off and left me and the girls to think you were dead in a ditch somewhere?"

"Now, Hank, aren't you being a little dramatic? I explained that I had to go away for a while, to be by myself and sort things out, and you know I was unhappy with our financial status."

"Oh yes, I knew that, all right! And my financial status, as you put it, was a lot worse off after you left, taking our savings with you!"

"Well, I had to have something to live on," Nancy pouted, turning away from the stove and placing a platter of perfectly fried eggs in front of Hank. "There," she said girlishly. "Over easy, just the way you like them, darling."

"Don't call me darling!" Hank yelled, slamming his fist on the table so hard the platter of eggs slid off the table and landed on the floor, splattering runny egg yolk everywhere.

"Good heavens! You have been repressing your anger, haven't you, dear? Well, don't worry," Nancy said, bending to clean up the mess. "Perhaps a few sessions with Doctor Ellis will help you learn to deal with your innermost feelings in a more productive way."

"I can deal with them very productively without any help from your shrink!" Hank raged. He stood up, so angry he was trembling. "I'm going to work," he said. "When I come home I sincerely hope you're gone, but this time leave an address where you can be reached, because my attorney will be serving you with divorce papers very soon!"

Nancy watched Hank back out of the driveway, and shook her head. Hank was much angrier than she had expected. He'd always been a mild-mannered, easygoing man. What on earth had changed him so? Well, it was an unexpected hurdle, but nothing she couldn't handle. She sat down and picked up the telephone. Dr. Ellis would tell her what to do.

Pat sat by her front window. She watched Hank drive away in a cloud of dust, and she waited, hoping and praying that the little red car would be next. But the car never moved, and finally, at one o'clock in the afternoon, hunger forced Pat into moving away from the window and into the kitchen.

So! She was staying. That could mean any one of a number of things. Perhaps she and Hank were trying to work out a divorce settlement, or maybe he was just letting her stay there long enough to be reunited with her daughters or maybe . . . and this option was the one that sent shocks of pain through Pat's heart, maybe Hank and Nancy were going to put their marriage back together.

Well, so be it, if that was what they both wanted. Personally, just a couple of minutes with Nancy had told Pat that the woman was all wrong for Hank. Nancy was a good-looking woman, no doubt about that, but there was a brittleness, a coldness about her that worried Pat. Even if she and Hank went kaput, she didn't want to see him get back into a situation that could only bring him unhappiness. Because no matter what happened, she knew Hank was a good man, a loving man who deserved to be loved in return.

The men arrived to give Pat an estimate on a new heating system at three o'clock. As she let them in, Pat saw that the little red car was still parked in Hank's driveway. Something inside her shriveled and died.

"Come in," she invited the workmen politely. "I've been waiting for you."

By the time the men left an hour later, Pat held two written estimates in her hand. One for a gas heating system, another for an electric system. Her head was spinning with the pros and cons of each, with specifications and projected costs, and she was thoroughly confused. She'd never dealt with things like this when Clifford was alive. She felt her lips twist bitterly as she remembered. She hadn't been a helpmate in her marriage, she'd merely been a pretty ornament. Window dressing. Well, she'd come a long way since Clifford's death, and she could handle this, too. Only, she'd hoped to get Hank's input, not because she couldn't do this alone, but because she valued and respected his opinion.

Well, forget that, Pat, she told herself, staring out the window at the little red sedan. Her eyes narrowing, Pat decided that red cars were incredibly ugly, and anyone who owned one must have horrible taste.

Hank pulled into the driveway, his muscles tightening in painful spasms as he saw the red car. Now what? How could Nancy possibly think that she could waltz back into his life with a weak apology and a wistful smile?

He felt ten years older than he was when he slid out from behind the wheel, and he couldn't help glancing over toward Pat's house. He felt a twinge of pain in his chest when he saw that her minivan was gone. Then he shrugged. Maybe it was just as well. He needed to straighten out this mess with Nancy before he went to Pat.

"Of course I'm thrilled to have you here," Celia said, hugging Pat tightly. She had lost more weight since Pat had last seen her, and she looked wonderful, except for the deep sadness shadowing her eyes.

Pat gave her sister an extra squeeze, then stepped back. "How are you really, dear?" she asked gently. "I've been worried about you."

Celia took Pat's hand and led her into the living room. They sat down on the overstuffed sofa. "One day at a time," Celia said quietly.

"I just take each day as it comes. Some days are better than others."

Pat nodded. "I know. It was that way for me at first. But it is true what everyone says, sis. Time heals."

Celia nodded. "That's what I keep telling myself. I'm glad I've got Mortimer. I don't know what I'd have done without him these past few weeks."

Pat laughed. "And now both you and Mortimer will have company," she said. "Are you sure you can handle three lively dogs?"

"Of course. Didn't you tell me that Ink and Spot were exceptionally well behaved?"

"I did," Pat said, flushing as Celia backed her into a corner. "Well, they are . . . usually. It's just that once in a while they get a little rambunctious . . ."

Celia rolled her eyes heavenward as the three dogs fought over a pair of socks she had knotted together for Mortimer to play tug-of-war. "There goes two more pairs of socks," she said, groaning.

"I just couldn't bear to leave them in a cold, impersonal kennel while I'm out in California. Dale offered to take Cat, and Pete is baby-sitting Tweetie, so I thought . . ."

"Stop apologizing, Pat. If I didn't think I could handle them, I'd say so. Have you ever known me to be shy?"

Pat grinned. "Now that you mention it . . ."

Celia chuckled, and for a minute the sadness in her eyes dimmed just a little. "Don't even think about that!" she cried. But a moment later, she sobered. "I would have thought Hank would keep the dogs. He has all those kennels, and he certainly knows a lot about dogs."

"I didn't ask him, Celia," Pat said slowly. She needed to talk to someone desperately, but she wasn't sure Celia would understand. "He . . . his wife is back." There. She'd said it. If Celia wanted to say "I told you so," let her.

"Oh, Pat! What happened? I thought he didn't even know where she was?"

"He didn't. I think, no, I'm sure Hank had no idea she was going to turn up on his doorstep. If you could have seen his face . . ."

"You were there?" Celia's hand went to her throat. "Oh, Pat! You weren't . . . she didn't walk in on . . ."

Pat laughed, but it was a harsh, bitter laugh, without a trace of mirth. "Don't worry. She didn't catch us in a compromising situation, if that's what you're thinking. Actually I walked in on them . . . oh, they weren't doing anything, but she was there in his kitchen, acting as if . . . as if she'd never left!" Her voice broke on a sob, and Celia gathered her into her arms.

"Oh, Pat! This is exactly what I was afraid of!"

"We thought she was . . . dead," Pat sobbed. "She's been gone more than three years, and she never even got in touch with her daughters!"

"Oh dear, this is terrible," Celia said, her forehead puckered with worry. "What are you going to do?"

"I don't know," Pat said, dabbing at her eyes and straightening up. "How about a cup of tea? Didn't Mom always say that would cure anything?"

Later, over tea and some of Celia's homemade sugar cookies, Pat and her sister talked their hearts out.

"If it weren't for the fact that I'm committed to this day-care center, I don't know what I would have done," Celia admitted. "It's as though a vital part of me is missing. You know how close Jake and I were. He could start a sentence and I could finish it. And sometimes, at night when I can't sleep, I blame myself for not insisting he see a doctor. I knew something wasn't just right, but he'd always been so strong and healthy. I guess I couldn't imagine anything getting him down."

Celia lowered her eyes, and her voice was almost a whisper. "I'm ashamed to admit this but . . . sometimes I feel so angry at Jake for leaving me this way. He always promised me we would grow old together, and now he's left me to do it all alone."

Pat nodded. "Anger is a normal part of the grieving process, hon. It's good that you can admit what you're feeling. It shows that in time you will heal."

"Well, I'm doing my best. But what about you, Pat? What's going to happen with you and Hank?"

"I don't know," Pat said, setting her cup back in its saucer. "I was starting to think that Hank and I might be able to have what you and Jake had. But now . . . well, even though he assured me had no feelings left for Nancy, how can I be sure? And if there's a chance they can get back together I have to back away. You know how I feel about the sanctity of marriage, Celia. I would never do anything to undermine that."

"My goodness," Celia said, shaking her head in bewilderment, "how could a woman just walk out on her husband and children and let them think she was dead?"

"I don't know. But I was planning to fly

out to California in a couple of weeks anyway for Cliff's show, so I decided maybe I should leave now and give Hank a chance to work things out, without worrying about me hovering in the background."

"Maybe that's best," Celia said. "You know, dear, if it weren't for these animals, I'd be tempted to go to California with you. Jake and I always planned to take a long, leisurely trip out there someday, but now . . ."

Celia's voice trailed off wistfully, and Pat had a sudden inspiration. She couldn't imagine why she hadn't thought of it herself.

"Celia, we can do it!" she said excitedly. "If you can leave things on hold with the day-care center for a few weeks, we can go and have a wonderful time, and we deserve it!"

"Oh dear! But what about the animals? I thought you didn't want to put them in a kennel?"

"I don't," Pat said, "but maybe we won't have to. Let me give Pete a call at the shelter and see what he and Dale can do for us."

A hour later, Pat hung up the phone and faced her sister with a triumphant smile. "They'll take them," she said happily. "Dale will look after Ink and Spot at his home, and Pete will take Mortimer. They promised to give our pups lots of TLC. We're going to do it, Celia! California, here we come!"

The next morning, leaving Celia in a flutter deciding what to pack for the trip, Pat drove the three dogs to the shelter.

"Now promise you'll give them their doggie biscuits every morning," she reminded Dale worriedly.

"Relax, Pat, you're talking to an expert here. Anything I don't know about looking after dogs hasn't been invented."

"That's what I love about you, Dale, your modesty." Pat laughed and hugged him, then dropped to her knees to hug each dog in turn. "I'll be back," she promised. "I'll be back."

She couldn't resist driving past her house. She told herself she just wanted to check on her property, but in reality she wanted to see if the red car was still parked in Hank's driveway. She grimaced when she saw that it was. Well, that told her something, she thought sickly. If Hank wasn't interested in patching things up with his wife, he'd have booted her out, but he hadn't so . . . Pat decided she didn't want to think about it, and she pulled into her driveway, hopped out of the car and hurried to her back door. Hank always used the back door, and that was where she'd left the note. It was still there, and the imprint of her coral lipstick was still vivid. Sealed with a kiss—and Hank hadn't even seen it. He hadn't even bothered to come by to explain. The sickness intensified as Pat impulsively ripped the note off the door and tore it into tiny pieces. She watched, dry-eyed, as the fragments fluttered away in the wind. Over. It was over.

Eighteen

"Are you sure we have everything?" Celia asked, looking around her living room as though something would suddenly jump out at her. "Every time I go on a trip I forget something."

Pat laughed. "Not this time. This time you have me with you to keep your head on straight. Oh, Celia, I'm so happy you agreed to come with me! We're going to have a good time. I was halfway dreading this trip, but with you at my side . . . well, I think I can get through anything."

"Mom! Aunt Celia! What a surprise!" Cliff beamed at his mother and aunt when he met them at the airport. "Gosh, I wasn't expecting a family rooting section. This is great!"

Celia hugged her nephew, then stepped back to allow Pat the same privilege.

"I'm glad to see you, son," Pat said softly. "I persuaded Celia to join me and we thought we'd explore your new home state."

"I couldn't be more pleased," Cliff said, sobering. "I'm still working at night, you know, so I won't be available to squire you around. This works out perfectly."

"If your show goes well, maybe you can give up that job soon, Cliff," Celia said. "I'm so happy you're finally going to realize your dream."

Cliff grinned boyishly. "Me, too," he said. "Although sometimes I have to pinch myself to be sure it's really true. Doug says . . ."

Pat saw the flush that colored her son's cheeks.

"I mean . . ."

"It's all right, son," Pat said gently, laying her hand on his arm. "Aunt Celia and I both are eager to meet Doug. Is he working today?"

Cliff's smile was blinding. "Yes, he is. He has an agent now who is interested in marketing the book he's working on, so his big break may be just around the corner."

"That's wonderful," Pat said, surprised to find that she meant it.

Cliff drove them to their hotel in his old pickup truck.

"What is it with you men and your trucks?" Celia complained good-naturedly. "Jake always claimed he needed a pickup, although what for I could never figure out."

Cliff grinned. "It's handy for transporting my paintings back and forth," he said.

"Well, if your show is a success, and I know it will be, maybe you won't be doing so much transporting," Pat said. Maybe she should offer to help buy a new truck. This one didn't seem to be in the best of health. She bit her lip, wondering if she dared broach the subject to him. When Cliff left home, he declared his independence, and although Pat was sure he had endured some very hard times, he'd stuck to his guns and refused to take any help from her or his father. Would it be different now? She didn't know, and she decided not to worry about it. A new truck was the least of her worries at the moment.

Cliff helped them get settled in their room at the hotel, then, looking extremely uneasy, he broached the subject that had apparently never been far from his mind.

"Doug and I would like to take you to dinner tonight. There's a great new Italian restaurant not far from this hotel and . . . well, I know you're probably tired from the flight, so if you want to beg off . . ."

Pat wondered how many times Cliff had practiced his little speech in front of a mirror. She was tired, and if the circumstances had been different, she probably would have taken a rain check. But circumstances weren't different, so she smiled brightly. "That sounds wonderful, Cliff. If it's all right with Celia, I'd be delighted to have dinner with you and Doug. What time shall we be ready?"

Cliff's relief was almost palpable. "Hey, that's great! Can you be ready by six-thirty? I'll make reservations for seven."

"Fine," Pat said, then she gave her son an extra hug. "I'm glad I came," she said simply.

"Me, too," Cliff said happily. "I mean, so am I."

"Good work, Pat," Celia said, nodding her approval when Cliff left. "I'm proud of you."

"Don't give me too much credit too soon," Pat said, suddenly feeling exhausted. "I think I'll lie down for a while."

Doug turned out to be an extremely handsome and charming young man. He appeared to be about five or six years older than Cliff, and he treated Pat and Celia with quiet respect. As the meal progressed, she found herself relaxing and actually beginning to enjoy herself. Then Cliff asked about Hank.

She felt the color wash out of her face. "He . . . I'd rather not talk about Hank right now, if you don't mind."

Cliff looked bewildered. "Oh. Well, sure. Whatever you say, Mom. Uh, how is the work at the animal shelter coming?"

As it turned out, Doug was an animal rights activist, involved in protesting the use of animals for laboratory experiments. After outlining her work at the shelter, Pat listened as Doug explained what the group he belonged to was doing to protect helpless animals.

When Doug paused to take a breath, Cliff laughed. "I was so impressed with your work at the shelter that Doug and I have adopted a couple of pets ourselves. Wait until you see my dog, Arnold."

"Arnold?" Pat asked, laughing. "Well, I suppose it's not as bad as Mortimer."

"Mortimer is a perfect name for a dog," Celia protested. "At least it's perfect for my dog. Mortimer loves his name."

Doug grinned. "I adopted a dog that already had a name. Rover is just a plain, ordinary dog, but he's great."

Over dessert, Cliff filled them in on the plans for his art show. "Three other artists will also be showing their work. It's a major gallery. I'm still having a hard time believing they really liked my work."

"He's much too modest," Doug said. "I keep telling him his talent is remarkable."

"As yours is," Cliff said quickly, smiling. "Did I tell you that Doug has an agent interested in marketing his work?"

"That's wonderful," Celia said. "My, I do admire creative people. I've never been able to create anything more exciting than an apple pie!"

Both young men laughed.

When Pat and Celia finally began to succumb to jet lag, Cliff insisted they call it a night. "You two are going to pass out on your feet if you don't get back to the hotel and get some rest," he said, "and we've got plenty of time to do this again."

"Yes," Pat said, knowing now that they would get together again, and that the next time she would enjoy herself even more than she had this evening.

After telling them good night, Doug waited in his car while Cliff walked the two women up to their hotel room.

At the door, Cliff impulsively hugged Pat. "Thanks, Mom," he said softly. "Tonight was great."

Pat patted his cheek. "I love you. I'm glad I came."

"Oh my, I'm really done in," Celia said, flopping down on her bed after Cliff had gone, "but I had a wonderful time tonight, Pat. I really did. Cliff's friend is very nice."

"He is, isn't he?" Pat asked incredulously. "I'm not sure what I expected, but I actually forgot that he's . . . that he and Cliff . . ."

Celia smiled gently, and reached out to touch her sister's hand. "Let it go, Pat," she said. "Forget about that and just enjoy visiting with your son. They're just people, you know."

Pat nodded, her lips curving in a smile. "I'd almost forgotten that," she said. "Thanks for reminding me."

Nineteen

Pat and Celia had a wonderful time the next few days. They shopped, lunched in little restaurants, and most evenings they had dinner with Cliff and Doug. On her third night in California, Pat agreed to visit Cliff's apartment and have dinner there.

"Be grateful Cliff's the chef," Doug joked, as he greeted the two women and took their coats. "I'm totally helpless in the kitchen."

"My, I never would have imagined Cliff would turn out to be a gourmet chef," Celia said. "My husband enjoyed cooking," she added.

"I'm sorry I didn't get to see Uncle Jake when I was visiting Mom, Aunt Celia," Cliff said, passing around a tray of canapés.

Pat forced herself to relax. She had been tense all day. She'd been able to accept Doug as a pleasant, personable young man, but being in the home her son shared with him was something else. It was as if she was being forced to come face-to-face with the intimate side of her son's life. She accepted a glass of wine from Doug and managed a weak smile.

"Jake was very fond of you, Cliff," Celia said. "He would have been so pleased at your success."

Pat took a deep, calming breath, and the tightness in her chest eased. Dear Celia. She'd come to the rescue once again, reminding Pat of the real reason they were here in California.

"Yes," she said, nodding in agreement, "Jake would have been almost as proud as Celia and I are."

The meal was excellent. As she tasted the delicious flan Cliff had made for dessert, she mentioned that Ashley had also become quite a good cook.

"I was amazed," she said, "because when she lived at home she didn't know the difference between a spatula and a fork, but I guess that's what living independently does for you."

Cliff laughed. "It helps if you like to eat." He and Doug exchanged a brief smile, and Pat felt the tightness back in her chest. She had to stop this! She had to accept what she had no power to change. Cliff was not her baby boy anymore. He was an adult. He was capable of making his own decisions, and mature enough to handle the consequences of his actions. That was what she had to remember.

They made it an early evening, and Pat felt a rush of relief as she stepped out into the night air. Cliff had offered to drive them to the hotel, but Pat insisted on calling a taxi, and now she slid into the car gratefully.

"Another hurdle," she mumbled, leaning her head back and closing her eyes.

"You're doing beautifully, Pat," Celia said, patting her hand. "I know how difficult this is for you. I'm proud of you."

"I don't want to hurt Cliff," Pat said quietly. "He got enough of that from his father."

Celia sighed. "Pat, Cliff seems very happy, and he's living his life the way he sees fit. That's what you have to remember."

"I keep wishing there was some way I could get Cliff and Ashley together. When I'm gone I'd like to think that they'll have each other."

"I think that's an issue they have to work out for themselves," Celia said. "It's not something you can force."

"I know," Pat said, "but it hurts to see them separated this way."

The next day Pat and Celia got up early and took a bus tour to the San Diego Zoo. Like children they oohed and aahed over the animals, the cuddly koalas, the huge hippos, and even the slithery snakes. At noon they found a bench and flopped down gratefully.

"Whew! I must be getting old," Pat said. "I'm exhausted. Oh look, isn't that a hot dog stand over there? When was the last time you had a hot dog, Celia?"

"Before I started my weight-loss program," Celia admitted. "I know I can't make a habit of this sort of thing, but one wouldn't hurt, would it?"

"Shall we?" Pat asked eagerly, already fishing some money out of her purse. "Oh, I wonder if they have sauerkraut?"

They ate hot dogs and drank lemonade and recharged their batteries by resting on the bench and watching the other zoo patrons stroll by.

"This is delightful," Celia said. "I almost feel like a kid again. I'm glad you asked me to come along with you, sis."

"Me, too," Pat said. Then, a sudden, sharp pang of longing pierced her heart. Celia was a wonderful companion, but she couldn't help wishing Hank was beside her. He would have had a wonderful time at the zoo.

"Missing Hank?" Celia asked.

"Yes. Stupid, isn't it? Even though I know he's probably all wrapped up in Nancy, I can't help wishing . . . well, I'll get over it. I have to!"

"If Hank does get back with his wife, won't it be difficult to live there, right across the street from him?" Celia asked, her forehead puckered with concern. "I mean, I'd think it would be awkward at best."

Pat nodded. She hadn't thought that far ahead yet; she was just trying desperately not to think about Hank at all.

"I'll cross that bridge when I get to it," she said quietly. "Right now I'm just trying not to worry about anything but my son."

"Good," Celia said, nodding in agreement. "I think that's best."

Then, almost before they realized how much time had passed, the day of the show arrived. When Cliff hesitantly informed the women that the affair would be formal, Pat and Celia went shopping.

"Do you realize how many dresses like this I donated to the thrift shop?" Pat asked, laughing, as she held up a black gown with abundant sequins.

"Oh dear," Celia said. "I haven't worn a dress this fancy since my senior prom." She flushed prettily as she held up a soft blue chiffon.

"I love that color with your hair. Are you going to take it?"

"I don't know. It's terribly expensive, and where would I ever wear it again?"

A spasm of pain clutched at Pat's heart, but she just shook her head. How could she admit to Celia that she'd started to dream about marrying Hank, and that she'd envisioned Celia standing up for her as her maid of honor? And the blue dress would be perfect.

"Please take it. It will be my treat. After all, it's for Cliff's show."

"Oh, I wasn't hinting," Celia said, flushing. "I can pay for it."

"I know you can, but I'd like to do this. Please let me have the pleasure."

Celia grinned, running her fingers over the silky soft material. "Why not? If it makes you happy, how can I say no?"

Pat passed up the black dress in favor of an ivory crepe, adorned with pearls.

Then, giggling like schoolgirls, they hurried off to the beauty salon to have their hair done.

They were ready and waiting long before Doug arrived to pick them up. "Cliff went on ahead to make sure everything was properly set up," he explained.

"Cliff must be a bundle of nerves," Celia said. "Oh, I do hope everything goes well."

"I'm sure it will," Doug said, smiling. "Your son is a very talented man, Pat."

"Yes, I know. He was interested in art even as a small boy. I'm glad someone finally saw his talent."

They rode the short distance to the gallery in relative quiet.

Pat had her fingers crossed that Cliff would realize his dreams. Her son had persevered despite the obstacles life put in his path, and now it was time for him to receive the recognition he deserved.

Doug parked the car and came around to help Pat and Celia out. Celia began walking toward the gallery entrance, barely able to contain her excitement. When Pat would have followed her, Doug laid his hand on her arm.

"Thank you," he said simply.

Pat nodded. There was no need for words.

* * *

When they entered the gallery they saw Cliff surrounded by several elegantly dressed patrons. Pat felt her heart swell with pride. Cliff wore a tuxedo, and he looked incredibly handsome and happy. She allowed Doug to propel her and Celia toward the group.

"Doug!" Cliff's eyes were shining, then he turned to Pat and Celia. "Everyone," he said, his voice filled with pride. "I want you to meet my mother, Patricia Melbourne, and my aunt, Celia Browning." He laughed. "And, of course, you all know Doug."

Doug stepped to Cliff's side, and Pat felt a momentary stab of pain, then it was swallowed up in good feelings as Cliff's new friends heaped congratulations on him.

Later, when the first flurry had died down, Cliff took Pat and Celia on a guided tour to point out his work. Pat felt the color drain out of her face as she saw the first painting.

"Oh, Cliff!"

It was a dark, sad painting depicting a small boy cowering in a corner with a tall, stern-faced man standing over him with a hunting rifle in his hands.

"It's all right, Mother," Cliff said quickly, pointing toward the rest of his paintings. "This one was done shortly after I came out ıere. I was pretty unhappy then, and it showed in my work. I wasn't going to hang t, but my sponsor thought I should." He ugged Pat away from the painting and pointed to the next one.

"This is one of my most recent works," Cliff said, unable to hide his pride. "What do you think?"

It was a landscape, soft and pure and filled with light and sunshine.

"It's beautiful," Pat said, awestruck. This was the first time she had seen her son's work, with the exception of his childhood drawings, and those more closely resembled the first painting. As they moved from one painting to the next, Pat saw that they were all light, happy renderings. There was one of a small boy and girl sitting on a lawn that was particularly poignant.

"That looks very much like you and your sister did at that age," she said, speaking around the lump in her throat.

Cliff nodded and squeezed Pat's hand. "I know," he said softly.

White-coated waiters served champagne and canapés, and soft music played in the background. Pat moved easily among the crowd, memories of her past life putting her at ease. She was so terribly proud of her son! Her heart felt as though it would burst with pride as she watched Cliff greet admirers. And always, nearby was Doug. Pat watched her son turn to his companion from time to time, as if seeking reassurance. She watched Doug smile encouragingly, and once she saw him make a victory sign. And as she watched, trying desperately to understand, her aching heart eased. Her son was loved. What more could any mother ask for?

Then, just as she placed her empty champagne glass on a tray, she felt Celia's hand on her arm.

"Pat, look! Over there! Isn't that . . . my God, it is! It's Ashley!"

Pat spun around, convinced Celia had tippled one too many glasses of bubbly. Her mouth opened, but nothing came out. It was Ashley, and she was heading straight for Cliff!

A crowd of people separated them, and there was no way Pat could reach them in time. She could only stand helplessly as Ashley determinedly marched up to her brother.

She saw Cliff turn, saw the amazement in his eyes, saw the color rise in his cheeks, and then, praying her knees wouldn't cave in, Pat watched in awe as her daughter threw her arms around her brother and hugged him.

"Oh my!" Celia said, her hand at her throat. "Oh my!"

Then the two women were threading their way through the crowd, and when they finally reached Cliff and Ashley, Pat saw that both her children had tears on their cheeks. And Cliff's arm was tight around his sister's slender waist.

Ashley smiled through her tears. "I had to come, Mother. This is my brother." She looked up at Cliff then, and her smile said it all.

"Now everything is perfect," Cliff said, hugging his sister. "This really is the happiest night of my life."

"I still can't get over the way Ashley just walked in and hugged Cliff," Celia said the next day. "I almost fainted."

Pat laughed. "You and me both, but oh, Celia, wasn't it wonderful? I'm still in a state of shock."

"As Cliff said, it made everything perfect. But what a shame that Ashley had to fly right back to New York."

"Yes. I was hoping she could stay on with

us until we leave, but she has such a hectic schedule."

The next three days flew by as Pat and Celia crammed as much sightseeing as possible into every waking hour. Then the morning of their departure arrived. Grinning sheepishly, Celia admitted that she was ready to go home.

"This has been lovely," she said, "and I'm so glad we could have this time together, Pat. You know, all those years when Clifford was alive, I sometimes felt very separated from you."

"I know," Pat said. "I realize now that I did a lot of things wrong during that time, but you and I are going to spend a lot of time together from now on. But you're right, you know. It is time for us to go home. I miss Ink and Spot, and even Tweetie's blabbermouth."

They had said their goodbyes to Cliff and Doug the night before, and now there was nothing left but to pack the souvenirs they'd purchased.

Celia dozed during the flight, but Pat was wide awake, her mind spinning. Saying goodbye to Cliff had been emotional, but not as sad as she had once thought it would be. Finally, after years of embarrassment and abuse, Cliff was free. He was marching to his own drumbeat.

And seeing Ashley and Cliff together had been the ultimate gift to a mother's heart. All in all, the trip had turned out far better than she could have hoped, and now she was on her way home. Her heart twisted as she remembered Hank and Nancy, and the way Nancy had looked in Hank's kitchen. So confident, so at ease.

It was her kitchen, too, she reminded herself and maybe by now . . . no, she couldn't bear to think of it. Yet, when she closed her eyes horrible images flashed in front of her. Hank smiling down at his wife . . . putting his large, calloused hands on her shoulders . . . bending his lips to hers . . .

"He belonged to her before he belonged to you, Pat," she muttered, wishing it weren't true, but knowing it was, and if Hank wanted to reconcile with Nancy, she certainly wouldn't stand in their way. She had always believed marriage was a sacred trust between a husband and his wife, and even Clifford's infidelity hadn't changed that.

"I'm sorry, sis," Celia said softly, laying her hand on Pat's arm. "I know you cared for him."

"Yes, I did." She didn't tell Celia that she

still cared . . . that even if Hank went back to his wife, she would still care. She loved Hank, and love didn't die that easily.

Twenty

They took a taxi from the airport to Celia's house, then they drove to the shelter to pick up their pets.

Dale and Pete hugged Pat in turn, and then, almost before she was ready, they turned the dogs loose.

Ink and Spot were so excited they piddled on the floor at Pat's feet. She laughed helplessly as she hugged and petted both dogs.

"Oh, Mortimer, look at you," Celia said, her eyes shining. "I believe you've gained weight!"

"Hank was here," Pete said quietly, drawing Pat aside, after the animals' first excitement subsided. "He was frantic wondering where you'd gone."

Pat stiffened, remembering the note she'd torn up and thrown away.

"What did you tell him?"

"The truth, of course, that you and your sister went out to California to visit your son." Pete shifted his feet uneasily. "Look, Pat, I know your private life is none of my business, but I . . . well, Dale and I really care about you, and unless I'm losing it, so does Hank. He seemed really upset. I just . . . well, is there anything Dale and I can do?"

Pat smiled gently. "Thank you, no, but I appreciate your concern. I'm sure I'll be seeing Hank one of these days. Things will work out, one way or another."

And they would, she told herself sternly, as she drove home after dropping off Celia and Mortimer.

Clifford's death and discovering his infidelity had taught her a lot. Life didn't always turn out the way you expected, and you had to roll with the punches. Sighing, Pat glanced at the two dogs sleeping in the back of her minivan. She grimaced as she watched Tweetie's cage sway dangerously as she rounded a corner. At least she still had her pets, and Ink and Spot were real good at keeping her feet warm on a cold winter's night.

* * *

Hank had come home from work the day Pat left for California fully expecting his house to be empty, but no, Nancy's little red car was still parked in the drive. Anger stiffened his jaw. Nancy sure had guts to think she could waltz right back into his life and take up where she'd left off. Well, she was in for a surprise. He was finished with her little games. He had Pat now, or at least he did until Nancy showed up. He prayed he could get things straightened out with Nancy before Pat got fed up and took off.

He looked across the road as he pulled into his driveway. Pat wasn't home, but that didn't mean anything. She might be at the shelter, or even in the city visiting Celia. She'd said something about that a few days earlier.

The minute he opened the kitchen door he smelled it. Nancy's famous Hungarian stew. Once it had been his favorite, but now his stomach churned.

She was standing by the stove, looking younger than her fifty-three years in a soft pink shirt and dark slacks, with a frilly apron protecting her clothes.

"Nancy? What the hell do you think you're doing?"

"Oh, Hank, stop growling like a grizzly

bear. I know you're tired and hungry. Why don't you take a nice warm shower? You'll feel better."

Hank opened his mouth, but the words he wanted to say wouldn't come out. Finally he slammed his lunch pail down on the counter furiously. "I'll be down in a few minutes," he yelled, "and then we're going to talk!"

He let the shower run for a long time, hoping the warm water would loosen his tight muscles. He felt like a rocket about to blast off into the atmosphere. How could a woman possibly think she could just walk back into her marriage after three years of silence? Did she even care that he and the girls had been frantic, thinking she was dead?

No, of course she didn't. Even as a young wife and mother, Nancy had put her own needs and wants first. Part of it was because of the way she'd been brought up, with all the privilege of wealth . . . with her every wish granted the minute she voiced it. But through the years he'd kept hoping she'd change, that she'd grow up and get her priorities straight, only she never had, and then she left.

"Oh, there you are," Nancy said brightly, carrying the soup tureen to the table. "I was starting to think you'd climbed into the bath-tub and fallen asleep."

"You know I don't like baths," Hank growled, sitting down at the table. The smell of the stew made him feel like he was smothering. "Take that off the table please," he said, waving his arm at the tureen. "I can't eat it."

"But . . . you always loved my Hungarian stew," Nancy said, a puzzled frown marring her still smooth complexion. "You must be hungry. Aren't you hungry?"

"Not for that," Hank said tightly. "Please take it away."

Her eyes sparkling with tears, Nancy carried the tureen to the sink. "I don't see why you have to be so nasty," she mumbled. "I'm doing everything I can to make up for what I did."

"Make up? You think a pot of stew can make up for three long, lonely years? Are you crazy?" Hank was sure his blood pressure was about to go through the roof. He'd had some problems right after Nancy walked out, and for a while he'd had to take medication, but finally he'd gotten it under control with diet and exercise. Now he felt the tension mounting.

Nancy smiled sadly. "Oh, Hank! See? You

just admitted that you've missed me. You admitted that the last three years were long and lonely. And I missed you, too. That's why I came back. I knew that if you and I just sat down and talked this whole thing out, we could come to a mutual agreement."

"Mutual agreement?" Hank's face twisted. Now he felt like Pat's lovebird, mimicking everything it heard. "About what?"

"Why the way you . . . we live, of course," Nancy said brightly. "You really must be getting tired of those smelly dogs by now, and even though my parents are still hurt about the way you refused their help, they're willing to forgive and forget. Why, Daddy said he'd be delighted to have a brand new house built for us, anywhere we like. We can start over, darling. And with the girls grown and on their own, we'll be like honeymooners again."

"You honestly expect me to sell this house, get rid of my dogs, and move into a house your father pays for?"

"Well, of course I wouldn't expect you to get rid of the dogs overnight. I know you'd want to find good homes for them."

Nancy looked around the big country-style kitchen. "Wouldn't it be lovely to have a nice new kitchen with all the latest appliances?

All new plumbing and electricity so you wouldn't have to spend all your time making repairs, and doing maintenance. I know you wouldn't want a great big house like we had before, and that's fine. We don't need that much space now that it's just the two of us."

"No," Hank said quietly, his hands clenched tight at his sides.

"What? Darling, if you really insist maybe we can find a place with some ground where you can keep those precious puppies of yours. Although why you want to tie yourself down to a smelly kennel, I'll never understand."

"I mean no to all of it, Nancy. No to the new house, to getting rid of the dogs, and no to our getting back together. It's too late."

"Of course it isn't. Don't be silly!"

"I mean it. I want you to leave tonight. I'm sure you can afford a hotel until you decide what you want to do, and if not you can always charge it to Daddy, can't you?"

"I won't give you a divorce," Nancy said, her eyes narrowed. "It's that woman, isn't it? The one who came bopping in here the other night. Are you having an affair with her? Is that what this is all about?"

"You deserted me, Nancy," Hank said quietly. "There isn't a judge in the country who wouldn't grant me a divorce."

The color drained from her face. "I can't believe you're acting this way. You worshipped me when we were first married. Don't you remember? You called me your little princess."

Hank nodded, and he felt every bit of his fifty-seven years. "Yes, Nancy, I remember," he said, "but that was a long time ago, and we were two different people then. It's just too late to go back."

"You really want me to leave? You really want a divorce?"

"Yes," Hank said. "I want my freedom."

Hank saw the tears in Nancy's eyes before she turned away and busied herself at the sink. "Well, far be it from me to stay with a man who doesn't want me. I'll just tidy up here and then I'll go."

"Thank you," Hank said wearily.

Pat pulled into her driveway, and heaved a sigh of relief. Jet lag was catching up with her, and she was incredibly glad to be home. She let the dogs out of the car, then reached in back for Tweetie's carrier. "We're home, Tweetie," she said.

"Hot damn!" came the squeaky reply. "Hot damn!"

Pat turned on all the lights and raised the thermostat on the new heater. Thank goodness she'd had it installed before she left for California, because it was bitter outside.

She settled Tweetie back in his regular cage and filled his feeding dish with sunflower seeds. Then she fed the dogs, flopped down on the sofa, and kicked off her shoes.

"It's good to be home," she said, scratching Spot between his ears. "I missed you guys."

It was only then that she remembered she'd forgotten to pick up Cat. Well, he'd be okay until morning, and right now all she wanted to do was sleep.

By eight-thirty Pat had doused all the lights and was cozied up in bed with both dogs lying by her feet. She felt completely exhausted, and she couldn't even worry about what Hank and Nancy might be doing. She was asleep minutes after her head hit the pillow, and she never heard the screeching tires as Nancy peeled out of Hank's driveway. She didn't even hear the telephone when it rang a few minutes later.

Twenty-one

Hank drove off to work the next morning wishing he didn't have to go, but they were busy right now and he couldn't afford to lose his job. He wasn't sure what divorcing Nancy was going to cost him, but it was something that had to be done. He had to put a closure to that part of his life and get on with it.

He thought of Pat, his hands tightening on the wheel as she remembered the look of stunned hurt on her face as he looked at Nancy prancing around his kitchen as though she belonged there.

Would she understand? He thought so. Pat was an intelligent, reasonable woman.

Suddenly a new thought struck Hank. As a reasonable, intelligent woman, maybe Pat had already decided that she didn't need the hassle of being involved with a man who was smack dab in the middle of what could prove to be a nasty divorce. He had a sinking feeling that Nancy wouldn't give up gracefully, that if there was any way to make herself look like the injured party she'd do it. Sighing, Hank decided that he would have to take things one step at a time, and whatever happened, happened. What else could he do?

Pat woke to the sound of the telephone shrilling in her ear.

"You forgot your Cat," Dale sang. "The poor thing is brokenhearted."

Pat laughed and rubbed her eyes. She still felt as though she'd been drugged, but hopefully a hot cup of coffee would fix that. "I'll be by to pick him up later," she said. "I didn't notice he was missing until I got home, and I was too tired to go back for him. He's okay, isn't he?"

"Sure. Pete and I have been giving him lots of TLC."

"Good. Okay, let me get some coffee so I can prop up my eyelids and I'll see you this afternoon."

"Great, and welcome home, Pat. We've all missed you."

Smiling as she measured water and coffee, Pat gave a furtive glance out the window at

Hank's place. Her hand flew to her mouth when she saw that the red car was gone!

But that didn't mean anything, she reminded herself a moment later. For all Pat knew, Nancy could be grocery shopping, or having her hair done, or meeting Hank for lunch. Then she wrinkled her nose, remembering the way Hank always looked when he got home from work. She couldn't help chuckling. No, Nancy was definitely not meeting Hank for lunch, not if the things Hank had said about her were true.

Pat poured herself a steaming mug of coffee, let the dogs in from the backyard, and sat down at her kitchen table.

She didn't know what was true and what wasn't anymore, she decided. She had to believe that Hank was as surprised by his wife's sudden appearance as she was, because if she knew anything, it was that Hank was an honest, honorable man. And given that, he might feel obligated to give his marriage another chance.

Pat ran her hands through her hair distractedly. One thing at a time, she reminded herself. She was home and mighty glad of it, despite the fact that all things considered, it had been a glorious trip. But there really was no place like home, especially with her new heating system humming away and keeping her warm. Best of all, she handled the choosing and buying all on her own, without any help. She felt good about that, and confident of her ability to handle whatever life flung her way, even losing Hank.

She stood up. There were several loads of laundry waiting to be done, and Cat to be picked up, and the house needed a good dusting. She'd keep busy doing those things, and the situation with Hank would resolve itself when the time was right. That's what she had to keep telling herself. That's what she had to believe.

"So, the trip was good?" Pete asked, feeding Cat a kitty treat. "How did your son's show go?"

Pat beamed. She was still glowing with the thrill of Cliff's triumphant debut. "He was a smashing success," she said proudly. "I'm his mother, and even I didn't realize just how talented he is. I think he has a wonderful future ahead of him."

"That's great," Dale said. "Now, how about if we bring you up to date on what we've been doing around here?"

Pat listened avidly as Pete and Dale told

her about the six adult dogs they had placed with Janet Marlborough.

"One of them was a real beauty," Pete said. "A German shepherd who looked purebred. The guy who brought him in said he was moving and couldn't take the dog along. Anyway, Janet was thrilled with him. She said she thought he'd make a great companion dog for someone who is physically challenged."

"What a nice thought," Pat said happily, "And six dogs placed! That's wonderful."

"Yeah," Pete said. "Somehow, the working conditions around this place are a lot nicer these days."

Pat blushed, knowing she'd just gotten a backhanded compliment. And she was so glad the situation with Janet Marlborough was working out. Every adult dog that was placed was one that wouldn't have to be put down.

"Well, guys, as soon as I get caught up at home I'll be back to pester you. I missed this place, and the two of you."

With Cat safely inside his carrier, Pat drove home.

As she turned onto Robin Lane she saw Hank's pickup parked in his driveway, and the red car was still missing. Her heart began to pound.

"Pat, you are really losing it," she chided herself. "Every time you come home you look for Hank's truck. Talk about nosy neighbors!"

She got out of the car and discovered that her legs felt like jelly. Her hands were shaking as she lifted Cat's cage from the back of the van. "Home sweet home, Cat. Let's get you inside before I cave in."

She just made it. She turned Cat loose and sank down on the closest chair. It was ridiculous to feel this way, she told herself. Absolutely crazy to let any man get under her skin the way Hank had. Where were the lessons she'd learned from Clifford?

Then she heard the sweetly familiar tap-tap on the kitchen door and her blood galloped wildly through her veins. Hank!

His face was so dear, so pleasantly familiar. She stood there drinking in the sight of him, oblivious to the frigid air swirling around them.

"May I come in, Pat?" Hank looked shy and uncertain, and his hands worked nervously as he waited.

"Oh . . . of course. I'm sorry. I . . . yes, please come in."

Like wary strangers they stared at one another. Pat's heart was thumping crazily inside her chest, and she wanted nothing more than to fling herself into Hank's strong arms. But was that what he wanted? What if he'd come to say goodbye?

"Pat, I . . ."

"I missed you," she said, heedless of the consequences of showing him her heart. "My trip was great, but I missed you."

"Oh, Pat!"

She was in his arms then, crushed tight against his broad chest. She could feel the heat of his lean body even through the heavy jacket he wore. Home. She was home and she was in Hank's arms where she belonged.

"This is crazy," Hank said, with a soft, happy chuckle. He kissed her gently, reverently. "We have to talk, Pat. There's so much I have to tell you. So much I need to explain."

She refused to let go of his hand. As he shrugged out of his heavy jacket she tugged him into the living room and over to the sofa.

"I just want to look at you," she said. "I thought . . . I was afraid what we had was over."

"Never," Hank said vehemently. "Unless you decide you don't want me anymore, this is for keeps. I'm in this for the long haul, Pat. You're the woman I want to spend the rest of my life with."

She leaned her head on his shoulder, inhaling the scent of him. "Where's Nancy?" she asked softly.

"Gone," Hank said, "only this time I told her to be sure and leave a forwarding address, so my attorney can send the divorce papers."

"Did she agree to a divorce?"

Hank chuckled. "Not with good grace, that's for sure. She had some crazy idea that we were going to take up where we'd left off."

Hank smoothed Pat's hair off her forehead with his big hand and sighed. "I don't know. In a way I suppose I feel kind of sorry for her. She really thought we could just sweep three years under the rug as if it never happened. It turns out that she was seeing a psychiatrist before she left, and he advised her to go away and find herself."

"Did she?" Pat asked, trailing her fingers up and down Hank's arm. It felt so good to be close to him, so right.

She felt Hank shrug. "I don't know. I'm not sure what she was looking for in the first place. At least she saw the girls. According to her, they were very understanding." Another heavy sigh. "I guess it's normal for girls to take their mother's side."

Pat touched Hank's cheek. "I'm sure they were just relieved to see that she was alive and well. Hank, do you . . . are you sure a divorce is what you want? I wouldn't want you to cover up your true feelings because of me."

"My marriage was over before I ever met you, but these last months, knowing you, being a part of your life . . . well, I know what I want to do with the rest of mine. I want to grow old with you, Pat."

"Oh, Hank, that's what I want, too. While I was in California I thought about what I would do if you went back to Nancy. I know we never made any promises to each other, but I felt as though we were growing closer every day. When I saw Nancy in your kitchen I didn't know what to think."

Hank's hold on Pat tightened. It was as if only by joining his body with hers could he believe that what he felt was real, and not just a wistful dream.

"Pat Melbourne, I'm in love with you," he said, his voice deepening and sending thrills through Pat's eager body. "In the beginning I only wanted you as a friend, now I want all of you, for all of me. Do you feel the same?"

"Do you really need to ask?" Pat said teasingly, pressing closer to Hank so that he could feel the way her breasts yearned for his touch. She was warm and ready to receive him, and suddenly she was as wildly impatient as he.

"Upstairs?" she asked softly, nodding toward the two dogs who were watching the human antics with interest. "It will be a little more private."

"Mmm, if I can make it that far," Hank said. He was so aroused he wanted to take her right there in the living room, on the floor if necessary, but Pat was right. Counting Tweetie, there were four pairs of eyes watching their every move, and he wasn't too keen on a cold, wet nose poking him at the wrong moment.

But every moment with Pat was right, he thought, as they made their way upstairs, holding on to each other as though they were afraid it was all a mirage.

Pat had just a moment to be glad she had changed the sheets on her bed that morning, and then she and Hank were tumbling in the middle of the bed like anxious, eager teenagers.

"Oh Lord, do you think we'll be this bad when we're old and gray and hobbling around with canes?" Pat whispered against Hank's neck as her fingers busily worked the buttons on his shirt. "What if all this excitement is too much for our aging hearts?" She nuzzled his chin, inhaling and savoring his scent. She couldn't get enough of it, the clean, fresh male scent of him, the feel of his leathery skin under her fingertips, the hard planes of his body against her own feminine softness.

"Oh, Pat, you're making me crazy," Hank moaned. "Can't you hurry?"

Then it was his turn to revel in the sight and scent and feel of her. It seemed like years had passed since the last time he'd held her. He was hot and greedy and his arousal was hard and demanding against her thighs where her skirt had ridden up. Smooth, bare flesh enticed him, making him fumble as he tugged at his zipper. Then he was warm and throbbing against her, and Pat cried out.

"Oh yes, Hank, hurry," she urged, stripping off her own clothes so she could feel him against her. She looked at his face just before he bent his head to kiss her. There was such love and need in his eyes that she felt herself melting.

Then his body moved to cover hers, and all

coherent thought was suspended as feelings took over. There was a physical excitement and eagerness that continued to amaze her. Hank was a grandfather for heaven's sake! But even more than the physical pleasure she derived from Hank's body was the feeling of homecoming, as though this truly was the man she was meant to spend the rest of her life with.

"You're perfect," Hank murmured softly, feathering tiny kisses down her neck until his lips moved to pull a taut, quivering nipple into his mouth. "Ahhh."

Pat writhed against him impatiently. She loved long, slow, sweet lovemaking, but not now, not this time. This time she needed to blend her body with Hank's, she needed to feel him deep and warm inside her. She needed to feel that no one could take him away or tear them apart. She needed to be totally connected.

"Now, darling," she pleaded, urging him into position as she opened to receive him.

"Yes, now!" Hank said, groaning as he let himself sink into her sweet, welcoming warmth. For a moment he lay still, reveling in the sense of rightness, of completeness, then he began to move.

Pat moved with him, and together they

raced up and over the mountain, and together they held each other as they slowly and gently descended the other side.

Hank laughed softly as they lay quietly, their heartbeats slowing in unison, their breath mellowing into a steady cadence. "I was worried about my blood pressure a few days ago. Nancy had me so stirred up . . . whoops, sorry. That was poor taste, wasn't it? Mentioning Nancy at a time like this."

Pat propped herself up on an elbow. She shook her head. "No. I'm glad you feel comfortable enough to talk about her. I realize what happened between the two of you is really none of my business, but . . ."

"I'm afraid it is your business," Hank said, sobering. He looked at Pat earnestly. "I meant what I said earlier, about wanting us to spend the rest of our lives together, but it may not be smooth sailing all the way. I have a feeling Nancy isn't going to give up without a fight."

"She deserted you," Pat said calmly. "I doubt she has a legal leg to stand on."

Hank grinned. "That's right. You were married to a lawyer. I tend to forget that."

Pat traced a line down Hank's arm with her fingernail. "In the beginning I wanted to forget everything about Clifford, but now, well, somehow it doesn't seem to matter very much, especially not now when I've got you right where I want you."

Hank laughed as Pat rubbed against him suggestively and gave him a decidedly wicked leer.

"Not yet, sweetheart," he said apologetically. "I'm afraid, that although the spirit is more than willing, the flesh is a little weak. How about saving something for dessert?"

"Oh my goodness! I forgot all about dinner! You must be starved," Pat cried.

"Well, I was, but some of my hunger has been appeased, for the moment at least." Hank kissed Pat tenderly, wishing he could wrap her in silk and steel and protect her from what might be ahead. He hated the thought of involving her in a mudslinging session, and he knew that it was a definite possibility. Nancy had never taken rejection kindly. He didn't expect her to now.

"What was the big joke about Hungarian stew?" Pat asked later, as she and Hank cleared the remains of their impromptu scrambled egg dinner.

"It was what Nancy had waiting for me the other night when I got home from work. It was always one of my favorite dishes, and I guess she thought it would soften me up."

"It didn't?" Pat asked, wiping the counter.

"The smell turned my stomach," Hank admitted. "I never did eat any dinner that night. Nancy was so put out she poured the whole pot of stew down the garbage disposal."

"Then I'll cross that off the list of recipes I want to try in the future," Pat said. "I'm really getting into cooking, you know. If it weren't for my work at the shelter, I'd probably turn into a real housefrau."

"Would that be so bad?" Hank asked, pouring them each a mug of coffee laced with cinnamon.

Pat sniffed the coffee appreciatively. "There's so much in the world that needs doing, you know? And I'm very fortunate. I have enough money to be able to make a difference."

Hank sat down on the sofa and nodded. "And you're the type of person who will put her money to good use, but that is something you and I will have to discuss, Pat." He sighed. "Money. It crops up at all the wrong times."

"What's bothering you, Hank?" Pat asked, sitting down beside him. "I thought we had the matter of my money in perspective."

"I thought so, too, but divorcing Nancy is

going to be expensive, and although she always hated the house, I'll probably have to sell it to settle things. I'm not in a financial position to run out and buy another. I don't know what I'll do about the kennels." Hank's eyes took on a bleak, dark look. "I may have to give them up after all."

"Oh no!" Pat cried. "You can't do that. Those dogs mean so much to you. That's not fair!"

"Maybe not, but Nancy and I were married nineteen years when she took off, and although things weren't always rosy, as far as I know she was a faithful wife and a good mother. I'm sure the courts will think that counts for something."

"But she doesn't need money, does she? Didn't you say that her family is well off?"

"They are, and Nancy will inherit quite a bit someday, but I have a feeling she is going to be vindictive about this divorce."

Pat fell silent. She didn't know what to say, or how to reassure Hank. If he weren't so sticky about finances she could offer to help, and certainly she wouldn't mind. She had more money than she needed for her own comfort and security, and she had already made sure that Ashley and Cliff would be taken care of after she was gone, so there was nothing to stop her from helping Hank . . . nothing except his male pride.

Hank slipped his arm around Pat's shoulders and nudged her head down onto his shoulder. He couldn't predict what the future held, but he was pretty sure there were some rough seas ahead. He wasn't looking forward to stormy weather, but as long as he had Pat as his mate he knew he could ride it out.

"Don't give up on me, sweetheart," he begged softly. "Somehow, someway, we'll get through this."

"I know," Pat said softly. "I'm not a bit worried."

Twenty-two

Pat dove back into her day-to-day routine with pleasure and fresh enthusiasm. She could sit in her sunlit kitchen and begin to smile for no apparent reason, and as she went from room to room in her small home, she realized just how much it had come to mean to her. It was all hers, her sanctuary. It was decorated in her favorite soft pastel colors, the furniture was casual and comfortable, and the flowers that would bloom come spring had been planted with her own hands. She loved it. She loved her new life. Her animals, her work at the shelter, the new friends she'd made, and most of all she loved Hank.

A warm glow spread throughout her body as she remembered how they'd spent the past few nights, wrapped in each other's arms like eager, impatient teenagers. Only Pat had never been that kind of teenager. She'd been dreadfully shy when she met and was swept off her feet by the young, handsome, charismatic Clifford. She'd allowed him to mold her into the perfect lawyer's wife. Sleek, chic, and always ready to do whatever was necessary to be a credit to her husband and children.

Dusting the coffee table in the living room, Pat chuckled. She was certainly making up for all she'd missed now, and there definitely was a lot of truth in the old saying, "better late than never."

She couldn't seem to stop smiling as she moved from one task to another. Hank. Dear, loving Hank. He'd given her so much, and he didn't seem to realize it. He worried about the difference in their financial situations, when what they shared was beyond price.

The strident ring of the telephone interrupted Pat's musings, and she hurried to pick up the receiver.

"Mrs. Melbourne?"

Pat frowned. The voice was totally unfamiliar, and she hadn't been called Mrs. Melbourne in a long time. "Yes. Who's calling, please?"

"This is Becky. Hank Richards's daughter. I have to talk to you, Mrs. Melbourne. It concerns my father and it's very important."

"Well, I . . . well, of course. When would you like to get together?"

"This afternoon, please," Becky said. "I'll come to your house, if I may?"

"Yes, of course. I'll see you then."

Pat hung up the phone, her brow furrowed. Hank's daughter. And she had sounded almost frantic. Her frown deepened. Something told her this was not going to be a pleasant little tea party.

She was dressed and waiting long before 2 P.M. when Becky had said she would arrive. It had to do with Nancy, of course. What else? Had Hank's ex-wife gone running straight to her daughters hoping they could change their father's mind? What kind of woman would use her child this way?

"Easy, Pat, old girl," she told herself. "You don't know what this is about yet, and it's silly to start imagining things."

The doorbell rang and Ink and Spot started to yap.

"That's a bunch of bull!" Tweetie screeched. "A bunch of bull!"

"Becky?" Pat questioned softly a moment later, smiling at the young woman standing on her doorstep. "I would have known you anywhere. You look a lot like your father."

A hint of a smile tugged at the girl's lips. "That's what everyone has always said. May I come in?"

"Please," Pat said, stepping back. Hank's daughter was dressed in expensive designer jeans and a fur-trimmed suede jacket, and her gray eyes skimmed Pat's little home curiously.

"I made tea," Pat said. "It's been so cold lately and I always enjoy a cup of tea this time of year."

Becky nodded, tossing her jacket carelessly over the back of a chair. Then, as though she wanted to say everything she had to say before she lost her nerve, she whirled to face Pat. "You have to stop seeing my father! If it weren't for you he and my mother could get their lives back on track. Mother is willing to compromise with Daddy. She even said he could keep his kennels."

Pat sat down quickly. She wasn't sure exactly what she'd expected, but certainly not this. Becky looked like she'd rather be anywhere else than where she was, and tears sparkled in her eyes.

"Please," Pat said. "Won't you sit down and have a cup of tea? I know you had a long drive, and I honestly think you're laboring under some misconceptions. I'm not a sorcerer, you know, and I didn't seduce your father. We've been friends since I moved here, and from what I understand his marriage was over before we ever met."

Becky sat down, then she popped back up. "No . . . no, that's just what Daddy thought. He was hurt by the way my mother left, but it was all just a . . . a misunderstanding. If Daddy would just give Mother a chance to explain . . ."

Pat poured tea and shook her head. "Your father has talked about you quite a bit, Becky," she said. "I wish we could have met under different circumstances."

"None of this is any of your business," Becky cried, tears streaming down her cheeks now. "You don't know me or my sister, or my mother, and if you'd just stay out of things we could be a family again!"

Pat swallowed, feeling sick. Becky could have been Ashley. She was younger, but the girl's pain was terrible to see, and what could she say? Look, kid, your father and I are sleeping together, and all he wants to do is get rid of your mother.

"I'm afraid it isn't that simple, Becky," she said slowly. "Your father is a grown man, and he has something to say about all this. You can't decide what he should do with his life, you know."

"My parents are still legally married," Becky insisted. "It's not as though they're divorced. And Mother is sorry she left the way she did. She wants to make it up to all of us."

Pat sipped her tea and wished it would ease the ache around her heart. She didn't know this young woman, but she was Hank's daughter, and she knew the way Hank had agonized over his separation from his daughters. Now, after such a brief respite, it might be happening all over again, and this time she would be right in the middle of things. And she didn't want to be. She didn't want to be the "other woman."

"I knew this wouldn't work!" Becky cried, grabbing her jacket. "You're one of those women who just can't wait to get their hooks in a man, and it doesn't matter to you whether he's married or not! I told Mother this wouldn't work!"

Before Pat could move Becky was heading for the door. She yelled, "You'll be sorry!" over her shoulder, as Pat blinked frantically to hold back her own tears.

So. Nancy had put her daughter up to this. Somehow, Pat wasn't surprised. It tied into what little she knew about Nancy. A woman who went after what she wanted with no thought of the consequences. A woman who would use whoever she had to to get her own way.

How was it all going to end? Would Hank be able to divorce his wife and still keep his daughters?

She had supper ready that night when Hank got home from work.

"Mmm, you smell good, and so does whatever you have simmering on the stove," he said happily.

He smelled of soap and crisp, citrus after-shave and Pat was reluctant to let him go. For just a moment she buried her head on his shoulder wishing she could freeze the moment.

"Pat? Honey, what's wrong?" Hank moved her away and looked deep into her eyes. "You're trembling. What happened? Celia and the kids are all right, aren't they?"

"Yes, they're all fine," Pat managed. "it's your daughter, Hank. Becky. She was here today. Nancy sent her." It had never occurred to Pat not to tell Hank. She knew how he valued honesty, and he needed to know what Nancy was up to.

"Becky was here? What happened? What did she say to you?" Hank paced Pat's small living room. "Oh Lord! I knew Nancy wasn't going to give up gracefully, but I was hoping she'd leave the girls out of this. What did Becky say to you, Pat? Was she abusive?"

Pat quickly shook her head. "It wasn't anything like that. She's just hurt and confused and scared. She wants her parents back together. It's perfectly understandable."

Hank groaned. "This is so like Nancy! To send Becky to do her bidding. Well, it won't work. I'll have to see the girls myself. I'll explain everything to them. I'll tell them about us. They're not kids anymore. They're old enough to understand that I'm entitled to a life of my own, that I have a right to some happiness for myself."

Pat busied herself dishing up the beef stew she'd made. When the food was on the table, she turned to Hank. "Please don't tell your daughters about us, Hank. Not yet. It will only make everything worse. They know there's something between us, but if you throw it in their faces . . ."

Rank sank wearily into a chair, and suddenly the rich, savory smell of Pat's stew made his stomach lurch. Pat's face was pale and strained, and the sparkle was gone from her lovely eyes. The sick feeling intensified.

"I've got you into a real mess, haven't I?"

he asked softly. He didn't voice the rest of his thought, that maybe Pat was regretting her involvement with him. But it nagged at him all evening, and later, when he tried to make love to Pat, he was unable.

It was the worst humiliation of his life. The only other time it had happened was with Nancy, just before she walked out. He'd sensed her pulling away then, and it had frightened him, because he didn't know how to stop it.

"Hank, it's all right," Pat said, kissing his cheek. "You're upset. You're letting this thing with Nancy get to you. It's all right. There'll be other times."

Maybe. And maybe not, Hank thought as he dressed and made an excuse about getting home to the dogs.

But Pat knew. Hank wasn't running to the dogs. He was running away from her, from the ultimate masculine humiliation.

"Celia? How are you? How's the day-care center coming along?"

"Oh, Pat, you wouldn't recognize this place! All the playground equipment arrived yesterday, and I've been interviewing for helpers. I've just about decided on one young woman, and there are more applicants coming this afternoon. But how are you, dear? I've been so busy I haven't had a chance to call since we came home. Do I dare ask about 'you know who'?"

Pat sighed. "That's a long story, sis, and I'd rather not go into it right now. I just called to make sure you were okay, and you sound great. Busy as a bee."

"Oh, I am, and I know it's the best thing for me. When I fall into bed at night I'm so tired I go right to sleep." Celia managed a small laugh. "I'm sure that is just exactly what Jake would have prescribed for me. Oh, and I lost three more pounds. I'm only fifteen pounds from my goal weight now. I can't thank you enough for helping me the way you did, Pat."

"It was my pleasure," Pat said, "and I'm glad you're keeping busy. You're right. It's the very best medicine."

When she hung up, Pat went into her bedroom and changed into her work clothes. As she zipped up her jeans and buttoned her soft, plaid flannel shirt, she smiled. Work was the best cure for what ailed you, and things would straighten out eventually. She just had to hang in there.

* * *

"Look at this, Pat," Dale said late that afternoon. He beckoned Pat over to a cage where he was keeping a female rabbit and her new litter. Six babies.

Pat watched the infants nurse and shook her head. "I'm sure glad we women don't have six or eight at a time."

"Cute aren't they? We probably won't have any trouble placing the babies because it's getting close to Easter, but what happens when they're not too little and cute anymore?"

"I know. People buy baby bunnies and chicks indiscriminately at Easter time, and then in a few weeks, when they're not babies anymore, all our cages will be filled with rejects."

"I've been thinking," Dale said. "People need to be educated about things like this, and the best place for education is with the kids, right?"

"I suppose. What's on your mind, Dale?"

"I was wondering if I could go around to the schools and speak to the kids about the responsibilities of pet ownership."

"That's a great idea. Would Pete be interested in getting involved with you, or would you be doing it on your own?"

Pete came up behind them. "Count me out on that one, Pat. I'm not much for public speaking. I'd rather work with Janet and the companion dogs."

"That's fine. I think they're both worthwhile projects. And speaking of Janet, whatever happened to that little cocker spaniel you took home to your neighbor's son, Dale?"

Dale flushed. "A match made in heaven. Janet was right when she said he was the perfect pet for a young, energetic child."

Pat smiled. "Another happy ending. Good. I can use about a bushel of those right now."

"Anything you want to talk about?" Dale asked soberly. "I know Pete and I are young, but we do care about you, Pat."

"I know, and I appreciate your concern. It really isn't anything I can talk about right now, but I'll keep those broad shoulders in mind."

Pete winked. "You do that, Pat. We'll always be here for you."

Getting into her minivan that night, Pat was all set to head home, but something stopped her. The dogs had plenty of fresh water. If she were an hour or so late they would be fine, and she just couldn't go straight home. She couldn't face another night of sitting and waiting to see if Hank would come over, if he would take her in his arms and kiss her, if he would want to make love to her.

Impotence. She'd read about it, and had even laughed at jokes about it, but it had never touched her before, until now. Pat sat for a minute before starting the car, her eyes closed, trying to shut out the sight of Hank's stricken face. He'd been so embarrassed, so devastated by his failure. But why did it have to be viewed as a failure? Pat wondered. It was only a temporary lapse. Why did men give one incident such enormous power?

She would have been perfectly happy to hold Hank and have him hold her throughout the night. When they had sex it was wonderful, warm and exciting and pleasurable, but there was so much more to their relationship than a romp in the sheets. Didn't Hank realize that? Didn't he know that she loved him, and not his prowess as a lover?

But it was a male ego thing, or at least that's what she had always read. Men took even temporary episodes very hard, and what could a woman do, except wait and be as loving and supportive as possible?

Pat squared her shoulders and started the van. She was hungry and she didn't feel like cooking, especially when she would probably end up with a refrigerator full of leftovers. No, tonight she was going to please herself. There was a great pizza parlor around the corner from the shelter and that's where she headed. Extra cheese and pepperoni, she decided. And a tall icy Coke . . . and not diet either!

Twenty-three

Hank sat in Pat's kitchen, his hands wrapped around a mug of hot coffee. He looked tired and much older than his fifty-seven years.

"She's determined to fight me on the divorce, Pat," he said. "And I don't have the money or the stamina for a long, bitter court battle."

"She deserted you, Hank. She left you wondering if she was dead or alive for almost three years. Doesn't that make a difference?"

"Ultimately it will, or at least that's what my lawyer said, but in the meantime it looks like Nancy can hold things up for a while. She's got a psychiatrist who is apparently willing to testify that she was undergoing a midlife crisis when she took off."

Pat stood behind Hank's chair, massaging his shoulders. It had been over two weeks since Hank had done more than kiss her cheek, and she missed the sweet intimacy they'd shared before Nancy came back to rip Hank's life to shreds.

"I can help you with the legal fees, Hank," she offered hesitantly. "I know how you feel about taking money from me, but it's crazy to worry yourself this way when it isn't necessary. Please let me help you."

"No." The word was flat, dark, and angry. Pat recoiled as though Hank had struck her.

"But . . ."

"Don't we have enough problems in our relationship now, without adding anything else?" Hank asked, his face twisted in agony. "I can't handle much more, Pat. I feel like I'm going crazy. I worry about Becky and Laurie. I hate knowing they think I'm . . . well, they don't understand about us, and they just want me and Nancy back together."

"Then maybe that's what you should do," Pat said quietly, her hands hanging limply at her sides. Hank was tired. Well, so was she. Either he wanted his freedom enough to fight for it, or he didn't. And if he didn't, she'd just as soon know it now before she wasted any more time and energy trying to be helpful and supportive. "Maybe you want to go back to Nancy and just haven't admitted it," she said. Pat hated the way she ached inside, but the words had to be said. She'd always thought of Hank as a strong man, but this thing with Nancy and the girls had shaken him badly. She felt she had to do or say something that would shock him into getting back into the ring for the final round.

"That's not true," Hank said quickly.

Too quickly, Pat thought as tears stung her eyes.

But then Hank was on his feet and he was dragging her into his arms and rubbing his face against her hungrily.

"You're the only woman I want, Pat," he vowed huskily, his hands holding her captive against him. "It may not have seemed that way lately, but it's true. I'll do whatever it takes to get free for you, darling."

Joy surged through Pat's trembling body.

"Hank . . . oh, sweetheart," she breathed, raising her lips to his. "You do love me!"

Hank hugged her tightly. "You better believe it," he said, raising his brows in a mock leer. "Do you think it will shock that bird too much to see two old fogies like us going at it, because I know I'm not going to make it upstairs?"

Pat willingly allowed Hank to pull her down beside him on the thick green carpet.

Her need was as great as his, and she had one moment of thankfulness that she'd put the dogs in the garage to have their dinner.

It was a wild, quick mating and just as she and Hank reached the pinnacle they heard it. The all too familiar screech of Tweetie.

"Hot damn!" Tweetie squealed. "Hot damn!"

"Whew! I hope that doesn't happen again," Hank said, when they finally caught their breath.

"You didn't enjoy it?" Pat asked, pretending to pout.

"Not that. The . . . other. You know, my inadequacy."

Pat touched a finger to his lips. "Don't say that," she scolded. "That's not what it was, Hank. You've been under a lot of stress. And your lovemaking is not all I love, you know. I like it when you just hold me. When we sit in front of your fireplace and listen to love songs. I love it when you tease me. Actually," she said, propping herself on an elbow, "I guess I just plain love you, Hank Richards."

"Oh, Pat, what did I do to deserve you?" Hank asked, kissing her before he sat up and began to pull on his clothes. "I've been a real mess these last few weeks, haven't I?"

"Well . . ." Pat cocked her head, pretending

to consider. "You haven't exactly been a barrel of laughs, that's for sure." Suddenly her eyes darkened. "What are we going to do, Hank? We can't go on this way, up one day and down the next. It's just too wearing."

There was a long silence, then Hank spoke, his voice so low Pat barely heard him at first. Then, as if he was slowly gaining strength, his voice became loud and clear. "I need your help, Pat," he admitted. "I don't think I can do this alone."

She knew it was a turning point in their relationship. Despite the lovely physical intimacy they had shared, there had always been a holding back, at least on Hank's part, and Pat had felt it was her financial situation that ultimately separated them. Now, at last, Hank seemed ready to accept the help she was only too willing to give.

She went to him and threw her arms around his neck. "Oh, Hank! I never thought I'd hear you say those words."

Looking a little puzzled at his own bravado, Hank shook his head, and his arms tightened around Pat until she was pressed close to the length of his body.

"This is hard for me," he said slowly. "I always looked at it as a sign of weakness for a man to take anything from a woman, financially, I mean. You know what people say about gigolos."

Pat began to laugh, and the freedom of it was wonderful. A gigolo! Hank a gigolo! It was just too funny!

"Oh, Hank, I haven't heard that word in ages!" She pursed her lips. "Gig-o-lo," she said, drawing it out. "My, it does have a nice ring, doesn't it?"

Hank had to smile. "Come on now, cut it out. I'm serious. Maybe I'm old fashioned, but it's what I always believed."

Pat nodded, sobering. "And there is a certain amount of truth in that, for some people. But not us, Hank. We're a team, remember? And we're in this for the long haul, together."

Sighing, Hank drew Pat back into his arms and rested his chin on the top of her head. "I just hate dragging you through this mess. I never thought it would come to this."

"What? That you and I would fall in love, or that Nancy would hang on this way?"

"Both," Hank replied, stroking Pat's back in a way that made coherent thinking very difficult.

"I think there's only one solution to this problem," Hank said, his voice deep and warm and enticing.

"Oh? What's that?"

"I think we should make love as often as possible. I read somewhere that good sex is great therapy, that it reduces stress."

"Oh? And is our sex good?" Pat asked teasingly, running her hands up and down his arms. She still couldn't believe it. Couldn't believe that this plain, ordinary man could turn her into a hot-blooded hussy, yet that's exactly what he did, with the merest touch of his hands or lips.

"Good?" Hank stepped back, letting his eyes roam leisurely up and down Pat's still slender body. He pretended to consider the matter. A smile twitched at the corner of his lips. "Good can't begin to describe how I feel when I'm with you, lady," he said.

They made love again, slowly and with great care this time, as if they needed to reassure one another of their deep love and commitment. Just before they reached the top of the mountain, Pat said the words. "I love you, Hank Richards," she gasped, "with everything that I have and everything I am."

Hank sighed his words of love against her neck as he held back from the final, mind-shattering thrusts. Then he let go and they soared up and over once again, holding tight to all that was precious and dear to them.

"Now I am worn flat out," Pat said later, as they relaxed in her bed. "And I'm definitely too tired to cook."

"Funny," Hank said, chuckling. "This kind of aerobic activity invigorates me. How about letting me cook tonight?"

Pat grinned mischievously. "I thought you'd never ask!"

They ate tomato soup and grilled cheese sandwiches with as much relish as if it had been roast pheasant under glass.

"This is nice," Hank said. "Just being casual and comfortable this way."

"Umm, I guess we're peasants at heart, aren't we? This is a lot more fun than getting all gussied up and standing in a receiving line smiling and shaking hands with people you don't even like."

Hank grimaced as he bit into the last corner of his sandwich. "Sounds awful, but seriously, Pat, don't you ever miss going to the theater and the opera and having dinner in expensive, elegant restaurants? That kind of thing is not my style, you know? Even if I had piles of money, I'd probably still prefer the golden arches. I'm just an ordinary guy."

"And you're ordinarily, absolutely perfect for me," Pat insisted. "Don't forget I had the other kind, and it wasn't all glitter and glamour."

"I guess I still can't believe my luck in finding you at this time in my life. When Nancy left . . . well, after I got over the first shock I just figured that part of my life, having a woman to share things with, was over." Hank laughed. "Can you picture me getting down and dirty in a singles bar? I wouldn't even know how to go about picking up a woman!"

Pat leaned close and kissed Hank's cheek. "You wouldn't have to. The women would probably be all over you in a heartbeat. You've got a special aura, Hank Richards."

"Ha! I sure do. It's called essence of oil and grease, with the odor of my favorite canines thrown in for good measure."

"Personally, I find it irresistible," Pat said, grinning as she stacked the few dishes in the dishwasher. "Ah, oil and dog, an absolutely unbeatable combination."

"And on that note, I am going to leave you and go home," Hank said, getting to his feet.

"Must you? I was hoping you'd stay awhile."

"Not tonight, sweetheart," Hank said regretfully. "I'd like nothing better, but there are some things I have to take care of."

"All right," Pat said, moving into his arms for one last embrace. "Then I'll let you go. Will I see you tomorrow?"

"I'm not sure. If there isn't too much work at the shop I may take off and go see the girls. I don't want to let things run on the way they did before. I don't want to lose my girls."

"You won't," Pat said firmly. "They're not just Nancy's daughters, they're yours, too. Right now they're confused and their loyalties are all mixed up, but I'm sure that underneath it all, they love you, Hank."

"I hope so. Because if Nancy causes me to lose the girls I'm not sure I can deal with it."

"That's not going to happen," Pat insisted. "Now go home and do whatever it is you have to do, and when you fall asleep, dream of me."

Pat finished tidying the kitchen, put the dogs out in the yard to do their business, fed Cat, and filled Tweetie's food cup with sunflower seeds. Then she brought the dogs in and checked the locks on the back and front doors. But it was too early to sleep and she was restless. After checking her watch to make sure it wasn't too late, she sat down and picked up the telephone.

"Mother?" Ashley sounded surprised and

concerned. "Is something wrong? Why are you calling?"

"Can't a mother call to say hello to her only daughter?" Pat asked. "You weren't in bed, were you?"

"At nine o'clock? Of course not. Actually, Fancy and I were getting ready to watch a television movie. Honestly, Mom, she's the best company."

"I know. I don't know what I'd do without my animals. So Fancy is behaving herself, is she?"

"She's getting more beautiful every day. I'm thinking of entering her in an upcoming dog show, but of course if I do that I won't be able to have her spayed. What do you think?"

"I think it's your decision, darling, but a female dog that hasn't been spayed can be a problem. What will you do when she's in season?"

Ashley laughed. "I guess I haven't thought that far ahead. It's just that she's so perfect it seems a shame not to show her."

"Well, you still have time to decide which way you want to go. I'm just glad you're enjoying her. I'll pass the word along to Hank."

"How is Hank?" Ashley asked, a hint of mischief in her voice. "You still see a lot of him, I presume?"

"You presume correctly," Pat said honestly, "but Hank is going through a rough time now. It seems his wife just walked out on him three years ago. For a while Hank and his two daughters didn't even know if Nancy was alive. Anyway, now she's back, and she wanted to pick up where they left off. Hank said no, and told her that he wanted a divorce, and now she's setting up all kinds of roadblocks. Hank's daughters are all upset again. It's a real mess."

"And where are you in all this, Mother?" Ashley asked, after a pregnant silence.

Pat managed a shaky laugh. "Would you believe that Nancy has Hank's daughters convinced that I'm the 'other woman'?"

"Are you?" Ashley asked.

"Of course not . . . I mean, all right, I suppose that technically I am, but it's not as though I deliberately set out to break up a man's marriage. Hank's life with Nancy was over before we ever met. I would never have gotten involved with a married man, especially not after . . . well, that's not my style."

"I know," Ashley said softly, "and I also understand what you didn't say, Mother. I know about what Daddy did, and I'm sorry."

"You . . . know? But how? I never wanted

to tarnish your memories of your father."

Pat's hand trembled on the receiver. She heard Ashley's sigh.

"Never mind how I found out, Mother. It doesn't matter anymore, does it?"

"I suppose not, but you were always so close to your father. I didn't want to do anything that would change what you felt for him."

"I know, and I think that's when I first knew just how much you do love me. When I realized you weren't going to tell me."

Tears stung Pat's eyes and she dabbed at them angrily. "Oh, honey, I'm sorry."

"It's all right, Mother. Everyone has to grow up sometime, don't they? And by the way, have you heard from Cliff since you got back from California?"

Bless her. She was changing the subject. Pat smiled through her tears. "Just a note saying how happy he was that his family was with him to share his special moments. And that's really the reason I called, honey. To tell you how happy I was to see you at your brother's side."

"I'm glad I went," Ashley answered, "and I am proud of Cliff's success, but I still have ambivalent feelings, Mother, and I'm afraid I always will."

"I understand, but the important thing is that we keep on loving Cliff."

"I know," Ashley said softly. "He called me after I came home. He thanked me for coming, and he said that he understood how hard it was for me, and that made my presence all the more special."

Pat nodded, forgetting that Ashley couldn't see her. "Your brother is a very thoughtful, sensitive young man," she said, "And I'm beginning to realize that his sister isn't far behind."

Ashley laughed. "Thanks, Mom. That was definitely a backhanded compliment, but I liked it just the same."

Pat was smiling as she hung up the telephone. Now she could sleep.

Twenty-four

Pat had just finished bathing Ink when the doorbell rang. "Damn! Now what do I do?"

As if to make sure Pat felt properly guilty for bathing him in the first place, Ink began to shiver and shake.

"All right, you old faker, you! I'll get rid of whoever is at the door and dry you as quick as possible, and you know very well it's not that bad!"

Wrapping the silky little dog in a huge old terry towel, Pat hurried to the front door. Why did salesmen always pick the worst possible times to pitch their wares?

Keeping Ink firmly tucked under one arm, she opened the door with her free hand and felt her jaw go slack.

"You!"

Nancy smiled grimly. "Yes me, and I can't

imagine why you're surprised. Did you really think I was going to lie down quietly and let you steal my husband from me?"

"I don't . . ."

"Oh for heaven's sake, let me in, won't you? I can see you've just given that creature in your arms a bath. You don't want it to catch a cold, do you?"

Pat stepped back numbly. This couldn't really be happening. It was like something from a TV sitcom. Irate wife shows up on the "other woman's" doorstep.

"Come in then," she finally managed, cradling Ink's shivering form. She felt like her brain was a blank canvas. What did one say to one's lover's wife?

Nancy followed Pat into the utility room where Pat grabbed a second towel to help dry Ink. "I suppose I can see what attracted Hank to you," she said disdainfully. "Apparently you both have an affinity for smelly, flea-ridden animals." Nancy wrinkled her nose when Spot came dashing in from the other room. "Two dogs?"

"And a cat, and an African Lovebird," Pat said, as she briskly toweled Ink's damp black fur. She was coming back to life. She could feel the anger rising. She fixed a cold, hard stare on Nancy and wrinkled her own nose.

Nancy had a dark ranch mink stole draped casually over her shoulders. "I would never dream of wearing animal skins," she said flatly.

Nancy smiled thinly and tugged the mink from her shoulders.

"Really? That's probably because you never had the pleasure." She rubbed her face against the smooth pelts. "I always say there is nothing like the feel of real mink."

"Is that why you pushed your way into my house today, to discuss how much you like wearing mink?" Pat asked, wrapping a fresh towel around Ink and leading the way into the living room.

The blow dryer was on the table next to the sofa and she sat down and calmly turned it on.

For a moment Nancy looked disconcerted. "Must you do that now?" she demanded.

Pat nodded. "Yes, I must. I don't want Ink to catch cold."

"Well, then I'll just sit here and wait until you're through," Pat said, "because I certainly don't intend to compete with that thing!"

Pat concentrated on drying Ink and tried to think of what she could say to Nancy. She'd never met anyone quite like her, and in her years as a successful attorney's wife, she'd met some pushy people. But Nancy was certainly unique. She walked off and left her family, didn't bother to contact them for three years, then popped back into their lives expecting to be welcomed with open arms.

Finally, when Ink began to squirm free, Pat was forced to turn off the blow dryer and face the music. She released Ink and turned to her uninvited visitor.

"What is it you wanted to say to me?"

"It's very simple," Nancy said, pulling a cigarette out of her purse and searching for a light.

"I'd rather you didn't smoke," Pat said quietly. "I have allergies and cigarette smoke doesn't agree with me."

"Oh for . . . all right, I suppose this is your home. Let me get right to the point." Nancy stuffed the unlit cigarette back into the pack. "I want you to get out of Hank's life. Leave him alone so he can get his thinking straightened out. Right now the poor man is thoroughly confused, and no wonder, both of us tugging and pulling at him. It's really very unfair, don't you think?"

"Yes, I do," Pat said agreeably. "So why don't you get out of Hank's life? It shouldn't be hard. You did it before."

"Why you . . . how dare you speak to me that way! You don't know what you're talking about!"

"I know what Hank has told me, and I know that when I met him he was a very lonely man." Pat stood up and brushed dog hairs off her jeans. "He's not lonely anymore," she added, smiling. And it was true. Hank laughed a lot more these days than he had when she first met him. He was more relaxed and content, or at least he had been until Nancy popped back into his life.

"If you have any feelings left for him, why don't you just agree to a quiet divorce and let him get on with his life?" Pat asked. "You're an attractive woman. You shouldn't have any trouble finding a new love interest of your own."

"Well, aren't you sweet?" Nancy's handsome face twisted sarcastically. "You'd like that, wouldn't you? For me to just disappear into the woodwork and leave the field open for you. Well, it's not going to happen! Hank is still my husband, and when the court hears why I left in the first place I'm sure they'll agree that I deserve a second chance, not to mention the fact that our children want us back together."

"Your children are adults," Pat pointed

out, "and they are old enough to understand that sometimes you can't have things exactly the way you want them. If they care for their father, they'll want him to be happy."

"And you think his happiness is with you?" Nancy asked coldly.

"I know it is," Pat said quietly. "I love Hank and I accept him as he is. I'm not interested in making him over."

Nancy colored, and her voice rose. "I was very young when Hank and I married, and perhaps I did try to change him, but I'm different now. I know what's really important."

Pat sighed heavily. This conversation was getting them nowhere, and she was tired of it. "I would appreciate it if you left," she said. "Obviously you and I see things differently, and I don't see the point in our continuing this verbal sparring."

"Then you won't voluntarily give Hank up?" Nancy asked, her eyes narrowed with fury.

"The only way I'll give Hank up is if he tells me it's you he wants, and I really don't foresee that happening."

Nancy laughed, a tight, hard little sound that sent chills up Pat's spinal column. "Don't be too sure," she said, grabbing her mink. "He was mine a lot longer than he's been yours!"

Pat closed the door after Nancy and leaned against it weakly. Good Lord, had it really happened? Had she actually been confronted by her lover's wife? She couldn't even say ex-wife, because in the eyes of the law Hank and Nancy were still married. The implications suddenly smacked her square in the face. My God, she thought, I've been sleeping with another woman's husband!

"That's a bunch of bull!" Tweetie sang, hopping from perch to perch.

Pat smiled grimly. If only it were! But it had never seemed that way, not when Nancy had been gone for so long, when she had left the way she had. When Hank had seemed so alone, so . . . unattached. But he wasn't, and from the very beginning she'd known it. Celia was right. She should never have allowed herself to get involved with a married man. She was asking for trouble and now she had it.

She broiled lamb chops for dinner that night, with new potatoes and peas, and while she waited for Hank she vented her frustration on a loaf of banana bread.

From her seat by the front window she saw Hank come home, and she waited, knowing he would shower and change and take care of the dogs before he came over. And then she would have to wipe the smile off his face by telling him of Nancy's visit, or, she wondered, as a new thought came to her, maybe she shouldn't tell him. What good would it do? What could he do about it? He'd get upset. His blood pressure would rise, and their time together would be ruined.

I won't tell him, she decided, as she saw him come out the front door and head across the street.

"Mmm, I'm glad you're here," she said, when she opened the door to him. "Somehow this house feels different when you're in it."

Hank smiled, the warm, loving smile Pat had come to love.

"I love coming home to you," he said, holding her close to his heart. "It makes everything else worthwhile."

Pat laughed softly and kissed his cheek. "Well, come in and sit down before our dinner gets cold. You must be hungry."

She needed to keep busy, needed to keep her hands moving, and her mind centered on the logistics of getting the food to the table.

And then, finally, she was seated across

from Hank. I'm not really being dishonest, she told herself. I'm just avoiding an unpleasant scene. But she felt dishonest. She felt almost as if she and Nancy were conspiring against Hank behind his back.

"Honey? Something wrong?" Hank asked, knife and fork poised over his lamb chop, his gray eyes vaguely troubled. "You seem a little jumpy tonight. You didn't have another visit from Becky, did you? I swear, sometimes she can be a real sweetheart, but she can also be a little bitch when she wants to."

Pat buttered a roll and shook her head. "No. No more visits from your daughter, and I don't believe she was really trying to be bitchy, Hank. Her loyalties are being torn in two different directions. That would be difficult for anyone."

"How can you be so understanding?" Hank asked, shaking his head. "Most women in your situation would be pitching a fit."

"I have children of my own, remember, and my relationship with them has not always been smooth sailing. I just tried to picture Ashley in the same situation, and when I did that, it was pretty hard to stay angry with Becky."

"Well, I'm angry, and I wish I'd been able to get over to see the girls this afternoon, but there was just too much work at the shop. I guess I'll have to wait until this weekend."

"Don't be too hard on them. This is rough for everyone, you know?"

"Yes, I do know that," Hank said, accepting the cup of coffee Pat poured for him. "But the girls have to understand once and for all that I am not the villain. Nancy left me, of her own choice. Now, just because she wants to come running back, they expect me to be filled with gratitude. Well, damn it, I'm not! I'm glad Nancy is alive and well, and I'm glad she finally had the decency to contact the girls, but I don't want her back in my life, and Becky and Laurie have to accept that."

Pat busied herself clearing the table while Hank drank his coffee. Was she wrong in not telling him of Nancy's visit? But look how upset he got when he talked of the girls and their attitude? What would happen if he found out that his wife was waging her own campaign to win him back?

"Hank?"

"Umm? What is it, sweetheart? Something on your mind?"

Pat quickly shook her head. She couldn't do it. For the moment, Hank was calm and relaxed. She couldn't shatter that and send him over the edge into helpless rage.

"I just wondered if you had room for a slice of banana bread," she said. "I made it fresh this afternoon."

Knowing that Hank was planning to visit his daughters on Saturday, Pat got up early and drove into the city to visit Celia.

"Sis!" Celia enveloped Pat in her arms and hugged her tightly. "Just the face I needed to see, and you're just in time to help me set up the playroom. All the stuff I ordered is here and now it's just a matter of putting it in place."

"Sounds like great fun," Pat said. "But how about a cup of tea first and some sisterly advice?"

Celia led the way to the kitchen, a big, old-fashioned room that always made Pat feel warm and comfortable. "Are you giving it, or seeking it?" she asked. "The advice, I mean."

"Seeking it, but you've got to promise you won't say I told you so."

Celia's eyes narrowed, but she nodded. "Agreed. It will be hard, but I'll hold my tongue. What's wrong, hon?"

Pat tugged at the neck of her shirt. She suddenly felt uncomfortably warm. "Everything," she said, without stopping to think. "No, forget I said that. It's not true. It's just this situation with Hank and his wife. She . . . came to see me a few days ago, and I didn't tell Hank."

"Good heavens, why not?" Celia asked, her hands stilling on the teakettle. "I don't think you should keep things like that from him."

"I know you're right, but Hank gets so wound up. When I told him about Becky's little visit he was livid. And he had trouble with his blood pressure when Nancy first walked out on him. I worry about him."

"Oh, Pat! This is what I was afraid of!" Celia said, sitting down across from her.

"I know. I guess I just never thought Hank's wife would be an issue, and I didn't set out to fall in love with him, Celia. At first it was just friendship, but he was so lonely, and he is such a good man! I . . . couldn't help loving him."

Celia's expression softened and she quickly moved to Pat's side to hug her. "Of course you couldn't, and it's not as though you stole him away from her. She'd already thrown him away."

"That's what I thought, and that's why it didn't seem wrong to let myself love him." Pat stirred sweetener into her tea. "It's different now than it would have been if I were twenty-five or thirty, Celia. You know what I mean, don't you?"

Celia nodded. "You mean that every day is precious. When I was in my twenties, life seemed endless. Time just stretched ahead of me like an unending strip of ribbon. I was convinced that there was plenty of time for me to accomplish all my dreams. Now . . . well, I knew Jake and I were getting on, but I never expected to be left alone so soon." She laughed. "Goodness, I haven't been this philosophical in ages, but you know what I mean, Pat. And I know what you mean. At our age, there's no time to waste. If we see something that's going to bring us happiness, we'd better grab it pretty quick!"

And that's what Pat had done. She'd grabbed Hank, and now Nancy was trying to grab him back.

"Anyway," Pat said, "do you think I did the wrong thing not telling Hank about Nancy's little visit?"

Celia refilled their teacups and nodded. "Hank seems like a man who values honesty, sis. Sooner or later he'll find out, and he might not like your keeping things from him." Celia's brow furrowed in a frown and her smile was hesitant. "Please don't take this the wrong way, Pat, but do you think . . . well, after all those years with Clifford, with him calling all the shots, do you think you're trying to be in control this time?"

Pat's cup rattled in its saucer as she set it down. In control? Of Hank? What on earth had put such an idea in Celia's head? Pat knew she'd never been a controlling person, and just because she'd changed her life-style didn't mean . . . her thoughts drifted off in confusion.

"Do you think that's what I'm trying to do?"

"I don't know, hon," Celia said quietly. "It's just that I know how hurt you were when you discovered Clifford's betrayal. I know how anxious you were to put a period to that stage of your life, and it would only be a normal, natural reaction for you to want to take charge in this relationship."

Pat felt as though she was looking into a giant, magnifying mirror and seeing all the flaws in herself. Was she really trying to control Hank?

"I don't think . . ."

"Just think about it, hon, and ask yourself why you really don't want to tell Hank about Nancy's visit. Sometimes we can't be objective about our own feelings, you know?"

"Of course."

Pat stayed with Celia until early afternoon, helping her set up the playroom for her little day-care charges. When she decided it was time for her to go home, they were almost finished.

"All I really need to do now is hang some bright pictures and plaques," Celia said, "and put some hooks in the wall for the sleep mats. Oh, Pat, isn't this wonderful? I'm getting so excited! And I've got two of the nicest, most enthusiastic young helpers lined up. If everything goes as planned, I should be able to open my doors in a few weeks."

Pat smiled. "You're a natural for this kind of thing," she said. "You were always great with kids."

"And so was Jake," Celia said, her eyes wistful. "My only regret is that he won't be able to share this with me."

"I know, dear." Pat hugged her sister. "I really do have to go now, but I'm glad I came today. I needed to see you. You've always been able to make me see even the things I didn't want to see about myself."

As she drove home, her sister's words ran circles in Pat's head. Deep down in her subconscious, did she want to control Hank? And if so, why? As a way of getting back at Clifford? But that was stupid. Clifford was gone. He would never know or care about what Pat did with the rest of her life, and anyway, she'd forgiven him, hadn't she?

When she pulled into her yard she saw that Hank's truck was still absent. He'd mentioned he might stay overnight, and his next-door neighbor would tend to the dogs.

Pat let herself into her little house, and her spirits lifted as Ink and Spot came racing to greet her as soon as she let them out of the garage. She bent to pet them, then let them out into the yard to run. After hanging up her hat and coat, she put the teakettle on. It was definitely a day to drink tea and do some soul-searching. It was only when the kettle started to whistle that she noticed the blinking light on her answering machine.

Pat pushed the button to play her messages and gasped when she heard the harsh, grating voice. "Husband stealer!" the voice screeched. "Whore! How can you sleep at night, you hussy?"

Shaking like a leaf, Pat turned the machine off and sat down before her legs gave out.

Nancy! It had to be Nancy, even though it didn't sound like her. Dear heaven, what was happening here? She'd thought of Nancy as a spoiled, self-centered woman, but anyone who would call and leave that kind of foul message on an answering machine was sick, and maybe even dangerous.

A terrible weakness gripped her, and she felt herself gag. Now she had to tell Hank, and heaven only knew what he would do!

Twenty-five

"Why didn't you tell me?" Hank demanded.

"I didn't want to upset you. I knew how worried you were about the girls, and I thought . . . well, I guess I thought Nancy would just give up, but she isn't going to, is she?"

Pat didn't have to glance in the mirror to know how she looked. She hadn't slept at all the night before. She'd lain awake waiting for the phone to ring again. And in the morning, when she saw that Hank was home, she'd called and asked him to come over. Now, her hands gripped tight around a mug of hot, strong coffee, Pat stared at Hank. She felt terrible. Nancy's phone call had made her feel dirty and cheap, and she wondered if she would ever be able to love Hank again without guilt.

"I know she was seeing a psychiatrist," Hank said. "Now I'm beginning to understand why. Only a sick person does something like that."

"What can we do?" A part of Pat wanted to run away and hide. A part of her wanted to wash her hands of the whole mess and forget she'd ever met Hank, but she couldn't. As she and Hank had promised each other, they were in it for the long haul. She'd never been a quitter. She wasn't going to start now.

Hank sighed. "I'll get in touch with my lawyer and have him put a restraining order on her so she can't harass you anymore. And maybe I should get in touch with that doctor she's seeing. Maybe he can help me understand what's going on here." Hank ran his hands through his thick hair. "None of this makes any sense, Pat. It's not as though Nancy and I had the love affair of the century. We spent most of our marriage arguing, and if anything my financial situation is worse now than it was when she left, so why is she so determined to come back? Doesn't she realize that all the old problems will still exist? Can't she see that there's nothing left for us to build on?"

Pat sipped her coffee thoughtfully. "Maybe it's just her ego. She can't stand the thought of losing, of someone else having the husband who once belonged to her."

"That sounds more like Nancy," Hank said. He stood behind Pat and began to massage her neck. "I never meant to put all this on you."

"I know, and none of this is your fault, but I have to admit that phone call threw me. Nothing like that has ever happened to me before."

Hank sighed. "I think I managed to make the girls understand where I'm coming from," he said, "but they're not happy. I guess they want to believe that Nancy and I can get back together and live happily ever after."

"You didn't say anything about us, did you?" Pat asked. Hank's daughters would have to know sometime, but not yet . . . not right now. They had enough to deal with now, without imagining their father with another woman.

"I wanted to." He stepped around in front of Pat so he could look into her eyes. "I'm not ashamed of what I feel for you, and I know if the girls would just be reasonable they'd love you as much as I do."

"Maybe someday they will, but right now their first loyalty is to Nancy. As it is, they're being torn in two different directions."

Hank nodded. "You're probably right. That's why I didn't say anything, but they know you're in my life, Pat. And Becky knows that it's serious."

"She's such a pretty girl," Pat said. "I'd like to think that someday we could be friends."

Hank looked doubtful. "That would be wonderful, sweetheart, but no matter what happens, you and I are going to be together. We're going to be married when this is all over, and we're going to live the rest of our lives the way we want to. If my daughters can't accept that, it's going to be their problem."

He held her then, but there was no thought of lovemaking. The emotions they both felt were too raw and painful.

Pat was grateful that Hank cared enough to stand up for their love, but at what cost? She didn't want to be responsible for his losing his daughters . . . didn't want them to start off their life together surrounded by bitterness and regret.

"I thought life was supposed to be easy and uncomplicated after middle age," Pat mused. "I thought once the early struggles of making a living and child rearing were over, you could just coast through the rest."

"Hmm, that's a nice thought," Hank said, holding her in a loose, yet comforting embrace. "Maybe all these roadblocks are coming our way to keep us on our toes."

"You mean, if things went too smoothly we'd become complacent?"

"Something like that," Hank said, nodding.

Pat wasn't sure what she had expected when she told Hank of Nancy's phone call, but his reaction had surprised her, and she couldn't help remembering her conversation with Celia. She hadn't given Hank enough credit. She'd treated him like a hapless child. He had every right to know what was going on, and if their relationship was going to work, it had to be based on trust. That meant no more holding back, no more weak attempts to shield Hank from the realities of this situation. If they were to overcome this problem, they needed to face it head-on. They needed to take charge and stand up for what they knew was right. And being together without guilt or shame was right, Pat knew. She and Hank belonged together. They both embraced the same interests and values. They were right for each other.

"How about a nice, long walk to work out some of the kinks?" Pat asked. "I feel like I need to get moving."

Hank nodded agreeably, then he grinned. "And after our walk, I have some nice, relaxing therapy in mind."

Pat shrugged into her down jacket and smiled. She knew all about Hank's therapy, and maybe that's exactly what they needed. Maybe they needed to make love and reaffirm their commitment to each other.

It was a cold, damp March day, and they bundled up warmly. Pat took Ink's leash and Hank took Spot's.

"This is a real treat for these two," Pat said. "Usually they get their exercise chasing each other around the backyard."

"I enjoy a nice long walk," Hank said. "I don't do it often enough."

They walked for more than an hour, until Pat noticed Ink and Spot beginning to droop, then they headed back home.

"I'm ready for spring," Pat said, pointing to a neighbor's yard where some crocuses were starting to poke their heads out of the ground. "I'm anxious to see the flowers I planted last fall come up and start blooming."

Hank gave Pat a quick hug. "A country girl at heart, hmm? Who would have thought it?"

"Who indeed?" A vision flashed in front of Pat. Memories of her life with Clifford, when wearing jeans and a sweatshirt around the house would have been unthinkable, when Clifford would have deemed it unseemly for her to putter in the garden and get dirt under her fingernails.

Linking her arm through Hank's, Pat rubbed her chin against his shoulder. "Sometimes I still can't believe the difference in my life-style. I'm so comfortable now, so relaxed." Suddenly remembering their situation, Pat laughed. "Well, most of the time I'm relaxed," she amended. "The house I lived in with Clifford was elegant, and Philadelphia is a wonderful city, but this . . ." Pat's words trailed off as she waved her arms at the open field they had just passed.

Hank nodded, and looked up at the dreary, winter-gray sky. Ordinarily a day like this, with an overcast sky, would have made him feel a little down, but now, sharing it with Pat made everything bright and hopeful. She took such joy in the smallest, simplest things.

"Did anyone ever tell you you're some special lady?" he asked, tipping Pat's chin up with his fist. "You've turned my life completely around."

"Oh, Hank!"

"Come on," Hank said, "Let's hurry and get home. I've got plans for you!"

And for a few hours it was as if Nancy didn't exist. They showered together. Pat giggled like a child as Hank soaped her back, then her giggles turned to soft, kittenlike moans as Hank's strong hands found their way to other, more interesting areas of her body.

"Do you know that Nancy and I never did this?" Hank asked. He had a large towel haphazardly draped around his waist, and he was intent on drying Pat in a very seductive way.

"Clifford and I never did it either," Pat admitted. "He was always in such a hurry to get to his law office." She grinned impishly. "Isn't there some unwritten rule about discussing one's past lovers with the current love interest?"

"Love interest? Is that what I am?" Hank asked, cocking his head and arching his brows comically. "Mmm, I don't think anyone has ever referred to me in just that way before, but I like it."

"If you don't stop torturing me this way, I'll be referring to you in a way you definitely won't like," Pat threatened, her limbs growing heavy with need. "Let's go to bed, my darling," she coaxed.

Hank threw the towel down and laughed. "I thought you'd never ask!"

"Mmm, is there anything better than lying in bed on a cold winter's day with a beautiful woman?" Hank asked later, nuzzling the tips of Pat's breasts with his lips. "You taste as delicious as you smell, my lady," he said huskily. "Maybe after I rest a little . . ."

Pat gasped. "Heaven forbid! Don't I get any peace at all? Don't you realize you're too old for marathon feats of lovemaking?"

She was wrapped in a delightful afterglow, her flesh still tingling from Hank's touch, her body fulfilled and relaxed.

Then the telephone rang. Hank tensed. Pat felt the tension radiate through his fingertips and onto her own skin. Please no, she thought. Not now!

Her hand was trembling as she lifted the receiver. "Hello?"

"Mother?"

Relief flowed through Pat's body like warm honey. "It's Ashley," she cried.

"Is someone there with you?" Ashley asked.

"Yes. Hank." Pat felt a warm flush color her cheeks and beside her, Hank chuckled wickedly.

"Never mind, Mom," Ashley said, and Pat could hear the laughter in her daughter's voice. "I just called to tell you that I'll be going back to California next week. I'm doing a shoot there. I called Cliff and told him, and we're going to get together for dinner. I thought you'd like to know. I'm trying to be a good sister."

"Oh, honey, that's wonderful," Pat said, sitting up and tugging the sheet around her. She shot Hank a warning look when he gave the sheet a tentative tug.

"May I speak to Hank for a minute?"

Ashley asked. "I want to ask him something about Fancy."

"Of course. Give Cliff my love when you see him, honey, and have a good trip. Call me when you get back, okay?"

Pat handed the phone to Hank and swung her legs over the side of the bed. She was starting to get hungry, and she thought it would be a good idea to make her getaway while Hank was occupied.

He joined her in the kitchen a few minutes later. "Ashley is thinking of showing Fancy. Did she tell you?"

Pat nodded as she diced onion and celery for a salad. "She mentioned it, but she was concerned about not getting Fancy spayed."

Hank went to the cabinet and began taking down plates and silverware. "That is a problem with show dogs, and especially for someone living in an apartment like Ashley. To tell the truth, I did my best to discourage her. Showing a dog is time consuming and it can be damned expensive as well. For someone who is breeding dogs to sell, it's almost a necessity, but with Ashley's career, I don't see how she'd manage unless she hired someone to train and show Fancy for her."

Pat nodded. "I don't think she has any idea what she'd be getting into. She's just so thrilled with Fancy." Pat shook her head, smiling. "I still can't believe it, my daughter the dog lover."

Pat took a package of chicken breasts from the freezer and laid them on a plate to thaw. She accepted the glass of wine Hank held out to her.

"You thought that phone call was Nancy, didn't you?" Hank asked. "I saw the way you froze."

"And I felt your tension. Do you think we're getting paranoid?"

"Maybe, but I think we're entitled. Like you said earlier, life should be straightforward and simple at this stage of the game."

They worked comfortably together as they prepared a simple dinner. This closeness and ease was what had been missing in her first marriage, she realized. She and Clifford had been more like business partners than husband and wife. Her life had been programmed, and she had been a robot. Well, thank goodness, it was no more! She was free to be herself, whoever that was. As she put the finishing touches on a salad, Pat realized she was still discovering herself. She was still learning what pleased her, the sights and sounds that made her smile involuntarily. And thanks to Hank, she was certainly enjoying a richly satisfying sex life. She chuckled to herself, remembering how she'd thought that part of her life was over when Clifford died.

"Do you realize I've undergone a sexual revolution?" she asked Hank, going up behind him and sliding her arms around his waist.

"Really? That's interesting. Do you realize that you've opened up a whole world of firsts for me?"

Pat leaned her head against Hank's back and let the warm strength of him soak into her own body. "You're such a solid man," she said. "Such a decent, dependable person. I like that."

Hank covered her hands with his own. "And you are the most unselfish woman I've ever known. Your first thought is always for the other guy. I'm still not used to that."

"Well, you better work on it, buster," Pat teased. "Because you're stuck with me. I'm not letting go."

"Thank the Lord, because I really don't know how I'd manage without you!"

Twenty-six

"Well, it's done," Hank said. "I had my attorney put a restraining order against Nancy. Hopefully, she won't bother you anymore."

"What about the divorce? How is that coming?"

"Nancy can't legally stop the divorce," Hank said, accepting the glass of wine Pat handed him. "Thanks, darling. It's been a rough day. Anyway, in this state there's no way she can stop me from getting a divorce if I want one, but she can make things rough financially. It looks like I'll have to sell the house and split the proceeds with her." Hank couldn't face Pat's probing look. "I'm going to have to give the dogs up," he said quietly.

"No! Oh no! Hank, you can't! Those dogs are the reason we met in the first place. You can't do it!"

"I have to, Pat. Actually, the only thing I have that I can share with Nancy is the house and the kennels, and I suppose she is entitled to something. She's the mother of my children."

"Of course she is, but you told me she always hated that house, and it's not as if she needs the money."

"No, but she'll take it just to be vindictive. She knows that if I sell the house and the kennels I won't be in a financial position to start over." Hank grinned ruefully. "I really don't have much to offer you, Pat. You may want to reconsider this relationship. I'm just a middle-aged auto mechanic. I'm not especially good with words and . . ."

Pat smiled. "Don't worry. I already have reconsidered, thousands of times, and I always come up with the same answer. I'm hooked. My fate is sealed. You're the man I want, Hank Richards."

Hank put down his wineglass and opened his arms.

But he was unusually quiet the rest of the night, and Pat knew that the decisions he was being forced to make were weighing heavily on him. Although he'd never actually said it in so many words, Pat knew that the kennels were a very special, important part of Hank's life. If he lost that, there would be a big hole in his life, and he wouldn't be the same man.

Hank went home early. Before he left he held Pat close. Pat hugged him, feeling his pain deep inside her own heart. "Don't worry," she said softly. "Everything is going to work out. You'll see."

"As long as I have you, I'll get through this," Hank said, but Pat thought there was a trace of uncertainty in his voice that hadn't been there before.

As soon as Hank had gone, Pat looked at the clock on the kitchen wall. Nine-thirty. Too late to call Bruce Howard at home. She decided she'd be in her attorney's office first thing in the morning. There was only one way to save Hank's kennels for him.

"As I'm sure you realize there's no problem with the money, Pat," Bruce Howard said the next morning, after Pat explained what she wanted to do. "But are you sure this is what you want to do? Running a dog kennel must entail a great deal of work. I know you've become quite an animal lover, but . . ."

"I won't be doing this all alone, Bruce," Pat said, smiling as she thought of how relieved Hank would be when he realized he would be able to keep his kennels. "I'm going to marry the man who presently owns the kennel."

"I see. No, actually I don't. If you're marrying this man, why do you want to buy his kennels?"

"It's complicated. He's in the middle of a divorce and he needs to sell the property to settle things with his wife. But he doesn't want to sell and . . ."

Bruce nodded. "Now I get the picture. Does your . . . does your intended know what you plan to do, Pat?"

"Well, not exactly. Not yet anyway. I wanted to make sure there wouldn't be any problems before I said anything to him."

"Pat, you can certainly afford to do this, if you insist, but I feel I should caution you. There could be repercussions to a business arrangement of this sort. Are you sure you don't want to think this over?"

She shook her head. "I know this is the right thing to do. Hank may be a little reticent at first, but he'll come around. I'll make him understand that this is the only way. I'll get back to you when I find out the listing price, and I'd like to make the transfer as quickly as possible."

Bruce nodded, but his eyes spoke volumes. "I'll do my best, Pat, but as I'm sure you know, there are certain legal aspects related to a closing that take time. But I'll rush this through as fast as possible, if that's what you want."

Pat drove to the shelter humming happily. At least one hurdle had been successfully jumped. She would have liked to instruct Bruce to put the property in both her name, and Hank's, but under the circumstances, that simply wasn't practical. Perhaps later, when Nancy was permanently out of the picture, she could fix things so that the house and kennel belonged to both of them, but for now the deed would have to remain in her name alone. It was the only way to protect it from Nancy's greed.

"Well, Pete and I were starting to think you'd deserted us, Pat," Dale said, giving her a hug after she'd hung up her jacket. "How are you?"

"I'm making it," Pat said. "How about some of that terrific coffee of yours. I've been tasting it for the last hour."

"I'm glad you stopped by, Pat," Dale said, joining her and Pete in the office. "There's something I need to tell you."

Pat looked at the young man curiously. "Uh-oh, this sounds ominous."

"Not really," Dale said. "Actually, at least part of it is very good news. I'm getting married. Remember my neighbor, the young widow with the little boy?"

"The one you gave the cocker spaniel to?"

"Yep. That's the one. We're getting married, and I'm going to be a stepdad. What do you think of that?"

"Dale, that's wonderful! I'm happy for you, but you said that only part of your news was good?"

"Yeah. Well, I'm going to be leaving the shelter, Pat. I'm going back to school to become a veterinarian. I got sidetracked there for a while, but now that I'm going to be a family man, I realize that I've got to move forward."

Pat shook her head. "Talk about ambivalent feelings! I'm thrilled for you, Dale, but how are we ever going to replace you here?"

"We've been thinking about that," Pete said, "And we were wondering if you'd consider Dale's job? The pay isn't all that great, but the fringe benefits are nice. You'd get to work with me, and you know you love my coffee."

"That I do," Pat said, laughing. "Wow! This is really a surprise, and I'm flattered that you want to work with me, but I'm afraid I can't do it. I'm making some changes in my life soon, and I'm going to be pretty busy."

"Let me guess," Pete said, grinning mischievously. "The change wouldn't be spelled H-A-N-K, would it?"

"In a way," Pat hedged, "but I'm going to

be working at Hank's kennels, and that will take a good chunk of my time. So, I think you'd better start looking for a coworker."

"Okay. Does this mean we won't be seeing you at all?"

Pat laughed. "Are you kidding? Do you really think I could stay away from this place? I'm addicted, just like you guys. What do you want to bet Dale starts volunteering his time once he's a practicing veterinarian? No, I'm not deserting you. It's just that I can't commit to full time."

"Well, that's a relief. I don't think I could take losing both you and Dale," Pete said.

On the way home from the shelter, Pat stopped at a small grocery store she sometimes used when she was in a hurry. She wasn't really in a hurry tonight, but Petrie's had the most delicious cheesecake she'd ever tasted, and it was Hank's favorite, too. She smiled, picturing Hank's relief when he found out he wouldn't have to give up his beloved dogs. They definitely had something to celebrate!

Stashing the cheesecake in the refrigerator, Pat let the dogs out into the yard. She sang as she filled the animals' food dishes, and gave Tweetie an extra helping of sunflower seeds.

"Hot damn!" Tweetie squawked. "Hot damn!"

"Same to you, little pal," Pat said, laughing.

She continued to sing as she showered and searched her closet for something pretty and feminine to wear. Hank swore he adored her in jeans and a flannel shirt. He claimed he loved the way flannel felt when he rubbed his hands over it, but there was definitely a time and a place for silks and satins and sweetly erotic perfumes, Pat thought, and this was definitely the time. She wanted to bowl Hank over. She wanted him to be absolutely, totally besotted with love for her, and not just because she was giving him his kennels back. No, tonight she wanted Hank to see her as all woman. She wanted him to know that she was soft and warm and willing, all for him.

It was Hank's turn to cook, and he'd promised her a special treat, so Pat put her coat on over her raw silk green jumpsuit and carried the cheesecake over to Hank's house.

She knocked and it was as if he'd been standing by the door just waiting for her.

His eyes lit with pleasure when she shrugged out of her coat.

"Well, what's all this? You didn't tell me we were dressing for dinner tonight. Shall I change?"

Pat wrapped her arms around Hank's neck and laughed. "Don't you dare. You're perfect just as you are." She kissed him, a quick kiss that left her wanting more, but she was bursting with her news, and there was a long, beautiful night ahead of them.

She picked the cheesecake up from the table where she'd deposited it. "This needs to be refrigerated," she said. "Mmm, what's that yummy smell?"

"That's my surprise." He took the cheesecake from her and turned her toward the living room. "Stay out of the kitchen," he instructed. "There's cheese and crackers and some wine on the coffee table."

"You're not joining me?"

"In a few minutes," Hank said. "There's something I have to do first."

Pat sat down on the sofa and helped herself to crackers and cheese. She felt a surge of pleasure as Princess sauntered into the room and came to rest her head on Pat's lap.

Completely recovered from whelping, Princess had her full Samoyed coat, and she looked as though she'd just been brushed. Pat scratched behind's the dog's ears and wondered how anyone could look at an animal this beautiful and not be moved. Her pleasure intensified as she reminded herself that she would soon be part-owner of Princess and her lovely kennel mates. Technically, she supposed she would be the sole owner of the Royal Sam Kennels, but as far as she was concerned, these dogs would always belong to Hank, no matter what the papers said. He loved them and they were a very real and important part of his life. How could Nancy not see this? How could she be so vindictive to want to take this away from Hank?

"Ah, two of my favorite females," Hank said, joining them a few minutes later. "About fifteen more minutes and we can eat. Have you figured out what I'm cooking yet?"

"I haven't a clue, but whatever it is, it smells wonderful." She poured Hank a glass of wine and handed it to him. "Sit down. You look a little tired."

Hank nodded, and some of the light went out of his gray eyes. They looked dull now, the color of pewter, and something painful stirred in Pat's chest.

"Hard day?" she asked.

"Wicked, but not at the shop. Things are a little slow right now, and I guess it's just as well. I'm having a hard time concentrating on alternators and dead batteries and burnt-out transmissions. I signed on with a realtor today, Pat. They'll probably put a sign up tomorrow."

Pat nodded wordlessly, her surprise trembling on her lips, but she wanted to wait for exactly the right moment. She wanted to be in Hank's arms, with her head on his shoulder when she told him.

So she began to talk about her own day, omitting the trip to Bruce Howard's office and telling Hank about Dale's upcoming marriage, and his plans to go back to school.

"He'll make a wonderful veterinarian," she said.

"Did they offer you his job?"

Pat laughed and sipped her wine. "Actually they did," she said, setting her wineglass on the table, "but I declined. I explained that I have other plans."

"Oh?" Hank's brows rose questioningly.

"Not now," Pat said, putting her fingers to his lips. "Later. Right now I want to taste whatever it is that smells so delicious out in the kitchen."

"Well, I guess I can take a hint. I'll go see if I can rustle up our dinner."

And rustle he did, the most delicious, delectable assortment of Chinese dishes Pat had ever tasted. Chicken and walnuts, Pepper steak, and Egg Foo Yong with Shrimp.

After dinner, they sat in the living room with coffee and tiny, crystal brandy snifters. A fire crackled in the grate, and it was as if they were the only two people in the world.

"This is what life is all about, isn't it?" Pat asked. "Two people who care about one another, sitting in front of a fire, warm and comfortable and full of delicious food."

Hank laughed softly. They were on the floor in front of the somewhat shabby blue sofa, with their legs stretched out toward the fire. Princess was beside Pat, and Frosty was next to Hank, getting his head rubbed.

"I'm going to miss the kennel," Hank said, sobering. "I was thinking I'd keep these two as pets. Giving them up would be like giving my children up for adoption."

Now. Now was the right moment. Pat sat up a little straighter until her eyes were level with Hank's. "You don't have to give any of them up, darling," she said softly. "I figured out a way for you to keep the kennels." Her eyes were sparkling with excitement now, and she didn't notice how still Hank had become.

"I went to see my attorney this morning. It will be no problem for me to buy the kennels. It will have to be in my name, of course, at least for a while, until we're sure Nancy is out of our lives for good, but, I can sell or rent my house out and move in here with you. I can look after the dogs while you're at work and . . ."

Hank's face was stark white, his eyes chunks of granite sunk deep in their sockets. "You want to buy my kennels? You?"

A queer sensation crept up Pat's backbone

and despite the warmth of the fire she shivered. "Hank, what's the matter? Aren't you pleased? Don't you see that this is the answer to your problems? This way you can take the money from the sale and give Nancy her share. She'll be satisfied, and you'll be free and we can be married . . ." Pat's voice trailed off as Hank's anger exploded.

"No!" he cried. "Dear heaven, Pat, didn't you hear any of the things I told you about my first marriage? Nancy practically emasculated me! Are you trying to do the same thing?"

"I . . . no, of course not! I thought . . . I just want to help!"

"By castrating me?" Hank asked, his voice harsh with pain. "I'm not for sale, Pat. I know I'm just an ordinary man. I don't know much about stocks and investments. Hell, I wouldn't know a portfolio if I fell over one, but what I do know is that no woman is going to stamp *bought* and *paid for* across my forehead again! Not even you!"

Twenty-seven

Pat was shocked speechless. She'd never imagined Hank reacting this way. She'd expected him to protest, perhaps even be a little embarrassed, but she had truly believed that when she explained everything to him, Hank would understand that this was the best way.

"Hank, you . . . you said that you needed my help to get through this . . . you said you couldn't do it without me."

"Oh, Pat! I meant moral support. I meant that I needed you by my side, through good and bad. I wasn't talking, about your money! That's what ruined my first marriage. Didn't you understand that?"

The lovely mood was spoiled, all the peace and happiness Pat had felt just moments earlier was shattered. It seemed she'd made a terrible mistake, but what other alternative was there?

"There was more than money involved in the failure of your marriage to Nancy, Hank," she said quietly, "and if you haven't realized that yet, I feel sorry for you. I honestly thought that you and I were past all this 'my money-your money' stuff, but it looks like I was wrong. Well, if you're waiting for me to apologize for the offer I just made, you'll have a long wait. I did what I did because I love you, Hank Richards, and I thought we were going to spend the rest of our lives together. I know how much you love the dogs and the kennel, and I wanted you to be able to keep it. What I did I did out of love, and not because I want to buy you, Hank. If you can't figure that out, then I guess there's no chance for us, regardless of what happens with you and Nancy. I let one man hold me hostage. I'm not up for that again."

Pat struggled to her feet, furiously blinking back tears. "I have to go," she said, her words choked. "I've got to get out of here!"

And once back in her own house, Pat let the tears flow. Maybe Hank had been right in the beginning when he said they were from two different worlds. Maybe there really was no way they could meet in the middle and blend their lives. Maybe Hank would always resent her financial status . . . maybe it would always be there between them, like a sleeping snake, coiled and ready to strike at anytime. Well, she didn't want to live that way, and she wasn't going to. She'd be better off alone, than living with that kind of repressed hostility and tension.

Suddenly Pat was so tired her legs felt weak. All she wanted to do was go to sleep and forget everything that had happened. She put the dogs out in the yard for their last run, and picked up the cloth she draped over Tweetie's cage every night.

A soft whistle made her look at the bird. Tweetie's head was cocked to the side and he seemed to be studying her. Then he burst forth with the new sentences Pat had been teaching him.

"Pat loves Hank," Tweetie squealed. "Hank loves Pat."

Pat nodded. "True, but sometimes love is not enough, Tweetie."

"That's a bunch of bull!" Tweetie squawked.

Hank woke feeling like he had a king-size hangover. Pat's words hammered at him, arguing with the deepest feelings he'd never been able to completely bury.

"Maybe that's the trouble, old man," he told himself. "Maybe burying all this garbage is not the answer. Maybe you need to dig deep and get it all and throw it out."

It sounded good, Hank thought, but how was he supposed to go about this mental housecleaning? And who was right, him or Pat?

God knows he knew that Pat only wanted to help. She was just about the kindest, most generous woman he'd ever known, but how could he expect her to understand how he felt whenever financial matters came up? Years of being under Nancy's father's thumb, and the vicious verbal battles he and Nancy had had when he finally put his foot down, and the way he'd never, ever been able to satisfy Nancy, not even in the bedroom.

God, he hadn't thought of that in years, at least not consciously, but maybe it had been lurking in the back of his mind all the time, just waiting to jump out and whack him with the deepest humiliation a man could know. It would be hard for a woman to understand, Hank knew, especially a woman as warm and loving as Pat. Hadn't she taken his temporary impotence in stride and done everything she could to reassure him? And didn't she make him feel like a king among men every time they made love?

And now he'd probably lost her for good. He saw her face, the shocked hurt when he'd so rudely thrown her love gift back in her face. And that's what it had been, a gift of love, a testament to her faith in them and their future together.

"Oh, Pat, what have I done?" Hank moaned. "What have I done?"

Pat decided she was definitely coming down with something. It was either the flu or a severe case of unrequited love. She thought it was probably the former. She hadn't felt this sick and old for a long time. Her head hurt, her throat felt raw, and her bones ached. It was an effort to move, and the thought of coffee, usually the first thing she wanted in the morning, made her stomach lurch.

She finally settled for a glass of juice and as she slowly sipped it, the memories of the night before came rushing back. Hank's face . . . his masculine outrage . . . the anger he flung at her. Pat shivered. She couldn't think of it now. Moving slowly, she took care of her pets and made her way back to the bedroom. Sleep, she thought, as her eyes closed. That's what she needed. A little more sleep.

Someone was knocking on the door. It

seemed to take forever, but somehow she got out of bed and slipped on her robe. Ink and Spot danced around her feet, nearly tripping her as she moved to the door.

"Pat!" Hank looked shocked. "Oh, honey, what's wrong? You're sick!"

He closed the door behind him, and gripped her shoulders just as she felt herself start to fade.

"I've never fainted in my life," she mumbled thickly, "but my legs . . . feel funny."

"I don't wonder," Hank said, scooping her up as if she weighed no more than a little stuffed teddy bear. "You're burning up with fever. Why didn't you call me?"

"Why didn't you go to work?" Pat asked.

"I did," Hank said. "It's six-thirty at night, Pat. Have you been asleep all day?"

"I don't know . . ."

Hank deposited her on the bed and tenderly tucked the covers around her. "Just lie still and rest. I'll take care of the animals and be right back."

Pat nodded. Hank was here. She was safe. Hank would take care of her. She was drifting, but she could hear him moving around in her kitchen. And then she heard a thin, reedy little voice squawking. "Pat loves Hank! Hank loves Pat!" She tried to smile, but her lips felt like they were numb. She wished she could have seen Hank's face.

"All right, the animals are all fed and taken care of. Pat? Are you awake, sweetheart? I made you some soup and here's a cold glass of ginger ale. Can you try to eat?"

He was peering down at her anxiously, and she wanted to reassure him, but she was just too tired. Then she, felt him lifting her, propping her against a nest of pillows so she could taste the soup.

Dimly she remembered opening her mouth when Hank prodded her, then she sipped the cold ginger ale. Then Hank was sliding her down under the covers again. She felt herself sigh. She was warm and the pain in her joints seemed to be lessening. She floated away to a lovely dream. Hank was kissing her, his lips soft and gentle against her forehead. She felt the tender touch of his hands on her breasts, then, like a brief butterfly's kiss, it was gone.

"Ah, you're back," Hank said, his voice thick with relief. "The doctor said . . ."

"Doctor? What doctor?" Pat struggled to sit up. Her body felt curiously heavy, but that awful headache was gone, and when she blinked her vision cleared.

"I had to call a doctor, sweetheart," Hank explained. "Your fever was dangerously high and you were delirious."

"What was it, the flu?"

Hank nodded and handed her a cold glass of orange juice."Drink up. You need all the vitamin C you can get. Whew! You sure had me scared, Pat!"

"Haven't you ever been around anyone with the flu before?"

Hank's face softened and he shook his head. "Not anyone I love as much as I love you."

"Oh." Pat sipped the juice in silence. What could she say to that? She still felt a little fuzzy, but the memory of what had happened the night she got sick was sharp and clear. It sounded like Hank had undergone a change of heart, but why? Was he just saying these things because she'd been sick?

"Hank, we have to talk."

He nodded, his gray eyes dark and sober. "I know, and we will, but not right this minute, okay? You need a few days to get your strength back, and I need a little time to get my head on straight once and for all. I haven't thought of anything but you and getting you through this for the past three days."

"I've been like this for three days?" Pat asked incredulously. "But . . . it seems like just last night . . ."

"The fever," Hank explained. "You were really burning up."

"Well, thank you," Pat said quietly. "I guess I owe you."

"No, sweetheart. The debt is all mine."

Twenty-eight

"All right, I'm coming!" Pat hurried to answer the front door. It was the first day of really feeling human again since she'd gotten sick, and it felt so good to be up and around she had to keep reminding herself of Hank's warning not to overdo.

She opened the door and felt her jaw sag. Becky, and beside her, looking decidedly uneasy, was a young woman who could be no one but Hank's oldest daughter, Laurie.

"I . . . what is it? What do you want?" she asked, her hand at her throat.

"Please, may we come in?" Becky asked. "This is my sister, Laurie. We'd like to talk to you, Mrs. Melbourne."

"Pat. My name is Pat. All right, come in, but if you're here to ask me to stop seeing your father . . ."

"No. Oh no, that's not why we're here,"

Laurie said quickly. "We didn't come to argue with you."

Pat led the way into the living room. She remembered the day Becky had come to ask her to leave Hank alone. She felt like she was reliving a nightmare.

When she was seated across from the two young women, she shrugged her shoulders. "What did you want to talk to me about?"

Laurie looked so much like her mother it was eerie, and Becky was a female version of Hank. Pat felt her lips twitch in the beginnings of a smile. Then Laurie began to speak, and she sobered.

"We . . . Becky and I want to apologize for the way our mother has been behaving. We didn't know about the phone call until Dad came to see us."

"It's certainly not your fault," Pat said, knowing she sounded a little stiff, but she couldn't forget the angry, hurtful words Becky had hurled at her so recently.

"I'm sorry about coming to see you and the things I said," Becky chimed in. "At first, when Dad tried to explain why he and Mom couldn't get back together we figured it was just because of the other woman in his life. We were pretty mad at you, Pat." She smiled disarmingly.

Pat couldn't help smiling back. What child wouldn't be angry in such a situation.

"But, well, since our mother has been back we've noticed things, and we realize that she's got some problems. It was awful of her to call you and say the things she did, and it's mean of her to make Dad sell his house and the kennels. It would be different if she needed the money."

"We're trying to get her to back off," Laurie said. "I don't know if we'll be successful, but we wanted you to know that we realize you're not responsible for the breakup of our parents' marriage, and if you're the person Dad wants to spend the rest of his life with . . . well, we won't do anything to stand in your way."

Tears stung Pat's eyes, and she wished she had the nerve to take both girls in her arms. But perhaps that would come later, if she and Hank could work out their differences, and if he could come to terms with her financial situation.

"Thank you for telling me that," she said gently. "I want you to know that I do love your father very much. He's a good man, and he loves the two of you. That will never change no matter what else happens in his life."

Becky nodded, her eyes glistening with unshed tears. "We wasted a lot of time being angry with Dad for something that wasn't his fault. We're not going to let that happen again."

Pat smiled. "I'm glad." Her smile softened as the girls stood up to leave. "I don't know anything about your mother," she said quietly, "but she must be quite a lady to have raised such wonderful, loyal daughters. I truly hope she can find the happiness your father and I have found together."

Becky nodded. "That's what Laurie and I want for her, too, and we're trying to convince her that the best thing she can do is let Dad go and start a new life."

"Thank you for coming and telling me all this," Pat said. "I know it must have been hard for you to come here, and I know you must think of me as an outsider, but I hope that someday we can all be friends."

Both girls nodded. "We'd like that," they said in unison.

When she closed the door after them, Pat leaned against it weakly. Would wonders never cease? A visit from Hank's daughters was the very last thing she had been expecting, and unless she was reading the signals all wrong, it looked as if the girls wanted to be friends as much as she did, so maybe it could all work out.

But then the final decision lay with Hank, Pat reminded herself. She'd made her decision a long time ago. If Hank could accept things as they were, then the commitment she had made to him months earlier was strong and valid. If he couldn't . . .

She looked out the front window, hungry for the sight of his truck. But he wasn't home yet, and when he did come home all she had to look forward to was a brief phone call. Since he'd deemed her well enough to be left alone, he'd called to check on her every day as soon as he got in from work, but he didn't come over, nor did he invite her to his house. He'd said he needed time to get his head straight, but how long was it going to take? How long did he expect her to sit and wait?

When she finally saw the familiar pickup pull into the drive, Pat waited for the nightly call, but it didn't come. Her spirits fell. Maybe Hank figured she was well now, and he didn't have to check on her. She was filled with disappointment. She hadn't realized how important that brief contact had been.

"Well, if he's too busy to call, so be it," she said, moving away from the window, "and I'll be darned if I'll sit here like a reject waiting for the phone to ring!"

Pat fed the dogs and Cat, listened to Tweetie sing a short, off-key rendition of "London Bridge," then she stared at the contents of her refrigerator listlessly. Yogurt, a couple of bruised apples, a carton of milk, and three eggs. Definitely time to go shopping.

The pantry was a little more interesting, thanks to Hank. He'd stocked it with nonperishables, and now she stood, debating between vegetable beef soup and chicken rice.

Then, she heard the knock on the front door.

Hank! It had to be Hank. Had he finally gotten his head on straight? Was he here to tell her what he'd decided about their relationship?

She hurried to the door, peeked out the side window to make sure it was Hank, then opened the door.

Smiling, he hurried inside, a thin flurry of snowflakes following him. "Last snow of the season," he said, brushing flakes off his coat.

"Here, let me hang that up for you." Her heart was hammering, and her throat felt dry, but this time it wasn't the flu, it was just the way she felt about this man, the way she'd come to need his dear presence in her day-to-day life.

"How are you?" Hank asked, lifting her chin so he could look into her eyes.

"I'm fine." And then she couldn't help it. "I'm germ free if you want to kiss me," she said shamelessly. She stood on tiptoe to make it easier for him.

Hank hesitated for the space of a heartbeat, then he gathered her against him. "Oh, Pat, my Pat! What did I ever do to deserve you?"

Pat's heart leaped, then settled down into a steady, reassuring rhythm. "Does that mean you . . . you've decided to keep me?" she asked. She wrapped her arms tight around Hank's neck and held on. She had to. Her legs had suddenly turned to jelly.

Hank laughed, then he kissed her. It was a light, gentle kiss, a kiss filled with promise. "Let's go inside and sit down," he said. "I have a lot to tell you."

"I saw my lawyer today," Hank began quietly, when they were seated next to each other. "I laid everything on the table. I was frank about my financial situation. I told him about you, and about how much the kennels mean to me . . . how it would be like giving up a part of my life to part with them. I asked him if there wasn't some way I could keep my home and the kennels, and still give Nancy a fair settlement."

"Is there?" Pat asked, leaning forward eagerly.

Hank nodded, the joy in his eyes nearly blinding Pat as their gaze met and locked. "He thinks he can get Nancy's attorney to talk her into taking a monthly payment. I will have to pay Nancy a set amount each month until she's collected her half of the value of the property. I may need to work some overtime to make the payments, but . . ."

"Hank, you wouldn't have to. I could help," Pat said.

"No, I do have to. Maybe it's wrong of me to feel the way I do, Pat, but my life with Nancy was separate from what you and I have, and I need to take care of this on my own to keep it that way. Do you understand?"

"I'm trying to," Pat said, "but let's face it. Unless you win the lottery I'm always going to have more money than you." She shifted nervously. She didn't want to rock the boat when things were going so well, but the money issue wasn't going to go away, not unless she took a vow of poverty and gave it all to charity, and she knew she wasn't that noble. She enjoyed the freedom her money gave her, and the things it could buy. "I don't want to feel guilty because I'm fortunate enough to be financially well off, Hank."

Hank shook his head and gripped both Pat's hands. "You don't have to. I don't want you to. I've done a lot of thinking. I thought I was handling things pretty well after Nancy left, and even after she came back. I didn't realize how much emotional garbage I was carrying around until the night you told me what you wanted to do about the kennel. Suddenly, for just a moment, it was like you were Nancy . . . like it was happening all over again. I panicked. After you left, when I realized I'd dumped on you, I knew I had to get the poison out once and for all, if you and I were to have a future together. And I want that more than anything, Pat. I can't promise you your money will never be an issue between us. I guess I'll carry the bruises on my male ego for a long time." Hank grinned. "But I promise I'll do my best to think before I open my mouth. Can you live with that? Can you live with me? I'm bullheaded at times, my hair is starting to thin, and I'm not the snappiest dresser in town, but I do love you, Pat. With all my heart I love you."

"Oh, Hank! Darling! "I'm so happy. Everything is going to work out for us, isn't it?"

Hank's rugged features softened and he reached out to gently trace the line of Pat's cheek. "With all the love between us, how can it not?" he asked. And then he stood up, tugged her into the warm, protective circle of his arms and kissed her.

Pat sighed, a mere whisper of contentment against Hank's lips.

Who said there were no miracles?